Marcella Bell is an avid reader, a burgeoning beader, and a corvid and honeybee enthusiast with more interests than hours in the day. As a late bloomer and a yogini, Marcella is drawn to stories that showcase love's incredible power to inspire transformation—whether they take place in the vast landscapes of the west or imagined palaces and exotic locales. When not writing or wrangling her multigenerational household and three dogs, she loves to hear from readers! To reach out, keep up, or check in, visit marcellabell.com.

Emmy Grayson wrote her first book at the age of seven, about a spooky ghost. Her passion for romance novels began a few years later, with the discovery of a worn copy of Kathleen E. Woodiwiss's *A Rose in Winter* buried on her mother's bookshelf. She lives in the US Midwest countryside with her husband—who's also her ex-husband!—their baby boy, and enough animals to start their own zoo.

SNOWBOUND IN HER BOSS'S BED

MARCELLA BELL

THE PRINCE'S PREGNANT SECRETARY

EMMY GRAYSON

MILLS & BOON

First published in Great Britain 2022
by Mills & Boon, an imprint of HarperCollins*Publishers* Ltd,
1 London Bridge Street, London, SE1 9GF

www.harpercollins.co.uk

HarperCollins*Publishers*
1st Floor, Watermarque Building,
Ringsend Road, Dublin 4, Ireland

Snowbound in Her Boss's Bed © 2022 Marcella Bell

The Prince's Pregnant Secretary © 2022 Emmy Grayson

ISBN: 978-0-263-30104-5

10/22

MIX
Paper from
responsible sources
FSC™ C007454

This book is produced from independently certified FSC™ paper
to ensure responsible forest management.
For more information visit www.harpercollins.co.uk/green.

Printed and Bound in Spain using 100% Renewable Electricity
at CPI Black Print, Barcelona

SNOWBOUND IN HER BOSS'S BED

MARCELLA BELL

MILLS & BOON

This book is dedicated to my Gold family.

Not everyone is so lucky in the family they marry.

I am eternally grateful to have become a part of yours.

CHAPTER ONE

MIRIAM HOWARD SUCKED in a quiet gasp as she took in the immense property below.

Her stomach did a somersault while the plane began its descent, as if she rode over a hill in a car, rather than coasted smoothly toward the runway below.

Even blanketed in a light sheet of snow as everything was now, or maybe because of that, the expanse of development stood out in sharp contrast against the ocean of forest it was nestled within.

She had never before seen a private residence so large—and she was from Los Angeles.

She had also never seen so much snow.

Both were more unnerving than impressive.

When she had been informed yesterday that she would be making the trip to Aspen this morning, she had assumed that she would be landing at a small private airport akin to the one from which she had taken off in LA only hours before.

Instead, while the runway below was indeed small and private, it was not to an airport that the pilot delivered her, but to the far end of what she could only surmise was Benjamin Silver's Colorado compound.

Miri shivered, despite the comfortable cabin temperature of Mr. Silver's private jet.

Descending upon Mr. Silver's famously private sanctuary, she wondered if there was such a thing as *too much* money.

If Mr. Silver wasn't proof of the possibility, over the past twenty-four hours he'd done a fair job of making the case.

Prior to 4:45 p.m. yesterday, Miri had had no travel plans on her horizon.

Now she was moments away from landing at a private compound in the isolated forests outside of Aspen, Colorado on a private jet—all because of Mr. Silver.

She didn't imagine the facts that the trip was both inconvenient and undesired—she had evening plans for the first time since she'd been hired as the new events director for the Los Angeles Jewish Community Foundation two weeks ago—particularly mattered to Mr. Silver. He was a self-made billionaire, after all. It was unlikely that he'd made it as far as he had by prioritizing the desires and convenience of his underlings.

And an underling was most definitely what Miri was to him—even if he wasn't her direct boss.

She didn't report to him for day-to-day things, but he was the board chair of the JCF, the *head* head honcho, and that meant that she—and everyone else on staff, when it came down to it—reported to him.

He could have any one of them fired at any time.

And, making matters worse for Miri in particular, while she didn't report to him, she was tasked with working directly under him to coordinate and execute her most important responsibility as events director: the annual fundraising gala.

She had to jump when he said jump, not just to impress him, but in order to get the job done. She unfortunately needed whatever time he made available to her.

And, if their brief phone call the day before was to be any indication, Miri had gotten the distinct impression that Mr. Silver's time was extremely limited—and that he didn't want to spend much of it with her.

Never mind whether or not I want to spend mine *with him*, she mentally grumbled.

But, as board chair, Mr. Silver was the board member assigned to liaise with her, as well as the one to give official approval for any of her plans.

They had to work together, and his time was worth more than hers.

Hence her impending arrival at his mountain fortress.

Calling the private residence a fortress would have been a bit hyperbolic in most cases, but not here.

Fortress wasn't even truly enough to describe the compound. Really, even that word needed some kind of modifier. *Monstrous*, perhaps? Or maybe *gargantuan*?

The largest building was at least the size of a hotel.

How was it even possible that such a structure was a private residence?

Miri couldn't fathom a family actually living in such a huge structure, even a wealthy one.

With that much space, a family could go weeks without running into one another.

Her own family was large and close-knit, and they had always done fine with just three bedrooms and a finished garage.

And while it had been a long time since Miri had lived at home with all of them, her absence hadn't created any more space. Especially not when her siblings were out there busily populating the world with her plethora of nieces and nephews, all of whom were happy to take the place she'd left.

Now that she lived alone, her entire personal life fit easily within the confines of a microscopic one-bedroom apartment. She had a tiny kitchen, a shower rather than a bathtub, and a bedroom that was too small to fit anything over a full-size bed, and it was still sometimes too much space.

And what if it were just him, all alone out here in the snow?

Miri blinked to clear her mind of the image. It was eerie and lonesome, and the last thing she wanted to think about before spending time in his company.

A place this massive with no family or friends nearby would make a person wonder if *they* were a ghost haunting the halls.

Family—born into, reconstructed or completely made up—was what gave a person the strength needed to navigate landscapes that were vast and filled with pitfalls.

That was true whether the setting was the endless forestland of Colorado's mountains, or the concrete jungle of Los Angeles.

His success was a clear indication that he had successfully navigated his fair share of vast landscapes. There had to have been somebody around, quietly supporting that.

Therefore, she was glad she'd brought doughnuts.

She had taken the risk of waking early to pick them up from a place in Highland Park that everyone had been raving about on her way to the airport that morning.

While under normal circumstances she would not have brought doughnuts along with her to a last-minute meeting with a billionaire, the current context made it seem not only appropriate, but shrewd.

As opposed to what she had learned about the JCF's offices, where contributing to the break room's baked goods collection was not only considered professional but simply the right thing to do, she was not under the impression that sweet treats would impress Benjamin Silver.

She *did* think, however, that there was a chance they might impress his family—whoever they happened to be.

Their meeting was taking place on the first day of Hanukkah at his sprawling private residence; whoever was around would appreciate doughnuts.

Impressing everyone that she met while wearing the hat of events director was not simply a fun exercise to break the ice, nor an attempt to win friends—at least not yet.

Her job was on the line.

She was only two weeks into her new position, a position that was critical to her being able to pay her rent.

To compound the pressure, she had barely secured the position in an extremely competitive hiring process in which she had been neither the favorite nor the most experienced candidate.

But—the result of her being desperate, loaded with more degrees and certifications than any one person had any business having, and inexperienced enough to be foolhardy—she had promised something that the other candidates had said couldn't be done.

She had promised that she could pull off this year's famed annual gala even though the date was only two months away and all the work that had been done up to her hiring had imploded in the fallout of a scandal.

She had projected confidence in making her promises, sensing that she had the hiring committee's attention.

The JCF had been planning to announce the cancellation of the gala.

And so they had taken her up on her bet, provisionally hiring her on the spot—the provision being that she delivered on her promise and gave them a gala the likes of which would make the community forget all about the fact that the former executive director and events director had both been fired upon the discovery of their years-long office affair.

The JCF was still reeling from the fallout among its community of supporters, their faith in the administration of the organization at an all-time low.

Only something transformative could distract and redirect their attention and restore their confidence.

Miri had promised a gala that would be just that.

So she needed Mr. Silver not just on her side, but behind her with full support.

She needed him wrapped around her little finger when it came to ideas and plans—at least if she had any hope of preserving her job.

Unfortunately, she was not off to a great start when it came to the billionaire, whom she had only been able to speak to for the first time yesterday—after emailing and reaching out to him multiple times a day every business day for the past two weeks.

Even more unfortunately, the moment had not been at her best.

"Virtual meetings leave questions, and I don't have time for follow-up calls," the man on the other end of the line had said in the kind of voice that narrated women's fantasies.

Deep and smooth, each perfectly modulated word vibrated with power and wealth.

Even, apparently, when he was being unreasonable.

Miri held back her frustrated sigh.

That he felt that way was a problem. As the board liaison assigned to the annual gala, Mr. Silver was the man she needed to work with.

He also currently resided outside of Aspen in Colorado, whereas she was operating out of the foundation's primary offices in Los Angeles.

"I have two hours to spare for this," he'd continued, the smooth chords of his words reaching through to the phone to once again wrap around her. "And that means we need to get it all done in one go, rather than meet virtually or exchange a thousand emails."

As gorgeous as it sounded, he chastised her with his

mention of emails—of which she had sent many—before carrying on with his baritone bulldozing.

"You're going to fly out here tomorrow morning. We will spend a couple of hours making necessary calls and final preparations for the gala, and then you'll fly home. You will have the rare privilege of my complete attention, after which I don't expect to hear from you again until we meet again on the night of the gala."

Nothing about his suggestion was at all reasonable.

The following day, the day he was proposing they meet in person, was the first day of Hanukkah. And as if that weren't enough reason not to demand a sudden meeting, Miri already had a full day scheduled. Not to mention the fact that, in keeping with the tradition they'd started in their undergraduate days, she and her closest friends were getting together in the evening to celebrate the holiday.

These days they saw one another so infrequently, she didn't relish the possibility of missing it due to travel sna-fus.

Plus, getting tickets and a car rental at this stage would be an expensive nightmare—even if it was going on her business credit card.

But, smiling through her slightly locked jaw, Miri had said, "I'd be happy to fly out to Aspen, Mr. Silver. I'll co-ordinate travel immediately."

On the other end of the phone line, Mr. Silver had laughed.

"That's adorable, but no. Do you know how long it would take you just to get through the airport, let alone get a seat on a commercial plane at this time of year? I did mention that I have just two hours, did I not? It would take you that much time just to get to my home from the airport via car. No. You'll take my plane. Are you ready for my airport's address?"

"Sir, really, it's no trouble," Miri had pressed back.

She didn't even like sharing rides around town. The idea of being at the mercy of someone's plane for out-of-state travel sat even less well with her. If she was doing this at all, she was making her own arrangements.

"The flight from LA to Aspen is not long and I don't mind a red-eye," she'd added.

Miri hated to feel indebted to or reliant on anyone— especially for the experience of a luxury that she hadn't asked for. When you owed people, they had a hard time allowing you to change.

If Miri was going to pull this gala off, she needed him to be open to change.

Irritation energized Mr. Silver's voice, but the edge of it only enhanced its spine-tingling nature.

Voices like his belonged in the entertainment industry, not on the board of directors for a nonprofit organization.

"I told you we don't have the time," he'd said, with a firmness to his words that set off a little flame of defiance in Miriam.

He wasn't the only one who was irritated.

"Private planes are far more likely to crash," she said drily. "I imagine my death would create a bigger delay than the cab ride from the airport to your home office."

Then she'd clapped a silent hand over her mouth.

Exasperation had momentarily clouded her good judgment.

She was going to get herself fired.

The last thing she needed was to give the impression that she was difficult, or, God forbid, *sassy*.

Either alone could spell death for a Black woman in high-level nonprofit work.

Mr. Silver, however, had surprised her.

He'd laughed.

The sound was as rich, warm and well-rounded as his speaking voice, but unlike his voice, the modulated and controlled cadence of which sounded like money, his laugh was the open joy of a regular person, rolling out of him as if he could recall what it was like to go to grocery stores and pay parking tickets.

As if she had been joking, he came back with his own sarcasm and humor. "If you're so concerned about the plane, my helicopter is always available…"

"I'll pass on the helicopter offer, thank you," she said quickly, shuddering even at the idea while simultaneously relieved that it appeared that she hadn't put her foot in it after all.

Nonetheless, it had been time to get off the phone before something even more disastrous happened.

"I'll be at the location you gave me in the morning," she said.

"Excellent. I'll see you tomorrow. And don't worry, you have my word that you'll be back in Los Angeles long before dark, no risk of missing even a moment of Hanukkah with your family. Two hours, no more."

He had hung up without saying goodbye, and at the click, Miriam had let out a sigh of relief.

She could have told him that that particular concern was unnecessary because, while she had a family, they wouldn't be celebrating any holidays with her any time soon and her friends wouldn't mind her being late—but did not.

Benjamin Silver had no reason to care about her personal life.

The only thing he cared about was getting everything they had to get through done in two hours, and if they were going to do that, she had a lot of prep work to do.

Fortunately, that meant a lot to distract her from the fact that she would be attending a meeting with the sixth-richest man in the world.

A long night in front of the computer had to be enough to dull the stress of the idea.

They would meet for no more than two hours, and then she could return home, that much closer to securing her position with the JCF and done with Mr. Silver.

The next day had arrived very quickly, though, and now, as the plane touched down, Miri wasn't sure if her reassurances might have been a bit premature.

Staring in awe at the wintery world outside the comfortable private jet, she was reminded that, in truth, her time with Mr. Silver had not even begun.

CHAPTER TWO

"A CARDIGAN?" he asked incredulously, adding, "You thought it was a good idea to wear a cardigan on a business trip to Colorado in November?"

Exasperation was just one of many emotions Benjamin Silver felt upon laying eyes on Ms. Miriam Howard. Among the surge, however, exasperation was the most straightforward and direct.

He preferred communication that was clear and to the point.

Therefore, he made it clear what he thought of the cardigan.

While the snow was just a light blanket over the ground this early in the year, it was, nonetheless, *snow*.

Closing his eyes, he exhaled through his nose, allowing himself a respite from the effort of not devouring her with his eyes.

Her appearance had somewhat stunned him.

When he focused on the cardigan, however, rather than the fact that her figure and face would have made the proud subjects of a sensual oil painting, he could handle himself.

She stood above average height, which appealed to him as a tall man, and had glowing skin that looked soft enough to touch.

And she wore a cardigan to Colorado in November, he reminded himself.

And in what should have been a more compelling fact, she was his subordinate.

Ms. Howard had been an emergency hire. This was their first meeting.

His reaction was inappropriate.

But she was nothing like what he had expected.

A cardigan, he repeated mentally.

Taking her in, he wondered if the foundation had simply added fuel to the fire that was this year's gala in selecting her for the position of events director.

She looked incredibly young, her clear brown skin bright and dewy, even in the crisp dry mountain air of Colorado.

She certainly did not present the kind of mild-mannered mid-career executive image that would have reassured their supporters that the JCF had left its sexy and salacious days behind it.

She was the sexiest woman he had ever encountered.

Even in budget business attire, she gave the impression of lushness.

Shaking himself, he wrestled his mind back to the cardigan.

And, young though she might look, it wasn't a naive newbie who answered him when she finally spoke. Her irritation obvious in the words that squeezed through her clenched teeth, she said, "I was under the impression that we would be meeting inside."

She might be inexperienced, he acknowledged, *but she has spine.*

She revealed it now, as she had when they'd spoken on the phone the day before.

If anyone knew how far spine could take a person in this world, it was him.

He'd built an empire on spine.

If she possessed enough of it, she might even be able

to deliver on the bold promises she had made to the hiring committee.

Her cardigan, however, did not convey spine.

It conveyed poor planning, and planning was her job.

"It's November. In Aspen," he said, giving her no quarter even as he allowed her stubborn streak to impress him.

In response, her stunning topaz eyes narrowed, flashing against the warm brown backdrop of her skin.

He had never seen eyes like hers before—warm whiskey, rimmed with deep obsidian.

"Forgive me for not packing my skis," she retorted.

Flushed heat then came to the satiny apples of her cheeks, bringing a subtle duskiness to their warm expanse, and the pressure in Benjamin's veins ticked up a notch not for the first time since he had been in her presence.

Perhaps that reaction was what was behind the pleasure he found in goading her.

A part of him recognized her as a woman worth romantic pursuit.

The remainder of him, however, was committed to the success of the annual gala.

And attraction to the new events director, after what had happened with the previous, was entirely inappropriate for that goal.

Even if she was nearly six feet tall in the heels she wore and had the curves to carry it.

Benjamin tore his mind away from her body and returned it to her clothing.

Clothing was innocuous and safe.

Her outfit consisted of a blouse buttoned low enough to give hints of what looked like a lace-edged beige satin camisole beneath, both of which were tucked neatly at the narrow waist of her black pencil skirt.

Her heels were skinny and also black. And to bring it all together, she wore her ridiculous, flimsy beige cardigan.

Everything she wore was thin.

And she was carrying a bright teal box.

A faint smile coming to his lips, Benjamin replied smoothly, "I've got plenty of skis, if it comes to it. What I haven't got—" the edge returned to his words "—are spare women's parkas."

Though, of course, between the staff and his guest supplies, Benjamin would not have been surprised to learn that he *did* have spare parkas.

"I'm sure I'll survive," Ms. Howard replied smoothly, her voice as dry and cold as the air around them, and Benjamin nearly chuckled.

Her sartorial wisdom might be questionable, but she was funny.

And she had backbone.

The traits could only help her get her job done—as long as she knew how to create the kinds of events that schmoozed wealthy donors like himself into opening their wallets.

Getting started toward that end was why he had driven out to the runway to pick her up himself, rather than send someone.

He had not braved the elements in order to criticize her choice in clothing, but in order to get working.

But with her teeth chattering as they got in the car, he instead turned the heat up and yet again adjusted his expectations.

Ms. Howard was necessitating quite the number of adjustments.

She was nothing like what he had pictured when he'd spoken to her on the phone yesterday.

Her Southern California accent was so reminiscent of the women he'd gone to school with as a suburban kid in Los Angeles that he'd assigned her a figure and persona to match.

Instead, stealing a glance at her through the corner of his eye as he drove them to his home, Benjamin could not remember ever meeting a single woman who looked like the one currently riding in his passenger seat.

Certainly not the entire package she presented—the remarkable eyes, the height, the willingness to push back at him.

Currently, she thrummed with a swirling blend of righteous indignation and professional poise he found mildly impressive.

Pulling into the circular driveway at the front entrance of the closest thing he had to a home anymore, he smiled when she let out a little gasp.

He was proud of his getaway in the trees, though no one had ever visited it.

The compound was a testament to all of the hard work he had done in his life to get there.

Going around the car, he opened her door and offered her his hand.

She took it, stepping outside to take the structure in.

Her palm slid into his, cool and smooth with a whisper of something that had him leaning in to hear before he had the presence of mind to pull back.

Ms. Howard did not appear to notice his proximity, however, her attention instead focused on his home.

The front entrance had been designed to inspire wonder, and it appeared to have done the job with Ms. Howard.

Her heavily lashed almond eyes widened as she stared.

The enormous building boasted beams that seemed to have to have come from trees from another epoch, their incredible girths anchored into equally massive rounded river stone bases. The real estate listing had described it as "an elegant log and stone cabin on a large private forested property outside of Aspen," highlighting its classic exposed-beam design, vaulted ceilings and rich natural materials.

He'd purchased it on sight, feeling instant ease with its immensity and lack of facade.

Growing up in a city that grew illusions, he had longed for authenticity.

It pleased him that Ms. Howard was impressed.

Closing her car door behind her, he then led her through the front door and into the vast foyer with its wall of floor-to-ceiling windows that stared out into miles and miles of forest.

To offset some of the heavy, closed-in feeling that log cabins—even enormous ones—could sometimes have, he'd had his designers incorporate white accent walls of smooth adobe throughout the home, their rough natural surfaces blending well with the thick rounded beams of the mountain estate.

He had also added more than two dozen new windows and skylights to the existing impressive number, brightening the interior and bringing even more of the vast forest into the many hallways, dining rooms and sitting rooms that he now led her through.

He did not give her a tour, though.

As much as he was enjoying her little noises of astonishment and awe, she was not here to look at his house.

She was here to work.

To that end, passing several sitting and specialty rooms and hallways without comment, he brought her to his office.

Located in the deep interior of the sprawling chalet, Benjamin's office was connected to his personal suite via thick French doors that were currently closed.

He had had the private wing of the cabin remodeled to meet his exact specifications, including the office.

The desk was his preferred height, built into a bay of windows that overlooked the forest.

Built-in bookshelves lined the walls, fabricated to the exact size required to house his favorite works.

A fireplace and seating area were set up in the corner for his comfort.

His office space was more closed in and cozier than much of the home, which he preferred.

Closed-in and cozy reminded him of where he had come from. It connected him to the drives of a younger, poorer version of himself.

His office reminded him that he had achieved what he had because it had been his parents' dream that the world know his name—not because he was trying to be someone he was not.

Whether he was one of the most powerful men in the world or, as he had been when they were alive to bear witness, one of the most anonymous—he knew who he was and he was comfortable with it.

Ms. Howard, however, appeared to be less moved by his most revealing space than she had been by the rest of the house.

She likely saw only that it was less awe-inspiring than the other areas, not realizing that it represented the essence of him.

To her, in all likelihood, it was merely the room that housed a desk and computer.

She wouldn't necessarily see that the computer and what he did with it were worth more than the entire compound—as well as the reason he could afford it all in the first place.

"This is where we'll be working," he said, observing her as he spoke. "You can sit there."

He pointed to a chair at his left.

Ms. Howard nodded and went to the seat, placing her teal box on the desk to the side of her shoulder bag.

The bag had seen better days.

Unlike the foundation's previous events director, a woman who had owned a seemingly endless supply of immaculate designer briefcases and handbags, Ms. Howard's accessory had cracks in the leather of its handles and fraying seams.

In fact, like the rest of her attire, it appeared rather threadbare.

"What's in the box?" he asked, unable to keep a taut note from entering his voice as he took a seat at her side.

"Oh," she said, taking a quick glance at the box as if she had momentarily forgotten about it. "Doughnuts from Grease Monkey. It's the new *it* spot in LA."

Lifting a brow, he remained silent, staring at her for a moment before smirking at the direction of his thoughts.

She would have no idea bringing doughnuts would touch a nerve.

She was probably just eager to impress.

"Do you usually go through a box of doughnuts in a two-hour meeting?"

A frown swept across her brow at his question. "Absolutely not."

He chuckled. "So they're for me, then?"

Shaking her head in another quick negative, Ms. Howard denied quickly once again, "No."

"Then who were you hoping to impress with doughnuts from LA's latest hot spot?"

Frown deepening, Ms. Howard looked around as if she expected someone to appear in the deep inner sanctum of his house. "They're for your family. With the holidays kicking off tonight, I thought…"

Benjamin stilled.

She had brought doughnuts for the loved ones that she assumed he would be around for the holidays.

It was a sweet gesture.

There was just no one left in the world that he loved.

He had been blessed with two sets of adoring parents in his life—and he had lost them both.

Neither set had left him with any grandparents, cousins, aunts or uncles, and being twice orphaned had left him leery of going for a third shot and making a family of his own.

And if all of that meant an isolated existence for him, it also meant there was no family to compete with his work for his time.

There was no one to make demands of him, no one to disappoint.

He could disappear into the woods and no one would come looking for him.

He could lose himself in work and no one would find him.

But, of course, she wouldn't know any of that.

And he intended to keep it that way.

Mystery was more powerful than pity.

For anyone to pity him was absurd.

He had been blessed with more love, happiness and success in a single lifetime than the vast majority of humans on the planet.

What did it matter if all that remained now was success?

Concealing his thoughts behind a polite smile, Benjamin did not answer the unspoken question about his family. Instead, he commented, "Thoughtful of you. Obvious, but thoughtful."

Ms. Howard whipped around to face him, her eyes widening at him in offense in the process.

He wanted her offended. Offended was better than curious about his life.

She opened her mouth, but he spoke before she could. "I've buzzed my assistant to retrieve them. I'm sure they'll be appreciated."

He did not mention by whom.

She need not know they would simply be set out for his staff to enjoy at a later time.

"Shall we get started, Ms. Howard?" he asked.

She gave a decisive nod, then reached into her bag to pull out a dinosaur of a laptop. Setting up in front of her, she opened the ancient device and began a slow process of starting it up and loading programs. "What's the Wi-Fi password?" she asked without looking at him, and Benjamin was amused.

He appreciated these brief moments in which she seemed to forget just who he was and treated him like a colleague, as opposed to her wealthy supervisor.

He answered her question as he continued to observe her.

She opened impressive, color-coded spreadsheets, electronic brochures and a number of emails.

Her fingers flew across her keyboard at an administrative clip, her well-shaped nails just long enough to click against the keys.

Her hands were softly padded and elegant, her simple manicure tasteful if not of the highest end, fingers moving with confidence and assuredness.

She continued to prepare, focused on the work in front of her, until his assistant arrived to remove the doughnuts.

At the interruption, Ms. Howard looked up with a smile and a warm, "Thank you."

As she spoke, her cheeks lifted, her entire countenance brightening with the expression, and Benjamin found himself momentarily surprised, right alongside his assistant.

That Ms. Howard's smile was enough to stop even his hatchet assistant in her tracks, an aging mountain woman who utterly lacked a sense of romance, spoke to its power.

Turning to Benjamin, Ms. Howard's expression transitioned to one of focused seriousness, her eyebrows drawn slightly together as she asked, "Where would you like to begin, Mr. Silver?"

But though he had recovered from her arresting smile, Benjamin nonetheless did not answer her immediately.

Before that, he slid out the chair beside her and took it, reaching forward to press the subtle round button in the desk's surface. Soundlessly, a panel in the center of the desk opened and his large, thin monitor rose from its compartment within the desk.

"Let's begin with the venue," he said before booting up his own system with the voice command, "Load!"

The system, and the wealth of very proprietary coding contained within it, was programmed to respond only to his voice. For additional security, his keypad, which rose from its own panel within the desk at his word, responded to his fingerprints alone.

He was a man who appreciated his privacy, his security and his world programmed exclusively to himself.

Fortunately, he had enough money to ensure all three.

With his system up and running, he turned back to Ms. Howard, covering the strange jolt he had felt each time he laid eyes on her with a frown.

"Where are we with that? Concept? Progress? All of it in two minutes," he commanded.

Frown flashing across her own face, Ms. Howard turned her gaze to the many tabs, images and pdfs open on the screen in front of her. With a faint shake of her head her eyes flashed from detail to detail, the wheels of her mind obviously turning as she bent herself to the unexpected task of trying to so succinctly summarize the bulk of her work for the foundation thus far.

Benjamin, however, did not modify his request.

If she could not summarize her efforts, she did not have command of the situation.

Could she deliver?

When her eyelids lifted there was a steady resolve in her bright amber orbs.

Her gaze, direct and clear as it was, rattled him, shaking him as if she had some power to influence the tectonic plates of his subconscious, but he processed the impact in the back of his mind, keeping his primary focus trained on her full lips.

Moistening them before she spoke, she said, "I reserved Vibiana. They're full service and since time is short, I thought it best to take them up on that. Because it's a decommissioned cathedral, it's got a lot of very old-world European detail, so I have been conceptualizing a Secret Garden theme. I looked through previous files and it has never been done before. It's pretty and festive, but still far from Christmassy. Picture lovely architecture and detail, mosaics, greenery all around. There is also an outdoor garden area that will serve as the ballroom floor, so to speak."

Her ideas were fresh, possibly exciting—as long as they were carried off with taste as opposed to kitsch. They were certainly nothing like anything the foundation had done before.

There was a big gap between a good idea and a solid execution, however.

"You're telling me the plan is to gather the city's wealthiest Jews together in a Roman Catholic cathedral?" he pushed.

Had she thought her plan through, or was she merely carried away in imagery? Did she understand what was at stake, or did she think this event was merely an opportunity to plan an almost-wedding?

Her frown deepening, Ms. Howard repeated and emphasized her first word when she spoke. "*Decommissioned* and now one of the trendiest event spots downtown, so yes, it is. The location is ideal, the full service and reputation for excellent catering is beyond a time-saver, and the capacity is exactly what we need for this event. It's large enough for the dinner service, while also offering private and intimate spaces for smaller groups to gather and converse. Honestly, it's better than we could have hoped for. That they could even fit us into their calendar was a matter of dumb luck and cancellation. They have a kosher kitchen, and the chef is well versed. I really can't see how we could have done better, especially given the circumstances."

Benjamin appreciated her thinking, though he continued to search out any flaws in her ideas.

"It's not the Getty," he said.

Letting out a little noise of frustration, Ms. Howard's response was both sharper and quicker than her previous. "No. It's not the Getty. And, as I've discussed with the rest of the senior staff, as well as some of the more involved donors who somehow got word, given the situation we're presently dealing with, not to mention the fact that it is now absolutely unavailable to us, the Getty is unfortunately no longer an option on the table."

There was that interesting spine of hers again.

Benjamin allowed a small smile to tilt the corners of his mouth upward. "That's a rather politic way to describe a scandal," he said.

Ms. Howard gave an unconcerned shrug. "My job is to ensure that the foundation's events continue to run smoothly, now and into the future. I'm not interested in rehashing the past."

"Well said," Benjamin replied, "and, as *I* said, politic."

The previous events director had been fired due to the revelation of her ongoing affair with the foundation's married executive director.

Fraternizing between employees was prohibited at the JCF.

Both actors had been fired, deeply damaging the reputation of the foundation and rattling community faith in its capacity to carry out its mission.

Ms. Howard wasn't the only new hire, nor the most important.

But, as opposed to Ms. Howard, the hiring committee had gone with the most experienced and proven candidate for executive director in order to re-instill faith in the community and steer the organization through the rocky transition.

The former executive director had bowed to the decisions of the board, cooperating and supporting it with as much grace as she could.

The former events director, however, had not been so accommodating.

Choosing vengeance, she had taken her contacts with her when she left as well as sullied the foundation's name among her network of service providers.

And after fifteen years in the position, the woman's network had been extensive.

In attesting to have the skill to clean up the mess, the newly hired Ms. Howard had agreed to not just race against the clock, but to buck the flow of how things were normally done.

The foundation's largest donors, however, did not tend to be fans of bucking the flow.

"You're going to need that when we announce a new venue," Benjamin added.

If she had been comfortable around him, she might have sighed in commiseration. Her eyes said as much, even while outwardly she merely held herself still and took a long blink.

"I've gathered as much," she said. "At this point, though, I have sampled menu options and walked the space myself, so I am confident that the experience will change hearts and minds."

"And what about those who will refuse outright? This

is LA we're talking here. Never put it past people to simply not be willing to drive downtown."

Without missing a beat, Ms. Howard replied, "That's where you come in. This year it is more important than ever that you reach out to our most important donors with personal invitations. I can give them a gala they won't forget, but you need to sell it."

Benjamin held back a full smile after getting yet another glimpse of the steel in her.

She had communicated the same message, earnestly and with urgency, in the many emails she had sent him. Though she did not realize it, he had done better than respond to an electronic message. He had given her his direct time.

He wanted this to succeed as much as she did.

"Ah, yes," he said, warmth cracking some of the hard lines of his face. "A personal invitation from the billionaire. Well, if I am to whore myself out, it's likely time to get into the details."

"So I have your approval for the venue and theme?" she confirmed.

She needed it—his approval—and so he knew she listened for his response carefully. It appeared she was the type of person unwilling to jump to conclusions.

He appreciated the trait.

It revealed that she was keenly aware of the time constraints she was working within and would not risk losing any to mistakes or misunderstandings.

He nodded, confirming with a "yes" but no further elaboration. She need not know that not only did he approve, but that he found her ideas a refreshing change from the glitz and glam aesthetic of previous years.

Ms. Howard's eyes lit with a spark of real joy. "Excellent. Now, for food. Given the time frame, it seemed best to go tried and true for the menu, sticking with the chef's most popular option of a three-course meal with seafood, red meat and vegetarian options, fruit and chocolate dessert selections, and a very open bar. If you agree, it's a simple matter of letting the chef know—"

Stopping her, Benjamin held up a hand. "What are the options?" he asked.

"Salmon, filet mignon and vegetable risotto," she answered, eyebrows drawing together as she looked from her screen to him.

Benjamin shook his head. "No. Absolutely not. Your concept thus far has been interesting and fresh. I expected better from the menu. The donors will, too."

"Excuse me," she said, her right brow lifting slightly, arguments reading themselves in her eyes. "It's my judgment that with the event less than four weeks away we don't have the time to experiment with a menu and the subsequent tastings. The classics done right blow people away, time and again."

"No," Benjamin repeated, more certain he was right with every word he heard. "If we give them what they might have delivered to their doorstep on any given Tuesday night, the letdown will be what people talk about afterward, no matter how many pretty flowers you surround them with. Your menu bears no relationship to the concept. By that alone, it breaks the continuity of the evening and theme, makes it clear that the recent scandal was a sign that the foundation is indeed faltering and disorganized. It is more critical this year than ever that every detail reflect competence or they're not going to hand over their money. Anything that hints at haphazard or thrown together at the last minute will have lasting impacts. And more than that, it's boring. Give me something better. That idea is lazy and below your standard."

That idea is lazy and below your standard...

The words rang in Miri's head, stunning in their blunt censure—even if they were true.

How dare he say so? What did he know of her standards?

The classic catering offering idea *had* been lazy—intentionally—because Miriam had seen the menu as the best place to save time in the miracle she was trying to pull off.

There simply wasn't time to reinvent the wheel, and food was a place where people preferred the usual.

Or so she had determined.

Mr. Silver clearly did not agree.

Unable to fully hide the faint edge to her tone, Miri said, "I apologize, but I'm going to need you to clarify. Are you asking me to come up with a new menu right now?"

He nodded impatiently. "It appears I was crystal clear. What you've got now is basic and has nothing to do with your theme."

Miri pressed back. "I won't argue those points. It was a sacrifice I felt was warranted considering our time constraints."

With a dismissive snort, Mr. Silver waved her words away like so many excuses. "I don't care what your reasons were. I told you to do better."

Miri's mouth dropped open.

The man was out of his mind and mad with power. It was the only explanation—for any element of her day, honestly, from the unrequested flight to the fancy desktop, to this right now.

How dare he speak to her like a child?

Like he was some kind of mentor pressuring her into higher performance.

And this was *after* all of his comments about her cardigan.

Thank God they were only meeting for two hours. And that she had a night with her closest friends to look forward to when it was all over.

He's been complimentary of the concept thus far, a timid internal voice offered.

Miriam stamped that voice out.

The last thing this man needed was someone inside *her* head making excuses for him.

Autocratic, bad-mannered, out of touch, toxic man... Her mental litany continued as she forced her face into a smile.

"Why certainly, Mr. Silver. Recalling that the theme is Secret Garden, we should obviously have a menu built around lush produce prepared simply with fresh herbs, botanical cocktails, and desserts inspired by the overflowing bounty of a summer garden, throwing in honey berry drizzles and edible flowers here and there throughout it all for the whimsy. Is that more along the lines of what you were thinking?" She said it all brightly, but the flat tone of her voice said exactly what she thought.

She thought he was being outrageous. Everything about him.

His demands, his mountain fortress, his power, his ability to make her forget that everything depended on making a good impression with him and instead respond with a more authentic version of herself—all of it.

Without his cooperation, there was no way she would keep her job. Without her job, the only place she had to go was back home. Pride had pushed her to stay in her car the two weeks immediately after graduation rather than go back to her family home before she'd gotten her apartment, but she knew she didn't have enough pride for a second round of that.

She would rather do whatever it took to keep her apartment and the new job she was already in love with.

She wanted those things more than she was interested in chasing any wild thoughts she might be inclined to think about Mr. Benjamin Silver.

He might be good-looking and have a great voice, but he also lived on a different planet from the one she inhabited. He was entirely out of her league—both because of the foundation and because of his wealth.

He was not a man she could afford to be a more authentic version of herself with.

He was a man she had to be the sharpest, most impressive version of herself with.

He held her gaze for a moment silently, his clear blue eyes dancing with a light that could have been temper or humor.

It flashed through her mind that under different circumstances, she wouldn't have minded knowing him well enough to know the difference.

Then he smiled, slowly, one corner of his mouth lifting at a time, offering Miri a glimpse of his straight white teeth, and she had her answer: humor.

Even as she attempted to shore up the foundation of her professionalism, his grinning eyes promised he could handle a little pushback.

"Exactly," he said. "Much better, Ms. Howard." He continued to grin as he elongated the *Ms.* in a way that could only be interpreted as insolence. "That's much more in alignment with the event you've put together thus far."

"I'll update it accordingly, sir," she said, exhaling through flared nostrils with irritation even as a part of her was pleased at what was ultimately a show of real buy-in to her plan.

Here again was the contrary sense of humor that she had encountered on the phone.

He joked, but he was also serious.

He meant every word he said, even when his delivery was shameless.

Sighing out the last of her irritation on the point, she

updated her spreadsheet, elaborating and specifying the menu she had rattled off to him facetiously.

Eyeing the updated menu with narrowed eyes, a part of her grumbled, knowing the necessary tastings would have to be squeezed into her already tight schedule.

The rest of her acknowledged that the revision was an improvement over the original.

With his input, the new menu was more interesting and memorable, and far more aligned with her concept.

"Wonderful work, Ms. Howard. Now that's sorted, please continue. I believe we had arrived at entertainment."

He spoke as if he were a king, generously doling out his approval, and Miri resisted the urge to roll her eyes.

She didn't know why it was so hard to maintain control of her reactions when it came to the man at her side.

It was probably just that everything he said and did was provoking.

If he could have managed to stop behaving as if the entire world worked for him for more than three minutes, it might have been easier to keep a handle on herself.

Never mind that she *did* work for him.

They continued through the remaining elements of the gala in generally the same manner—Mr. Silver waving his dismissive hand of approval to most of what she presented with periodic breaks for criticism that goaded her into improvement.

That he seemed to understand her intentions without needing explanations only made it that much more irritating each time he lambasted the elements of her plans that were merely acceptable or expedient.

But to both of their credits, the event improved at each and every point at which he stopped her.

When they were done, Miriam was confident that if this gala didn't blow its attendees away, it would be because those attendees were dead inside.

Unfortunately, her neck was also stiff and tense from the effort it had taken to rein herself in every time her mind wanted to dash off on a wild tangent related to his voice or brace for his next critical interruption.

Bringing a hand to rub her neck, she checked her watch, only to startle at the time.

They were late—by an hour.

How had they gone over by a whole hour?

By the way Mr. Silver had gone on and on about how limited his time was, she would have expected him to have set an alarm to keep them on schedule.

As it was, going over the hour threatened to put even *her* off schedule.

Yes, flying by private jet saved a lot of time, but losing an hour meant losing the chance to get home and change her clothes before she headed out to meet her friends.

But out loud, all she said was, "It looks like we've gone over our two hours."

She packed her things back into her bag with a new urgency.

"What?" His response was swift, that stunning voice of his filled with genuine and not exactly pleased surprise.

Even caught off guard it was kind of sexy.

Shocked at herself at the thought, Miri moved with even more purpose.

She needed to get out of Colorado and back to Los Angeles. A warm night with friends would wash this whole encounter away—which she obviously needed.

They might work well together, but she was grateful it wasn't going to be an all-the-time thing. Three hours in the company of Mr. Silver was simply more than her body and mind could handle.

Men were not supposed to both be as rich as he was and look the way he did.

Where was the equality in that?

He needed more flaws than the habit of delivering criticisms with the bluntness of a baseball bat.

He should not have been blessed with the kind of voice that belonged on television, nor should he have had the physical features to match.

He should not have had bright azure eyes, as clear as a glacier.

He should not have worn his hair long so that its soft mink-brown waves framed and feathered around his face and thick broad shoulders.

He should not have had full lips and straight dark brows, or his incredible height.

He was supposed to be an arrogant software guy approaching midlife.

Instead, he was attractive even when his behavior wasn't.

And after three hours that were supposed to have only been two, it had finally short-circuited her.

Miri was exhausted—by his energy, his exactitude, his commands, his gorgeousness and her reactions to it all.

For his part, Mr. Silver had the decency to look a bit worn himself.

Looking at his watch, he frowned, the expression flaring in his cool blue stare not the surprise of a man caught unawares by how much time had passed but the irritation of a man used to total control, especially over the clock.

He was offended that time had gotten away from him.

Well, good, Miri thought. *It's about time someone other than me was offended.*

"It cost an unexpected hour, but we made excellent headway." She didn't know why she made an attempt to comfort him when he could stand to be reminded that the elements didn't bend to his will, but she did, adding, "It will be just like you said on the phone. We won't need to connect again until the night of the gala."

He only nodded absently, frown still firmly in place, lost in his own thoughts.

Well, if he wasn't pleased with their progress and lack of need for further contact, Miri was.

They'd done good work, which, simple as it was, was something she took pride in.

She wasn't made for last-minute flights on private planes and private meetings with billionaires. She was made for working in an office with a shared break room that was always stocked with baked goods.

She was made for water coolers and event planning and proving her value by showing the funders a good time.

She was made for good work, intimate dinners with longtime friends, quiet nights at home curled up with a good book and finally establishing some real independence in her life.

In all of that, she was not, as the afternoon had made painfully obvious to her, equipped to withstand the onslaught of an ice king richer than most world leaders and hotter than an A-lister.

Was it any wonder she was losing control of her mind?

And to make matters worse, she still had to brave the perilous and freezing journey through the snow to get back to Mr. Silver's plane and private runway.

Once she was on the plane, though, she would be able to breathe a sigh of relief away from the hawklike blue gaze of Mr. Benjamin Silver and focus on the warm and relaxing evening ahead of her.

Where, thank God, there will be wine, she reminded herself.

Miri sighed out loud in anticipation, and Mr. Silver gaze shot to her, a quizzical look in his eyes.

He really had the most arresting eyes.

Miriam would not have been surprised to learn he could see straight through everyone he encountered.

"Private joke?" he asked, leading her to the office door they'd entered not two, but three, hours before.

Shaking her head, Miriam said, "No. Just getting a little delirious. Air is thinner here," she added lightly.

Self-deprecating, he smirked. "Is that a nice way of saying I suck the oxygen out of a room?" he asked, and though she didn't know him well—at all, really—Miri knew he was joking.

She smiled and shook her head lightly but said no more.

From another man, the joke might have been charming. But not from him. She couldn't allow him to be charming.

He was too powerful—had too much sway in her life to be charming from a safe distance.

Charm could be fun, but it was also dangerous.

Charm disarmed. It was fun and made you feel pretty, and it was also fickle and liable to abruptly leave you alone in a lurch.

She had an ex-high-school-sweetheart fiancé who had been charming until he wasn't, and the experience had taught her that charm was something she could allow into her life only under strict parameters.

Alone in the woods with a man with enough power to have the world literally at his fingertips, a face and physique that belonged on the silver screen, and a voice that made her want to take off her clothes—whether it was demanding more of her or calling her out or simply exchanging pleasantries—were not those parameters.

"This place is so big, inside and out. No single man could take up all the air. Is that why you like to spend so much time out here?"

He laughed, the sound deep and resonant, and Miri once again questioned her decisions.

Making him laugh was a bad idea.

"You've found me out," he said, still smiling, his eyes

glittering like ice in the moonlight. "Here, even a man such as myself is humbled by the surroundings."

He was mesmerizing, like something beautiful because it was dangerous, and for a moment she was frozen looking at him.

It took her several seconds to shake free once more.

She had never encountered a man around whom walking the line was so exhausting.

And once again he was telling the truth even as he joked.

There was real respect for the awe-inspiring landscape in his humor.

When she had collected her things in her shoulder bag once more, he led her toward the office door. "Despite our additional hour, you should still arrive back in LA with plenty of time to spare before sundown."

Miriam nodded, relieved again at the prospect of a night celebrating Hanukkah with her friends after the intensity of her meeting with Mr. Silver.

Opening the door, he stepped aside to let her through, only to stop in his tracks upon finding his assistant standing on the other side of the door, a severe frown on her face.

"I'm sorry to be the bearer of bad news, sir," the woman said, without preamble or a hint of remorse in her voice and as blunt as her employer, "but a storm swept in. They're calling it a full-on blizzard. Chuck says he doesn't know when he'll be able to get back into the sky, but it's not going to be today."

Mr. Silver stilled. "There was no warning?" he asked, censure heavy in the question.

His assistant remained unfazed. "The do-not-disturb alert was on," the older woman replied with a shrug, as if that explained her not poking in to let them know of an impending storm that had the potential to prevent Miriam from getting home.

In response, however, Mr. Silver nodded, accepting the response as if it were perfectly reasonable.

But it was not reasonable.

It was completely unreasonable.

Blizzards weren't the kind of thing that happened to her.

They should have been warned. She needed to get home. To her friends, and the sun, and Los Angeles.

And most of all, she needed to get away from Mr. Benjamin Silver—before she did or said something to get herself fired.

CHAPTER THREE

"How LONG AGO did it roll in?" Benjamin asked his assistant, irritation in his voice though none of it was for the messenger. He knew where the fault lay, and it wasn't with the bearer of bad news.

He had been very clear with his staff about his expectations when the do-not-disturb light above his office was lit. He was not to be disturbed—under any circumstances.

"About thirty-five minutes ago, sir," his assistant replied with her characteristic specificity.

It was exactly as he had immediately assumed.

Had their meeting concluded on time, Ms. Howard would have beat the storm.

He despised lapses in scheduling.

He knew that a difference of an hour could be the difference between life and death.

He had learned that the hard way, long ago and too young, with the death of his parents.

A wasted hour of fuel and you woke up more than half-drowned to the loss of everything you held dear. A wasted hour was enough to make a man wish he were dead, too.

But Benjamin was not dead.

And because of that, he did not waste time.

But somehow, he had with Ms. Howard.

An entire hour had slipped past him unaware while he

had been absorbed by the fascinating mind and mannerisms of a woman who was nothing that he expected.

And because of that lapse, she would not be going home tonight.

Because of that, she would spend the first night of Hanukkah with him, rather than whatever else she had planned.

Turning to her, his frustration making his delivery less smooth than it might otherwise have been, he said, "It appears that you *will* be missing the first night of Hanukkah with your family, after all. Feel free to reach out to them via any of the numerous means available. I will have my staff prepare a room for you for the night, and it goes without saying that you will be compensated for your inconvenience."

His assistant turned on her heel at his words, reacting to the situation with her characteristic pragmatism.

Ms. Howard, however, was dealing with the revelation in a different way, her whiskey eyes flashing and narrowing at him.

It was obvious she placed the blame on him.

He shouldn't be surprised. She had shown herself to be an intelligent and quick-thinking woman over and over again through the past three hours.

Three hours…not two.

She was likely recalling the fact that he had been the one to insist she travel to him for the meeting—a meeting that he had arrogantly assured her would last no more than two hours.

Pride had come before his fall. First, they had gone over time, and now a blizzard.

It was enough to crave a drink.

But there would be no silent night of unwinding by the fireplace with something on the rocks tonight.

He had a guest.

"Thank you," Ms. Howard replied thanklessly, her voice flat, before finishing her thought with, "I'm sure my phone will suffice, though. Rather than impose on your family, I'll plan to stay in my room for a quiet night." Her expression turned abruptly serious then. "Really, I'd prefer that. It's been a long day of travel and work and I don't want to be the unexpected guest that impacts your holiday celebrations."

Did he detect a hint of censure in what she said, faint chastisement in the words *travel* and *work*?

He thought he did—because she had spine.

Her use of the word *unexpected* he found interesting too.

The concept clung to her, enveloping her with its many meanings.

The woman, the work, the blizzard—all thoroughly unexpected.

A further example of which was the fact that he had not expected his earlier omission to come back around to him.

Ms. Howard remained under the impression that he had family hidden somewhere in the wings, waiting for him to light candles and hand out gifts and eat doughnuts from LA's newest hot spot.

Now, despite the excuse she had offered him, he would have to correct the misrepresentation.

Once again, Ms. Howard had necessitated a change of his plans.

Rather than correct her impression immediately, however, he said, "We can certainly have that arranged, though it will take a little bit longer before your room is fully stocked and prepared. In the meantime, with work done, we might as well go track down those doughnuts."

Cheering her in the face of the situation was reason enough to manage the memories the doughnuts would stir up.

The question was, would she follow, or would she insist on waiting to hole up in her guest room until the storm passed?

He took his first step, turning to her to with a look in his eyes that challenged her to come along.

Her warm amber eyes flashed.

Of course she would meet his challenge.

Already she had proven she was the kind of woman who met challenges head-on.

She closed the door of the office behind her as she left, the click of the latch engaging echoing around the two of them in the hallway.

The sound signaled that their workday was done, while the silence after it asked *What's next*?

Early as it was, just past 3:00 p.m., the remainder of the afternoon and the long stretch of evening lay ahead of them.

Up until moments ago, they had been colleagues. Now they were a man and a woman alone at his place.

Had these been normal circumstances, he knew exactly what he would suggest they do.

But these were not normal circumstances.

Ms. Howard was not his paramour of the hour, and he typically did not have the forces of nature to thank for a romantic opportunity.

Besides, he didn't entertain in Aspen.

Aspen was his personal retreat, reserved for working creatively and recharging after bouts of making the rounds socially and professionally.

Aspen was for warm fires, and privacy, and building things that had never existed before.

The idea to invite Ms. Howard to meet him here—while he was in the midst of designing a new software project— had only come to him when she had picked up the phone, eagerness to turn the gala around as obvious in her voice as it had been in her emailed correspondence.

She had the kind of goal-oriented energy he appreciated while working and had acted off the cuff, inviting her because he was willing to welcome that energy into his private sanctum.

His impulse had not been wrong.

The three hours he had spent with her had flowed smoothly within the atmosphere he had created in the woods—too smoothly, if the extra hour was any evidence.

Until she had gotten stuck here, of course.

The extension of her visit necessitated a bigger shift than he could have predicted.

"Really," she said again, obviously still thinking of the family he didn't have, "I don't want to impose. There's no need for introductions."

She had gone from no imposition at all to one that was profound, but nowhere near the way she thought or could understand.

Of course, none of it was her fault—and he had been raised to ensure she did not feel as such.

To that end, it was time to clear up her misconceptions.

"You're in luck on that front, Ms. Howard," he said, "as there are no introductions to be made."

"The doughnuts are not with your family?" she asked, offense in her tone.

He chuckled at the censure. "They are not. I believe my assistant planned to distribute them to the staff. Hopefully we are in time to intercept."

He had not intended to reveal his lack of family to her or host her in his home, but circumstances had forced him to shift gears.

Fortunately, he could not have gotten as far as he had in life without learning to pivot.

"Not good enough for the Silvers?" Ms. Howard asked, her eyebrow lifting at the word *staff*, and he realized she still had not yet heard what he was really saying.

Laughing at her pique, he shook his head, before saying more clearly, "Of course not. Benjamin Silver comes from humble beginnings, if you will recall from my legend. Your doughnuts would have been more than acceptable to anyone in my family. I, however, am the only Silver."

Ms. Howard stopped in her tracks at his side. "You're here alone?" She looked not at him as he spoke, but around the two of them, her warm gaze spanning the massive ceilings and exposed beams.

He would have brought a palm to his face if the motion were not likely to irk her even more.

She was still not getting it.

Nor did she appear to approve.

His lips curved up at her expression.

With a small nod, he said, "I am."

"All by yourself in the middle of the woods and snow?" She shuddered lightly on the word *snow*.

Again, he nodded in response to her question, eyes laughing though he did not let the sound escape. "Not a fan of snow?" he asked.

She shook her head. "I'm not a fan of being cold."

Angling his head at her, he teased her. "Strange. One would think you would dress appropriately for the weather if you didn't like being cold."

Scoffing, she retorted, "I dress for occasions, not weather, and that is because I am a civilized person from a civilized place in which the weather accommodates. I am perfectly dressed for a business meeting."

"Spoken like a true Angelino," he said with a smile, voice warm.

Ms. Howard waved him away with an expressive palm. "That *is* where I live."

His smile faded.

Los Angeles *was* where she lived, and where she should

be nearing even now as they spoke, looking forward to enjoying the holiday and sleeping in her own bed.

"The bigger question—" she broke into his thoughts unaware of the direction they had turned "—is what is an Angelino like *yourself* doing out here all alone for the holidays? Shouldn't you be attending or hosting a new glamorous party every night for the next eight nights?"

It was a Hollywood image, and probably even enjoyable, for all that it was nothing like his reality—which she persisted in misunderstanding.

Likely, the concept of family was so secure and immutable that she could not imagine that one could be without it—that the whole of it could be suddenly and violently torn away from you.

He envied her that.

It was not his experience.

But he tried to keep it light with his reply of, "Some people *like* the snow." The words sounded more pinched than he would have liked, but reasonably casual.

Ms. Howard's eyes, however, shot to him with a flash of concern and pity embedded within them.

But then, with a small smile, she surprised him by backing off the subject.

"Figures…" she said, her voice now lit with impersonal humor.

It was too late, though.

He had seen the expression beneath.

Whatever the backstory she had concocted for him, it led her to pitying his lack of family for the holidays.

But there was nothing pitiable about him. And certainly not from her.

Her career was just starting out and struggling while he was firmly established in his field as well as one of the richest men in the world.

How could she possibly pity him?

"Oh, there it is," she exclaimed, her expression of shock distracting him from his thoughts once more.

They had rounded the hallway corner, coming into the open kitchen and informal living area.

Sitting on the shiny marble of his countertop, mirror-reflected against its glossy surface, was the bright teal doughnut box she had brought with her, but the box was not actually what had caught her attention.

Instead, she stared out the wall of windows that revealed the storm that raged outside.

It was a full whiteout, visibility a joke of the past, the snow so dense and wild it looked like a sea that you could look deep into—a churning ocean of wind and ice and snow.

It was otherworldly, like being dropped into the great storm of a foreign planet.

The weather in Colorado was the main event here—a bigger celebrity than any attention-hungry star or man with more money than he knew what to do with.

Like Ms. Howard, it was unexpected and unignorable, and Benjamin appreciated it.

Colorado, and storms like the one that whirled around them, kept him humble. LA tried to make him into a false god.

Ahead of where they stood, offset to the right, a massive fire roared in his oversize fireplace, filling the space with warmth and light that somehow held its own against the raging storm outside.

His assistant would have arranged that it be lit according to his preference.

He liked a nightly fire.

It was the closest substitute that he had yet to find for the comfort of the family he had lost. It might not be able to embrace, but it was alive and warm, as ever-changing as it was steady and dependable.

Stepping out of the hallway and into his private living area, what had seemed luxuriously cozy at first pass was now a scene of power and wonder—the storm outside a primal reminder that even in this day and age, huddling together remained mankind's greatest strength against the forces of nature.

"I've never…" Her words, as much fearful as they were astonished, trailed off, shaking Benjamin from his own regard of the storm.

"I've never seen anything like this," she finished.

And, he noted, taking in the alertness in her body and pallor of her cheeks, she was sensible enough to tremble in the face of it.

He believed in looking unflinchingly at the harsh power of the world around him and demanded the same of the people he allowed in his company. Looking away didn't make things better.

But he didn't want her to be afraid.

In fact, he had the unusual urge to make her feel safe.

Keeping his voice steady and nonchalant, he gave a light shrug as he said, "I've been through worse out here, but the first one I encountered after coming from LA? It was certainly an experience. And foolish me, back then I did not have the forethought to bring doughnuts."

Her face whipped toward his, her eyes their own form of fire, humor with a trace of relief alive in them.

Lifting a brow, a half smile on her face, she asked, "So which is it, wise forethought or an obvious move to curry favor?" referring to his earlier comments about the doughnuts.

Pleased with the return of her fighting spirit in the face of the storm, he countered with a slow grin, "It can't be both?"

She laughed as if she couldn't help herself, brow crinkling as it came together over her smiling eyes and mouth.

Again, he was momentarily stunned, her expression and the sound of her laughter sparks of joy that, like the roaring fire, held their own against the icy storm outside.

Inconveniently, she was more than attractive.

Her spectacular body of curves stacked upon curves—all of them sumptuous and well-formed—was mingled with the flames of her temper and joy that were contained, for the most part, within the bounds of her diligence, intelligence and competence.

It was a knockout combination.

In the face of both derailment and mild terror, she dazzled him, her eyes alive in the firelight, the whole of her thrumming with vibrancy and heat at least equal to that of the flames.

The attraction that had been a mild irritant throughout their meeting was clearly growing more potent after hours.

Shaking himself, he brushed away the snapshot his mind had taken of her smiling, recalling the fact that he was more than capable of controlling his baser urges for a night.

In making the years-long transition from skinny computer programming major from the California suburbs to one of the richest men in the world, he had both overindulged and learned how to manage his appetite for romantic company.

He knew how, and when, it was appropriate to express interest in a woman, and how to ensure that she liked it when he did, and he used those talents according to the preferences of his life. And his main preference when it came to romantic entanglements was that they not to get too serious.

He had no intention of starting another family that could be lost and made it a policy to be clear about his intentions with the women he got involved with.

Women who were not off-limits to him, as Ms. Howard was—due to both the foundation's nonfraternization policy, as well as the scandal that had led to her hiring in the first place.

"A man who understands nuance," she said, speaking not to his thoughts, which she could have been, but to his teasing. Referencing another earlier comment of his, she followed with, "I might not be able to go through a box of doughnuts during a two-hour meeting, but I bet I can give it a good go in front of a fireplace after-hours."

"Three hours," he corrected automatically, wondering if she knew that it sounded like she was talking about something else when she said *I can give it a good go in front of a fireplace after-hours.*

Or was only his mind rolling around in the gutter?

Snorting again, she rolled her eyes. "The time's gone either way. The doughnuts, however, are right there," she said, waving a palm toward the bright box on the counter.

And then she was moving toward them and opening the box, helping herself.

He joined her as she chose a pillowy and plump-looking confection, lightly coated with powdered sugar.

He watched her bite into the treat, closing her eyes in delight as she did, and his stomach tightened.

Her entire posture changed in pleasure, softened and eased, and he realized it was not bravado that had driven her to the box but the need for comfort.

Could he blame her? An unexpected and last-minute business trip had been even more unexpectedly extended and now she was trapped with a supervisor she barely knew for the first night of Hanukkah.

Whatever her original plans for the evening had been, he was sure they had been more comfortable than where she found herself.

But like steam rising, a measure of tension evaporated from her form as she chewed.

He wished a bite could be so effective in the face of losing control of a situation for him as it appeared to be for her.

"Mmm…" she hummed, and when she finished, she opened her eyes, the expression in them easier and brighter. "Lives up to the hype, even hours old, abandoned and *obvious*. You should try one." A grin spread across her face as she finished speaking, gesturing toward the open box with her palm. "They're not all jelly, but it seemed appropriate to get a half dozen, tonight being the first night of Hanukkah."

She had meant to encourage him to grab a doughnut, but instead reminded him of so much more: of his family, of almost-forgotten family traditions, of the fact that she was here, isolated with him, as opposed to celebrating the holiday with her own family back at home.

Offering her a smile that did not reach his eyes, he reached for a doughnut, grabbing at random to humor her while his thoughts circled once more around the inconvenience of the storm.

However, as soon as he bit into the fried dough, perfectly prepared with exquisite filling, his mind paused.

It was delicious.

He could remember the last time he had eaten a doughnut.

It had been his last Hanukkah with his adopted parents—the parents who had raised him from early childhood, after his birth parents had left him an orphan the first time.

And of course, by chance, he had grabbed a jelly.

"Delicious," he said, though the flavor was tinged with something bittersweet, before adding, "almost worth the change in plans."

Once again, she snorted. "Speak for yourself. My evening had wine on the docket."

There was humor in her voice, and he appreciated it, but there was also disappointment.

Whatever her evening plans had entailed beyond wine, she was sad to be missing it.

He couldn't replace her loved ones—he knew from personal experience the impossibility of that enterprise—but he had a world-class wine cellar. "Do you like rosé?"

Nodding and smiling, she was nonetheless cautious as she said, "I do."

He smiled. It felt good when he was right about Ms. Howard. "I've got a Sangiovese dominant, a Tempranillo dominant and a Syrah dominant. All of which would pair well with these." He lifted the bright box.

She considered, a slight frown creasing her brow.

"Melon and floral, meaty, or olive and cherry," he offered.

"Olive and cherry," she responded decidedly.

"Good choice." He gestured to the down-stuffed sofa in front of the roaring fire. "Go, sit," he said. "I'll bring the rest."

An expression he could not read danced across her face before she nodded, and he found himself watching her as she turned to make her way to sit.

Reading people came as naturally to him as reading code or print.

But not with Ms. Howard.

He wondered how long it would take him to get used to the sensation.

CHAPTER FOUR

MIRI SANK INTO the sofa, swallowed by its cushioned designer warmth. In front of her blazed the largest in-home fireplace she had ever encountered.

Plush, heated and inviting, the sitting area was a far cry from the hard-lined modern-style particleboard couch she'd purchased secondhand for her own living room, as well as the cracks in the plaster, mostly covered by thrifted artwork, in her 1920s single-story apartment walls.

Mr. Silver joined her with two chilled glasses of delicately pink wine and the box of doughnuts she'd brought.

He had asked her earlier if she normally made it through a box of doughnuts in a meeting.

She had never finished anywhere near to a full box of doughnuts before in her life, but it looked like that might be changing over the next few hours.

Given that this was her first time in a blizzard, snowed in with a supervisor, she couldn't even find it in herself to feel like she shouldn't.

In fact, given the day that she had had, she couldn't even say doing so would ultimately register as one of the big firsts.

It certainly fell below drinking wine with an astronomically wealthy colleague in front of a fire in his private residence, as well as below being flown out to Aspen in a private jet.

In the face of all of that, what was eating half a box of doughnuts?

She took the glass from him with a "thank you," unsure if she was grateful or not.

While a nice gesture, rosé and delicious doughnuts were still no substitution for her annual night with her friends.

He sat down beside her, placing the doughnuts on the marble-topped table in front of them as he did.

Beneath their feet, a thick sheepskin rug glowed like a bright pearl in the flashing light of the fire, just begging her to curl her toes into its silky softness.

But one had to be barefoot to curl one's toes into a luxurious rug, and Miri still wore her pumps.

Despite the rosé and the doughnuts and the fire and generally opulent coziness surrounding them, there were cracks in the image of winter holiday bliss they presented.

Mainly the lack of bliss or basic familiarity with each other.

Abruptly, her life didn't seem to make any sense anymore.

She sat on a plush sofa alone with a man she barely knew, drinking wine, their bodies angled toward each other.

Finding herself in this position with a man she had only just met was unheard-of for her.

Miri went slow with things, taking her time with love and friendship and anything else that the crush of modern life would let her get away with.

Rushing and being hasty and trusting too soon were things that she had learned the hard way to avoid from the man she had thought she was going to marry.

Her former fiancé had taught her that even three years was not enough time to truly know if someone was trustworthy and steadfast enough to give your heart to.

She had thought it was, but it wasn't.

And she had known Mr. Silver for mere hours.

And yet the alternative to sitting here with him would have been waiting out the storm alone in one of his many guest rooms.

Sometimes circumstances forced unusual behavior.

"Cheers," he said, breaking into her thoughts and jolting her back to the present moment that she had been reflexively denying.

The present was surreally romantic and ideal, a cozy and rom-com-esque situation in which to find herself in the wake of all of the unexpected events that this man had set off in her life over the last twenty-four hours.

"To the gala, and the first night of Hanukkah," he continued his toast, "and the end of this snowstorm, of course."

His glacial eyes had melted somewhat in the light of the fire, warming even further the longer they held hers.

She should have been on her way to West LA to spend the night catching up with the dear friends with whom she didn't get enough time these days.

Instead, she was staring into the eyes of one of the richest men in the world.

She touched the top rim of her glass to his before drawing it back, maintaining his hypnotic gaze as she drank to his words.

The fire crackled, its light dancing across their profiles, and his expression deepened, darkened.

The chilled wine danced across her tongue and her cheeks heated with the sensation, her breath fluttering for a moment at the intensity of him.

Outside the storm raged, powerful enough to make it unclear as to whether or not the sun still hung in the sky. This late in the year, however, the simple time of day— approaching 4:00 p.m.—meant that the star's descent had to be near.

Hanukkah would officially begin soon.

And here she was.

Her experience with Mr. Silver thus far had been surprising and compelling and challenging and stimulating.

She could think of many words that might be used to describe the man in front of her—powerful, attractive, intelligent and demanding came to mind—but she wasn't here to do that.

She was only here because of the gala and because the hand of fate had forced it, not to spend time with Mr. Silver.

"The rosé is fantastic," she said into the silence that had stretched out around them following their toast and first sips.

"Thank you," he said. "I've only recently begun to add them to my collection."

"Rosé not high enough brow for your collection?" she teased, but he smiled.

"On the contrary. You keep forgetting that I don't come from money. There's very little that I'm too highbrow for. I simply had not yet had time to learn about it. I choose my own wines—it makes it that much more personal to drink them."

Miri was glad her skintone kept most people from noticing her blushes.

Anyone who was astute or knew her well would see it right away, but that wasn't most people.

Most people just thought Black people didn't blush.

She didn't think Mr. Silver would be one of them, but they had also just met. He didn't know her.

"It's easy to forget your humble beginnings when you're living out here in the isolated wilderness like only somebody with money would," she teased. "Nothing says old money like minimalism and luxurious isolation."

With a laugh, Mr. Silver gestured around the plush enormity within which they lounged and said, "As you can see, I'm no fan of minimalism…"

"But the isolation," she countered. "*Regular* people prefer to spend their time with loved ones rather than snowy mountains."

But instead of laughter, as she was coming to expect from him in response to pushback, a shadow came to his chill gaze. "And here again, rather than disproving your theory, I am the case in point. I would spend my time with my loved ones lavishly, had I the opportunity. Unfortunately, I do not, as they no longer exist."

"What do you mean they no longer exist?" she asked, something in her resisting the obvious.

He had told her many times now, she realized, in different ways. His mention of being the only Silver, but she had assumed he meant the only Silver in residence. Not the only Silver at all.

"I mean they are dead." He confirmed what was only now dawning on her. "My most recent parents died in a boating accident just after I finished high school."

"And you don't have any siblings?" she asked, barreling on insensitively as if she had lost her mind.

It was just so unbelievable that this incredibly powerful and wealthy man could actually be alone in the world.

Shaking his head, he said, "No. I was a later-in-life adoption for the two of them, raised and doted upon as an only child. Neither of them had siblings of their own and their parents had passed away long before they had even considered adoption."

As fractured and disjointed as her experience of family felt at times, she still had it.

They might not always know where she fit into the family portrait anymore, now that she was grown and branching out on her own, but there remained people to stand beside.

Compassion and sympathy, however, were not what he wanted from her in this moment.

He had told her multiple times now, casually, thrown out as if it did not bother him, and she had not understood.

Now that she had unwittingly pressed him into stating the obvious, he stared at her as if ready to assess her merit based on how she responded to his sad story.

He had not sent her doughnuts on to family as she had assumed he would because there was no one to eat them.

He was out here alone on Hanukkah not because he chose to keep himself apart, but because there was no one for him to be near.

But he didn't want her pity; she could see that in his eyes, and she even understood it. So she said, "Well, that explains no one else eating the doughnuts."

A small smile cracked the intensity of his expression. "But that means there's more for us," he said, reaching for another. "It's been years since I've had *sufganiyot*," he remarked as he finished the jelly doughnut, eyeing his still faintly powdered fingertips thoughtfully, his expression seeming to hover somewhere between the present moment and memories of long ago.

Each word reverberated through her fire-and-wine-warmed body, while her eyes remained riveted on his expression.

Nostalgia and distant joy mingled in the curve of his wide mouth, and Miri found herself wishing that she had purchased an entire box of jelly doughnuts after all.

Eyes that normally froze her in her tracks looked like a crisp clear summertime sky over the ocean now.

The furrowed brow that so well communicated just how unimpressed it was possible to get lifted and softened now, revealing a character that was as vulnerable as it was masculine and beautiful.

"My mother loved them. She could easily polish off a

box over a business meeting." His smile stretched slightly as he spoke, his voice warm and soft and dangerously normal—easy to relax into—and…also beautiful.

"She had no self-control when it came to *sufganiyot*, and she knew it, so she refused to buy them. *Why tempt myself?* She'd ask herself, and us, over and over, more and more times each day as Hanukkah drew near," he continued.

Miri couldn't have stopped her own smile, nor the quiet laugh that accompanied it, if she had wanted to, and she didn't want to.

It was a good story. A happy memory.

"And did you all suffer along with her?" she asked, but he only shook his head.

"Every year on the first night of Hanukkah, my father would pick me up from school and we'd get a box of them on the way home. It became a tradition, the first night of Hanukkah, every year."

Miriam's breath caught in her throat.

She had unwittingly brought him *sufganiyot* for the first night of Hanukkah.

If the unexpected deliciousness of the evening did not, then the kismet of that fact at least made up for her thwarted plans a little.

Her friends would miss her, but they would still have one another.

Mr. Silver would have been entirely alone if not for her and her ridiculous doughnuts.

Her presence mattered more where she was, she realized, than even where she should have been.

Seeming as stuck in the moment as she felt, his eyes caught hers once again.

"The box never made it past that first night at our house, which I would say is a testament to our self-control today," he said, brushing the powdered sugar off his fingertips before reaching for a glazed cruller, his smile turning mischievous and indulgent, perhaps distancing from the vulnerability of his memories. "Then again, though, Hanukkah hasn't even truly begun yet, and we've already broken the seal. We never did that growing up." He bit into the cruller, making a noise of enjoyment that vibrated through Miri with a different kind of frequency than his childhood memories had.

Was his voice the real secret behind his success? she wondered, still feeling the sound of it along the skin of her arms. Did he simply hypnotize people into believing he was a brilliant software designer when really they just liked listening to him talk?

Judging by the wealth on display all around her, she imagined he probably knew what he was doing when it came to software as well, but with that voice of his, it was easy to believe that it was something more supernatural.

Reaching for another doughnut, she was surprised when she leaned back to find him refilling her glass.

Had she finished the first so quickly?

It had gone down so easy, she couldn't recall.

She might have been more concerned about that had his wholesome story not still been playing in her mind— the heartwarming indulgence of it, the togetherness, the normalcy lulling her guard down.

Each detail reached through time, their compulsion even more powerful than the voices inside that cautioned her not to get too comfortable around this powerful man.

She remembered family moments like that, Christmases with the whole group of them crammed together and piled on top of one another—eating, singing, laughing, bickering, sharing love via a myriad of warm gestures and sweets. Easter egg hunts with cousins from across town, birthdays and celebrations, all of that had been not just present but at times overwhelming in her life growing up.

Any excuse to gather had been taken, and closeness had been the result.

Her family had been what motivated her to succeed growing up—to make them proud—and what she had looked forward to in order to refresh and recharge her system when succeeding wore her down.

Of course, that had all been before college—before she had converted, and everyone got awkward about the fact that they tended to gather around religious holidays.

They continued to love her and would never think of disowning her, of course; they just didn't know how to fit her into the picture any longer.

She missed having a place held for herself. She missed the open, easy feeling of belonging. Thank goodness for their Fourth of July and Labor Day barbecue traditions.

She couldn't imagine what it must be like for Mr. Silver, not merely to have had his relationships strained and altered by time but taken away altogether.

Taking a decadent bite of Boston cream, she banished the creeping melancholy and made her own sound of enjoyment. "That's a really sweet story. I bet she really loved that you guys did that."

"She complained that we were the reason she couldn't fit into her old jeans with every bite, but I think she did. We loved to make her smile like that, and thankfully, it was easy. Hanukkah was always her favorite. She was a kid at heart."

Hearing him talk about his mother was making it harder to hold on to the image of *disapproving taskmaster* that she had mentally assigned him, but Miri was high enough on doughnuts and good wine and sweet stories to not care for the moment.

She could remember who he was, and who she was, and who he was to her, when she got back to LA.

Tonight, they were the shared parts of something bigger.

And as such, she wanted to break out of the professional box she'd put herself into, too.

"I don't have any sweet family Hanukkah stories like that, but the year of my joining, the group of us got together to celebrate each night of the holiday. We were all still undergrads at this time, before any of us had husbands or kids or careers, so it was easy to spend that much time together. That first year we actually made *sufganiyot* from scratch, with all the oil stains and burns and sticky jelly and sugar you can imagine would be involved in the process. We learned how to cook something different each night of Hanukkah that year. *Sufganiyot*, latkes, brisket, kugel, roast chicken, matzo ball soup...we even made gelt. There were seven of us who joined that year, all undergrads, and a lot of wine that was much, much, much cheaper than this—" she held up her glass "—so it was chaos, but it was also really fun and kicked off our annual tradition. I'm sure none of us could fit into our pants after, either."

In telling the story, Miri realized she hadn't shared it with anyone before. That year had started a tradition and been the seed of what had become her family of friendship.

It was important to her, life path–defining even, but she had never had anyone to share it with before.

And oddly enough, sitting here drinking wine and eating doughnuts that somebody else had made with the boss she barely knew, no pan full of hot grease or bottle of cheap wine in sight, there was a hint of the same kind of warmth.

As if she were missing it, but not missing out completely.

That could just have been the result of the fire, though.

And the really good wine.

Or maybe it was a Hanukkah miracle, lighting up something inside.

It's just the wine, she assured herself.

It really was amazing wine.

Because it couldn't possibly be the company.

A half smile on his face, he tipped his glass to her. "I'm impressed. I was born a Jew and I've only ever made half of those things."

Snorting, Miri waved the statement away. "You had a mom to cook it all for you. We were all just a bunch of orphans bouncing around together. The blind leading the blind, if not for our fearless mother hen of a rabbi."

"You were all orphans?" he asked, his face more serious than it had been a moment before.

Startled by the shift in him, though she shouldn't have been, given the history that he had shared, Miri said slowly, "Figuratively. None of us came from Jewish families," eyeing him as she did. She knew now why the concept of orphanhood was a literal one for him.

Immediately his posture relaxed, the stiffness that had come to him exiting almost as suddenly as it had entered.

"That's what you had meant by joining," he put together now. "You're a convert."

He said it like it suddenly made sense, and she tried not to take it personally.

Going through any religious or sacred process was not part of the general modern experience of most people—it stood out and she was used to the fact.

Just like she was used to the fact that most people didn't expect a Black woman to be Jewish.

So while she wouldn't have minded if people could have been a little less weird about both, she understood.

Nodding, she said, "I did, early in college."

She braced herself for the typical question that came next: *Why?*

But Mr. Silver instead concluded, "So no sweet family Hanukkah stories because your family is not Jewish, not because you don't have a family. I had wondered when you said that."

The deduction also wasn't what she had expected.

Shaking her head, she confirmed, "No. My family is alive and well and growing by the minute, it seems. My sisters keep having kids and my parents love to have their grandbabies around. I swear their house is louder now than even when we were all little."

"And none of them celebrate Hanukkah with you?" he asked, his opinion on what the answer should be clear in his tone.

Bristling on behalf of her family, Miri replied primly, "None of them are Jewish."

Mr. Silver was unimpressed. "Hanukkah is an easy holiday to celebrate in solidarity. Many non-Jews take part. Kids love it."

Miri snorted. "Not *my* family."

Lifting an eyebrow, he challenged, "Why not your family? Shouldn't your position as a convert make them even more likely to take part?"

Miri had thought so, privately, in the deep recesses of her mind, but she would never say so.

Not to her family, or anyone else.

"They're pretty stuck in their ways, but it's not like they've shunned me or anything like that. We get together regularly, once a month for big family dinners at my parents' house. They still don't really understand my choices, but they support me as best they know how to."

"What's so hard to understand about becoming a Jew?" he asked. "The food is great, and we know how to have a good time."

Miri laughed, saying, "Clearly, I was convinced," even though once again, his question was a penetrating one that she had privately asked herself more than once.

But unlike her family, she had a better understanding of what was going on beneath the surface.

She encountered it a lot more than they did, and because

she had transitioned from a non-Jewish to Jewish identity, she had unique insight into the fact that many people thought anti-Semitism had ended with WWII.

Most people, her past self included, had no idea how many of their own ideas of Jewishness fell between incorrect and vaguely uncomfortable to outright anti-Semitic.

Encountering Jewish people directly, born or converts, confronted and agitated those below-the-surface ideas.

Even when there was no doubt they loved you, she reminded herself.

And from her vantage point, able to see what was going on, she could forgive them for it.

She didn't get the impression that Mr. Silver would be so forgiving. He would challenge it directly, every time he encountered it, ice in his veins.

But not, perhaps, his soul.

Because right now, his eyes smiled as he spoke, striking Miri with just how warm and deep they could be. The contrast between them now and their typical icy sharpness made it even seem possible that he burned hotter on the inside.

But that was ridiculous, of course, because he was Benjamin Silver, billionaire software developer.

He wasn't a man whose passions burned.

He was a man cold enough to become rich.

Miri tried to remind herself of that—and to believe it—despite the fact that she was too comfortable with him and enjoying herself too much to give it any backing.

"Well, as evidenced this afternoon with your impressive plans, it is clear you have excellent taste and discernment."

Her cheeks warmed at the compliment, but Miri tried to focus on the work part of it. "Thank you. As much pressure as there is, I'm looking forward to the gala."

Staring at her, his stormy eyes changed once more, deepening and heating even as they conveyed respect. "It will be unlike anything the foundation has done before. People will be talking about it for months to come."

She didn't know if it was the wine or the fire or the compliments, but she was overheating.

She leaned forward to set her glass on the table and stretched her arms upward as she came back, saying, "As long as everything goes according to plan, of course. I might be often right, but occasionally things don't go according to my plans."

Eyeing her with amusement clear in his gaze, he asked, "Such as?"

"Well, let's just see here," she began, listing with her fingers as she dared a cheekiness that she certainly wouldn't have had had they still been in his office. "Going with classic options for the gala dinner, nearly marrying my high-school sweetheart, running away to join the circus and flying out for a brief meeting with Mr. Benjamin Silver are just a few that come to mind," she said, openly naming some of her most disastrous ideas alongside the storm to soften her joking about the fact the she was stuck here when they were both still dealing with the fallout— trusting the part of himself that he had shown her multiple times now, the part with a strong enough sense of humor that he was willing to laugh at himself.

He did not disappoint.

"Yes," he said, mock serious. "It does seem that *some* of your plans go awry. Thankfully, it's only the terrible ones. That dinner, for example…" He trailed off, grinning at her. "At least in that case you had me to lead you back to excellence."

Miri's bark of laughter was natural and loud, even as she rolled her eyes—for a moment entirely forgetting that this was not a close friend she spoke to and instead was Benjamin Silver—her body shaking with mirth. "It's so refreshing to meet a humble rich man," she said, wiping a tear from the corner of her eye.

"We're a rare breed," he said with a glint in his eye that was as seductive as it was humorous.

She couldn't remember the last time she'd laughed like this.

It was hard to believe that *the* Benjamin Silver was the same man who'd just made her laugh so hard she cried.

He was nothing like she had imagined and all the more fascinating because of it.

He certainly made it hard to turn away from him, sable flowing locks and all.

So she didn't. She just watched him. Was there to witness that glint of something more turn sly.

"So, what happened to the high-school sweetheart?" he asked, one corner of his mouth lifting higher than the other, revealing a hint of his sparkling white teeth, and Miri cringed, somehow still smiling.

For the first time in their acquaintance, he asked a common question.

She couldn't blame him, though. It was human nature.

Whenever the subject of her former engagement came up, questions always followed—and she'd been the one to bring it up.

She usually didn't, though.

In fact, the only times she had in the past had been with those she'd wanted to maintain a clear and open slate with.

Mr. Silver seemed to exist in a world with different rules—even the ones she set for herself.

And she couldn't find it in herself to be mad.

Grimacing for effect, she said, "I changed a lot in early college, and after all of that, he said he could no longer envision me as the mother of his children."

She didn't usually feel comfortable sharing these hurts with people, even those she trusted the most.

And here she had with Mr. Silver.

Maybe it was the storm that was changing all the rules?

She didn't know; she just continued, "*Unfortunately*, he realized that in the process of becoming intimate with another woman. They're married and have children now, though, so it seems like he was right."

It no longer hurt like it had—going through the initial emotional agony, there were times when she literally thought she was having a heart attack from the pain of it all—but sitting next to the man at her side, it was nice to realize that time and distance had finally worked their magic.

Just as Mr. Silver's expressive, arresting voice worked its own kind of magic as he lifted his glass and said, inventing a tone that was equal parts sarcastic and sexy as he did, "Congratulations on extricating yourself from a dire situation before it became even more complicated, Ms. Howard. Things clearly worked out the best for everyone involved in the end."

Surprising herself, Miri laughed again—not as loud or as overwhelmingly as before, but therapeutically none the less.

It was nice to be able to make a joke of it.

That was another one of those things she hadn't been able to do with other people before. Her family and friends had gone through it with her and were too tender to joke about it now.

They felt bad for her and uncomfortable with the details of the story as well as when she mentioned the current life of her former fiancé.

They didn't congratulate her on dodging a bullet.

But she had needed to be free to laugh about it with someone like this.

She realized it in the doing.

She had needed the unusual moments of connection

in their conversation as much as Mr. Silver had needed company.

It was something that even her holiday with friends could not have given her.

Laughing lightly, at herself as well as the audacity of the man beside her, Miri said, "At the time I thought the extrication *was* the dire situation, but now I agree."

"So who was this high school Casanova?" he asked, dry and biting and hilarious.

Laughing, Miri said, "A young man I met through youth group."

"Obviously," Mr. Silver nodded, grave, and she hit his shoulder.

She continued. "We met in middle school—"

"Middle school?" he barked, shock clear in his voice, and Miri laughed more. "Is that legal?"

Nodding, she picked back up, "It is. And we didn't go on our first date until high school, and that date was chaperoned by our parents. Our whole relationship happened beneath the watchful and adoring eyes of our parents. Nothing inappropriate." Her chuckling probably weakened the assurance, but she wasn't lying.

"Like I said, lucky to get out before it went too far. It sounds like your fiancé was an idiot. I'm surprised you didn't know it."

Once again Miri's laugh sounded more like a bark, tears sprouting in her eyes at his frank delivery. Shaking her head and wiping at them, she said, "I'm not even sure I quite see how he is now. Weak-willed, maybe. But an *idiot*?"

Mr. Silver shrugged. "He questioned your motherhood potential. I have not known you long, but even after just a short time of working with you, I can tell that you would be an excellent mother. You're dedicated, passionate, innovative, creative, determined, and you know how to hold a line in the face of challenge. Those are the makings of an excellent mother."

She wasn't laughing now, was for a moment instead brought to stunned silence.

She had hurt so much over so many things at that time in her life, but she hadn't realized how much that particular knot had bothered her—not until now, at least, as a virtual stranger massaged it out.

Her cheeks heating, she tried to wave his compliments away. "Like you said. It worked out for the best for everyone."

He nodded. "And even more fortunate, now you don't have to worry about having a stupid man's stupid children. Thank God you practiced good contraception prior to your escape."

Miri gave him a playful punch in the arm. He was terrible.

And yet he had also somehow made an experience that had truly been terrible for her not just bearable, but something she could laugh at.

That might be a Hanukkah miracle.

"Look at you," he insisted, a grin tilting up the corners of his mouth. "You've got an unusually high number of degrees and certifications, an important job at a large foundation, you have a found family of converts, and you're living your best life. Sounds like a happy ending to me." He tipped his glass to her, and she rolled her eyes, looking away so that he could not see her continued blush.

Despite the nighttime glow of the wild snow outside, there was no longer any doubt as to whether the sun remained in the sky.

Night had fallen in Aspen.

Los Angeles would be only hours behind and her friends would be well into their beloved annual tradition. She had sent messages letting them know what had happened and not to expect her—it had happened occasionally over the years that one of their party might not be able to make it, though this year would be Miri's first time as the absentee.

And there will always be next year, she promised herself.

"They'll be lighting candles soon, I imagine," she said, looking out at the storm only a little wistful.

Next year, she repeated to herself.

"You would have been with them tonight," he said, causing her breath to catch.

Turning away from the window to face him again, the darkness of the storm outside forgotten in the alarm of being understood by this man. How long it would take for her to get used to his level of penetration? He saw and pieced together so much more than the average person.

Nodding her head in the face of the acuity of his mind, she could do nothing but answer honestly, authentic words and feelings spilling out without guard. "I would have. The group of us still meet up for the first night of Hanukkah every year. Some of us have families now but we still all just pile into the house of whoever has hosting duty for the year and cook together. It's a silly tradition, but I guess I hadn't realized how much I was looking forward to it."

She didn't say any of it angling for an apology, but he said, with all seriousness, "I apologize for my role in the circumstances that have led to your having to miss them this year."

He excelled at what no one else could do—surprising her, and in a good way.

She hadn't needed an apology, and initial frustration aside, she hadn't *really* blamed him—the storm was out of his control—but she appreciated that he understood what she was missing out on and said so.

She wouldn't have thought Benjamin Silver would apologize to anyone—let alone the new hire who had yet to prove herself.

He didn't have to.

But he had, and because of it, her respect for him grew.

"Thank you for saying so. You really don't have to, but I appreciate it." She accepted his apology with the same sincerity that he had delivered it. "Like I said, it's helped me realize how important the tradition is to me and how much my friends mean to me. Those kinds of lessons are what the holidays are all about."

"Spoken like a Hallmark card," he teased with a light grin, "but true. I can't give you back what you've missed out on this year, but I can promise that you will be taken care of well for the time you are here, Ms. Howard. Anything within my power to provide is yours for the duration."

Given who he was, he had just promised her only about half of the world, and she could see in his eyes that he was serious in the offer.

The restitution mattered to him.

He felt like he owed her, and something in her knew that he was the kind of man who repaid his debts.

And something whispered in her that she might like it.

The power of it sent a strange thrill through her veins.

It was a good thing she wasn't one to use power for evil.

But there was nothing she really needed but to get home as soon as possible and make sure that this gala went off without a hitch, even if, at the moment, the world lay at her fingertips.

"Really, it's fine," she insisted. "It's still just one night in the grand scheme of things, and I can handle the disappointment. And, please, call me Miri." After the scope of their conversation, calling each other by their surnames felt silly and formal.

None of the resolution left his gaze, though his smile

took on a warmth that his teasing grin had not had before. "I appreciate your altruism, *Miri*, but I'm not a man used to disappointing. I'm certain there is a way I can make up for it, and when the time comes, it will be done. In the meantime, call me Benjamin." He made her name a sensual experience and followed it with a series of words that rippled through her like an erotic promise—even though she knew he didn't mean them that way.

Despite sharing more with him than she did with most people, at best, the two of them were colleagues in the endeavor of repairing the reputation of an organization they both cared about.

It was impossible that the innuendo she heard in his words could be anything but imaginary.

They both knew what was at stake.

But if someone had told her that she would be on a first-name basis with Benjamin Silver to kick off Hanukkah, she would have responded that *that* would have been a miracle.

If they had said she would be drinking exquisite rosé, reminiscing and making revealing confessions to him, then she would have called security to have them removed.

The idea of it alone was almost as ludicrous as the fact that she could have sworn she saw the same realizations mirrored in his own eyes.

This was *Benjamin Silver*, her project supervisor and one of the richest men in the world.

He was demanding and critical and had no regard for the fact that he had completely disrupted her last twenty-four hours.

He was nowhere near a close friend, let alone a confidant.

He was not someone she could relax around.

And yet here she was.

Eating doughnuts and drinking gorgeous wine in front of a roaring fireplace together.

Relaxing.

Alone in the middle of a storm.

Eyes locked.

Were they breathing in sync with each other?

That would be absurd.

And yet…

The moment stretched longer than it should, longer than two people in a new platonic relationship should stare into each other's eyes in a setting like this, and yet they did not stop.

Emotions that could not be expressed in words skittered across both of their gazes.

It was impossible.

They barely knew each other—had only met in person for the first time that day, had only spoken with each other for the first time within the last twenty-four hours.

He was Benjamin Silver, one of the richest, most sought-after men in the world.

And she was a teetering on the edge of broke forever-student, barely two weeks into a new job.

The current pulsing between them could not be what it seemed.

He couldn't be looking at her like he was promising to make up her thwarted plans to her in an intimate way.

She couldn't be holding her breath in anticipation.

They both knew better.

The lines were drawn in the sand and clear as day.

This couldn't be happening.

So why were they leaning into each other, their gazes drifting toward each other's lips?

Did she make contact first, or did he?

Would she ever know?

Did it matter?

Their lips connected, touched, hers soft and pliant, his wide, strong and full.

One of his hands came to her face, his fingertips tracing the line of her jaw, while he reached around her with the other arm, lifting her chest as he pulled her toward him to clutch her against him, her breasts flaring to life as they pressed into his chest.

With her hand, she gripped his forearm, holding him in their kiss. Her other hand she fisted into the thick silky brown locks that fell to his shoulders.

He growled into their kiss as her fingers tightened in his hair, the sound of his approval egging her on.

Like he had in the office that afternoon, he demanded more from her now—more passion, more access.

As she had earlier, she dug deeper, opened further, and delivered.

His tongue plundered, exploring her, dominant as his mouth made the kind of promises that only full bodies could keep.

Her nipples pebbled against the warm solidity of his chest while she spiraled not out, but *into* him.

Their breath entangled, leaving them both gasping as they angled for deeper connection.

He tasted sweet and heady, like doughnuts and wine, as implacable as the storm outside.

As with work, he wanted her best from this kiss.

Nothing else would he tolerate.

The challenge, spoken in the movement of lips and press of bodies, woke an answering intensity in her.

She would give him above and beyond.

Pouring herself into it, she unleashed all the repressed and unspent sensuality of her past.

It had been over eight years since she'd learned about her ex-fiancé's betrayal and in the interim, while she had been on dates multiple times, she had found it too hard to trust to do anything more physical than offer sweet goodnight kisses.

There was nothing sweet about the kiss she gave Benjamin Silver.

Theirs was the kind of kiss that led to more, to hands slipping beneath shirts and needing to slow down, lest inhibitions be forgotten in the heat of the moment.

It was the kind of kiss she hadn't had since the days of being a high-school sweetheart skirting the line of chastity with good intentions and fast-beating hearts.

It rushed, flooded her with heat and recklessness that was less concerned with the circumstances and more concerned with what it would feel like if her skin was touching his.

What would his hands feel like on her breasts?

Lower?

She should have been scandalized, a relative innocent clinging to the rational in order to avoid exactly the kind of mess that she had been hired to clean up.

She wasn't.

She was hungry and hot and light-headed on a combination of wine and the sensuality of the man she embraced.

His voice had been seducing her since she'd first answered the phone, his face from the moment she had disembarked the plane, and the hard planes of his body since she'd realized how much rigid strength they held.

He handled her with skill and ease, maneuvering her now as he wanted, running his hands along the curve of her back and down, along her hip, to grip and lift her until he held more of her weight, her very balance in his hands.

He teased her, keeping her teetering on the edge of falling, drowning in the pleasure of his mouth and hands on her body, until she was certain she could take it no more.

Pressing into him, her own hands exploring him through the boundaries of his clothing.

Her fingers found the buttons of his shirt and before

she could even register what she was doing, she had begun to unbutton it.

His quiet growls and rasps of pleasure encouraged her, goaded her to continue by virtue of her own power. He was as helpless to her in this moment as she was to him.

Around them, both fire and storm roared and crackled, and yet neither matched the unlocked desire pulsing between the two of them.

Locked up for too long, stirred and repressed and restricted for years, she knew why she was overcome, but why was he?

How was it possible that he could seem as powerless as she was to it?

As his arm once again tightened around her waist, drawing their bodies even closer together, the sounds of the fire and the storm and their chopped and heavy breathing swirled around them like a funnel, only furthering the sense of isolation. Just the two of them existed in the center of this remote universe.

Abruptly, Miri understood what people meant, what her fiancé had meant, when he'd said that he had forgotten about every promise he had made in the heat of the moment.

Feeling Benjamin, tasting him, breathing him in…listening to him…

Oh God… She breathed a sound that was half moan, half sigh into him.

Touching him—the many hard and muscular lines of his body highlighted and accentuated by her hands in a way that his perfectly tailored alpine wear could never hope to achieve—she felt like a teenager again.

And at the same time, like so much more.

The years between now and then, the things she had achieved and the knowledge of self she had gained, shored her up, made her confident and bold in going after what she wanted in a way she had never been back then.

Rather than simply drift away in the pleasure he set off with his lips, she rode the waves, leaning into the swells, an active participant in feeling good.

He let her know he approved by growling into their kiss before bodily rearranging their position, moving her until he had her where he wanted—face-to-face, breast to chest, her knees bent astride him, her skirt hiked past hips to accommodate, core pressed to hot core—refusing to release her lips as he did.

Bringing a hand up to grip the back of her skull, he lifted his hips against her and she saw an explosion of stars behind her closed eyelids.

She gasped and he consumed it, managing her with chiseled control even as she felt the shudders coursing through him through the fabric that separated them.

It didn't matter that they both remained clothed.

She had been naked to him since the moment they'd begun talking.

Since before that, even.

Since he'd told her to do better.

Since he'd seen into her mind through her work and demanded she show him more.

But insightful as he was, she still had depths he'd yet to see, secrets he would have to work much harder for.

She could still do better.

Pressing into him, she wound her hips, slow and deliberate, as much for herself as for him.

She could remind him that he had not had the best of her yet at the same time she drowned in the sensations he elicited in her.

She moaned as he did, his hand tightening in her hair.

Finally, he broke, pulling back for air. Unable to speak, he stared into her wide eyes like he had never kissed a woman before this moment. Like he had had no idea it could feel like this.

A rush of heat flooding her center, Miri could only pant and stare back. She hadn't known.

She had had no idea.

They breathed like high schoolers on the brink of going too far, staring, until he reached for her again, cupping her head gently in his hands to bring them forehead to forehead.

Closing their eyes, they moved in sync, drawing in a deep breath together and releasing it slowly. After another, they opened their eyes again.

"We can't do this, Miri," he said, his smooth voice rough and deep.

In time, she would be humiliated—would reimagine herself sitting astride him wantonly as she was, breathing hard, and be mortified.

She knew that.

But that time wasn't now.

Now she breathed heavy and fought the urge to argue.

Of course they could do this.

They were consenting adults.

No one had the right to tell them they couldn't.

But she *could* get fired.

Creeping hints of the coming humiliation sprouted in the soil of her subconscious.

Leaning back, she brought her palms up to press her face into them.

She was going to get fired in scandal less than two weeks into her job.

Her stomach knotted.

"Miri, I..." Whatever he was going to say was lost as he trailed off.

Rubbing her hands down her face, she started the slow work of disentangling her leg from his lap in the plush sofa, careful to avoid as much contact as possible between her heated, sensitive skin and his body as she went.

I just lost my job.

The thought looped in her mind.

She was straightening her skirt when he reached out to grab her wrist.

The skirt stopped where it was, still hiked up one thigh.

She couldn't avoid his gaze, was once again entrapped in its blue depth.

"Miri. That was absolutely my fault and will absolutely not affect your employment with the foundation."

For the first time in her experience of him, he looked frazzled. His eyes at once imploring—clearly intent on assuaging the most obvious of the concerns that had just sprung up between them—and hot, sparking like blue embers each time they tripped back to her lips or lower.

He didn't want to stop any more than she did, but he clearly had more sense and self-control in the matter than her.

Her stomach quaked and rolled.

All of the times she had forgotten herself in conversation with him—when she'd let snappiness creep in and when she'd spoken too casually—and now this?

He could only conclude that she was completely out of control—totally unprofessional.

Never mind the fact that derisive judgment was not what burned in his eyes as he watched her.

He wanted her, would have had her, she realized, if she had been someone else, someone whose job wasn't on the line in the having.

She could see it in the way the thrum of his body warred with conscience in his eyes.

They had kissed.

A kiss between single adult coworkers was a far cry

from a years-long extramarital affair, but nevertheless, both were against company policy.

He wouldn't tell.

His darkened blue eyes promised that.

He would not threaten her employment with the foundation by revealing what had happened between the two of them here in his remote cabin.

She had to simply trust him on it.

And what was more alarming to her than even the fact that they had crossed the line in the first place, was the fact that she was tempted to do just that.

She couldn't trust herself to be alone around this man if it could get to this point.

For whatever reason, she clearly lacked even basic self-control when it came to him.

And they were snowed in together.

It felt like some kind of cosmic trial.

She needed to get away from him.

Reading her mind, he spoke, his voice thick and raspy. "My assistant will show you to your room, Miri. A good night's sleep and this will be a blip we both eventually forget."

Nodding like making out with strangers on couches was a normal enough thing in her life she could forget about, Miri said, her own voice bearing signs of fading passion, "Thank you."

And when his assistant arrived to take her to her room, after they'd had enough time to gather themselves back to being presentable and fallen into a dense silence in front of the fireplace, she nearly made it into the hall before she turned to say, "Good night, Benjamin."

She shouldn't have used his name—not when the embers between them needed only a little fanning to flame back to life. She should have just gone, girding herself for the incredible awkwardness ahead of them if the storm did not pass by tomorrow morning.

She should have been cold to reinforce the fact that any heat between them was inappropriate.

But she couldn't.

It didn't feel right, not after everything they'd shared—both right and wrong—to leave without saying good-night.

When his voice reached out from behind her, wrapping around her to trail along her arms and leave her shivering in its wake, she somehow wasn't surprised.

"Good night, Miri. Sleep well."

CHAPTER FIVE

BENJAMIN WOKE TO a wall of white and a pounding head.

The wall of white—the storm through his massive bedroom windows—confirmed that, as predicted by the previous night's late weather forecast, it continued unabated.

According to those same predictions, Miri was likely be his guest for at least another day, if not another night.

His pounding head prayed that it would not be another night.

Her kiss was the kind of thing that drove a man to things—and if it wasn't going to be her, which it couldn't be, drink was the only remaining accessible option.

So in the end, he *had* had that hard drink that he'd fantasized about in the afternoon. It had just happened hours later than imagined and after polishing off two bottles of wine with her.

And then he had had a few more after that.

As if he had not already learned this lesson in college, mixing his alcohols had not been his brightest idea—no matter that each of his selections had been far above top-shelf.

There were some things money could not save you from.

Not many, of course, but some.

A hangover was one if you were as determined to get one as he had been last night.

Sitting up gingerly, he squinted against the bright light drawn in through the wall of windows facing his bed.

Under normal circumstances, there was nothing he liked more than to be greeted by the sun rising over the rolling sea of mountains and trees before him each morning, but normal circumstances for him did not usually include being hungover in the middle of a whiteout.

Storms like this were rare.

As his eyes slowly adjusted to the glare, what had looked like a solid wall of snow transformed into a sea of flurries, with huge snowflakes flying in every direction and visibility of no more than a foot.

As capricious as storms could be, Benjamin did not foresee it lightening anytime soon.

Not only would that mean another day and night with Miri, but likely more still after that.

What was he going to do with her?

As sexy as the images that filled his mind in response were, they were unhelpful.

Kiss or no kiss, those were not the kind of things he could do with Miri.

Last night a combination of drink, nostalgia and confessional had led them into forbidden territory.

Things had gotten out of hand, but certainly not as out of hand as they could have. They had shown restraint.

Admirable restraint, really, when one considered that it was just the two of them here, isolated in the snow far from the watchful eyes of anyone who would ever care or have the authority to do anything about it.

They were a man and a woman with obvious attraction between them and the only barrier was whether or not they could both keep a secret.

Perhaps they had shown *too much* restraint.

The good behavior certainly hadn't made him feel any better the next morning.

It did, however, continue to protect the foundation.

He had to remember that the foundation was what this was all about.

Miri would never have even been to his home to become snowbound were it not for the foundation.

The tiny nonprofit that had coordinated his adoption, a group that did the legwork of connecting Jewish children that fell into the system with Jewish families, had been funded by the foundation.

When he'd reached a place in life in which he had money to give away, he had given it there.

And when he'd reached a place in life in which he had become coveted for boards of directors, he had offered his time to the foundation.

Surely his lifelong gratitude and appreciation for, as well as his now longtime participation with, the group were reason enough to keep his hands, and mouth, off Ms. Howard.

Miri.

His mind corrected the attempt at distancing her immediately; her first name had already become the auto default.

He liked the way it sounded, how it felt in his mouth.

She wasn't Ms. Howard—the new hire he was assigned to work with to salvage the gala. She was Miri—a woman who loved rosé and tasted like vanilla sugar.

He liked her saying his name almost as much.

He felt it as it left her mouth, running along his skin like satin in the silk of her low register, lifting the hairs on his arms as it went.

Each time, it rang through his ears like a preview of what could be, what it might sound like were she gasping it, and paired with the kiss they had shared, left him in a state of mild pain with wanting.

He had intended to give her two hours of his time the day before, no more.

Now they faced days together.

He should be designing software.

Instead, he was mentally rearranging his day to play host.

He had told her he would show her a good time.

He would, and though it was crass, he knew he already had.

A woman didn't respond like she had if she wasn't having a good time.

Now all he had to do was actually deliver on the original intention of his statement when he had told her she would be well taken care of for the duration of her stay, which had not been seduction.

He'd intended to feed her well and keep her company while she was stranded in his home.

He was man enough to provide that, even in the face of their professional breach.

He trusted that they were both mature enough to navigate their morning after, so to speak.

They had to. Both of them would continue their work with the foundation, so they had to.

It would have been easier if he didn't already know what she felt like in his arms.

So he simply would not think about that.

He could not wipe the slate of experience clean—wouldn't want to, in all honesty—but he could certainly set it aside. He was Benjamin Silver.

And he had a guest to feed.

Ringing his assistant through his centralized intercom system, he confirmed that Ms. Howard did not appear to have woken yet and instructed his assistant to have breakfast prepared for them in the formal dining room.

The long table would remind him to show her the kind of good time that could be discussed over the water cooler.

They could eat and make small talk and Ms. Howard would have a pleasantly impersonal experience for the rest of her time here.

Miri lay in the utter darkness of the room with her eyes wide open, staring up at a ceiling she couldn't see.

She and Benjamin Silver had kissed.

No. That wasn't right.

They hadn't kissed.

They had made out like a couple in the honeymoon phase on his couch in front of a roaring fire.

And then she had slept at his house—not with him, *obviously*, but at his house, and woken up still under his roof.

If she could have taken a walk of shame out of his house to hail a cab home, she would have sneaked out the window without saying goodbye and done just that.

As it was, there was no way out but through him.

And that meant she was trapped forever because there was no way she would ever be able to face him again.

How would she be able to look him in the eye when she had moaned into his mouth the night before?

They had to work together.

Bringing her hands to cover her face in the dark, she muffled a groan.

How could I have made such a stupid mistake?

He was her direct supervisor, the long-standing leader of an organization still recovering from a fraternization scandal.

And she had fraternized with him!

There was no way he could continue to see her as a good fit for her position. He couldn't help but doubt her integrity.

She couldn't help but doubt her integrity—no matter that nothing like this had ever happened before in her life.

Her days of getting hot and heavy on couches were as far behind her as her days of being someone's fiancée.

As a college dater, she'd kept things to the realm of flirting in bars and the occasional good-night kiss at the door.

No man that she had encountered seemed willing to accept the pace she set on intimacy—emotional or physical—so her relationships had a tendency to fizzle out before they got past that point.

She refused to compromise.

She respected herself.

She had set boundaries around trust and a boundary was only as powerful as it was enforced.

Except for, apparently, when she was willing to throw it all out the window.

She had revealed so much and taken things so far with Benjamin the night before that there was no way he could think of her as anything but attention-starved and desperate.

And unless the storm had passed, she was literally stuck with him—no getting out without seeing the judgment in his frosty stare.

Maybe the storm passed overnight?

He was a busy man, busy enough that he'd had only two hours to spare for her and the gala.

He had already gone far over that allotted time, first during their meeting and later, spending hours with her drinking wine and talking.

If the storm *had* passed overnight, then wasn't it entirely possible that he would have to get back to work? That he would have no more time to spare for her and could have his assistant arrange her return to Los Angeles?

A woman could hope.

A woman could also get out of bed, open the curtains, and find out one way or the other.

But if the storm had not passed, getting out of bed

would be taking a big step toward facing Benjamin, which was something she honestly wasn't certain that she could ever do again.

If the storm continued, there would be no escaping the awkwardness of the morning after.

Miri groaned again.

What had she been thinking?

The simple answer was that she had not been thinking.

She hadn't been thinking about the precariousness of her position, or the importance of the gala, or the scandal that had been the catalyst for all of it.

She hadn't been thinking about her boundaries and rules, or being guarded, or holding back at all—not with the doughnuts, not with the wine and certainly not with the man.

They had talked about things she didn't talk about with anyone and done things she had only ever done with one other person.

Yesterday afternoon they had met for the first time and by nightfall they were making out on his couch.

Outside of coeds, who did that kind of thing?

She hadn't even done that kind of thing when she *was* a coed.

And she had been a coed for almost a decade!

But lying in bed prolonging the inevitable was not helping her either.

She had to face both what lay outside the window and the man who dwelled inside the winter castle, if she wanted to get home.

And she desperately wanted to get home.

At home she could give herself the dressing-down she deserved for her insane and reckless behavior with Benjamin Silver.

At home, she could settle into the uneasy belief that he wouldn't tell and that she wouldn't tell and that the memory of their little secret would fade into the background until neither remembered it all.

Forgotten, exactly as it should be.

It would be easier to believe in her tiny apartment with a fresh change of clothes on—clothes that didn't still bear traces of his scent from the night before.

Once she got home, she could put it behind her entirely—just as soon as she had a moment to go over every detail of it again, in the privacy of her own space, far away from the man at the center of it all.

She needed both—the examining *and* the forgetting.

And she needed to do it on her own turf, where the ground stayed exactly where it always had—beneath her feet.

And that meant she had to get out of this sumptuous bed and open the curtains.

Bolstering herself, she swung her legs free from the smoothest sheets she had ever slept in, enjoying the feeling of her toes curling in a plush rug.

Benjamin's home really was comfortable—all the way down to the little details.

When she had first laid eyes on its monstrous size, she had thought there was no way it could be comfortable.

A structure so large would have had to be strange and cavernous, she'd thought, more like an industrial warehouse than a home, but it wasn't so.

He had just made sure that all of the regular elements that made a building a home—windows, rugs, linens, pillows—were oversize and over-the-top to match.

Without a change in clothes, or her sleep bonnet, she had piled her hair up in a high bun and stripped down to her camisole to sleep in. As an option in a pinch, it had worked, but her hair would need some TLC when she got home, and her cami had definitely lost some of its shape through the night.

Maybe if she hadn't spent so much time tossing and turning…

But it was no use grumbling.

Tossing and turning, alternating between wishing they hadn't stopped and wishing they had stopped sooner was the obvious consequence of making out with your boss.

Padding over to the window, she took a deep breath and then reached out to take the curtain edges in her hands.

Flicking them open in sync with her exhale, she blinked against the sudden brightness in the room, squinting to limit the incoming light.

It was not a bright sun in a blue sky that had her wincing, though.

It was the continued whiteout of the blizzard.

She wouldn't be going home quite yet.

And without the possibility of an impersonal exit, she was going to have to face Benjamin Silver again.

Heat flooded her face and neck.

Pressing cool palms first on her cheeks before moving to her forehead and neck, she sighed.

It was her own fault.

I should have had more self-control, and word-control, and body-control…

There was no point in delaying it further, though.

Her time would be better used putting herself together to face the day, at least as best as she could.

Without her hot-air brush, flat iron or any hair product, there wasn't going to be a lot she could do about her curled and lifted baby hairs and added volume.

Yesterday she had done her usual morning routine and had arrived at the meeting with her normal office look of glossy soft curls—exactly so because she gave herself a mini blowout every morning before leaving the house and didn't skimp on the sheen spray before she used her flat iron to create soft wave curls that framed her face, neck and shoulders.

Taking her clothes into the adjacent bathroom, Miri flipped on the light and took in her sleep-messy bun and lace cami-clad reflection.

She looked like she had spent the night before making out with a man in front of a fireplace.

Her hair was going to require some creativity.

Rummaging through her purse back in the room, she found a few bobby pins and a small tin of cocoa butter she kept on hand to use as a quick moisturizer.

She used the cocoa butter to moisten the soft curling hairs that framed her face before twisting sections in the front back and away from her face, fixing it with the bobby pins just above her ears.

She repeated the process for the other side and smiled at the result in the mirror.

It wasn't the polished shine she normally liked to present at the office, but it was at least appropriate.

She didn't look like she was trying to seduce anyone.

A knock sounded at her door while she took advantage of the bathroom's complimentary toothbrushes.

Jumping, she paused mid-brush to say, "Just a minute."

As she moved, however, a giant dollop of sudsy toothpaste fell out of her mouth and straight down her chin and front, leaving a streak of white froth in its wake.

Fortunately, the disaster had missed her cardigan.

Unfortunately, it had missed neither her camisole nor her button-up blouse.

Double unfortunate was the fact that both were made of silk and would most definitely reveal the disaster— even if she managed to get the white discoloration from the toothpaste out.

"Damn it," she muttered to herself, reaching for a nearby washcloth to dab at the toothpaste residue.

She didn't have time to take it off and rinse it out because there was someone at the door.

Left with long streaks of darkened and wet fabric down her front, she quickly managed to get *most* of the dregs of toothpaste out, but could still make out a faint chalky discoloration through the fabric.

It was the best she could do for now, though.

Rushing to the door, she was slightly out of breath when she opened the door. "Sorry. I was in the bathroom."

On the other side of the door, Benjamin's assistant gave her a flat once-over, but said nothing to that. "Saw the light beneath the door and figured you were up. Breakfast will be ready soon. It'll be in the formal dining room, down this hall and to the left. Think you can make it there on your own?"

Miri nodded, gifted with a natural sense of direction as well as intimidated by Benjamin's assistant.

A tiny smile cracking her mountain-like face, the assistant nodded. "Good. Mr. Silver is waiting."

And then she turned on her heel and left.

For a moment, Miri stood in the doorway, staring after her.

And then she forced herself to pull it together and go out and face the day.

Mr. Silver was waiting.

Benjamin arrived first in the dining room, pleased at the spread laid out on the table. As pleasurable as their forbidden kiss had been, the sight before him was somewhat of a relief.

Breakfast was more akin to what he had meant when he'd told Miri that he would take care of her.

Growing up in Los Angeles had made him partial to farm-fresh fruit and vegetables, as well as avocados, and so he had had a state-of-the-art greenhouse installed on the estate and manned it with a staff of master gardeners.

Spending as many years in Colorado as he had now, he also had an appreciation for fresh beef and lamb—and had established an annual contract with a local rancher to buy a guaranteed percentage of his product each year to ensure he had ample supply.

Between those arrangements and the poultry contract he had with a local organic farmer, Benjamin's table was always fresh, vibrant and flavorful—just like he liked it.

This morning was no exception.

Two enormous omelets with fresh goat cheese and basil rested in the large heated dish that was centered between the nearest two end seats of the long wooden table. The table was the focal point of the formal dining room, which, like most of the other rooms in his home, faced enormous picture windows that currently showcased the blizzard.

Around the scramble were platters of fresh fruit, bagels and lox with trimmings, rosemary lamb breakfast sausages, and large mimosas made with orange juice squeezed fresh.

A coffee and tea tray had been rolled out and prepared for them as well, and he was pleased with his staff's presentation.

Regardless of her dietary preferences, she could find something to her liking among the spread.

Rather than sit and wait for her arrival at the table and allowing the moment and his anticipation to build toward the impact of seeing her walk in, he stood beside the fireplace—within which blazed another large fire—and watched the storm outside.

Storms, if not this strong, and well-laid fires were common features of his time spent in Colorado.

Miri was not.

In fact, as the years had gone by, company of any sort—

regardless of whether it was here or in California—had become more and more rare.

As he had aged, surrounding himself with people had become less and less effective at disguising the fact that at the end of the day, the only people who cared very deeply about him were shareholders.

People were wrong when they said it was lonely on the top.

It was lonely no matter where one stood if one stood without family.

But here, lost in the woods, loneliness could also be peaceful.

It could be normal.

That did not stop him from turning, though, at the sound of Miri's heels clicking against the hardwood floors.

She wore her clothes from yesterday, of course, but she had changed her hair.

She had pulled it back on either side, revealing cute rounded ears and giving an overall impression of a medieval princess.

She was as striking as she had been the previous day, but softer and sweeter somehow as well.

Or perhaps the softening owed nothing to her clever remixing and everything to do with the fact that he had had her in his arms the night before.

He had clearly spent enough time this morning recalling the more licentious portions of their evening to be struck by her walking through the door.

It was a startling moment when a fantasy became real.

He wanted to touch and taste again what he had already thought too much about.

That was the problem with getting a taste. Once taken, it was hard to pull back.

He wanted to show her a good time again, the way

he had last night—not with a lovely brunch but with his hands and mouth.

But today, the second day of not only Hanukkah but of being snowed in together as colleagues, needed to be a reset rather than a repeat.

He needed to keep his hands to himself and his thoughts aboveboard.

He needed to remember he couldn't have her, even while she remained lush and vibrant and entirely entrancing.

"Good morning," he said, smiling with a gesture toward the table. "As delicious as our dinner of doughnuts was, I thought this morning we might have a real meal." He broke the seal on the topic of last night immediately and—he hoped—softly, in order to lance any potential for discomfort that might exist for her.

Unlike him, she had probably spent her night agonizing not over the fact that they had gone to bed in separate rooms, but because she had fraternized with her supervisor amid the fallout of a fraternization scandal.

He could expect no less.

She was smart and dedicated and clearly determined to keep her job.

He liked the idea of her burning for him more, though, and hoped that perhaps a small portion of her evening had included that.

"Good morning," she replied with a blush and the kind of automatic politeness that told him she'd grown up in an "old-fashioned manners" kind of household. "This looks delicious."

When her eyes fell to the mimosas, though, her voice filled with some of the sarcastic humor he had been introduced to last night.

Lifting a brow, she said, "I see you went with champagne instead of rosé this morning."

Had he been a younger man, he might have said something about hair of the dog, but as she was not aware that he had had anything more than a respectable amount of rosé last night—nor why he might be inclined to do so—he merely smiled smoothly and said, "It complements freshly squeezed orange juice so well."

The look she shot him communicated an eye roll without any such movement and he was happy they could engage this way following their encounter the previous night.

Some people would be too awkward.

He had known they could both be adults about things, that they could be friendly and cordial and still enjoy each other's company and still maintain a courteous distance.

"Spoken like a typical rich man," she teased, affirming his belief, before adding, "Regular people don't drink fine champagne at every meal."

He gave her a look of mock wounding before smiling and nodding. "It's true. Regular people don't drink fine champagne nearly enough. Have you heard the health benefits?"

She laughed out loud at that, the sound as warm and crackly as the fire, and his smile grew.

This was taking care of her—feeding her and making her laugh.

Not laying her down on the table and eating her like *she* was the meal.

This was what he would provide today.

Casual conversation, rather than confessions—of the private history variety and of the subjects of late-night tossing and turning.

They could make small talk and eat, and perhaps even pass some of the storm time quietly working together again.

She had what she needed from him for the gala, he knew, but his office was equipped so that almost anyone with a white-collar to-do list could work on-site.

And after all of that, hopefully the storm would be abated and he could send her back home knowing that while they may have pushed a few boundaries, there had been nothing more damaging done than a rather tame transgression.

His mind protested the word *tame* in respect to what had transpired between them the night before, but he fought it.

Her body in his hands might have proven to be even more decadent than it had promised to be, but in truth it had simply been a kiss.

One that he would will away if he had to.

Iron will—the kind he relied on to come back to a coding or engineering problem time and again until he had a solution—was the only thing that had stopped him from taking things further with her last night, as the taste of her had made him feel as if he had reverted to being a teenager.

She was responsive and active, full of brilliant heat and warmth, and a part of him would always feel like he had been a fool to let the opportunity to experience her pass him by.

Even if it was an opportunity that should never have arisen in the first place.

Thinking back on it, he could see that the beginning of everything had been bringing her out to Aspen.

He should never have done that.

It was too relaxed here, too at home and comfortable and isolated and natural for anything but actual intimacy.

Intimacy he'd had with Miri.

As soon as she arrived, it had been inevitable.

For his work to be truly creative, he needed an environment in which he could be himself, where he could free his mind and let his ideas roam without limitation.

Only in that space could he come up with the kinds of ideas that could change the world.

His home in Colorado was that place.

Miri's visit—with its losing track of time and honest conversation and passionate embraces—had made it clear, though, that he was *too* comfortable here.

He was too soothed by his fires and sense of home to recall just how big a risk it was inviting anyone into that space.

By necessity, his guard was down here, and without a guard, it was hard to resist Miri.

Which he would do even if she *wasn't* his subordinate at the foundation.

He wasn't looking for the kinds of relationships that the comfort and ease of feeling at home created—which was what Miri's very essence seemed to foster.

He appreciated women—fast-paced women who were not looking to settle down any more than he was—and casual friendships of the mutually beneficial variety that left everyone involved richer for the experience.

Usually, literally.

Unlike Miri, he was not interested in replacing the family he still missed.

As a child, he had lost not one, but two families.

The family of his birth he had lost to a car accident when he'd been just four years old.

Of them, he had only a few vague memories, warm and fuzzy images really, of a man and a woman, and scents that brought them back to mind.

That loss was scarred over and almost unfelt by now.

No, it had been the second time that his family had been stolen from him—fourteen years later when he'd lost his beloved adopted family—that had cauterized any urge in him to try again.

He refused to allow the opportunity for that kind of loss into his life again.

He did not want confidants.

He wanted meaningful work.

He did not need intimacy.

He had his fires.

He wanted to fulfill the promises he had made his parents and enjoy the fruits of his labor in peace.

And to that end, there would be no more inviting colleagues to Aspen.

His compound would return to being solely his private retreat. Anything else risked the kind of feelings he refused to welcome back into his life.

And yet when he had been alone, after Miri had gone to bed last night, with just the remnants of the doughnut box and her empty rosé glass to remind him that he had spent most of his day with a woman he had only just met—even going so far as to lose track of time with her—it had not been regret that he felt.

Or rather, it *had* been, but not regret that he had brought her into his sanctuary.

It had been regret that he *hadn't* taken her back to his room.

Last night he had been willing to admit that he had enjoyed her company.

Today, however, he would remember the fact that he was not allowed to.

He might be one of the richest men in the world but enjoying Miri's company in any way beyond the brunch they shared now or long planning meetings could get her fired.

And entirely willing to blame the truth of it on Colorado, he already cared enough about her that he couldn't let that happen.

They ate in relative quiet for most of the meal, each enjoying the well-made feast in front of them, with a brief moment in which they each paused to gaze into the incredible storm outside.

"Doesn't seem like it's letting up any," she said quietly, and he shook his head.

"No, it doesn't, and neither is it predicted to anytime soon," he replied.

Moistening her lips, she opened them to say, "It's incredible. So powerful. Able to make it seem like the entire world has disappeared."

She was right, he thought, responding to her words with a nod as he, too, stared at the force outside.

It was easy to imagine the estate was a world of its own—and they the only people in it.

Noticeably shaking herself free from the storm's hypnosis, she gestured to her near-cleared plate. "Everything was delicious. Amazing. Like a restaurant," she said, finishing the last of her plate before leaning back with a champagne glass in her hand. "Thank you," she added.

"I'm glad you enjoyed. I'll pass the word along."

"You have enough staff to cook a meal like this, but I never see them around," she noted, looking around the room that held only the two of them.

The decor of the formal dining room was dominated by natural wood and large beams, and also like the rest of the space, he'd lightened the heavy impression of both by installing massively enlarged windows and utilizing white accents.

He shrugged with a smile. "There's a lot of space and I only hire those who are efficient."

"You like a lot of space, don't you?" she asked, offhandedly thrusting them back into the dangerous territory of personal divulgence.

Did she mean to ask such personal questions?

He doubted it. She was just making conversation.

Of course, making conversation was where things had started yesterday, as well.

"LA sprawls, and yet there is no room," he said, choosing his words carefully so as not to fall into the trap of divulgence. "I'm drawn to the contrast here. A sprawling natural environment in which human spaces are compact. Where they know their place."

"'Know their place,' huh? That's not a loaded statement or anything."

Catching her eyes, he allowed himself a moment to wonder at their whiskey glow before he answered her, "I should say, where humans recall that they are subordinate to the forces and powers of nature. No man, no matter how wealthy or famous or powerful, how loved or cherished, is greater than all this around us." He gestured toward the storm outside and the hundreds of thousands of acres of mountainous forest it hid. "Or really ever in control," he added, appreciating the irony of that embedded in their current situation.

The storm was an exercise in humility.

As well as a reminder that he appreciated as a man with the world constantly at his fingertips.

Lack of control, however. Was a lesson he had been introduced to long ago, with the losses of his adopted family to the sea barely a decade past the loss of his birth family to a flash-flooded road before them.

Death was always a lesson in control.

In Los Angeles, it was too easy to think that a big dream, engineering and money was all that it took to switch things around—to give people the power over nature and life—but it simply wasn't true.

Nothing was ever really in anyone's control.

But Miri was a California girl, through and through.

Had she had a chance to learn that lesson yet?

He watched her face closely for what she might give away without words.

Her response disclosed little.

A half smile gracing her face, she said, "That's actually rather profound. I was expecting it to be more of a 'king of the mountain' thing."

Smiling, he shook his head. "The woman who raised me shudders in her grave at even the idea of that kind of arrogance. Among other things, she was a Bay Area hippie in the sixties. Respect for nature was her jam. I keep having to remind you that I haven't always been one of the richest men in the world."

Lifting an eyebrow, she challenged him. "It's just too impossible to believe that you used to be normal."

Raising his own brow to meet hers, he said, "Just a regular Joe, in every way."

"I doubt that. You have born and bred bougie written all over you."

Enjoying the spark that flashed in her eyes, he said, "If by bougie, you're suggesting I went to good schools, I won't deny it."

She snorted. "I'm suggesting *private* schools and a brand-new car when you turned sixteen. You probably grew up spoiled and don't even realize it."

He laughed but a shadow crept into the sound.

He *had* been spoiled, and even—to some extent—in the ways that she thought.

But mostly he had been spoiled in love and affection.

For which he was grateful.

It wasn't a claim a lot of two-time orphans could make.

But it did make it that much harder to remember the good times.

Some of that shadow crept into his voice, giving it a somber cadence despite his continued smile. "I'm very aware of my blessings," he said, "but my car wasn't brandnew. It was a ten-year-old Subaru my mom only agreed to let me get because of its safety ratings."

At that, Miri let out a bray of laughter, the outburst and volume of it breaking apart his tension at remembering.

"I can't picture you in a Subaru at all!"

"It was a wagon, to make matters worse," he added,

enjoying her surprise. "Imagine my sex appeal, showing up to my a.m. coding course skinny and driving a wood-paneled station wagon."

She shook her head holding up a hand, refusing his pitiful image. "Stop! It's too painful."

"Exactly. All-American teen hood, in a single image."

Laughing still, she gestured around her with an open palm. "Congratulations on how far you've come."

Her words echoed his from the night before, when he'd learned about the fiancé that she had narrowly escaped becoming a virtual child bride to, and he appreciated that she could give as good as she took.

She was smart and funny and determined—everything his father had told him to look for in a woman—and it was a strange thing to realize that.

He had thought of his parents—their advice and love—more over the past twenty-four hours with Miri than he had in years.

He wondered why that was.

Was it just because it was Hanukkah, or was it because of her?

He was usually better at keeping the memories, and the associated longing they brought up in him, in the back of his mind.

And yet while they remained bittersweet, something about the way she drew them to the surface was gentle.

Nodding, he agreed. "How far, indeed."

A shift went through her at his words, her eyes narrowing, focusing in on him in a way that set warnings off.

"You miss them a lot, don't you? Your parents," she said.

It did not occur to him to deny it, though he kept his nod short.

Of course he missed them. It would be foolish to claim otherwise, and it was normal to miss lost loved ones, but he was by no means haunted by his loss.

The evidence was all around.

He had not ceased to function, or abandoned his goals, or given up on life.

He had dealt with the pain and picked up the pieces, wiser because he had survived.

He had found a way to be happy again, even through a loneliness that was as impenetrable as the storm.

Everybody was lonely.

He had built a more-than-good life.

"I do," he acknowledged. "The ache has faded over the years, though. And though it doesn't make up for their loss, I *have* had the benefit of not having to explain myself to anyone for the past twenty or so years. But we've digressed. As financially transformative as my story is, it's also boring."

Miri laughed. "Not to those who haven't figured out the formula yet."

"Are you the type to look? I can give it to you for free. It's simple. Hole up wherever you happen to be living for inordinate amounts of time and practice something that can make you rich. Also, have a source of independent financial stability and no one to answer to."

Now she snorted outright. "At least you're honest with yourself," she said, laughing.

"Where else does honesty begin, if not with the self?" he challenged, catching her eye.

Swallowing, a faint blush dusting the apples of her cheeks, she nodded. "So wise. Honesty begins with admitting who we are."

Her voice had gone slightly light and airy, her skin brightening, and he knew she was thinking about last night—and not in agony over it happening but the other kind of agony.

The kind that wished there had been more.

Licking his lips, a thrill lifting his pulse though he

maintained a steady hand of control on himself, he said, "And what we want."

Blinking and clearing her throat abruptly, Miri broke the stare first, reaching for her mimosa as she did so.

"It's a good thing we want the same thing," she said, quickly adding, "A good gala, I mean, that is." Stumbling over her words for the first time in his acquaintance, her voice pitchy in its forced lightness, after taking a swig.

CHAPTER SIX

"You wouldn't happen to have a roomful of clothing in every size that rich people always seem to have in the movies, would you?" Miri asked wistfully, aware of the toothpaste stain on her shirt, as they exited the dining room.

"Unfortunately, no. Not here, at least," he said. "At my Palisades home I retain a personal stylist on staff who generally does maintain a wardrobe for guests to choose from, but I don't entertain here."

At his Palisades home... He had a house in the Pacific Palisades?

Pacific Palisades wasn't the wealthiest neighborhood in LA, but it was the most beautiful, in Miri's opinion.

Keeping her reaction to a small choking laughing fit, Miri shook her head.

"It's all right. I'm sure it will pass sometime between now and tomorrow. I can bear another day in old clothes."

As if her words had sparked a memory, he said, "I can't offer designer attire, but I do have a few less traditional options."

Perking up a bit, Miri said, "Yes?"

"There is a near-endless supply of robes in the spa. I discovered them there on my last use."

Laughing again, at both the idea that he had not known he owned a stockpile of robes as well as the thought of wearing nothing but a fluffy white robe, and said, "No, thank you, though I appreciate the offer. Somehow it feels wrong to wear solely robes through a blizzard…"

Not to mention the fact that the idea of wearing nothing but a spa robe around him set off the kinds of sensations she had been trying to forget about since last night.

Laughter warmed his eyes, his smile remaining, as he said, "Absolutely understandable, and in that case, my second option: I think I have some of my old things from high school that might fit you. It may take some unearthing, but they have a better chance than anything from my current wardrobe. I've filled out since then," he added, a flirty light in his eye that Miri couldn't help but respond to.

"I consider myself generally more filled out than a teenage boy, as well," she said saucily, only partially joking, but his smile only grew.

"You'd be surprised what a height advantage can do to tailoring," he said. "You're a tall woman, but I've still got plenty of inches on you."

She loved being tall and full-figured—had been praised and lauded for both through her development into a woman—but it often meant she stood eye to eye with the men around her in more than a metaphorical way.

But not with Benjamin.

As he pointed out, he had her by more than six inches.

Focusing in on him now, her attention was drawn to the fact that his height and broad chest were traits she admired in a man.

Not that she spent much time admiring men.

Through a combination of scholastic busyness and her insistence on moving at a snail's pace romantically, dating had happened only sporadically amid her collecting of degrees, moving out on her own and finding a job.

It had just been too hard to get to know someone while juggling all of that, and she refused to be intimate with someone she didn't feel like she knew.

And now that she had a job, she had a gala to save.

She figured she would turn her attention to the awkwardness of modern dating once her career was secure and she had a few years with the foundation under her belt.

At that point her life might have space for the process of coming to trust someone.

But it really didn't now.

And it particularly did not with Benjamin—no matter how much of an ideal height he might be.

He was a man with no time, and she was a woman who required a serious investment of it—once she had some of her own to spare, that was.

As a man, Benjamin was distinctly off-limits.

But wearing his clothes when she needed a change of them was not the same thing as forgetting that.

It was merely a reasonable and pragmatic thing to do under the circumstances.

Facing him with a smile that was probably too big, she said, "If you think they will work. I would certainly appreciate it."

With a nod and a smile that seemed equally forced and overly friendly—as well as an odd mismatch to the heated darkening in his eyes—he gestured in a new direction than they were walking down the hall.

Miri refused to read anything into the look.

You don't have to worry about there being anything more than what's on the surface between the two of you, she assured herself.

They were grown-ups who knew the difference between a heated moment and full-blown attraction.

Today, they weren't anywhere near crossing any lines.

The room was bright and there was literal and appropriate distance between them—social and professional.

They weren't sitting together in front of a fire drinking wine again.

It was different now.

What had happened was behind them and they could put it out of their minds.

All they had to worry about was when this storm was going to end.

The conviction became harder to hold on to, though, when he led her up some wooden stairs and into an attic where he handed her a forest-green hooded sweatshirt with gold lettering that he had unearthed from the third box he opened.

"From high school spirit week, senior year," he said, his mind clearly in a different place than her own with regard to the sweatshirt. "I swear my mom kept everything," he murmured.

Miri didn't point out that it looked like he had kept everything that his mother had.

Instead, she took the hoodie gingerly, running her fingers along the golden letters sewn onto the breast, proudly declaring the wearer attended California Polytechnic State University.

Only one other time had another man offered her his hoodie, though in fairness, she wasn't sure it was accurate to call her ex-fiancé a man.

He'd barely been nineteen when they'd broken up.

Back then, she had worn his sweatshirt proudly around town, around the house—around everywhere.

It had quickly become one of her most cherished garments.

Kneading Benjamin's sweatshirt between her fingers, she recalled the texture and familiar thickness of a university pullover, but it wasn't her ex-fiancé's image that came to mind.

Instead, it was Benjamin's, from the night before.

Dragging her mind once again away from the past, Miri responded. "She must have been proud."

Continuing to search through boxes in the climate-controlled attic storage space he had taken her to, he nodded without looking up from what he was doing.

"They were both very proud. Perhaps too proud, ultimately."

The last bit sounded like an afterthought, and yet it carried a heaviness that made it seem ominous to her.

"Their pride was a lot of pressure?" she guessed, unable to stop the part of her that always wanted to take care of everything.

This time, he paused with the boxes, looking up at her as if truly startled out of the task at hand for the first time in their conversation. With a brief shake of his head, he said quietly, "No. Their pride was a wonderful mantle. Unfortunately, it had terrible consequences. They died when the yacht they'd chartered to celebrate my graduation capsized."

Squeezing the sweatshirt to her chest, Miri grimaced. "That's awful. I'm so sorry."

His expression shuttered at her words, and he shrugged. "Bad luck. But it never would have happened if they'd been a little less proud."

"I don't think—" she started to argue, to deny that correlation equated to causation in this case, but seeing his face harden even as she spoke, she realized it was a useless exercise—and probably foolish.

Who was she to know better than him?

She didn't know him.

They weren't friends.

She just worked for him.

And kissed him.

But that didn't make her anything to him or give her the right to push.

"That's a hard way to lose a family."

There was no pity in her words this time, just acknowledgment of the injustice of it.

To lose one's parents in such a horrible accident, and on the eve of college—it wasn't fair, for any young person.

His shoulders relaxed, the line of tension that had stiffened his spine curving back into a natural S.

He smiled at her and it felt like there was respect in that smile.

But had she done the right thing or simply the easy thing by not pushing back against such an obviously erroneous conclusion?

It doesn't matter, she reminded herself.

It wasn't her place to challenge his long-held notions.

He returned to hunting through the boxes for something for her to wear over her legs, and she pushed the question from her mind.

It wasn't her business.

Triumphantly, he held up a pair of sweatpants in the same forest green as the sweatshirt she held.

Between the hoodie and the sweatpants, her attire was going to be a long way from professional, but putting on clothes that didn't have dried toothpaste on them would still feel like a small miracle.

"Thank you," she said. "I appreciate you going to all this trouble," she added, gesturing to the attic and freshly opened boxes.

Closing the box, he rose to his feet with a shrug. "It's the least I could do. I'm sorry I'm not better prepared."

With a dry chuckle, she said, "I'd be worried if you were..."

Turning his neck from one side to the other, stretching out the kinks, he smiled. "I was a wilderness scout, you know... Always prepared."

Miri rolled her eyes, about to say, "Of course you were," when a box tipped over behind him with a loud clatter.

Miri winced as it landed. It sounded like whatever was in there was both dense and breakable.

The fall dislodged the tape that had held it closed, leaving one flap slightly higher than the other and through the sliver of open container, Miri could make out the green plastic lid of a storage container, but not much else.

"I could have sworn that was stacked securely," Benjamin muttered as he crouched to lift and return it to its place, in the process opening the lid fully to take a quick scan of its contents.

Righting it, he let out a dry chuckle, and said, "Irony of ironies."

Curious, Miri asked, "What's that?"

"It's a box of pictures, including, I'm sure, one of me in the station wagon. And my mom's menorah."

Miri laughed, even as a shiver went up and down her arms. "What are the chances?" she said, and wondered what they actually were.

The random coincidence of that particular box falling over on this particular day—the second night of Hanukkah when they had only this morning been discussing the station wagon—felt a little less random than it should.

"Indeed," he said under his breath as he removed the box of photos. With a remote and oddly robotic efficiency, he sorted through a few photos before handing her one, his eyes still in the box.

In the picture stood a young Benjamin Silver.

Tall and lanky, as he'd claimed, he stood proud beside an old Subaru wagon, wearing the bright and crisp Cal Poly hoodie that she currently held in her hands.

He was obviously himself, and yet it was hard to believe that the man she had spent the past twenty-four hours with was the same person.

It wasn't that he had physically transformed—although as he had said, he had filled out, losing every trace of slenderness in his long body—as much as he had hardened, become more distant and colder.

Especially the eyes.

It was there that he had changed the most.

In the picture, he was a boy, young and clearly eager for the future.

In the present, he was Benjamin Silver, a man with a gaze like an iceberg—chilly, hard and far more intense below the surface.

Had it been losing his parents so young that had done that to him, or was it the ruthlessness required to get as far as he had? Miri wondered.

"There are candles, too. Of course. She was forever worried about running out of candles…" he said, the box containing what she assumed was a menorah in one hand, and unopened box of slender blue and white candles in the other.

Making every move as if he intended to pack it all away, he began to put the candles back into the box, the man he had become was incapable of seeing the magic in the fact that they had stumbled upon a menorah and candles while stranded together on Hanukkah.

But the version of him that stood in the photograph—the same version that was hopeful and bright and went with his dad to get a box of doughnuts for his mom—would have.

He said he wasn't scarred from his loss, but he had just built up so much hard tissue he couldn't feel it anymore.

Surprising herself, Miri said, "Don't put it away. We should take it down with us."

"What?" he asked, looking from her back down to what he held in his hands, as if only now realizing what it was.

"The candles and the menorah. We should take them down," she repeated. "It's Hanukkah."

She tried to keep it casual, sensing that she trod in sensitive territory despite the fact that there was no outward change in him at her suggestion.

"I don't think—" he started, only to trail off for the first time in her acquaintance with him. He picked back up with a shake of his head. "No. No. There's no need for that. This evening is likely your last here and I won't light them after you're gone. There's no need to get wax all over everything and have to clean it up for one night."

Professionalism and basic respect for privacy urged her to leave it at that, but a rogue impulse in her drove her to continue. "I don't mind cleaning up afterward. There's a trick to it I learned during the years that my friends and I were still meeting every night."

She was laying it on thick, reminding him of the event the snowstorm had forced her to miss.

"You're a guest. Guests aren't supposed to clean up."

Miri snorted. "Since when? Everyone is supposed to clean up after themselves."

"Not according to my mother."

"You don't think your mother would be all about lighting those candles?" Miri asked, lifting a brow as she did.

"She also would have fed you a homemade meal for dinner instead of a box of doughnuts. I don't see how any of that's relevant."

"I think we should do it. They fell out of the box, for goodness' sake." She didn't know where the audacity to continue push like this came from, but as usual when it came to Benjamin, Miri could not seem to stem the flow.

"People were burned as witches based on coincidences like those," he said flatly.

Still she didn't give up.

"I don't think we're in any danger of starting a new inquisition."

"It's a waste of time," he said.

"Isn't that what we're looking for as we wait out the storm?"

"Between the room lighting and the fire, you'll barely notice the light of the candles."

"I'd like to, Benjamin," she said, soft and final.

He shut his mouth, pressing it into a straight line. Closing his eyes, he let out a breath, then opened them again. "I'll take them down."

"Fantastic!" She clapped as she said it, warmth blossoming in her chest at the victory, the sensation of it expanding outward like a huge bloom within her, not out of gloating but actual happiness.

It wasn't the battle of wills—hers against his—that she was glad of the outcome.

It was the battle fought inside him, between the hard Benjamin and the open Benjamin.

Angling his wrist to check the time in the hand that held the box of candles, his voice was gruff but had a hint of humor in it—even if it was a self-deprecating kind. "I told them to have dinner prepared at six tonight," he said. "If you want to change and have a little time to yourself and light candles before that, we should head back to the west wing. We'll pass the spa along the way and can grab a robe, in case I'm wrong about the sweats," he added.

Still emboldened after her menorah win, Miri teased, "Not so certain about being right anymore?"

Glancing at her out of the corner of his eye, he shot her a cocky half grin. "It pays to be careful, even if, like you, I am almost never wrong."

It didn't seem like he was talking about the fit of her clothing options anymore, but for the life of her, Miri couldn't pinpoint exactly what it was that he *was* talking about.

He'd assessed her as he'd spoken, eyeing her like she

had once again surprised him, but she had no idea why or how.

Leading her on the somewhat long walk back through his home to the west wing, he made small talk about the rooms they passed, including a private theater, a few bowling lanes, both heated and unheated indoor pools, and indoor skating rink.

Along the way, he stopped outside yet another wooden door and went inside, returning with a brilliantly white, gorgeously plush, bathrobe.

For an instant, Miri considered wearing the robe.

The hoodie suddenly seemed thin and rough by comparison.

But as one expected from a robe, its only fastener was the tie at its waist.

A body like Miri's needed far more coverage than that.

Benjamin left her at her room door, something strangely sweet and gentlemanly about the action, before parting with plans to meet up again for dinner in the private dining area, adjacent to the couch and seating area from the night before.

CHAPTER SEVEN

ONCE AGAIN, BENJAMIN ARRIVED before Miri.

Waiting for her for the second time in the same day, he wondered how she had spent the hour or so that they had been apart and considered the fact that a part of him had actually been reluctant to say goodbye to her.

What did that mean?

Despite his commitment to showing her a good time, he had needed the solitude after the incident with the menorah.

It was ridiculous, he knew, to have had such a strong reaction to the idea of bringing it down, but it had surged nonetheless. The last time he had placed candles in the menorah and lit them had been the last year his parents had been alive. There was something visceral in that, a kind of physical memory that could not help but remind him of things that were better off left in the back of his mind.

But to deny Miri's request, a simple and obvious one given the circumstances and time of year—two Jews stranded together over Hanukkah—would be to punish her for the fact that he had things he'd rather remained buried and forgotten.

If it weren't Hanukkah, she wouldn't have even suggested it.

He knew that.

It was a normal, logical idea.

Except that unpacking his old family menorah, freeing all the associated memories it held, wasn't a normal thing for him to do, at all.

And certainly not with a woman he barely knew.

It was an intimate thing to do.

Just like everything else that had occurred between them since their meeting had ended—an hour later than it should have.

For not the first time in his life, what a difference an hour had made.

It was the difference between appreciating the opportunity to work with a woman possessed of a body as fine as her mind and knowing what that woman felt and tasted like.

It was the difference between getting important work done and showing her a good time that was becoming progressively more personal.

He would put a stop to the momentum tomorrow, should the storm continue.

He would create some distance between them, blaming work if need be, to ensure there were no more slipups.

He had never had to be so diligent around anyone before.

But was it any wonder, really?

Even time worked strangely around Miri, flying by or stretching long in correlation to whether he was deep in conversation with her or anticipating the point at which he would see her again.

It was not an experience he regularly had in his life.

He had mastered time a long time ago.

The death of his adopted parents had been due to losing track of distance and time and running out of fuel in a rickety yacht just waiting to sink, and because of that he had disciplined himself into a man who was strictly aware of each minute as it passed, always knew where he was and insisted on high quality.

He controlled his time, he controlled his relationships, and through that, he limited life's capacity to surprise or hurt him.

But he was frequently surprised when it came to Miri.

At her door, to which he had personally led her through the multiple staircases and long hallways between the attic and her room because he hadn't wanted her to get lost, he had told her, "Dinner will be set for us at the informal table, near the fireplace where we ate the doughnuts."

Heat had come to her cheeks at the reminder of their night, as it had every time anything touched on what they had done on the couch, and she had clutched his old clothing to her chest, her glowing amber eyes racing with thoughts that she did not share. Instead, all she said was, "Great. I think I can make my way back there."

And he had wanted more, had walked away looking forward to the moment when he could have it.

And now he waited for her in the sitting area.

Since when did he wait for people?

He didn't wait for people.

Was there any greater waste of time than waiting for people?

A man could spend his whole life waiting and never get anything.

One had to act, and efficiently, to gain the kind of power and control to impact and save lives.

A man did not get there by waiting.

But, because it was Miri, he was waiting—and because it was her, the wait felt longer than it should have.

While he brooded on the couch and stared into the flames, his staff set the table and quietly left again, abandoning him once more to his private thoughts in his private living room.

"Things took a bit longer than anticipated." Her voice broke into his thoughts first, entirely too welcome. "Turns out this was one of those rare times you were wrong. The high school attire didn't fit and then took me a while to squeeze out of."

Turning in her direction, all thoughts immediately disappeared from his mind.

How was it possible for a woman to look so absolutely stunning wearing a simple spa robe?

The short robe was wrapped and cinched tight around her waist, stretching across her chest at the same time it hugged her hips and skimmed across the tops of her thick thighs, barely covering her gorgeous ass.

On her feet, incongruously and painfully sexy, she wore her work pumps.

Clenching his fists at his sides, he swallowed, his own thighs flexing and releasing as he focused his entire strength and will on not leaping at her.

He had already acknowledged that she was put together like no other woman he had ever encountered.

Now he was forced to admit that he might be developing some kind of kink around it.

At the very least, she had become the prototype for a new fantasy overnight.

"Don't worry about it," he said, forcing himself to be a host instead of a pervert, and she smiled.

The smile was a reward on top of her delicious body, and one that he didn't deserve.

Not when he didn't have the strength to redirect the flow of his thoughts.

"I figured we'd do the candles first," he said, voice rougher than he had intended.

Or perhaps it was as rough as it needed to be, given the fact that she was standing over there looking the way she did when they were about to light candles in his family menorah for the first time since he had lost his family.

There was only so many stimuli a man could take.

"Sounds good to me," she said softly, crossing the space between them, past the set table, to stand beside him in front of the fireplace.

The menorah rested on the mantel, candles in place.

Retrieving a lighter from his pocket, he held it up, gesturing with his other hand for her to do the honors.

Their eyes locked and though he would have thought it impossible only an instant before, for a moment he forgot about even the titillating robe.

Her eyes were so beautiful.

They were warm and boundless, tough and compassionate, brilliant and sexy.

They were the eyes of a woman with good ideas, a welcoming heart, and the strength of will to be honest and real.

They were eyes, he realized, that he couldn't imagine tiring of, even should they be snowbound for the entire duration of Hanukkah.

She moistened her lips, reminding him of what it had been like to explore her mouth, and reached for the shammash.

He struck the lighter.

To the side of them, the fire in the fireplace made silhouettes of them both, two backlit and shadowed profiles gazing into each other.

She tilted the candle wick into the flame, holding it sure and steady until it caught.

Releasing the lighter, Benjamin watched her, attention focused and detailed, noting everything about her in this moment.

Her hair, the robe, her satin skin glowing in the firelight, her eyes bright—everything about her radiated.

Smiling upon the lighting, she turned to him.

She lifted her chin, angling her face toward his, taking a step toward him—opening her mouth to recite the blessings. It was natural for him to tilt toward her in return.

As if drawn by a force outside of their control, their mouths neared each other—until suddenly she blinked, gave her head a small shake and cleared her throat.

"Maybe it's enough to just light the candles tonight?" she said breathily.

This time she had been the one to come to her senses.

Shaking himself, Benjamin flashed her a sardonic smile before looking up and away, staring into the storm in the darkness outside rather than the woman who was a flame to his moth.

"Certainly," he said, his voice not his own, thick and gruff. "I'm sure you're hungry. The table is ready if you are."

Nodding, she jumped on the subject eagerly. "Yes, starving."

He led her to the table and held out a chair.

She sat delicately, careful to ensure that the short robe continued to cover her ass as she did.

Clenching his hands around the chair, he swallowed as he gently pushed her in.

"Thank you," she said. "Once again, everything looks wonderful. I hope we didn't let it sit too long."

Her voice was airy and light.

"Nothing to worry about. Hot plates," he said, gesturing to the well-set table, each dish sitting on a state-of-the-art warming plate kept at its own perfect temperature.

"It looks delicious," she said, drawing in a deep inhale. "Smells delicious, too."

Recalling her story from the previous night, Benjamin had ordered a slow-cooked matzo ball soup for the night, with sides of grilled fish, roasted vegetables and fresh baked bread.

And once again he had selected the wine for the night, choosing from among the bottles he had the most anticipation around.

The wine was delicious.

The food, however, was unexpectedly disappointing.

Miri didn't think so, however, based on her commentary and sounds of approval.

"It's good," he said, unwilling to disparage his chef in the face of what was arguably a delicious soup, "but something is not quite right."

She laughed at that, the sound blunt and casual and comfortable, and teased, "It's not your mom's."

And though he had stopped being sentimental about his mother's cooking a long time ago—if only because he could no longer remember what it tasted like—he realized that Miri was right.

He had thought he had forgotten it, but tasting the soup tonight, he knew that what was in front of him wasn't it.

Miri, however, leaned back from her plate with a contented sigh. "That was fantastic. It's just too bad we ate all those doughnuts last night."

Laughing that she could crave more doughnuts after their smorgasbord the night before, he said, "No doughnuts tonight. But the chef did put together some delicious blackberry pie and fresh vanilla ice cream. The vanilla comes from my home in Seychelles."

She snorted. "You know they also sell it at the grocery store."

He laughed out loud at that.

There again was that spine, and it was even sexier showing up when she wore nothing but a robe.

"Wait until you taste it before you say that," he challenged, appreciating the way her cheeks shone in the firelight and the aftermath of wine. "I can guarantee you've never put anything in your mouth quite like it."

A familiar duskiness came to her cheeks, a blush darkening them without diminishing any of their glow.

On the surface, he spoke of vanilla but they both knew he suddenly made promises that didn't have anything to do with dessert.

They both understood it, and they were both curious—at least, according to the look in her eyes and the heat of her cheeks.

Watching her, he fought the sense of possession that rose within him.

She was not his, regardless of the fact that she wore his robe and had eaten the food of his world.

Persephone had not been allowed to leave after consuming pomegranate seeds.

They'd had multiple meals now.

Didn't that mean she couldn't leave?

He was surprised to realize he didn't want her to.

Aspen was his private sanctuary, but he was enjoying sharing it with her.

Across from him, Miri cleared her throat, and then shocked him with the words, "So what are we waiting for, then? Time to put your money where your mouth is."

She had to have been aiming for something else, something tough or playfully combative, he guessed—not the provocative challenge that came out.

At least, that was what he surmised by the way her eyes widened after the words left her mouth and her face flamed even further, her plump lips dropping open.

He had kissed those lips only the night before, and she had ended up on his lap when he had.

Could the same happen two nights in a row?

The answer should have been a resounding and absolute no, but it was not.

Instead, he wanted to put the question to the test, to see where she ended up in that little robe.

But he would not act on his impulses.

Things had gone too far last night on impulse. There was no sense in pushing the boundaries for a second night in a row.

Rising, acutely aware of the pulse and throb of each blood vessel in his body, some of which were more insistent than others, Benjamin said smoothly, "If you knew how much I wanted to, Miri."

Words, it seemed, had abandoned him, too.

Whatever he'd been left with had him moving toward something he knew he wasn't supposed to have with unstoppable purpose, careless of all the reasons why he should not.

Turning to get her dessert was the only way he was able to take his eyes off her.

Retrieving their dessert plates from the covered and temperature-controlled containers his staff had left them in, he placed two delicate plates in front of her.

Their eyes locked again, and once again, there was a long moment in which they simply stared.

When she finally said, "Thank you," her voice was rough.

He nodded, replying, "My pleasure," before returning to his seat where his eyes found her again, dropping to the vee where the robe overlapped to cover her breasts.

As tightly as she had initially had it cinched, and it had been enough to bring his attention and appreciation to the way it emphasized the pinch of her waist, it had loosened over the course of their meal, now revealing a tantalizing hint of the swell of her breasts.

He was playing with fire and could not seem to stop.

"Mmm…" she moaned, and his eyes shot back to her face, his body abruptly and absurdly stiff in attention.

It was the ice cream she purred over, not him—her mind

far from the prurient thoughts that raced through his head upon hearing the sound—and it didn't matter.

Watching her enjoyment activated his own pleasure.

She savored each bite, balancing warm pie on her spoon with the creamy, smooth ice cream. And each time she closed her eyes, tilting her head faintly back.

She swallowed and he followed the movement of her throat, unable to look away.

Somewhere in the barrage of her indulgence, he managed to finish his own portion, barely tasting it for all that he knew it was delicious.

It did not compare to her.

When she had finished the last bite, she opened her eyes, the whole of her person radiating a satisfied glow. "You were right. That was absolutely delicious."

For an instant, speech evaded him.

Then, clearing his throat again, he said, "I like to deliver on my promises."

Her gaze darkened at his words, her pupils dilating, and she gave her head the tiniest of shakes.

Blushing, she pulled back, energetically as well as physically leaning back, and gave a forced sounding chuckle. "I guess that's how you became Benjamin Silver, self-made billionaire."

He didn't want to talk about how he'd distracted himself from loneliness for years, drowning himself in work in order that he not have time or space to think about all the irreplaceable things he had lost on the boat that day.

He wanted to unwrap the gift that was her robe and appreciate the present inside.

But they weren't supposed to.

It wasn't allowed.

There could be consequences.

She wasn't ready.

Her eyes were wide, and her breath was short, her breasts lifting with each inhale, but she held back.

And he would not push her. Something deep and primal within him knew he didn't really need to.

She wanted to come play with him.

She just seemed to be trying harder to recall why that was a bad idea.

The self-made billionaire Benjamin Silver, as she had called him, knew that sometimes you had to wait to get what you wanted.

"I made my money by having nothing else to live for outside of my calling," he said, joking but also serious. His passion had been the only bridge between his parents and life that existed for him for a long time. "Coding, software engineering, design, all of it came to me as if I had been born with the understanding. It was my parents' greatest wish that the world would recognize that someday. After they were gone, losing myself in my studies and personal projects were the only things I could do to feel like a working part of the planet anymore. By the time I came out of that, I had made my first million. It was easy after that."

He had not planned on being quite so revealing with what he told her, but when had he ever with her? She had a way of drawing more out than he intended to give.

She gave back just as much.

Compassion warred with disbelief in her face. "I don't know if I should be depressed, impressed or incredulous," she said, beautifully honest, as always.

Amused by her frankness, he smiled. "Incredulous," he challenged.

A spark lit in her eyes, and he knew she wouldn't shy away.

"*Easy*? I don't think you know how hard it is out here for some of the rest of us poor souls."

"Of course I do. I told you, I wasn't always rich."

"But you were never poor, either," she challenged.

Lifting an eyebrow, he pushed back. "And you were?"

"Recently, yes," she said, bringing her hands together and closing eyes as she recalled. "In the gap between graduation and getting the job at the foundation, I was holding it together with piecemeal part-time jobs, but barely. If I hadn't been hired by the foundation when I was, though, I would have lost my apartment. It was pretty grim there for a while, facing either moving back into my parents' garage or living in my car. But then I got this swanky new job that I must preserve at all costs," she said, smiling with a serious look in her eyes. "I can't afford to lose this job," she added, and in it, he heard unspoken concerns about the security of her position.

There were reasons to dislike being her boss, so to speak. He wanted a different kind of power over her, the kind that ruled body and mind, not paycheck. He resented the shadow of coercion the fact that he could fire her brought into their relationship.

He wanted things to be different between them because he wanted her—even more powerfully than he had their first night together.

And despite that, he focused on her seriously and spoke clearly when he said, "No word will ever come from me that you are not the ideal individual for your position. You've convinced me with your work, and I would never put the foundation at risk of losing you."

Her eyelids fluttered closed, and she exhaled a long breath.

He frowned while her eyes were shut, even more frustrated to have work exist between them.

And yet without the foundation, he would have never met her.

Causing her to fear for her future was not showing her a good time, however. Nor, even, was alleviating that fear.

He wanted to make her smile.

She opened her eyes, expression earnest, to find him staring.

A slight frown drawing her eyebrows together, she said, "Thank you. I was worried after last night..."

"We're fortunate in being hundreds of miles away from anyone who might care, and neither of us is interested in reporting what went down here. As to last night, you have nothing to worry about." It was a promise he would use his considerable power to ensure he kept.

And he would make her smile again.

Voice turning teasing, he prodded her away from the direction of her fears. "So, you've struggled, it sounds like, but only recently. What about in childhood?"

Lifting an eyebrow at his question, she eyed him warily as she shook her head. "As a kid, things were happy and stable. We were never rich or anything, but I didn't have to worry about my needs being met, and my parents were able to afford things that weren't cheap, like piano lessons and judo."

"What did your parents do?" he asked, increasingly curious about everything that made her *her*.

"My dad is a pastor with his own church and my mom works for him as an administrator and all-around helpmate. The congregation pays the bulk of their salaries, which while not crazy by LA standards, was enough for a happy childhood and a bunch of spoiled grandkids."

Lifting his brow in response, Benjamin asked, "A pastor?"

Cringing slightly, Miri nodded. "Yep. There's a reason religious holidays are so big with my family."

A deeper understanding of her feelings of unbelonging dawning on him, Benjamin was softer than he might otherwise have been upon learning the information.

Instead of sarcasm or dry humor, he offered, "I hope he

comes around to seeing the great value in interfaith celebrations in the future."

Startled, her face shot to him, her eyes widening as she moved. A look entered them that was part hopeful and part vulnerable, and she swallowed. "Thanks," she said, after licking her lips, and he could tell that as much as she might be afraid to, she hoped that vision would come true, too.

He could tell she missed being a part of moments that were simultaneously familial and sacred.

He was honored to understand that about her. He got the feeling she kept a lot of herself hidden from the world around her.

But she still wasn't smiling.

So he said, egging her on through his tone and arch look, "Judo? I'm intrigued. Piano fits."

Her expression lost a bit of its softness. "And how's that?"

"It's a proper activity for a good Christian girl," he said with a sly grin and a shrug. "But judo? So violent." He shuddered in mock horror and her eyes lit with humor.

"Those of us that went to public school needed to be able to defend ourselves," she teased.

"So you're a public school brat then," he said, pleased to see her lift her chin with a glint coming to her eyes.

"And proud of it," she said, the corners of her mouth finally lifting.

He smiled.

He hadn't had a guess in either direction; he'd simply wanted to see her with her dander up again.

She was beautiful when she sparked.

She was always beautiful.

Blinking to break the spell, he cleared his throat and gestured toward her plate. "Do you want any more?"

She started, confused for a moment as to what he referred to, before looking down at her empty plate. She looked back at him with a smile and a shake of the head. "I couldn't possibly, I'm stuffed. What I want most right now is a comfortable place to stretch out for a post-meal coma."

He chuckled, amused by her way of being frank without crass, only mildly taken off guard by the satisfaction it gave him to feed her.

Why should providing for her fill him with such warmth? She was his guest, and it wasn't like it was a challenge for him physically or financially. It should have been a basic, second-nature thing to see to his guest's pleasure, and yet the evidence of hers made him pleased and smug—more akin to a caveman providing for his woman than a wealthy contemporary man seeing to his guest's comfort.

The achievement of pleasing Miri felt more like a necessity than a nicety.

"That can easily be arranged. Shall I walk you back to your room and the large bed awaiting you?" he began, only for her to stop him with a quick shake of the head and blush.

"No, no, no. I mean, no thank you. I'm not quite ready for sleep yet," she said, her voice taking on a breathy note it had lacked before. After a swallow, she moistened her lips. "Besides, why go so far when there is that gorgeous sofa and fire just right over there? Plus, the candles haven't burned out…"

Her eyes were like candles themselves, burning bright, their fire searing through everything that covered him.

He swallowed.

They had gone to the couch once before and the results had been…heated.

They'd already been playing with fire—throughout the entire meal, in fact—and he was struggling to resist the effect she had on him.

"And what if we go too far?" he asked, unwilling to be

anything but direct, even in the face of the currents running through his veins.

"No one ever need know if just this once…" she breathed, words thick.

His forearms tensed.

They shouldn't, there were more reasons than one, but they wanted to, and she was right, for the moment, they were the only two people in the world.

"Is that what you want?" He forced the question even as he already knew his answer.

He wanted her more than he could remember ever wanting anything in his life.

But while it could be their secret, it must be the choice of both of them.

There would be no claims of being caught up in the moment, swept away by doughnuts and rosé.

Waiting for her to decide, however, was another torture. Watching her mind work, her silhouette outlined by the fire behind her, his breath bated because of her for the third time that day.

When she nodded, his breath caught, the muscles of his abdomen clenching at the same time.

Picking up the wine that remained in the decanter, he rose, gesturing for her to precede him toward the fire and sitting area.

Her gaze followed the path of his hand, her eyes and mouth widening as they landed on the sofa.

The scene of the crime.

Wise as she was, he knew there was still a chance she might change her mind.

Color came to her cheeks, and she swallowed, the closing and reopening of her lips a sensual thing.

Would her mouth be confident wrapped around him?

With a bodily shudder, he imagined it would.

She looked from the place they had kissed the night before back to him.

Lips remaining slightly parted, breath escaping her, she nodded again.

She stood and again he wanted to groan aloud.

The robe had loosened enough to reveal a hint of the lace brassiere she wore. Her heels clicked across the floor as she walked to the couch.

At the edge of the rug she stopped, and he held his breath, watching her, wondering what she would do next.

His question was answered when she slowly stepped out of the heels, one foot at a time, each one a sensuous rise and fall, before stepping barefoot onto the sheepskin rug and letting out a sigh.

The muscles of his lower abdomen tightened at the sound.

"Everything that happens here, stays here?" she reiterated before taking another step, her question hushed, her voice low and throaty and incendiary—the words heavy with everything they left undescribed. "I don't have to worry about my future with the foundation?"

Nodding though her back faced him, Benjamin did his own swallowing in response, his throat tight from the images her questions sent racing through his mind.

"Yes," he rasped, frozen as he watched her.

At his answer, she did her own nodding.

Without looking back, she moved deliberately then, crossing the rug to sit on the edge of the couch, tucking the short robe beneath her as she did so.

He followed her slowly, trying to rebuild his control along the way.

He had wanted her to smile. He had wanted her to follow him, to take the bait of his invitation to risk returning to the sensual paradise that they had stumbled into the night before.

Now that she had, he was the one who felt like he flirted with danger—like he put something at risk through their encounter rather than her, something far more serious than a new job.

But there was not enough time to think about that in the walk between the table and sofa.

Setting down their glasses and the decanter on the marble-topped coffee table, he poured them each a glass before sitting at her side.

Ignoring the wine, she moved toward him.

It was a small motion, something no one else in the world would record or remember, but he knew he would never forget it.

The reasons why they should not clearly no longer enough to stop her, she reached for him.

Only a fool would not have reached back.

He was not a fool.

Eliminating the distance between them, he gathered her scantily robed figure into his arms, lifting her onto his lap once again as he tilted her face up toward his.

Their lips met, fitting together like puzzle pieces while flames flickered and danced in the fireplace, bathing their bodies with motion-filled light.

Her hands fisted in his hair as their mouths tangled, neither of them reserved or withdrawn.

It might have been snow madness.

It absolutely was.

There had been ample warning.

They were colleagues, not allowed to be lovers.

And yet they came together with smooth and supple ease.

She had moved to him, and then opened like a flower.

He plunged into her, savoring a nectar that was as intoxicating as if it had evolved to attract specifically him.

She sighed into his exploration, pliantly invested, savoring the sensations he brought to her while her fingers gripped his shoulders hard—not, he sensed, in an effort to remain upright, but in order to not let him go. In order that he not stop.

But she was in no danger of him stopping.

He had no stop left in him, save the emergency brakes reserved for her.

Only she could stop him now, not because they shouldn't or couldn't, not because of her job nor his, and not because he wanted to keep her at arm's length.

None of those reasons was more compelling than she was.

None of them greater than his need to have her again—to have more of her.

He did not want a taste followed by another night of tossing and turning, and he was past worrying about it.

He wanted her naked, riding him like he suspected she could, or laid out below him, or presented in front him, on her hands and knees, her curves taking on the shape of the only kind of instrument he was interested in playing.

She looked so damn good in the robe.

It was a shame that it had to go.

Sliding its upper edges over her shoulders while she straddled him on the couch, their position a re-creation of the night before different only in that neither of them seemed to have any intention of slowing things down tonight and there were fewer layers of clothes between them to begin with.

Her beautifully rounded brown shoulders shone soft and smooth in the light, her large breasts looking like some kind of layer cake, dressed in a cornflower-blue lace bra.

Pooling at the base of her gently rounded stomach, accentuating the flare of her hips, moving the robe away had revealed a barely hidden goddess—the kind of woman who was built for everything a man might throw at her.

She had been sexy wearing the robe.

She was out of this world in just lingerie.

Running his hands along her shoulders, he caressed her arms—strong, soft and supple—before cupping her breasts to rub his thumbs along the lace-edge of the half cup. The contrast of her incredible skin against the rough delicacy of the lace sent charged signals up and down his arms but was nothing compared to the jolt he felt every time he crossed over the pebbled treasure of her nipples.

She moaned, her hips rolling on him with each pass, heat pulsing at the center of her.

He had all the money he could dream of, but that meant nothing.

Real power was the capacity to make Miri moan—to bring her to such a state of abandon that she forswore the rules and set them both free.

Unable to stop, he caressed her breasts to the increasing volume of her cries, each one leaving him harder than the last, until he could take it no more, reaching for the fabric belt at her waist.

He made quick work of the knot, flinging the robe away once untied, and beheld the treasure that had lain beneath.

Her panties were lace, the same cornflower blue as her bra, low-cut and stretched across the plane of her abdomen.

Naked but for the faintly transparent blue lace she wore, the reality of Miri surpassed even the fantasies she had already inspired in his mind.

She was shapely and long-limbed, buxom to the perfection of the word, and had miles of beautiful, soft brown skin that begged to be kissed and caressed.

He could have spent an eternity devouring her with his eyes alone, but he did not have an eternity.

He had only until the storm passed to savor her, perhaps only now.

Her head thrown back, eyes closed, as his hands worked

their magic, she was everything erotic and sensual he could want. He did not want it to end.

Who knew when they would come to their senses?

If he was half as good as he thought he was, it wouldn't be any time soon.

He would happily drive her out of her mind with pleasure if madness was the only thing keeping reason at bay.

Their bodies pressed together on the couch once more, but tonight it was no longer enough, not for what he wanted to do to her.

Sitting up, he caught her lips again, wrapping an arm around her waist and back, reveling in the press of her skin against his in the process.

Had he ever felt something so soft and begging to be touched?

He had, he realized, but only because he had enjoyed the pleasure of her breasts.

She was the softest material in the known universe, and for better or worse, he knew that now.

Continuing to kiss her, he let his hands slide farther, slipping beneath her thighs to grip her ass as he lifted them both from the couch.

Her arms tightened around him, and she gasped into their kiss but did not break it as he carried her around the marble table to lay her on the sheepskin rug in front of the fire.

He released her lips reluctantly, and even then, only in order to look at her lying beneath him.

He had pictured her like this while he'd been alone in his bed.

Once again, the reality put his mental images to shame.

Her lips were slightly parted, plump and vibrant with their kiss, as sure a sign of her arousal as was the writhing of her body and the roaming exploration of her hands.

He shuddered as she ran the cool silk skin of her inner

thighs along his flanks, her breath catching and sighing at the contrast in their textures—hers smooth and soft whereas he was rough and hard.

The satiny caresses were a glorious preview of what it would feel like to have her legs wrapped around him, but not what he wanted most from her now.

Before that, before he slid inside her and appeased the pressing demand of the beat throbbing low in his abdomen, he wanted to see her free from the frame of her lovely blue lace lingerie.

And before he lost himself inside her, he wanted to taste her, to thrill her, to bring her to the precipice and over, more than once.

He wanted to hear his name on her lips, his first name, husky and thick and desperate. He wanted her to lose herself, to break apart, losing every shred of her incredible control as she did.

He wanted to make sure she never regretted letting the rules that governed them remain outside of the storm, outside of this moment.

Opening her eyes, her amber orbs glowed up at him like bright burning embers in a fire. Her hair was fanned out around her, long and wavy and black, and her lips glistened.

She was phenomenal, and he wanted more.

Leaning down to capture her lips once more, he indulged.

CHAPTER EIGHT

BEING MADE LOVE to by Benjamin Silver was unlike anything Miri had ever imagined, and she'd had years too long to imagine.

And it was nothing like the chaste good-night kisses she had enjoyed throughout college, nor the youthfully exuberant boundary-pushing she had done with her high-school sweetheart.

The passion was there—stronger now even than it had been back then for having had time to ripen and mature—but along with it, there was a level of expertise and finesse that her ex-fiancé had lacked.

Benjamin was superior to every sensual encounter she'd ever had before.

He was intelligent, direct, and knew exactly who he was and what he wanted.

She felt the truth of it with his every exceptional touch.

He was strong and un-shy about what he wanted from her, his confident hands and mouth playing her body like she was an instrument and he a virtuoso.

He had carried her like she weighed nothing, adroitly maneuvering her body into increasingly pleasurable positions.

He knew when to press firm and when to caress lightly, when to command and when to tease, and she was a quivering mess because of it.

Her skin was on fire, even as she shivered across her body. The silken softness of the sheepskin rug against her exposed skin, the sensuality of his kiss, the pressure of his body pressing against hers, his hips against hers, the rub of his body against her sensitive inner thighs—it overtook her, transporting her out of her body even as it anchored her irrevocably within it.

She was no longer a woman—instead she had deconstructed into a series of sensations.

And yet this was the most womanly she had ever felt.

Like the earth, Miri was hot liquid at her core while the surface of her burst with life and expression.

She sighed and moaned and cried out into Benjamin's kiss as his hands trailed along and over her breasts, down her stomach, and lower to gently cup the mound, separated now by only a thin layer of lace.

Deliciously and torturously, he kept his hand still there, cupping and holding her growing heat while her hips helplessly thrust into his pressure.

Only when she thought she would go crazy from wanting more did he begin to gently undulate his hand, creating slow waves that swallowed her in an ocean of pleasure.

Beneath his expert handling, she writhed, rocking her hips, opening her mouth to his deeper exploration, gasping as he did.

He was relentless as he drove her from pleasure to pleasure, and then his mouth began to travel.

First she felt his lips at the corner of her mouth, then along her jawline, on her neck and her breasts, hot as they engulfed her nipples.

It was too much, and she never wanted him to stop—even as she craved each new thing that came next.

He moved lower, pressing deft kisses against her stomach, giving her no time to process, only time to feel as he tasted and savored her.

When his mouth replaced the hand that had held her core, her thighs clamped around his head of their own volition and she called out his name.

In response, he growled into her, his hands coming to grip her hips and hold her tight.

He ate her through lace, and she burst into a thousand thrumming pieces, her back arching high off the ground while she gripped his hair.

She collapsed back against the silky soft rug boneless, a half smile on her face while the low rumble of his laugh reverberated through her.

But he was not done with her yet.

Laying a trail of soft kisses along her inner thighs, he pulled up slowly, his movement a gentle caress as she came down.

He rose over her, firm and steady, a smile on his face while his eyes continued to smolder.

Wrapping an arm around her waist, he carefully lifted her, leaning back as he did, until she straddled his seated form with her knees bent while her upper body rested cradled against his chest, held secure and supported by the arm curving around her lower back.

Seated this way, the center of her weighted and stacked atop his, she could easily feel the steel of him through the layers of clothing that still separated them.

He kissed her neck, his hand in her hair angling her head for access, and she moaned.

His hand at her back released the clasp of her bra, sending the straps sliding over her shoulders.

Drawing back slowly, he watched hungrily as the bra fell away to reveal her breasts.

Heat flushed her chest beneath the blue flame of his gaze.

Then, once again, he devoured.

Without the thin barrier of her brassiere between the

heat of his mouth and the skin of his breast, she was sure she must be burning.

Heat flared throughout her system again, rising fierce and hot from the embers of her orgasm, and she writhed on his lap while he acquainted himself with her bare breasts.

Until it was no longer enough.

He moved beneath her dexterously, drawing her forward onto her hands and knees now while he knelt in front of her.

She looked up at him, her eyes traveling up his still-clothed form, slowing when they reached the rigid outline of him through his pants before making their way up to his.

He groaned when they did, his hand coming to rake into her hair, cupping the side of her head and gripping for a moment before releasing with an exhale.

"Turn around," he rasped, and she obeyed, though she had never been so exposed to another person before.

He brought his palms to her hips and gripped strong before raking his fingers up to the hemline of her panties to pull them down and over the curve of her ass, feeling as he went.

Abandoning the fabric as soon as he had revealed all of her, his palm once again came to cup her mound. As if she had not already detonated once from the way he touched her, her body wound up again, tensing and thrumming as the movement of his fingers along the edges of her goaded her higher.

Breath abandoned her when his fingers slipped inside of her.

Behind her, he let out a strained moan. "Damn it, Miri, I can't wait anymore. I have to be inside you."

His fingers working steady magic, all she could do was moan and gasp and nod.

Keeping steady hold of her with one hand, his movements took on a new urgency as he freed himself with the other.

The quick clinking of his belt releasing, and the crinkle of the condom wrapper echoed around her, and then she felt him, hot—so incredibly hot—and hard and silken at her entrance.

"Benjamin," she gasped his name, the entirety of her focus zooming in to the place where they touched.

"Be still now, Miri," he commanded, his body poised to plunder yet restrained. "It'd be so easy to slide inside you right now, we both know it, but we're not ready."

Miri tried to listen, tried to behave, and yet still her hips angled back, winding toward greater closeness.

"Naughty Miri," he chastised her softly, his voice low and sexier than she'd ever heard. "I'll forgive you this time, though," he added, guiding her hips where he wanted them with both hands now.

They no longer merely touched, surface to surface, but joined as he pressed into her and held.

"Are you ready, Miri?"

"I'll die if you don't," she choked, and behind her he chuckled low.

And then he was sliding into her and her whole body was shuddering.

He cursed, his voice strained, even as he went slowly, allowing her body time to accommodate him.

It was unlike any sensation she had ever had, stretching, tight, and filling her, even as it somehow made her realize what she had been missing this whole time.

Him.

She had been missing him, this—the perfection of their fit, the strength of him in the core of her.

Moaning, her mind spiraled inward, focused on every way she could feel him, until her inner muscles began pulsing and twitching again.

"Miri," he groaned, his body taut and still as she shuddered around him.

But she couldn't help it; the tide within her rose steadily once again and she could only drift out with it.

And then he began to move, slowly at first, and then with greater speed and depth, until again she dissolved into a million tiny pieces.

And once again, he rocked her steadily through the process of the pieces coming back together, stuttering only when she came back to herself completely on a sigh of, "Benjamin."

His name was both gratitude and awe in her mouth, and as she finished it, his fingers gripped deep into her hips as he thrust one last time before shuddering in the same way.

They remained joined, motionless, while their breath returned, and aftershocks twitched through his body and into hers.

And then he slowly pulled out, allowing her to collapse on the ground and him to lower himself to her side, his eyes swirling as they took her in.

"You're beautiful, Miri," he said as she snuggled into him.

"You're a sex god," she mumbled into his chest as she nuzzled him, mildly aware of the fact that she was naked while he still wore his clothes.

Chuckling again, he said, "You of all people should be clear on the fact that Jews are monotheistic."

Her laughter muffled by their snuggle, she smiled into his chest, filled with a warmth that had nothing to do with the fire and everything to do with feeling free in a way she never had before.

"We should move," he said, adjusting his arm to be more comfortable for her.

Still smiling, she nuzzled in. "No way. I'm not going to my room when you're right here."

Drawing her closer, there was a smile in his voice when he responded. "Of course you're not. I was talking about my room, where I envisioned we would freshen up before exploring further…"

Even as his words thrilled her, a shadow of apprehension clouded her face. "But just until the storm passes," she said.

His arm tightened around her at her words, though he agreed, "Anything we want, but just until the storm passes."

And for the first time since it had blown in, Miri didn't want it to.

CHAPTER NINE

FOR THE FIRST time in memory, Benjamin was awoken by the buzz of his assistant.

Adjusting so as not to disturb the still-sleeping woman at his side, he pressed the audio-only feed to answer.

"Yes?"

Glancing at the clock as he waited for her response, he was surprised to see that it was 8:00 a.m. He hadn't slept in so late since leaving college.

Of course, it had also been a long time since he'd stayed up so late, and so exuberantly, with a woman.

Within the world of the storm and the safeties of their agreement to suspend the rules of the one outside of it for the time being, Benjamin was happy in a way he had not been in memory.

There was a difference, it seemed, between satisfaction and happiness.

Waking beside Miri made him realize that he had been confusing the rush of the former for the warmth of the latter over his past years and doing so to his own detriment.

Happiness led to sleeping in late.

"It occurred to me that your guest might appreciate a trip to the wardrobe sometime today, since the storm's showing no sign of slowing down. Might be some moths in there with all the use it's gotten since, but Sharice set one up here like she did in California and Ms. Howard might appreciate a change of clothes." His assistant's gravelly voice came through the speaker with even more of its stony quality.

Curled at his side, a naked Miri looked up at him out of one opened eye.

Her eyebrow was lifted and even though she'd only been awake for an instant, there was a *look* in that eye.

"That's an excellent idea, Melba. Thank you. We'll have breakfast in the private dining room today. A repeat of yesterday is fine. I'll wake Ms. Howard."

"Sounds good, sir." And then his assistant was gone, and he was happy to have the world shrunk back down to himself and Miri.

Even with the look.

"You only have spa robes, huh?" she said, head lifted to face him now, both of her eyes open, her hair tousled and gorgeous, a smile beneath the sternness in her tone.

Unable to help himself, he laughed, and it, too, felt as unfamiliar as waking up happy.

"I had no idea. I told you, I never have company out here," he said, smiling. "You're the first."

Abruptly, her sass disappeared, replaced with a warm blush. "Well, today, I will most certainly be making a visit to *the wardrobe*," she said primly.

"And what about ice-skating after that?" he asked. "Or a movie?"

Wariness came into her eyes, even as he could sense her interest. "Are you sure that's a good idea?"

He nodded, sure. He was deliberate when he made a decision. Rarely did he look back once one was made.

"No one knows you're here. No one really even knows we know each other yet. While this storm rages, no one could even take a picture if they wanted to. We've already agreed that whatever happens while you're here will stay here. Why not take advantage and make sure everything

happens?" There was an eagerness in his voice, a mischievous enthusiasm and a kind of desperation for her to see
his logic that even he could hear.

She turned him into a teenager again.

Once again, she repeated their mantra. "What happens
here, stays here."

He resented it, even as it thrilled him.

He was used to convincing his paramours that it was
better to be circumspect when dating a man as wealthy
as he was but found the fact that it was necessary with
Miri distasteful.

He didn't want her to be more concerned with keeping
their secret than she was with enjoying it.

"Okay," she said, nodding, her lips lifting into a smile.
"But that means candles and Hanukkah, too. At least until
the storm passes," she added.

He knew he had clearly gotten the better end of the deal,
but he wouldn't be the one to argue.

"Now where did that robe get up to?" she mused, a
saucy glint in her eye that he was becoming familiar with.

"Breakfast can wait a bit," he said, grinning, rolling her
on top of him all the way.

With the evidence of what he thought it could wait for
pressed against her as it was, she only asked, "Again?"
with a level of surprise.

Rather than speak, he showed her the answer.

The wardrobe was everything Miri had daydreamed a rich
man would have and more. Rather than simply a piece of
furniture, as the name suggested, it was a huge walk-in
closet—more like a walk-in *room*—filled with outdoor
wear, indoor wear, shoes and accessories in a variety of
colors, styles and sizes.

"It's stocked for guests, so have your pick and come
back if you need to. You remember how to get here?" Ben-

jamin's assistant asked her, after delivering her to what amounted to a private designer mall.

Miri nodded. "I do."

The assistant gave a tiny smile and then made her way out of the room, leaving Miri to make her selections.

It was a shame the storm was keeping them inside, because Benjamin's guest wardrobe had some fantastic coats and snow gear. Passing those options in favor of something more comfortable for indoor wear, though, Miri still felt like a princess.

Who else but a princess had her choice from among high-end designers and cashmere and fine wool? And though she'd been afraid there would be a limit of options in her size, so far, everything she had been drawn to had been in a size that would work for her.

And Benjamin hadn't even known he'd had it.

Snorting, she continued to hunt, humming to herself.

"Don't forget, we're ice-skating today," he said, his voice startling her from the doorway.

She didn't know when he had decided to join her, but it didn't make a difference to her reaction.

Heat filled her at the sight of him.

It was incredible to believe that she had made love to this gorgeous man, with his silken hair and piercing blue eyes, his comfortable, well-fitting slacks and his classy sweatshirt.

Multiple times.

And they would again.

For as long as the storm lasted, and they existed in a world of their own.

One that included fantasy rooms full of free clothes.

"What exactly does one wear to ice-skate?" she asked, tilting her head to one side.

He smiled. "You've never ice-skated?"

Shaking her head, she said, "LA girl."

"There're rinks in LA."

"Not in *my* LA," she said with a grin.

His blue eyes were warm as they watched her, but he answered seriously. "It's chilly in the rink, but still climate controlled. I'd recommend something over the extremities, but you don't need to worry too much about keeping warm."

Taking him at his word, Miri picked out a pair of supple black velvet leggings and a rich creamy oversize amber sweater with a tag that revealed it was 100 percent cashmere.

"What do you think?" she asked, holding them up for his inspection.

Looking at her face, rather than the clothes she held, he said, "Perfect," and her breath caught.

There was no risk of confusing this special time for regular life.

Benjamin Silver was fascinated…with her.

Swallowing, she said, "Fantastic, I'll change into them now."

She turned reluctantly away from him, finding a private alcove in the room to change.

Along the way she found fresh underthings and was again grateful to whomever was responsible for stocking Benjamin's guest quarters.

They had made love again in bed, then again in his shower after that before breakfast, so while her sensitized skin remained alive and quick to fire, she felt clean.

Fresh clothes that cuddled every inch they covered in fabrics she couldn't usually afford almost turned her into a new woman.

She purred at the sensation, and he called from the doorway. "Is that an invitation?"

Flushing all over again, she laughed.

He was insatiable, and she was grateful. She was, too. As she was also acutely aware of how temporary it all had to be.

All of it would blow away with the storm.

The thought was a faint chill in the warmth of the moment, and she pushed it aside, crossing the room to him to take his hand in hers and smile up at him.

Bringing his hand to her chin, he angled her face more openly toward his and took her lips, kissing her deep and lingeringly before pulling back. "It was. You look beautiful and feel even better. The clothes are nice, too."

Eyes closed, she smiled up at him feeling his regard like the sun on her face.

Then she let her lids flutter up and dived into the beautiful blue of his.

"Nice? You're going to have to drag me out of this room kicking and screaming," she teased.

Laughing at that, he easily led her out of the room and down the hallway toward the east wing, where the ice-skating rink lay.

Window after huge window they passed showed that the storm continued on outside as fiercely as it had from the start, and squeezing his hand that held hers, Miri was grateful.

The only fear she felt now in the face of it was that it would end before she was ready.

Benjamin's ice-skating rink was the kind of romantic dream that could have been in a movie. Miri gasped when he opened the door to reveal a room of structured blond wood and massive picture windows, a gray stone fireplace—of course—all surrounding a pristine expanse of ice.

Because the storm continued, all that could be seen through the wall of exterior-faced windows was bright white, but it only highlighted how serene and cozy his private rink was.

The interior wall and ceiling were constructed of long straight planks of the same warm blond wood, almost like a sauna, while the far wall entirely comprised gray stone-work with a large floating fireplace at its center.

A seating area was set up in front of the fire, but for the most part, the room was ice rink.

It was all so beautiful that Miri couldn't work herself up about the fact that she'd never ice-skated before in her life.

"Let's get you some skates," he said, almost in response to her thoughts.

"I've never skated," she admitted, even as she still smiled at the room around them,

"I figured when you said you'd never been to a rink," he said with a charming one-sided grin. "Have you ever roller-skated or Rollerbladed?" he asked.

Nodding, she said, "Both, avidly."

"You'll get the hang of it then."

And as she suspected was the case too often, he was right.

Before she knew it, she was evading his capture on the ice, skating and laughing like they were a couple of kids.

"If I catch you, it means I get a kiss," he said as she narrowly escaped him yet again, laughing and breathing hard as she did.

Gliding safely out of his reach, she was cocky. "Tell you what. You catch me, you can have it all. I'm *that* sure you don't have a chance."

Triumph lit his eyes, and she only had an instant to con-template if she had made a mistake before she was forced to dart away from his grasp as his own skating seemed suddenly in overdrive.

He had not been so fast even moments before, but breathless and laughing as she did her best to elude him, she liked that he had been holding back until he had some-thing worth going full tilt for.

Mere heartbeats later, he caught her, twirling her into the circle of his arms before spinning the both of them around in the center of the rink.

Their eyes remained locked as they spun, saved from dizziness by being each other's anchor—the steady spot to return to.

Their breathing synced even as the momentum of their turn slowed, finally coming to a stop while they stared into each other's eyes.

He held her hand, had taken it sometime in their spinning, and her breasts were pressed against his chest.

Below them, the ground radiated a chill, but she was far from being cold.

But neither did that mean she was ready to strip and lie down on the ice. "You have to take me somewhere warmer to collect your prize," she said, breathless.

"No, I don't," he countered, angling her head to kiss her once more. This time, however, his kiss held notes that had not been there before. Sweet and tender, they gentled his passion. He kissed her this time as if she were a special treasure, something delicate and precious, like ice-skating alone in the world.

She sighed into him, her arms wrapped around his neck, fire and ice all around them. Her unexpected business trip to Aspen had become a beautiful daydream, even if it was one she would inevitably have to wake up from.

"Thank you for taking me skating for the first time, Benjamin." Her voice was soft and vulnerable because she couldn't help it.

In just under three days, he had become responsible for so many new firsts: her first private flight, her first trip to Aspen, her first meeting with Benjamin Silver, her first blizzard and her first time making love.

And he had made them all luxurious and memorable, fully prepared and equipped to ensure that all her needs were met, even those she had no idea to anticipate.

He was more than equipped to feed and clothe and care

for her, with everything at his fingertips in his palatial forest estate—from spare clothing to protection.

Enclosed in the circle of his arms, she was tempted to tell him, but she knew the words would only tangle on their way out. Some things resisted words.

But she was grateful, and she really didn't want it to end.

With their agreements, spoken and not, creating a bubble around them, any reservations that Benjamin had been able to hold on to had quickly dissipated, leaving him with only a sense of urgency to experience Miri in every way he could in the limited time they had.

He had only as long as the storm to build the kind of catalog of images of her that was supposed to last him a lifetime.

He had never resented the foundation before this.

The foundation was the reason he had found Miri—and it was also the reason he could not have her.

With each passing moment in her company, it seemed he wanted her more.

The way she looked up at him, flushed and glowing from skating, however, was an image worth preserving.

As was her laughter as they removed their skates, sitting together on a long cushioned bench.

"You were a competitive figure skater?" she asked incredulously.

He liked her incredulous. He liked her in each iteration he had encountered her, in fact.

"Only until I turned thirteen," he said, smiling in the face of her shock. "My mom grew up in the Midwest, skating all winter, and she wanted that for me, but the culture was different in LA, so instead of hockey, I did death-defying spins."

Miri snorted. "Death-defying?"

"More so than you realize," he said seriously, glad to see her smile grow.

"The rink was part of the reason I chose this property when I came out here," he added. "I missed skating."

Miri nodded, barely holding back her grin. "It's definitely not something that comes up a lot in LA, like golfing."

"Though I'm good at that, too," he said, deadpan and utterly without humility, and she laughed aloud.

"Of course you are," she said when she could. "And I bet there's a golf course somewhere around here, too."

"You would be correct, though it's only a nine-hole."

She let out the bark of laughter he was so fond of as she set her skates to the side and slid her fuzzy-socked feet back into the fluffy slippers she'd found in the wardrobe.

He couldn't say he wished he had known that his assistant had taken his order to set up his Aspen house the same as his California residence—because he would eternally be grateful for the robe she'd worn to dinner last night—but he was glad to have discovered it existed today, even if just for her excitement in picking out clothes.

He was wealthy enough to be an over-the-top host.

She made it meaningful.

"Only a nine-hole," she muttered, shaking her head, still smiling.

It was remarkable how easy it was to be around her—to talk to her, or not, to make love to her or simply enjoy her company—the only thing it was not easy to do around her was focus on other things, and that was a problem rare enough that he was intrigued.

Work would be there waiting for him when the storm passed.

Miri wouldn't.

So he would go with the way she rerouted the flow, and keep her naked for as much of it as he could.

And, like his past with his parents, he simply wouldn't think about the future.

CHAPTER TEN

"WE'RE COOKING?" MIRI ASKED, staring at the apron that Benjamin had just placed in her still-outstretched hand.

It was the third night of Hanukkah, the second since they'd made love, and they had just finished lighting the candles.

Like the oil and miracle of light, they would be lovers until the storm blew over.

And true to his word, Benjamin had been attentive about lighting them with her this evening—this time they even got through the blessings without devouring each other.

He had been serious when he'd said that until the storm ended, he wanted to experience *everything* with her.

It was phenomenal just how much progress they had already made toward that goal.

This far into the second day of making love to Benjamin Silver, she was even getting used to the fact that her cheeks heated every time she thought of it now.

In the less than twenty-four hours since they'd broken the seal on lovemaking, they'd spent so much time engaged in activities that were erotically sensual that it was a wonder she had not burned completely to ash.

But currently, their Hanukkah candles flickering stoutly on the fireplace mantel, bedroom activities were not on their agenda.

Right now, they were cooking.

"Correct," he affirmed, tying his own apron as he answered her question. "I gave the kitchen staff the night off and ran up and found my old family recipes while you took your post-skating nap," he explained.

He conveniently labeled it a post-skating nap, when in fact, it had been a post-afternoon-lovemaking nap.

He had drawn her from the rink back to his bedroom, where he'd worshipped her with a new kind of tenderness and fervor, going soft and slow and drawing the pleasure out until neither could take it any longer before he drove them both passionately over the edge.

They had fallen together that time, and afterward, he had gently kissed her lips and eyelids before cradling her in his arms like a treasure.

She had fallen asleep warm and safely secure there, listening to the sound of his heartbeat.

And when she'd padded back out to find him where she expected—the sitting area with a roaring fire burning—he'd handed her an apron.

"We're making latkes!" he added, gathering ingredients now. "And a brisket."

"Your mom's recipe?" she asked as she began to tie her own apron.

She recalled teasing him about it the night before, that only his mother's recipe would satisfy, but he shook his head.

"My grandmother's," he corrected.

Miri rolled her eyes with a snort. "Same difference."

Grinning, he gave in easily with a nod. "Same difference. I'm sure it was her grandmother's before that, too, back in the old country."

It was a common story, to have heritage dating back to the old country, but Miri wondered if he appreciated it.

Growing up, her family Bible held a handwritten record of her family's genealogy—at least her dad's side—

but there wasn't much beyond that. They had no wealth of old recipes and photographs to tie them to their history, like Benjamin.

"And what old country is that?" she asked, curious to know the story that had led to him.

Setting her up with onions and a cutting board before he replied, Benjamin began grating potatoes and said, "Ukraine and Eastern Russia. I'm Ashkenazi on all sides, biological and adopted, though my mom, the woman who raised me, I mean, was born in China."

"China?" Miri asked, trying to make sense of it all.

"My adoptive family fled Eastern Europe early, before World War II, going east and eventually making their way to the US through China and San Francisco, as opposed to Ellis Island. Because of that, my mom was born in the Jewish quarter of old Shanghai."

"Fascinating," Miri uttered, placing a wet paper towel on her cutting board to save her eyes from the onion. "And what about your biological family? How do you know about them?"

"Mostly through the adoption agency paperwork and genetic testing," he said. "Unfortunately, on that front I didn't have much to work with. It looks like both of my biological parents' families came the European route, and both came from families hard hit by the Holocaust. It's incredible what havoc an attempted genocide followed by a generation of low fertility can do to a family line."

"I guess it's lucky you even know what you do, then," Miri mused, and he nodded.

"I owe a lot of it to the adoption agency that handled my case," he said. "They focus on making sure Jewish children end up with Jewish families and are meticulous about record keeping along the way. We've lost so much already—they work hard to preserve what's left."

"It clearly made a difference in your life. I'm glad you

had people like that looking out for you," she said, and she meant it. The image of a child Benjamin alone in the world filled her heart with sorrow. Instead of falling through the cracks, though, he had had a second chance at a doting family and the support and understanding he'd needed.

For an orphaned child, that was as precious as it was rare.

"Me, too," he agreed. "That's why, years later, when I had reached the point at which I could give back, I chose the foundation. To this day they fund the agency that handled my adoption, and to this day, I fund them."

Despite the fact that the reminder of the foundation cast an unwelcome shadow in her mind, Miri smiled. "Fund it? You run it."

Catching her eye, his filling with the glint she was coming to recognize, he said, "I like to be in control."

Miri shivered, hearing the promise in his words.

She knew from personal experience what it was like to be under his control, and she couldn't say she didn't like it.

Clearing her throat, she refocused on the onions in front of her. "Well, I can see why the foundation is so important to you now," she said, and again, the statement carried a twinge of melancholy.

The foundation was important to both of them, something far more than just an employer and a position of prestige, and because of that, there was an inevitable expiration to their interlude.

But banishing the dread, if she had to accept that the most sensual and alive experience she'd ever had was doomed to end, she would damn well make sure she enjoyed everything it had to offer along the way.

She wouldn't waste their time being anticipatorily sad.

No, the only crying she would be doing would be because of these damn onions.

Smiling through the welling in her eyes—entirely the

onions, she assured herself—she changed the subject with the words, "It's a good thing latkes are delicious, because they're sure a pain in the butt to make."

Two hot and fragrant hours later, they sat at the dining table together again, but this time the meal before them was the result of their own blood, sweat and tears.

Taking it in excitedly, Miri exclaimed, "While I'm sure your chef would have presented it better, all of it looks and smells delicious! I can't wait to eat it."

Benjamin laughed, rumpled for the first time she had ever seen, in the way that only big cooking projects can create. "That's just starvation and hard work talking," he said, grinning at her and their feast.

For the third night in a row, they ate delicious food and drank too much high-quality wine and ended up together on the sofa in front of the fire.

"I could never speak a word against your phenomenal chef," Miri said, a giggle in her voice, "but I have to agree. Your mom's tastes better."

Benjamin tipped his glass to her. "I knew you were a smart woman from the moment I first heard you speak."

Miri's breath caught in her throat.

His mind, his looks, the things he said—he was so arresting. For a moment she could only stare.

In the firelight, his eyes and cheeks glowed with a relaxed ease and warmth that she would have thought impossible the moment she first laid eyes on him.

He was so different, in private like this, from the man who had greeted her on his private tarmac.

That man had been Mr. Benjamin Silver, tech billionaire and board chair of the Los Angeles Jewish Community Foundation—cold and exacting and on a schedule.

Here, though, he was simply Benjamin, no less commanding, but also sensual and easy.

Like lava versus ice.

Hot, he was even more compelling and irresistible than he was chilly.

It felt like so long ago now that she'd even wanted to resist him. It was foolish to resist him—not because it was hard, but because it was foolish to resist the wonderful and precious gift of feeling close to someone, of inexplicably knowing it was safe to place trust in them, even without having known them long.

It was that very balance of hot and cold that made him worth both opening up to and investing time in. Though he led with cold, the heat within him ensured he would never be devoid of life.

And yet that was the part of himself he kept hidden in the woods.

Tearing her gaze away from him, she looked into the fire and tried to get a hold of herself. The longer they remained in their magical storm, the more theatrical her thoughts became, apparently.

"It's a shame you don't have any family to share the recipes with," she said, trying to find some practical footing again. "They're so delicious and we might be the last people to know it."

At her side, she felt rather than saw him stiffen and turned to him in concern.

Some of the warm openness of his expression had seeped away, leaving something hopeless and grave in its wake.

"If you'd like, I could make you a copy," he offered, not looking at her but staring into the dark storm outside.

She wanted him to smile again.

"Honestly, I'd love that, but family recipes are meant to be enjoyed by descendants, connected people passing flavor and technique and pride down through the ages and all of that. That's what makes them *family* recipes and not just great ones." She'd kept her voice and goading light, to let him know she teased, but if anything, his expression only hardened.

"These are just destined to be great ones, then, because there is no family to carry them on."

"You count as family," she said, wondering if perhaps being adopted had made him feel the imposter, but his next words, his tone sharper than she had yet to hear from him, suggested otherwise.

"Of course I count as family," he snapped, harshness in how fast the words lashed out. "For a moment, I was their new hope for it even. My mom talked about it, how she looked forward to keeping the traditions alive with my kids, how it would keep both her and my dad's families going, blood or no blood." He let out an abrasive laugh. "But that didn't happen. Instead, they died and with them everything else."

"Well, not *everything* else," she said softly. "Not you. And we kept some alive tonight. As long as you're here, it's up to you what lives and dies."

Benjamin scoffed again, his expression dark. "Well, that's a sad state of affairs for them, then, because I'm not going to pass them on."

"Why not?" she asked, gentle, soft, like a deer padding quietly through his deep dark forest.

Turning back to her, anger and hurt in his gaze, lines of his face hard, he gestured around them. "What kind of family could I provide to anyone?" he asked, bitterly. "Resources are not the same thing as a safety net. Four loving parents could not keep me from ending up alone, and there is only one of me. What would happen to any family of mine, should I meet an untimely demise like my parents? It would be irresponsible."

Feeling as if she were stepping through an unexpected minefield, Miri said, "Perhaps that's a burden that wouldn't just fall on your shoulders. Your partner, for example, could provide that safety net."

"Partner?" He sneered at the word. "If the point is to pass on tradition, what is the likelihood that I'll find the *right* partner in my available romantic pool? I'm a billionaire. I don't move in regular circles and most people have something to gain from their association with me. So should I hand my grandmother's recipe to a model that I met at a movie premiere? I can't undo the effects of generations of oppression and trauma by having kids and it's ridiculous to think I could. My mom could have, but not me. It's a losing battle and the possible consequences aren't worth the risk. Fortunately for the world, however, I know my strengths and I've figured out better ways to make an impact than keeping one family's traditions alive."

For a moment, Miri could not think of a thing to say. So much of what he'd spoken sounded more like the logic of pain than the logic of reason, and yet she could hear his conviction—could hear nights and years of coming to such conclusions with no one around to push back.

A part of her thought to argue, but the rest of her suspected that whatever points she made wouldn't matter. Family, the idea of it, the loss of it, was too sore a wound for him.

And one she didn't have the right to prod.

They might be playing at being lovers, but they both knew the game would last only as long as the storm did.

Who was she to suggest that the real reason he didn't want a family was because he had never been able to get over losing the one he'd loved?

Who was she to suggest that he was afraid?

He was Benjamin Silver and she the events director for the JCF.

Finally, she said, "I've never thought of it that way. Not about traditions as part of making the world a better place nor about children as a tool to combat intergenerational trauma. I just love that it feels like you're part of something bigger and more meaningful when you celebrate together and through time, and the idea of introducing new life to how great it can all be makes me happy. You're right about changing the world, though. You've transformed the entire world, Benjamin. In a way you're already going to live forever, but sometimes it seems like you're afraid to be alive."

He stared at her quietly, his eyes burning with intense blue fire, his face as hard as it'd been before she'd opened her mouth, and yet inside, she got the sense that he was on the edge of shattering.

After what felt like an eternity, he blinked, then closed his eyes, bringing a hand up to pinch the space between his eyebrows. Then he let out a long exhale.

Then he looked back at her, and his eyes were wide open again and because of that, she could see that deep inside him was an agonizing mixture of grief and pain.

He sounded older, his voice faded in places, when he said, "I'm afraid to lose everything I love again."

His words reached through the space between them and into her—as if they were true for her as well.

Maybe they were?

Hadn't she kept men at arm's length since being hurt as a young woman? Didn't she ache for the familial ease she'd had before she had discovered who she was?

She realized now that she had kept herself from a great deal of enjoyment and connection because of that very fear.

He had shown her that, even if he struggled to access it himself.

And there was nothing she could do to reassure him.

Her words, triggering though they clearly could be, could not convince him that he was wrong in assuming the worst for all outcomes.

And even if she wanted to, she could not be the one to

show him that there were plenty of women in the world who were strong and true enough to help him carry traditions forward. The constraints built into their relationship ensured that she could not, guaranteed that everything between them would disappear with the storm—like Cinderella's magic dissolving at midnight.

She couldn't tease him, as much as the idea brought a sour taste to her mouth, that some of those women might even be models he met at a premiere.

How she wished she could, though—not tease him or convince him to believe in possibilities, but to be the one to prove them to him.

But that wasn't a role for her because she already had an assigned place in his life.

She was the events director of the foundation he was involved with. As much as she was coming to hate it, the truth was that everything between them was predicated on that being the primary and most important role in her life.

A few days ago, she couldn't have fathomed wanting it to be any other way.

What a difference a few days could make.

The difference between that and wishing there could have been room in her life to play a different role for him, a more important and permanent one.

She'd stumbled into facing her own fears with him over the past few days, but it had required a blizzard, unbelievable circumstances, and a lot of high-dollar wine.

She couldn't give him those things—he already had them.

She could only give him what she had right now—herself.

She could give him something to remember.

Gently she placed her palms on his shoulders and pressed him back against the couch.

Eyes still locked on hers, he allowed her to push him back until he met the plush arm.

Miri leaned forward to press a soft kiss to his lips and his eyes closed, head angling to give her access.

She touched him softly, featherlight and sweet, knowing he needed more of that in his life, but she remained in control, pressing kisses to his lips and temples, luring and teasing him into opening up and following him.

And he did.

He had admitted his deep truth to her and now he let her tend to it, let her comfort and lull him though he so feared letting his guard down.

She kissed down his neck, pressing her lips even against the soft, thin fabric of his sweater as she traveled south.

Breath escaped him when she came to his belt.

Lifting the hem of his clothing, she exposed the skin of his lower abdomen and kissed there, too, a jolt of electricity jumping between them as she did.

Inhaling him, she removed his belt and exposed even more of him to the firelight.

Then she took him in her mouth and showed him that—at least while he was with her in this storm—it was okay to be afraid.

CHAPTER ELEVEN

THAT IT WAS now the sixth day of Hanukkah and still the storm continued was beginning to feel like some kind of divine phenomenon.

"Have you ever been through so long a storm before?" Miri asked Benjamin where they once again watched the storm from the breakfast table. "Six days seems awfully long for a whiteout," she marveled.

But then again, maybe it wasn't? She didn't really know much about snow.

"It is longer than usual," Benjamin said absently, before turning to her, the grin that she found impossible to resist planted on his face. "Are you so eager for it to pass?"

She wasn't, which made the grin and the question feel even more like darts as they landed.

With each passing day, Miri wanted the storm to end less and less, and she knew that was unrealistic.

Since the moment she had taken charge in the sitting area, something had changed in Benjamin, and that change in itself was making it harder and harder for Miri to keep things in perspective.

Since that night, he'd filled their time with the kind of holiday joy and pleasure that was the stuff of movies, sharing every family tradition he could remember along the way and taking her body to heights and places she'd never thought it possible to go.

They'd baked, watched Hanukkah movies in his personal theater, they'd cooked meals that took multiple phases and hours to complete without having to wash a dish along the way, and they'd gorged on fare prepared at request by his personal chef.

They'd made love in the spa—where he'd discovered all those robes so long ago—and in the library and in the hot tub, and the hallway, *twice*.

Each passing day with him was slightly better than the last, and with each one the inevitable end of the storm crept closer.

Miri wasn't sure her heart or head could take the torment of that push and pull for much longer.

Maybe she *did* want it to end now, just to lessen the hurt inevitable when it did.

A storm like this couldn't hold out for the duration of Hanukkah, could it?

Eight days of whiteout was unbelievable—despite the fact that they were well on their way through six.

The end had to be near, could come at any moment really, and Miri wasn't ready.

But what else was there for it?

Her job was the key to her independence and stability. It was the achievement she'd worked years to be ready for and as much as she had come to appreciate Benjamin, she would not give it up for him.

She could not.

It might have been different if there was something else on the table—something real and lasting and tangible, like commitments and family—but there wasn't. She knew now, better than ever, how he felt about those ideas.

And nothing he had said or done had suggested there might be something different about what was going on between them.

No. In fact, if anything, it was explicitly otherwise.

They had agreed on something temporary and secret—and neither of those was a strong enough reason to leave a job she loved and needed.

When the storm ended, she had to return to the real world, where she was just another woman working hard to survive and he was Benjamin Silver.

Her Benjamin had made her into a goddess, placing the world at her fingertips, but that fairy tale couldn't last forever. For all that he was open and revealed, *her* Benjamin wasn't the real one.

The magic that let them playact would eventually end, at which point she would have to somehow figure out how to pretend like it was okay that everything was back to normal.

Normal would never be okay again, not after Benjamin.

Normal didn't even *exist* after Benjamin.

Normal for Miri was virginal and entirely focused on her job.

After six days with Benjamin, she wasn't sure she would ever be able to fully focus on anything else ever again.

The man had infiltrated her consciousness in a way that meant he could never be far from her mind again, and she was growing more and more certain that the end of the storm would bring with it not relief at the chance to finally go home, but unbearable heartache—of a kind she had never known before.

CHAPTER TWELVE

BENJAMIN LAY BESIDE MIRI, listening to her deep, even breathing.

His room was dark still, no sun yet to backlight the snow outside, the sheets entangled around them.

Though he could not see it, he knew that outside the storm continued. By this point he had come to recognize the sound of it, like constantly listening to a muffled ocean inside a shell.

It did not matter that the storm continued, though.

Whether it did or did not was irrelevant to everything that came after. He'd finally realized that, somewhere between her having her way with him on the couch all of those nights ago and waking now, fully alert in the darkness beside her.

He could not let her go.

It was utterly ludicrous and ridiculous that they both acted like it was even possible—or necessary.

They were modern adults, neither of them indentured to the foundation or under any obligation to let it dictate their personal lives.

In this day and age, it was incredibly rare to meet someone who it was possible to work alongside, laugh with and reveal deep fears to, and in Miri, he had found all three. He had risked being vulnerable with her, made himself vulnerable to her derision and mockery, and instead she had chased away the shadows in his heart with her heat—as powerful as the light of any fire.

It wasn't the kind of thing any sane man would walk away from—one didn't give another the power to break them and then just go their separate ways—especially not because of a set of rules that had never been intended to apply to him.

What he had discovered with Miri—honesty, openness, passion and safety—was far bigger and more valuable than even the foundation.

Only a fool would pretend otherwise, and he was no fool.

He was one of the most powerful men in the world.

At his side, Miri stirred.

"Quiet down, over there," she murmured, her voice as sleepy and soft as her body in the shadowed room. "You're thinking so loud, it's waking me up."

"I don't want to end things when the storm ends," he said. He had a reputation for being blunt.

Beside him, she sat up.

"What are you talking about?" she asked, though he knew she knew.

Just like himself, he'd caught her looking out the window, eyebrows drawn together in a frown, multiple times over the past few days and he knew it was because she was afraid to see signs of its end.

He couldn't be the only one feeling that.

"There's no reason we can't continue to see each other after the storm passes," he said.

She shook her head, and he felt the reverberation of it through the bed they shared.

"No, we can't. The foundation…my job. We can't. I could get fired," she said, sounding tired now whereas she'd sounded sleepy but alert only moments before.

"No one needs to know," he insisted.

She scoffed. "Just like with the last events director, huh? No. No. We both know it's a no. Someone would find out. They always do, and you're famous. I told you, Benjamin. I can't afford to lose my job. I don't want the storm to end any more than you do, but you should know better than to ask me that."

He resented the censure in her voice, even if it was deserved.

She admitted to feeling the same; she couldn't in the same breath speak to him like a child.

"What I'm asking is not out of line, Miri. We're two adults with something good going between them. I'm asking you to give that a chance because I like you."

"But do you respect me, Benjamin? Because right now it doesn't seem like you do. I told you, I *need* this job."

"And if you lose it, I have more than enough money to take care of you until you got a new one. You're a brilliant woman, Miri. You don't need the foundation."

"You'll take care of me?" she demanded, voice rising. "I'm just supposed to put my trust in Benjamin Silver to take care of me if I lose my job? Why would I do that? You're not my dad. You're not my husband. When all is said and done, you're a man I barely know. And like I told you, I *do* need the foundation. I need the foundation more than a man like you is probably capable of understanding, and what's more, I *want* it."

"I *want* you," he snapped, and could swear he heard her mouth shut. "And you want me," he continued. "It's outrageous for us to ignore that because of the foundation."

"And what about because it's what we agreed to do? Or do you want me more than you care about me?"

How could she ask that? he wondered.

Had he not just spent days revealing in small and large ways just how much he cared for her?

He had shared his family traditions with her, for God's sake.

"I want you *because* I care about you, Miri," he insisted. "More than any woman before you."

"Or do you just want me more than any other woman because you can't have me and it's driving you crazy? We had a deal, Benjamin. Only until the storm passes. You wouldn't be saying any of this if it didn't have an expiration date."

He heard desperation in her voice as she spoke but could not decipher its root.

Was she desperate he believe her, or was she desperate to believe herself?

Because there was a question, he could not backtrack.

If she simply did not share the same intensity of desire for him, that would be one thing, but he knew she did.

He saw it in her eyes whenever he looked at her.

He felt it when he was inside her.

But like he had been, she was afraid.

"That's a lie and I think we both know it, Miri. You're afraid."

"I'm not afraid," she rasped. "I'm practical. No matter how many times we make love, it doesn't change the fact that I'm a single woman living in an expensive city. It's misogynistic of you to ask me to put my stability at risk just because you don't want to stop fooling around, but I wouldn't expect you to realize that."

"Misogynistic? Come on, Miri. Don't be ridiculous. We both know that misogyny is the furthest thing from my mind when we touch, just like your refusal isn't about misogyny right now. You're just afraid to get hurt. You got hurt once a long time ago and just like me, now you're too afraid of getting hurt again to tell the truth. You're afraid to put your heart on the line."

She gasped in the dark and for all that he regretted them now, he knew his words had hit their mark. She had wielded truth gently when she'd pointed it out to him.

He'd used it like a baseball bat.

When she finally spoke, her voice was rough. "The only thing I know is on your mind when you touch me is sex, Benjamin. Nothing special or romantic or lasting, just sex. You don't want *me*, Benjamin, you just want to keep having sex with me, and only then until you inevitably get tired of it, like you've gotten tired of every other woman you've had sex with. You said it yourself, you don't want kids, you don't want a family, you don't believe there's a woman out there you can share your burdens with, and you don't want people making demands on your time or distracting you from your work. That means you don't really want *me* because *I* am the kind of person who wants all of those things. You only want me because I'm here. We'd both be fools to pretend like it's anything else. That's why even now you're not asking for anything real or a legitimate relationship. You just want me to continue being your secret lover, your mistress, and you know what, I'm finding that that's something I'm just not interested in." She punctuated the last by sliding out the bed.

Not expecting the movement, he reached for her too late. "Miri, where are you going?"

"Back to my room. I'm suddenly not feeling as comfortable as I was," she said, her words stiff and tight.

Panicking, he swung his legs out of the bed himself, standing on the opposite side of the bed from her, as naked as the day he was born. "I'll walk you," he said lamely.

He didn't need to see her to know she shook her head. The negation was clear in her voice. "I'll find it on my own, thanks. I know the way by now."

"Miri…" he started, but didn't know what else to say.

"What, Benjamin? Am I wrong? Did I get the wrong impression here? Are you asking me to be the kind of woman you can share your traditions and start a family with? Do you want me enough to commit to more than sleeping together? Are you willing to risk loving me?"

All of the peace and heat and certainty he'd felt lying beside her, listening to her breath—along with his own breath—fled him.

Abruptly clammy and chilled, the sinking in him now an echo of what he'd felt upon learning of his family's death, he reached an arm toward her voice in the darkness but could do no more.

Because he was not.

He could not.

The idea alone shot him back to the day in the hospital, waking up alone in a way he had never imagined he would be again.

He wanted Miri, was crystal clear on that fact, and more than he had ever desired a woman before in his life, but he could not risk that. Not again.

He wouldn't survive a third time.

As much as her words cut through him now, he could not fathom what it would be like to lose her after falling in love with her.

He said nothing.

When his pause had lasted long enough to become its own answer, she said, "Storm or no storm, I don't think we should do this anymore. I don't think it's—" Her breath hitched and the sound of it tore through him. "I don't think it's good for either one of us," she finished in a rush. "I'd like to leave as soon as possible."

He listened as she padded to the door then, cracking it open and slipping out without another word.

And because it was the way his life worked, when the sun rose on the eighth day of Hanukkah, it brought with it blue sky.

CHAPTER THIRTEEN

STANDING AT THE WINDOW, the curtains open, Miri pressed
the intercom buzzer in her room as soon as she saw the
first sliver of blue sky.

Benjamin wasn't the only one who could call his assistant.

Miri just hoped it worked out like she wanted it to.

It was a huge relief to hear the woman's voice crackle
through the wall speaker—even if the crackle had more to
do with the woman speaking than the intercom her words
traveled through. "What can I do for you, Ms. Howard?"
she asked.

Rubbing her palms against her thighs, clad again in the
skirt she'd worn to meet Benjamin for the first time, she
said, "I noticed the sky had cleared and was wondering if
it would be possible to return to LA today?"

"I'll have to check with the pilot," she said, disappear-
ing for a long few minutes while Miri continued to watch
the sunrise.

She had not returned to bed upon leaving Benjamin's
room.

There was no point; she couldn't sleep.

Not with their conversation fresh in her mind.

She supposed she should have been flattered that he
wanted her to be his mistress.

He was a world-famous sexy billionaire who had changed the world and who was she?

She was a woman who was not going to act like a fool because a man was good in bed.

Maybe he wasn't even good in bed. She had no comparison—because he had been the first man, unlike every other man she'd ever met, to make her feel safe enough to let her guard down.

Her heart squeezed in her chest with a steady, painfully rhythmic beat.

He was asking her to put her fate in his hands, for no other reason than he *wanted* her.

The universals of womanhood transcended even those of faith, and she knew how much store could be set in what a man wanted in any given moment.

Or what anyone wanted of her in any given moment.

Whether it was her former fiancé's want of her as a mother of his children, her family's want of her to celebrate their way, or Benjamin's want of her to be his mistress.

Wasn't it all the same thing?

In none of those cases had she been wanted as a partner and cocreator. In their own ways, each of them had made that clear.

But she didn't have to wait around at the whim of anyone's capricious wants. She owed herself as full a life as she'd challenged Benjamin to live. She deserved a family, and shared traditions, and commitment.

And she would go out and get them.

Even if it wasn't with Benjamin.

The knot in her chest threatened to stop her heart from beating altogether.

Excruciating as it was, she didn't know if she didn't just want to let it.

She let out a strained gasp at the sound of Benjamin's assistant coming back to the intercom. "Pilot says there's not enough runway to fly you home yet, but he could probably get you to the airport in the chopper."

A helicopter.

Of course, it would have to be a helicopter, and then a commercial flight after that, at best.

Commercial flight at best? Where did such a thought come from?

Now she was incredulous with herself.

Just a week with Benjamin and she was already disdaining regular air travel?

She could handle a short ride in a helicopter. The vast majority of helicopter flights made their itineraries, and she was obviously losing her grip out here with him.

And the time it took to get through the airport and home would give her time to adjust to her reentrance into the real world, where she had no idea what it was like to make love to Benjamin Silver and women like her moved slowly and deliberately through quiet lives.

"I'll take it. Thank you," she said, her cadence more like a sob than a sentence.

That was fine, too. There was no law against crying on planes.

"Sounds good, miss. He'll get it fired up. Probably be about thirty minutes till you're in the air."

Thirty minutes.

She could handle that.

It was short enough that she could tell herself there wasn't time to say goodbye.

It was barely enough time to pull herself together enough to make the trip.

Twenty minutes later, Benjamin's assistant drove a bundled-up Miri to the helipad in a snowmobile.

Even temporarily clad in outerwear from his incredible wardrobe, with hat and gloves and all, it was too loud and cold for either woman to have brought up Benjamin.

Did he even know she was leaving?

Miri assumed he did. His assistant reported to him, after all.

If he did know, he didn't come for her.

Outside, what had been a thin layer of snow when she'd arrived was now a transformed landscape.

Forests had disappeared, replaced by mounds and hilltops of sparkling powder dotted with only the tallest of frosted trees.

Benjamin's gargantuan mountain cabin needed only enormous gumdrops to have transformed into a massive gingerbread house, its immediate vicinity and walls kept clear of snow by what looked like some kind of ground-based heating, while its thick-beamed roof lay covered with even thicker sheets of bright snow.

It was so cold outside that it was almost hard to breathe, but the deadliness of the chill did nothing to diminish the beauty of the wintery landscape.

Miri was amazed.

She had never imagined that snow could be so beautiful, the storm that had created a world of its own for Benjamin and her leaving behind still yet another new wonder to explore.

It invited one to do classic winter things like sled and build snowmen and drink warm beverages but only when it was time to come in from playing—things Miri hadn't spent much time thinking about before, but now would forever regret having missed the chance to try.

Benjamin had ruined everything.

He'd ruined her disdain for the cold and winter and snow, just like he had ruined good wine and doughnuts and probably Hanukkah, too.

Thank God she'd gotten what she needed from him

for the gala, otherwise he probably would have ruined that, too.

That she would have to face him again at it certainly constituted a level of ruin.

Though she wore a thick jacket meant for the snow, she was shivering by the time they reached the helipad.

"Think you're going to want to keep that on for the ride. It's not bound to be the warmest today," Benjamin's assistant told her when she tried to return the jacket, and Miri sighed.

She didn't want to take anything from him, but she wasn't willing to freeze to death to make a point.

He hadn't known he'd owned it in the first place, so he probably wouldn't have even noticed it being gone.

Tears turned into ice droplets around her eyes as she geared up for the helicopter ride and that, too, was a first.

Ten minutes later, they were taking off.

Miri was glad it was too loud to hold a conversation, even through the headset.

She didn't feel like making small talk.

She felt like burying herself in a dark room and staying there for days. Unfortunately, because of the storm, she'd already done that and now she had to get back to work.

She'd have to hit the ground running for all the time she'd lost, though the work she'd done with Benjamin ensured she could get it done.

Benjamin…

She didn't want to think about him, but of course she had no choice.

Even now, she looked for him, wondering which of the massive windows in his home he stood behind and watched her leave from—if any.

Did he care? Was he angry? Or had he simply gotten back to work?

Watching his home grow smaller, she realized that each option hurt.

The farther she got away from him, the more everything hurt, in fact.

Why hadn't he come to her? Why hadn't he said goodbye? Why hadn't he stopped her?

He tried to stop you, a voice inside reminded her. *By making you his mistress.*

Was it possible to think about him and not end up wounded? she wondered, watching a tiny figure dash from the front of his home.

Moving fast, it made a beeline for the helipad, which continued to grow smaller.

Miri watched, momentarily confused by what she saw.

A figure waving frantically, flares in their hands.

What was going on? Was it Benjamin?

"Stop the chopper!" she yelled into the headset, pointing toward the ground below.

"What?" the pilot hollered, turning to look where she pointed.

Then he nodded, and her stomach did a somersault as he began to turn the helicopter and descend once more.

CHAPTER FOURTEEN

BENJAMIN WATCHED THE helicopter descend with ice in his veins.

He had felt this before, chilled to the bone before he'd passed out in the Pacific and woken utterly alone in a hospital bed—cold, afraid and so painfully alive.

He hadn't thought she would stop.

It was too good to be true.

No matter how much money he had made, he knew not to expect too good to be true.

People didn't come back once you'd lost them.

He hadn't thought she would simply leave, either, nor had he any idea of how much it would hurt to watch her go.

It had been enough to rob him of words and breath, so that he could only respond with agonized grunts and desperate motion, fighting the sensation of drowning even as he ran after her.

She took off into the air while he continued to sink further down below, watching her rise resigned to the fact that he had finally joined his parents at the bottom of the sea.

He'd been so afraid of being broken by losing love again that he'd chased his away.

It turned out it didn't matter what form the loss took, though, it hurt both ways.

Thankfully, this time, there could be an opportunity to

do it all better. His decision to live again had given him a second chance.

The Miri that disembarked the helicopter was not the one who had first arrived.

That woman, clad in a thin cardigan and bearing a bright blue box of doughnuts, had been a stranger.

The woman he saw now, bundled appropriately for the weather with her arms crossed in front of her chest, was the woman he loved.

In just eight days, she had sneaked past decades of his defenses and gracefully navigated the minefield of his fears to become someone who took his heart when she left.

Somewhere in the mad dash after her, he'd realized that it was too late to protect himself from her.

He loved her, and because of that, she didn't have to die to kill him.

All she had to do was walk away.

But as long as they were both still living, there was a chance for life.

He wouldn't let fear keep him from the love that was possible with her, not when there were so many with whom he didn't have a choice.

He owed it to the dead to not squander his opportunities with the living.

"Miri," he breathed her name, and it rang clear through the cold, crisp air.

"What are you thinking, Benjamin? You don't even have a sweater on!" she exclaimed. "You're going to freeze to death. This is Colorado."

And it was true.

He hadn't had time to appropriately clothe himself when he'd heard she was already lifting off.

Hypothermia was nothing compared to losing her.

"I don't want you to leave, Miri."

Releasing her arms from their protective position at

her chest, she lifted her hands in the air. "I know. You already said that. You want me to put my job at risk to be your mistress. Well, you know what, you don't always get what you want, Benjamin. Even you."

He didn't flinch at her words; he couldn't. He was too glad she was still here. Instead, he just shook his head, smiling like a fool in the snow. "No. I don't want that either. I want you to marry me, Miri. You were right about what I said earlier. I don't have a right to ask you to trust me. I'm not your husband. But I want to be."

She stilled, like a deer in the sights of a predator. "What?" she asked.

"I want you to be my wife, Miri, and the mother of my children. I want to build a family with you and keep my family traditions alive. I couldn't trust my grandmother's recipes to just anyone, but I can trust them to you. I've made a career out of understanding complex patterns that underlie function and trusting my instincts. I don't need more time to see your beauty or value, just like I can't pretend that you're not everything that I want just because the storm has passed. Losing you now or losing you at the end of a long life together feels the same, and in one case I end up a lonely old fool with more money than I can spend, too scared to have really lived."

"But…" she said, eyes wide and mildly stunned. "The foundation…my job…"

"You can keep your job, Miri. I'll step down from my role with the board citing my need for more time for private business projects, effective immediately. The foundation won't dare reprimand you when they see the endowment I'm going to leave them, nor after the spectacular gala you're going to throw for them. I don't need you to give up who you've worked to be, Miri, nor was this ever about you putting your job at risk or being my mistress. That was your label, not mine. I just didn't want to lose you, Miri. Death isn't the only way love can leave you devastated."

Her amber eyes glowing, she cleared her throat before she said, her voice still thick when it came out, "You're going to have to be a little more direct if you want to start throwing that word around."

She was trembling, he could see it, even through the warm jacket she wore, but would hold her line even through her emotion.

There was that spine he loved so much.

"I love you, Miri. Marry me."

It was so cold outside, he could see his breath, could literally witness the command hang in the air.

And then she nodded. And then she said, "Yes. Yes! Absolutely yes!" and ran to him, leaping into his arms.

He held her there, kissing her, standing barefoot in the thick snow beneath a bright blue sky, the lonely chill he'd always relied on his fires to warm gone.

Until she pulled back, horror in her face, and said, "No shoes and a T-shirt? And you gave me a hard time for wearing a cardigan," as she unwound herself from her coat to wrap a side of it around him, too.

Smiling, he said, "I dress for the occasion, which, in this case, was running as if my very life depended on it. Because it did," and kissed her again.

EPILOGUE

"I HAD A feeling I should have ordered an extra box this year," Miri said, wistfully patting the rounded top of her abdomen with one hand as she polished off the last of the *sufganiyot* from the teal box with the other.

Her husband of almost a year now wisely said nothing.

"There was just no way I could have known, though," she sighed. "Everything is so hit-or-miss right now, and I haven't had them for almost a year, so two boxes felt like too much a risk."

Beyond that, she really didn't need to be eating another box of doughnuts almost entirely to herself, even if she was eight months pregnant.

After spending the first night of Hanukkah with her friends in the city, she and Benjamin had returned to Aspen for the holiday, stopping for doughnuts on the way to their airport.

Normally, doctors advised against a woman in her late stage of pregnancy flying, but Benjamin had allayed their fears by insisting that a doctor accompany them on the trip, and only then after a pre-takeoff checkup and approval. He was concerned of what might happen, on the off chance they got snowed in.

Miri didn't mind. She understood and appreciated it, even. Benjamin would always be serious about keeping his family safe. There was no other way he could be.

And it had certainly been known to happen.

If it did, they would be prepared. He always was.

He was going to be an amazing father.

Miri had no doubts.

He was kind and thoughtful, strong and determined, attentive and adoring.

Everything she could hope for her child and more.

And he had been entirely correct about the foundation's reaction—to both his endowment and her gala.

The endowment had made jaws drop. Her gala had made eyes sparkle.

Not only had she secured her position with the foundation, but she had also earned a reputation as one of the best and brightest on staff—in both mind *and* body, because of the flawless dress she'd worn.

Her Secret Garden gala held the new record for most funds raised, as well as made the front page of the society section in the *Los Angeles Times*.

Offering just the right mix of exclusivity, unexpectedness and photo opportunities, both the press and attendees had had a field day with it. It even briefly trended in top hashtags in Los Angeles.

And to make matters even better, she'd looked fantastic in every photo, the two-toned silver and gold long-sleeved body-contouring dress she'd worn popping and glittering against the all-black attire of the man who refused to leave her side throughout the entire night.

The event was the most talked about thing around foundation offices for months afterward, with many of the large donors going out of their way to let Miri know how much they looked forward to what she would be putting together for them the following year.

Even after the buzz died down a bit, she remained one of the most popular staff members—her dreams of happy hours and work friendships blossoming beyond her imaginings.

And all of the recognition had even come with a little salary bump, too—not that money was something she had to worry about anymore.

Not since she had become the wife of one of the richest men in the world.

They were married a month after the gala and Miri found out she was pregnant the following March. Since then, her husband had hardly left her side, taking out an office building across the street from the foundation so he could work nearby.

Her work necessitated they spend most of their time in LA, but for Hanukkah only Aspen felt right. It was their first tradition, a celebration of their own special miracle that had occurred.

She couldn't wait for their baby to be born, so they could join in the celebration, too.

Of course, by the way they were flipping around in her womb in reaction to the doughnuts, she couldn't exactly say they weren't participating already.

Sighing, she decided that she really should have bought more.

Wrapping his arms around her from behind, teal flashed in the corner of her eyes as Benjamin said into her hair, "I knew," and placed a second box of doughnuts on the counter.

Spinning around in his arms, she smiled up into his laughing blue eyes, and he caught her lips with his.

Heat filled her, as it always did when they kissed. He tasted like sugar and stability and a special world for the two—soon to be three—of them, with no end in sight.

* * * * *

THE PRINCE'S PREGNANT SECRETARY

EMMY GRAYSON

MILLS & BOON

For my husband, always.

For Mom, Dad and Mama Pam,
for always believing in me.

For Nate and Kels, for listening to me panic
and supporting me during Deadline Week.

For Katelyn, Teddy and Laura, friends and
fellow writers, who helped bring Clara to life.

CHAPTER ONE

THE FURY BURNING through Prince Alaric Van Ambrose's veins surprised him with its intensity. He hadn't thought it possible to experience this level of anger unless it involved his useless sire.

But it wasn't his father staring up at him from the picture pulled up on Clara's tablet. No, it was his ex-fiancée, Celestine Osborne, in the arms of not one but two men on the dance floor of some ritzy New York club. One man had his hands on her waist, his hips pressed provocatively against her barely covered rear. The other man's hands rested just beneath the curves of her breasts, which nearly popped out of her plunging halter top.

Most women in that position would have been focusing on at least one of their admirers, perhaps even ducking away from the bright flash of the camera.

Celestine, however, had looked straight at the photographer, her tawny gold eyes defiant, her perfectly shaped chin raised as she smiled smugly. Some might find her apparent confidence sexy. But to him, her bared pearly white teeth reminded him of a piranha.

Slowly, he uncurled his fingers from around his phone and set it on his desk. He'd kept the photo pulled up when he'd called Celestine, a visual reminder to himself that he could no longer overlook her scandalous behavior. Their engagement of nine years had been a business agreement arranged by their fathers, but one he thought they'd both willingly entered into.

Except according to her and the acrimonious conversation that had ended with her screaming at him before terminating their engagement, marrying him had been the last thing she'd ever wanted.

What did it say that he was angrier that he'd wasted so many years waiting on Celestine and having her antics associated with the country he was trying to rebuild than mourning the loss of his future wife?

"I'm sorry, Your Highness."

Clara's cool voice soothed some of the tension tightening his neck. She had been his executive assistant for the past seven years. Dependable, professional and talented with words, she'd made herself indispensable.

But over the last year, whether it was the escalating tension with his father, the increasing audacity of Celestine's behavior or terminating his last affair with a Spanish oil heiress, something had changed. He'd found himself seeking her out more, asking for her opinion on government matters, enjoying her company.

Red flags. She was his employee, and he was engaged.

Was, whispered the devil on his shoulder as he looked up to see her approaching his desk. It didn't help that Clara was a beautiful woman. Usually, she wore pant or skirt suits, form-fitting enough to be professional but loose enough that he could easily dismiss thoughts that started to take on an inappropriate nature.

But tonight…tonight she wore a deep blue gown that reminded him of the North Sea just before the sun rose. The way the material wrapped around her slender body, clinging to her slight curves before cascading down into a swirl of silk around her feet, sent a bolt of forbidden desire through his body. Her pale blond hair, normally wrapped in a tight bun at the base of her neck, had been pulled up into an elegant twist with soft curls framing her elfin face.

She reached over and tapped something on the tablet. Celestine's arrogant expression, simultaneously lewd and immature, disappeared.

"I'm not sorry." He leaned back in his chair and scrubbed a hand over his face. "Actually, I am. I'm sorry that I didn't have this confrontation sooner. Linnaea deserves better from its future queen."

Clara's lips parted for a moment, then compressed together in a firm line. He arched a brow.

"What?"

"It's not my place to say."

He chuckled. Rarely did he let his guard down, but with Clara, it had become easy to do. The woman didn't pull punches. He always knew where he stood with her, and he also knew that she had both his and Linnaea's best interests at heart.

"When has that ever stopped you from saying exactly what's on your mind?"

The corner of her mouth slid up as something akin to a sparkle danced in her eyes.

A sparkle? Really?

"You deserve better, too, Your Highness."

The sentiment tugged at his chest and catapulted him back to that night eleven months ago when she'd said almost the exact same thing. When, if he was being honest with himself, things had started to change between them, at least on his end.

He stood and stalked over to the floor-to-ceiling window behind his desk. The lake glittered silver beneath the light of the frost moon. Snow had covered the ground since late October, dressing Linnaea's spectacular scenery in a veil of white.

There were two things Alaric had loved in his life; his

late mother, Marianne, and his country. It had been because of his love for Linnaea that he'd agreed to the engagement with Celestine in the first place.

A bird soared across the lake, dappled white wings spread against the night sky. An eagle owl, judging by the wingspan. It dipped toward the water before lazily drifting back up toward the stars. He envied the owl's languid pace, no schedule, committees or legislation to keep it chained to a desk.

No errant fiancées, either, constantly threatening what he'd worked so hard for since he was sixteen, old enough to realize that if anyone was going to save Linnaea, it sure as hell wasn't his father, Daxon Van Ambrose. Daxon liked the title of king well enough; he just didn't want to do the hard work that came with it, preferring to spend as if he had endless resources at his fingertips instead of the country's dwindling treasury. The primary reason why Alaric had agreed to an engagement with a woman he'd never seen.

Nine years. Nine years since he'd met Celestine and her real estate tycoon father before he had signed the contract agreeing to give Max Osborne the one thing his billions couldn't buy: a royal title. The contract allowed for up to ten years for the marriage to take place, with Max pumping money into Linnaea's economy through various projects until Celestine officially became a Van Ambrose. After the marriage, a dowry consisting of a couple billion dollars would appear.

He'd sold the role of queen to the highest bidder.

The target of his anger shifted from Celestine to himself. He'd been the one to agree to his father and Max's ridiculous contract. He'd been twenty-six and already as involved as Daxon would allow him to be in Linnaea's operations. Celestine had been all of nineteen, barely out of school and entertaining wide-eyed fantasies of being a princess. The moment he'd met her in the palace throne room, a little-used elegant hall Daxon had picked to impress his audience, he'd known she was too young to fully understand what she was agreeing to.

But he'd signed. He'd signed the contract and sold not only his soul but that of a young woman to two devils who cared more about their own interests than the well-being of a country.

The picture from the club flashed in his mind again. He might have made a mistake nine years ago, but Celestine had made her own choices in that time. Her behavior had grown increasingly erratic, the tabloid features more embarrassing, especially since she'd quit college.

When she'd answered the phone, her groggy voice had quickly sharpened into a razor blade as she'd asked if he was calling to be a "stick-in-the-mud." He'd told her he was done, that either she cease her partying and set a wedding date or he would call her father to renegotiate. She'd responded with four words: "Go ahead. I'm done."

A different kind of tension tightened his back. He kept his eyes trained on the mountain peaks beyond the lake. A familiar, dependable sight. Better to focus on that than the heightened awareness of his secretary.

Executive assistant, he acknowledged internally with a slight quirk of his lips. Clara despised being called "secretary."

"I'm a prince, Clara. Not a hero in a fairy tale. The engagement was never about love or even compatibility. It's always been about money."

He spat the last word out. He'd spent his entire life fighting to distance himself from his father's legacy of womanizing, drinking and spending what little wealth Linnaea had.

Yet here he was, obsessing over money. That one of his first thoughts had been satisfaction that, because Celestine had been the one to break the engagement, Linnaea would still receive a handsome payout from Osborne Construction, said enough about who he had become and what his priorities were. He'd almost dragged a very reluctant bride to the altar for her fortune.

Revulsion rippled through him.

"I've prepared an initial statement for your approval—"

"Send it."

He felt more than heard her huff.

"I need your approval."

"Granted."

A louder sigh.

"That's not how this works, Your Highness."

The quelling glance he delivered over his shoulder didn't stop Clara's determined march across the room. The closer she got, the tauter his muscles grew.

She stopped next to him and handed him the tablet, a document now replacing Celestine's photo. He focused on the black-and-white text. Better that than the tantalizing floral sweetness teasing him.

Prince Alaric Van Ambrose and Miss Celestine Osborne have announced they are no longer engaged. They wish each other the best...

His lips twisted. Celestine's voice, shrill and frazzled, echoed in his ears. Somehow her screaming that she wouldn't be caught dead in a marriage to a stone-cold bastard or stuck living in a frozen backwater country didn't align with "wishing him the best."

"Fine."

The tablet disappeared. Clara, unfortunately, didn't. Out of the corner of his eye, he saw her attention drop down to the tablet as she tapped something out. The glow of the screen lit her delicate profile.

He knew the exact moment Clara had gone from being trusted employee and confidant to something more. Someone he could depend on, someone he looked forward to seeing.

The first few years of their engagement, Alaric had kept his distance from his fiancée. Celestine had seemed so young. Neither of them had been in a rush to get married, not while Max's construction projects finally flooded some much-needed cash and prestige into Linnaea. Clara had told him after the signing of the contract that she intended to live the next few years as she saw fit, including dating. Given that he'd known her for less than an hour, he'd been all too glad to agree.

Idiot.

While he'd been busy building up Linnaea behind the scenes and indulging in the occasional discreet affair, Celestine had started to act out, each year getting worse and worse as they neared the end of the engagement period. The last couple of years, he'd ceased his romantic involvements and tried to get to know his future wife better. He'd despised what he saw: a pampered, spoiled heiress who could have done anything with her life and instead chose to overindulge in the same manner his father did.

But he was not going to go back on his word or risk Linnaea's financial future.

It was why a year ago, the day before the annual Christmas Eve ball at the palace, he'd sought solace in his private gym downstairs when Celestine had shown up to a dinner with Linnaea's top officials already tipsy and wearing a dress better described as a shirt given how little it covered.

He'd made it through that dinner. Barely. A guard had escorted Celestine to her room after dessert, not allowing her the opportunity to join the party in after-dinner drinks and further embarrass herself and him. He'd made his excuses, ignoring the mix of pity and condescension, and sought solace in the small gym in the depths of the palace. He'd been in the middle of beating the hell out of a punching bag, wearing nothing but sweatpants with perspiration pouring down his back, when Clara had walked in. He hadn't let up, for once not caring that he wasn't being seen in a princely light. Who cared about how people saw him when the future queen of Linnaea was making an ass of herself just a few floors above?

She hadn't run away screaming. She hadn't chastised him for leaving the dinner. No, she'd sat down on a weight bench in all of her evening finery, clasped her hands in her lap and asked if he wanted to talk about it.

He hadn't. Hence the punching bag. But for the first time in years, someone had cared. When he'd growled that he'd rather be left alone, she'd given him a smile tinged with sadness before getting up and heading for the door. It had pissed him off. He didn't want her pity, and he'd said so.

The gentle tinkling of her laughter still rippled across his skin.

You are not one to be pitied, Your Highness. You just deserve better.

"Sent."

"Thank you, Clara."

Her eyes moved up, then fastened on the owl as it continued its journey toward the pine forest on the south side of the lake. A smile crossed her face.

"Hard to believe that I live here sometimes."

The awe in her voice made his heart squeeze in his chest. He had yet to find someone else who loved his country as much as he did, but Clara came a very close second.

"Oh?"

"Linnaea's like a fairy tale."

The huskiness in her voice, tinged with a wistfulness he hadn't heard before, heated his blood. He'd done a damn good job keeping whatever emotions she'd stirred up under wraps, told himself it was the stress and lack of female companionship.

But when she talked like that, when he heard the mutual admiration in her tone and saw the happiness that softened her face and revealed her true beauty behind the efficient facade she wore so often, he found himself barely keeping his hands off her.

"Fairy tales usually have happy endings."

"Not the originals." Clara chuckled. "The originals were quite ghastly. Lots of blood and executions."

Alaric arched an eyebrow. Normally their conversations revolved around legislation or current events.

"When my father finds out his contract with Max Osborne is no more, there could very well be an execution in Linnaea's future."

He bit back a smile at Clara's unladylike smile.

"Your sister's marriage will bring money to Linnaea. And the Swiss ambassador just said he's willing to advocate for an alliance." She gently nudged him with her shoulder, a break from protocol that made electricity shoot across his skin. "Because of everything you've done, Your Highness."

He wanted to accept the rosy picture Clara was offering him. Discovering he had a long-lost half sister had been surprising but not a shock given his father's numerous affairs over the years. Really, the bigger shock was that weren't more by-blows running around. Briony had entered into a marital contract with Cassius Adama, a Linnaean who hadn't let his banishment from his home country stop him from accumulating his own fortune or his own royal title. Alaric had been against the arranged engagement from the start. There had been too many parallels between the arrangement his father had made with Max Osborn. He still didn't fully trust the younger man, but based on what he'd observed the last few weeks, Cass appeared to truly care for his sister. And Briony had impressed him with how quickly she'd not only adapted to royal life, but thrown herself into advocating for the downtrodden people of her new country.

There had been plenty of unexpected positive developments in the last few weeks. But that didn't mean there wouldn't be hell to pay, both with King Daxon Van Ambrose and Celestine's father, Max. Yes, Briony and Cass's marriage, coupled with the foreign support, would get Linnaea closer to the financial independence he'd been working so hard for. Still, Celestine's money would have gotten them even closer.

"Have you always been a secret optimist? Or is the situation that bad that you feel the need to give me a pep talk?"

This time her chuckle carried an edge, one that hinted at darker things in Clara Stephenson's past.

"Most definitely not an optimist. I prefer to think of myself as a realist." She gestured toward the window. "But even a realist can be moved by this."

That floral scent, hints of rose and sweetness and just a touch of spice, wrapped around him and wound a spell that lit the match and started a fire burning low in his gut. A fire that demanded he lift the curls lying so gently on her swanlike neck, press his lips to her skin and finally taste her before he went mad.

He needed to put distance between them. Now.

He started to turn away. A delicate pressure on his arm stopped him, rooted his feet to the ground as his body went rock hard.

Don't look. Don't look.

He wasn't thinking straight. Couldn't think straight with finding out he had a long-lost sister, entering into her own royal agreement with her new fiancé, having his own fiancée break up with him and continuing to put up with Daxon's antics. He was wound so tight that anything could set him off.

Could make him do things he shouldn't do.

"It will be okay, Alaric."

It was the use of his name that made him look, the first time he'd heard it on her lips. The sound of it charged the air around them, tension crackling as the rest of the world faded away at the sight of her pale hand resting against his black sleeve.

"Clara…"

His voice came out a growl, raw and on the verge of doing something very unprincely. It should have made her yank her hand away and run for the door.

Instead, her fingers tightened on his sleeve. Her sharp inhale echoed like a gunshot in the room.

Then he looked up, met those arctic-blue eyes with his own gaze, and the world burned.

Did he move first? Did she? Or did they both just crash into each other at the speed of light? One moment they were staring at each other, awareness washing over them in waves and drowning them in lust. The next their bodies were pressed together so tightly he didn't even breathe before his hands slid into her silky hair and held her in place as he slanted his lips across hers.

It wasn't a gentle, courtly kiss. It wasn't romantic. It was hard, possessive, almost punishing, as if to show her the animal he'd always feared he secretly was beneath the controlled exterior he presented to the world.

Like your father.

Then her hands came up and cupped his face, cool and gentle, soothing some of the angry passion smoldering in his chest. It didn't stop him from running his tongue along the seam of her mouth and invading when her lips parted for him. But it did stop him from flinging her away and ordering her to leave before he did something even more stupid.

Something like let his hands move from her hair, now tumbling in a blond mass of curls down her back to her waist, and pull her hips against his. Something like deepening the kiss when she moaned into his mouth and arched her lithe body against him.

The thinnest thread of sanity broke through. It gave him just enough power to pull back, to rest his forehead against hers as his chest heaved.

"Clara, we—"

Her hands rested on his chest, her touch searing him straight through the thin fabric of his dress shirt.

"Alaric."

The raw need in her voice made his grip tighten.

"Don't stop."

Had he thought he was on fire before? Because it was nothing compared to the inferno that blazed forth and scorched all rational thought at her words. He scooped her up in his arms, planting another soul-searing kiss on her lips as he moved to the desk. Her fingers delved into his hair, tangled themselves tight, the pressure making him groan as his lust urged him on.

He set her down on the desk with her legs draped over the edge. He fisted handfuls of silk, the material cold compared to the electrifying warmth of her thighs as he bared them to his touch and moved between them. His other hand wound around the back of her neck and kept her lips fused to his.

Somewhere in the back of his mind, common sense tried to break through. He almost stopped, stepped back from the precipice of desire.

And then his fingers grazed the silky skin between her thighs, damp, hot and completely naked. He froze.

"Clara."

He didn't recognize his own voice—harsh, grating, dark and heavy with a lust he'd never experienced.

She arched her hips against his touch. His fingers moved of their own accord, stroking her wet heat.

"I didn't…" Her voice trailed off as she started to pull back. Uncertainty flitted across her face. "I didn't plan for this—"

He silenced her with another kiss. It didn't matter if she hadn't worn panties to torment him or for some other reason. All that mattered here, now, was that she was *his*.

Her hips moved frantically, matching the thrust of his fingers as his thumb gently caressed her most sensitive skin. Dear God, she was so tight, so wet for him. When she shuddered, crying out into his mouth, he swallowed her moans of pleasure.

That's enough. It had to be enough. He couldn't let things go further…

Dimly, he heard the hiss of a zipper. A moment later, her fingers wrapped around his hard length and he couldn't hold back his groan. Her hand pumped up and down, a motion that nearly made him embarrass himself. He grabbed her wrist and stilled her movement.

"Condom," he ground out.

"I'm on the pill."

She started to reach for him again, her head lowering. The thought of her exquisite mouth wrapped around him nearly undid him once more.

"Next time." When she started to argue, he silenced her by kissing her mouth before trailing his lips across her cheek and along her jaw. "I need to be inside you."

Her legs spread, her body moving to the edge of the desk. He guided himself to her core, gently pressed against her, teasing both of them into a frenetic frenzy before he finally gave in to both their needs and plunged inside her welcoming body. She closed around him as if she'd been made for him. Her head dropped back, baring her neck to his lips, his tongue, his relentless need. She grabbed on to his shoulders, met him thrust for thrust as he took everything she gave and demanded more.

"Alaric… I can't… I'm so…"

He wrapped his arms around her, tangled one hand in her hair and kissed her senseless as she came apart in his arms. He followed a second later, growling into her mouth as he claimed her body and soul.

CHAPTER TWO

Five weeks later

THE TESTS WERE lined up like little toy soldiers, five in total. Each one said the same thing.

PREGNANT

Why, Clara mused as she drummed her fingers on the edge of the bathroom sink, *did they put that word in all capital letters?* Like the tests were shouting just how big a mistake she'd made.

Because she'd made a colossal one. Not only had she not planned on having a child anytime soon, if ever, but having her boss's baby catapulted the situation from *uh-oh* to catastrophic.

She turned sideways. Her stomach was still flat. She'd chalked the bone-deep exhaustion up to overseeing the royal wedding, her loss of appetite to the time of year. The anniversary of Miles's death always left her tossing all night, afraid of the nightmares waiting for her on the other side of sleep. Even though her brief marriage to the scion of Clemont Oil had been a deeply unhappy one, it didn't wipe away the guilt embedded in her bones.

Guilt that Miles's death had, at least partially, been her fault.

It's why she'd taken an herbal remedy every night the last month. It knocked her into a dreamless state that made life possible until the anniversary passed and the memories faded.

But that sleep had come at a price. After the fifth test, an online search had revealed that herbal remedy also decreased the effectiveness of the pill.

Panic fluttered in her chest. Should she wait to tell Alaric until a doctor confirmed her pregnancy? Or should she get the big reveal over with?

Alaric's handsome face appeared in her mind. Normally his dark, chiseled features were frozen in a cold mask, a permanent poker face that gave nothing away, including his innermost thoughts and desires. The first couple of years she'd worked for him, his harsh attractiveness hadn't fazed her. Her heart had been too battered and wary to entertain anything beyond acknowledgment that the prince was extremely good-looking. She knew, too, between his own hints and palace gossip, that he wasn't living like a monk in the years leading up to his wedding. Neither was his fiancée, although her indulgences had played out across the press with increasing frequency compared to the shroud of secrecy Alaric had conducted his affairs under.

Still, as she'd healed and started to regain threads of her lost confidence over the last couple of years, she'd been grateful for the rarely-spoken-of engagement. It kept her mind where it belonged: on her work and off her unattainable boss's broad shoulders, dark gaze and razor-sharp wit. Easier said than done the more he'd sought her out, talked with her and, most importantly, listened. A stark contrast from Miles's preference for her to be seen, not heard. And Alaric's passion for the country he would one day inherit added another seductive layer to the intoxicating mix that was Prince Alaric Van Ambrose.

But there had always been Miss Celestine Osborne in the background. Alaric's future wife.

Until last year. Until That Night, as she'd come to think of it. The night when the innocent little flutterings in her belly and enjoyment she received from their talks had crackled into something more intense.

The night Alaric had ceased being just a prince and shown her that he was most definitely a hot-blooded man.

The tapping of her fingers intensified as she remembered Alaric, stripped to the waist with sweat glistening on his back as he'd pummeled the punching bag in his private gym. When he'd looked at her, she'd barely stopped herself from tripping over her own two feet at the intensity in his gaze. A mix of heated anger and raw pain at complete odds with the calm, controlled prince who had dealt with both his fiancée's and his father's machinations with a disapproving yet bored air.

He hadn't let up on the bag, delivering blow after blow as he'd released all the hurt and fury that had to have been building for years. She'd felt like a voyeur, her eyes riveted to the ripples of muscle as his body had moved with lightning speed. Desire had wound its way through her veins with an intensity she hadn't anticipated. She'd never experienced that intoxicating, languid heat, so potent she'd almost felt bewitched.

"I don't want your pity," he'd snapped at her.

Anyone else might have mistaken his growl for an order. But she'd sensed the undercurrents running beneath his words. He didn't want her support, fine. But the man needed someone to tell him exactly what she had:

You just deserve better.

The tapping ceased as she grabbed the sink in a death grip. What on earth had she been thinking, crossing that line with him? An innocuous comment that had taken the spark they'd both ignored and fanned it into a slow-burning flame. A flame that had suddenly burst out of control into an all-out blaze that had shocked her to her very core.

Even now, despite the exhaustion that had etched dark half-moons into the skin below her eyes, her body tingled at the memory of how they'd melted into each other, his fingers tangling in her hair as if to anchor her against him, his mouth plundering, possessing, marking her with his passion.

She picked up the last test and walked into the kitchen. As she set about preparing the teakettle, she kept glancing at the screen, as though if enough time passed, the answer might change and free her from this hell.

But the word remained. The kettle whistled. She huffed her frustration and shoved the test toward the back of the counter near a vase of flowers before grabbing the kettle off the stove and pouring the steaming water into a mug. She would need to deal with it at some point.

Just not now.

A knock sounded on her door and startled her out of her musings.

"Just a minute."

"Miss Stephenson, open up."

Her heart leaped into her throat as Alaric's deep voice rumbled through her. She gripped the sink and made eye contact with her pale reflection.

"Get it together. You have a royal wedding to manage."

She sucked in a deep breath, released the sink and breathed out.

Straighten your shoulders. Smooth your hair. Be professional.

With that last reminder echoing in her mind, she walked out into the spacious main room of the suite she'd called home for the last seven years.

Another knock sounded, this one brisker and louder.

"Miss Stephenson."

Irritation chased away some of her fear. Not just because Alaric was used to getting what he wanted whenever he snapped his fingers. No, she was irritated because the blasted man had slipped easily from his brief role of lover back to heir apparent and prince without batting an eye. Even the camaraderie that had materialized and grown since the Christmas dinner debacle last year had disappeared, replaced by the proper boss-and-underling relationship once more.

Whereas she had spent the past five weeks fighting to keep her eyes on his face instead of drifting lower, her traitorous mind providing vivid memories of what lay beneath his tailored suits.

The doorknob suffered her wrath as she twisted it with extra force and yanked the door open.

Did he have to look so handsome and put-together all the time? With his nearly six-and-a-half-foot height and broad shoulders, he towered over almost everyone in the palace. Emerald-green eyes pierced her from beneath thick dark brows. His face, classically handsome with carved cheekbones, a square jaw and sculpted lips, was normally set in a cold, apathetic mask.

Which made his glower ten times more alarming. Normally his imperious expressions didn't have an effect on her. It's what had made her an effective executive assistant, her ability to withstand his firm manner and short-worded orders.

"Your Highness? Is everything all right?"

Alaric's eyes traveled up and down her body, taking in her bathrobe and bare feet. She resisted the urge to pull the robe tighter. Ridiculous that she should feel vulnerable after what they'd done in his study.

Specifically on his desk, her skirt around her waist, his masterful hands on her thighs as he'd teased her most vulnerable skin with gentle, fleeting strokes before he'd thrust—

"I didn't realize robes were acceptable wedding attire."

His pompous tone threw cold water on her heated remembering.

"It's seven thirty in the morning. The wedding starts at five." She released her death grip on her robe and casually put one hand on the door frame, filling up the doorway in a manner meant to keep him in the hallway and out of her private sanctuary. "Didn't you read the schedule I emailed yesterday?"

He lifted a brow. "I did. Isn't the florist arriving at eight?"

Oh, no. It took significant effort to keep her expression neutral.

"Meira is showing them into the ballroom."

Both eyebrows climbed up. "Since when do you let your assistant do anything without you hovering?"

"I trained her. And she's a friend. Of course I trust her."

He leaned down. The scent of pine teased her, woodsy and crisp, like walking through a forest draped in snow.

"Since when?"

Her frown deepened. "What's this really about, Your Highness?"

"What?"

"Why are you here, at my private apartment, the morning of your sister's wedding, asking about how I've organized the day when I've kept this palace running for seven years?"

Something flickered in the chilly, sharp depths of his eyes. But then he blinked and it disappeared as he straightened.

"Ensuring my sister's wedding day is going smoothly doesn't sound like an unreasonable request to me."

She bit back a sigh. No, it wasn't unreasonable. She had picked a horrible day to go off script and not be ready to go her customary thirty minutes ahead of schedule.

Plus, if she kept fighting him, he might start asking more questions. What if she didn't have an answer or, worse, what if she became flustered and blurted out something she shouldn't?

"I apologize, Your Highness. I just need to get dressed. I'll be in the grand ballroom in ten minutes."

She started to close the door, but Alaric put a hand up to stop her.

"I didn't come up here to chastise you."

The thinnest thread of apology in his voice nearly undid her. Exhaustion sank into her skin, penetrated her bones in one fell swoop.

"Whatever your reasons, Your Highness, you are entitled to them." *Now would you just go away?* "If you'll excuse me, I really must get dressed."

She must be more tired than she initially realized. Because as she started to turn away, she could have sworn she saw frustration tighten his mouth and darken his eyes. Alaric Van Ambrose didn't get frustrated. He didn't get excited. He didn't get anything. He was aloof, detached, unemotional.

Sometimes she wondered if she'd even imagined that night in the gym, read too much into what she had perceived as the more relaxed nature of their working relationship the past year. If it wasn't for the very physical proof of their lovemaking, she probably could have convinced herself that she'd dreamed about the burning heat of his gaze, the simmering passion that had boiled over as their bodies had joined in a frantic dance of need and pent-up desire.

"Clara."

It took her a moment to realize he'd said it out loud, the first time he'd used it since he'd growled it right before his lips had slanted over hers, sent a shock of electricity through her veins. She jumped, started to turn. A hand fell on her shoulder, pressed the fluffy material flush against her skin. She jerked away, her breath coming out in a sharp exhale.

"Clara!"

Hands closed over her arms, steadied her. She sucked in a deep breath. Her lungs filled with his scent, the woodsy smell calming the rapid beating of her heart.

"Clara, if you don't speak now, I'm calling the doctor and—"

"I'm fine, Your Highness." She blinked rapidly and her vision filled with him: strong jaw tight with worry, full lips stretched into a thin line, the fit of his black pants and navy sweater on his muscular build.

"You're not fine."

"Look, I didn't sleep well, and I'm just feeling a little under the weather." She stepped back but he didn't relinquish his grip on her arms.

"You're pale, you have bags under your eyes, and you just jumped out of your skin. 'Under the weather' is an understatement."

This time she managed to wrench free of his hold and took a large, purposeful step back.

"Just the words a girl needs to hear when she's sick."

Sick. Pregnant with your illegitimate child.

"I'm sending for the doctor." Alaric turned away. "You're right. Meira can handle the initial setup until you're cleared."

She stood there, mouth agape, as he disappeared from view. Then common sense returned and she rushed to the door.

"Your Highness, I—"

"That's an order, Miss Stephenson." The haughty jerk didn't even bother looking over his shoulder as he stalked down the hall. "One you'll follow if you want to keep your job."

CHAPTER THREE

ALARIC'S EYES ROAMED the ballroom. Somewhere among the designer dresses and tailored tuxedos, a pale-haired woman in a blue dress glided through the crowds and elegantly set tables. A stubborn woman with blue eyes that could cut a man down to size one second and make him drop to his knees the next with a seductive need that burned in his veins long after she'd left.

Christ, get a grip.

He was at his sister's wedding. His little sister's wedding, for God's sake.

White lilies and red hydrangeas bloomed from glass vases. Candles flickered on crimson tablecloths, creating an intimate environment in the massive grand ballroom hosting Prince Cassius and Princess Briony Adama's wedding reception. Chandeliers sparkled overhead, with scarlet roses placed strategically among the glittering strands. White-gloved waiters cleared china, refilled champagne glasses and passed out trays of chocolate-covered eclairs, slices of tarte aux pommes topped with sliced apples and melted apricot jam, and macarons.

Judging by the beaming smile on Briony's face as Cass swept her onto the dance floor, she was having the time of her life. Everything was perfect. It always was when Clara was involved.

So why, Alaric asked himself for the twentieth time that day, had he come down so hard on Clara that morning?

Because you can't stop thinking about her. Ever since their tryst in his office last month, he'd been disgusted with himself. Disgust that he had not only abandoned his scruples and had sex with an employee, but that he had done so in such a coarse manner.

Just like your father.

He swallowed a larger amount of gin than he'd intended, focused on the burn of the citrusy liquid. He would have to confront his actions, and his fears, at some point. Especially the intensity of his attraction to his secretary.

Executive assistant.

He frowned into his glass. His engagement to Celestine Osborne may have lasted for almost a decade, but he'd had no emotional connection to his betrothed. How could he when he'd only seen her a handful of times since their engagement officially started? Her telling him at that first meeting that she would be living her life as if she were single up until their wedding had certainly not made him inclined to entertain romantic thoughts, either. He hadn't blamed her; she had been just shy of twenty when her father had pledged her hand in marriage to Alaric.

When Celestine had told him her intentions, he'd been only too happy to follow her lead. For the next several years, he had conducted a couple of discreet affairs with women who knew marriage was off the table. They'd been pleasant, mutually beneficial and pleasurable relationships that had sustained him as he'd taken a more active role in Linnaea's government. A necessary move given how little his father, King Daxon Van Ambrose, bothered to involve himself in anything but spending the treasury's money. A habit that had been the driving force behind the Van Ambrose-Osborne marriage contract.

Except that insidious fear had crept in once more.

Am I like my father?

At first it had just been an adolescent worry. But it had started to rear its head as the people of Linnaea had started to look to him more, as his duties became clearer. He'd terminated his romantic liaisons two years ago not just because the deadline for his marriage to Celestine was drawing nearer, but because his fear had started to overshadow every encounter with another woman who wasn't his fiancée, no matter how atrocious her behavior or outrageous her antics. He'd made excuses long enough, but in the end, he was enjoying the company and beds of women he wasn't pledged to.

Just like Daxon.

No matter that Celestine had apparently more than outmatched him in the number of bedmates, and done so as publicly as possible. Unlike his mother, too, who had loved his wastrel of a father until her dying day, Celestine hadn't felt anything close to love for him. Those facts hadn't made a dent in the guilt that had dug into his veins.

Alaric loathed any hint of scandal. He could still remember hearing his mother's sobs through the hotel room door on a trip to London when he'd been all of four years old and his father had left a dinner with the wife of a Foreign Office official. It was the first vivid memory he had of the damage Daxon wrought with his selfishness, although he had plenty of moments to pick from since then. From using the illegitimate daughter he'd never met as a bargaining piece in yet another marriage contract to spending money on vanity projects like an art museum and a high-rise, Daxon seemed determined to outdo himself time and again.

Alaric made himself reach for a glass of water and take a long drink before indulging in another sip of gin. Reminiscing about the past, especially when it involved his father, made the idea of taking the edge off with a drink all too appealing. Daxon, thankfully, had excused himself at the beginning of the reception. Still licking his wounds, no doubt.

Oddly enough, Alaric's romantic interlude with Clara, coupled with the loss of the Osborne money, had propelled him to do what he should have done a long time ago: strip Daxon of his power. The members of Parliament, who could have best been described as window dressing until a month ago, had been all too happy to unite with Alaric and offer Daxon the choice of retaining his title of king but stepping down from any actual position of power and living out the remainder of his life with a small allowance and the few shreds of his dignity intact, or face a very public inquiry into his spending.

His lips tilted up as he remembered Daxon's shocked expression when Alaric had given him his two options. He'd granted the old devil the gift of sharing the news in the privacy of his office, even if a vindictive part had longed for a public outing in front of Parliament and the various committees who had worked so hard with Alaric to keep the country running the last few years. Daxon had blustered, argued, yelled and, for one horrifying minute, blubbered.

But the threat of censure, of finally having to face his decades of mistakes, had been enough. He'd stepped down from the public eye, citing his cancer diagnosis, and turned over Linnaea's government to Alaric and Parliament. The shackles that had kept Alaric's hands tied, loosened by Celestine breaking their engagement, had fallen away. Though it wouldn't have been possible without the money brought in by Briony's marriage to Cass and the new agreement with Switzerland.

Best not to look that gift horse in the mouth. The timing had been perfect. He, and Linnaea, were free to move forward.

Amazing the number of changes that had occurred since his engagement from hell had ended.

A flash of pale gold hair caught his eye among the sea of designer dresses, tailored tuxedos and overpriced jewelry. His eyes narrowed as he watched Clara dart about, checking in with vendors and making notes on her tablet.

The dratted woman had openly defied him that morning. When he'd returned to her apartment with the palace's physician, she hadn't answered. When he'd let himself in, worried she might have passed out, it was to find an empty suite of rooms. She'd ignored his calls, responded to his texts with as few words as possible and skillfully avoided him all day.

Why?

The second question that had been bugging him all day. The last five weeks Clara had been nothing but professional. She ran his schedule with the same ruthless efficiency she'd displayed the last seven years. She'd attended all of her meetings, addressed him formally and...

And acted as if she hadn't arched her body against his, her fingers tangled in his hair, his lips pressed in a heated kiss against the pulse pounding in her neck as he drove deep inside her.

Blood rushed through his veins as her husky moans and frantic murmuring of his name echoed in his mind. Thank God he was sitting down so the evidence of his lurid musings wasn't observed by his sister's wedding guests.

Had they not had wild sex in his office, he wouldn't have gone up to her room this morning. That had been a mistake. But then again, so had allowing her to slip under his skin over the last year, to pay attention to the subtle nuances of her character like the flash in her eyes when she got frustrated or the sharp wit in her texts and emails. Those indulgences, letting his guard down and treating her more as a partner than an employee, had ripped away his self-control in the moment when he'd needed it most.

His eyes found, then clung to her svelte form clad in navy blue. She moved through the crowd, confidence evident in the set of her shoulders, the lift of her chin.

What was it about her? Had the stress of last year's dinner made him latch onto the nearest woman who conducted herself with decorum? Had the unexpected breakup led to what could be chalked up as a simple bad decision?

Or was his worst fear true? That he'd inherited his father's uncontrollable desires? He'd spent years working to distance himself from King Daxon Van Ambrose and his legacy of selfishness and greed.

But perhaps he was more like his sire than he knew.

Coldness crept in and chased away the lingering warmth from the gin. If the last was true, and he had surrendered to nothing more than lust, he and Clara would have to evaluate whether reassigning her to another role in the palace would be in both their interests.

He didn't care for that thought. But being the heir didn't mean he always got his way. It usually meant the exact opposite.

Briony swept up to him, her smile more radiant than her gold wedding gown.

"Why are you over here by yourself?" she asked as she sat in a swirl of tulle and satin.

"I'm not the star of the show. I'm enjoying a rare moment of solitude."

Briony rolled her eyes. "Rare? You go out of your way to avoid people."

"Only ones I don't like."

"You don't like anyone."

His eyes drifted to where he had last seen Clara. When he glanced back at his sister, it was to see a suspiciously satisfied smirk on her face.

"What?"

"Nothing."

A childish urge to tweak a stray red curl made him clasp his hands around his gin glass. As much as he had come to care for his half sister, there were times having a younger sibling made him grit his teeth.

"Are you enjoying your wedding ball?"

The teasing glint disappeared as her green eyes, so like his own, lit up.

"It's magical," she breathed as she gazed around the candlelit ballroom. "It's hard to believe two months ago I was slinging drinks in Kansas."

"And that a prince would sweep you off your feet."

"That, too," Briony agreed with a light laugh.

Prince Cassius Adama, Alaric's new brother-in-law, appeared at her side and leaned down to press a kiss to his new wife's forehead. Alaric had despised Cass when the man had appeared out of nowhere and essentially blackmailed Daxon into letting him marry Briony. But surprisingly, not only had the two fallen in love, but Cass was genuinely invested in helping Linnaea reclaim financial independence.

Alaric nodded to Cass. He liked to think that confronting Cass the morning after he'd broken off his engagement with Briony had had something to do with the couple reuniting.

Cass returned the nod before glancing around. "Didn't mean to interrupt, but has anyone checked on Clara?"

Unease made Alaric frown. "Checked on her?"

"I just saw her leaving the ballroom. She looked paler than usual."

Alaric was on his feet and moving before either of the newlyweds could utter another word. What was the little fool trying to do? Kill herself with work? He'd always admired Clara's strength, work ethic. But she'd never been this stubborn before.

A mining heiress, several dignitaries and an American pop star interrupted his journey. He forced himself to accept their well wishes, frustration seething beneath his normally calm exterior.

At last, he extracted himself and reached the main hallway outside the ballroom. Some partygoers were clustered off to the right. To the left was an empty hall, save for the lone guard heading off any inquisitive guests who might want to access the royal family's private quarters.

"Cecil."

"Your Highness," the guard replied as he snapped to attention.

"Did Miss Stephenson come this way?"

"Yes, Your Highness. Less than five minutes ago."

"How was she?"

Cecil paused for the briefest of moments. He was new to the guard, barely out of university. Judging by the indecision on his face, Clara had warned him not to say anything.

"Cecil, I'm asking you as your future king."

"Yes, Your Highness. She looked ill. Said she was feeling faint."

Alaric swore softly.

"Thank you, Cecil."

He strode past the guard, turned right and headed for the elevator.

Until a glimpse of blond hair caught his eye. He stopped, keeping his face smooth even as his pulse started to pound at the sight of Clara sitting on a bench tucked into an alcove, her skin too pale, her chest rising and falling with her rapid breathing.

"Clara?"

Her eyes flew open, the blue even more vivid against the pallor of her skin.

"I just need to rest."

"You need a hospital," he ground out as he strode forward and knelt at her side.

"No, I don't," she retorted, her voice surprisingly strong. "And if you try to pick me up and carry me out to an ambulance, I will scream."

Despite the worry coursing through his body, his lips twitched.

"What if I gave you an order as your future king?"

"I'm a British national. You're my boss, not my king." Her face contorted and one hand flew to her mouth.

"I just need to lie down. I'm feeling a little sick to my stomach."

"Nausea?" he repeated. Something flickered in the back of his mind, a notion he couldn't quite grasp.

"Something I ate."

Her gaze skittered to the side. His eyes narrowed. Before he could press her, she pushed off the bench and teetered. He stood and wrapped an arm around her slender waist.

"Go back to the reception," she protested as she pushed at his arm.

"No. I'm making sure you get back to your apartment without passing out."

Her lips parted to argue.

"Nonnegotiable, Miss Stephenson." Blue fire flashed in her eyes as her mouth thinned into a straight line. But she didn't argue as he guided her to the elevator.

Worry and unwanted awareness thickened the air in the elevator. The palm of his hand, splayed cross the curve of her hip, grew warm as the heat of her skin seeped through the thin material of her gown.

Disgust tightened his throat as his body reacted. The one time he'd confronted his father about his affairs and the toll they'd taken on Queen Marianne, a month before his mother passed, Daxon had said he just couldn't help himself when he saw a pretty woman.

And now here he was, the faint scent of roses making his heartbeat quicken, as Clara grew paler by the moment.

Pervert. Selfish jerk. Bastard.

The words he'd leveled at his father before he'd stalked out of the room pounded through his head, each damning word making him want to revisit his gym and punch the bag until he collapsed from exhaustion.

He slowly loosened his hold on her waist and, once he was sure Clara wasn't going to topple over, released her completely. He needed to reassign her. Immediately. This wasn't her fault. No, it was his. His for letting himself lose control too many times, for not having enough strength to resist his own chaotic desires.

Clara deserved better.

When they reached her room on the top floor of the castle, she paused outside her door.

"Thank you, Your Highness."

"I will leave once I know you're safe."

The door swung open. Clara walked in, her shoulders tense as she moved into her apartment. He didn't bother to disguise his curiosity as he looked around, making sure to keep plenty of physical distance between the two of them even as he kept an eagle eye on her form should she suddenly start to collapse. When he'd been in there earlier, he'd been so focused on finding her, and then so incensed by her outright defiance, he hadn't bothered to take note of her residence. With Clara's toned-down style and ruthless efficiency, he'd expect a minimalist approach, lots of clean lines and white and black. Not the pale blue walls, dove-gray sofa scattered with colorful pillows or twinkling lights draped over the fireplace mantel.

His eyes drifted to Clara as she kicked off her heels and sank into an overstuffed chair by the fireplace. What

else did he not know about his assistant of seven years
and onetime lover?

Drop it.

Common sense chased away his curiosity. The more he
wondered, the more he blurred the lines between work and
his personal life, the more he courted trouble.

*Taking her on your desk didn't count as blurring the
lines?* a voice taunted in his ear.

Clara's shuddering breath broke through his thoughts.

"Thank you again, Your Highness."

He gritted his teeth. The formal address was appropriate
and a reminder of their stations. It shouldn't bother him.
Just another example that she was behaving professionally.

While he was remembering how incredible her body
had felt beneath his hands.

"You're welcome.'" A quick glance at her face confirmed that she was still too pale. "I'm going to get you a
glass of water before I leave."

She started to stand.

"I can get it—"

"Sit," he ordered as he crossed the room.

That she only shot him a minimal glare before sinking
back down into the depths of the chair let him know just
how exhausted she felt.

He walked into the kitchen and pulled a glass out of a
cabinet. He kept his gaze focused on the water flowing
from the faucet, not on the little details begging for his
attention: the photos on the refrigerator that hinted at a
life outside of the palace, a vase of flowers in the corner,
a book lying facedown on the counter.

As he turned off the faucet, something caught his attention—a little white stick sitting next to the vase.

A dull roaring built in his ears. The apartment faded
as his vision narrowed. He reached out, pulled the stick
closer and read the single word still visible on the screen.

His fingers tightened around the test as white-hot anger stormed past the walls of his usual restraint. How long had she known? How long had she concealed the truth from him? Clara had always struck him as honest and honorable. Yet she had hidden something that literally changed not just the course of both their lives, but the future of the country.

He breathed in, then out, tamping down the fires of his fury to simmering embers that he could control. Then, slowly, he turned and walked back to the mother of his child, keeping the test partially concealed in his hand.

He handed her the water, watched her drink it. She murmured a thank-you, handed him back the glass, then frowned as he pressed the test into her hand. He hadn't thought it possible for her face to turn any paler, but any color she'd regained disappeared as her eyes widened before flying up to meet his gaze.

His face settled into what Clara had once called his "ice mask." Frozen, she'd said, like his features had been carved from granite by the devil.

"You lied to me. So," he said as he sat down on the ottoman in front of the chair and put his hands on the armrests, caging her in, "we need to make some decisions, Miss Stephenson."

She swallowed hard but didn't look away. He despised the flicker of admiration in his chest. She didn't deserve anything right now but his anger.

"Like what?" she finally asked.

He smiled, the gesture anything but pleasant.

"Like when we should get married."

CHAPTER FOUR

CLARA STARED AT ALARIC.

Did he just say "married"?

"What?"

"Married."

Yes, he did.

She blinked a couple of times, her brain grasping for a response. It finally settled on, "Why?"

His icy smile disappeared, replaced by a quelling glance that all but shouted how foolish she was for not immediately realizing where he was going with this.

"You're carrying the heir to the Linnaean throne."

Her eyes drifted back down to the test. Over twelve hours had passed since her suspicions had been confirmed, and it still didn't seem real. She'd caught herself glancing at her reflection more than once as she'd moved throughout the day. But no matter how many times she'd looked, her belly had remained flat, her body showing no outward signs that a child was growing inside her.

"And?"

Alaric's muscles tightened, the material of his suit sleeves stretching across his biceps.

"And I will be damned before I allow my child to be born out of wedlock and see his or her legacy tainted by scandal."

The words whipped out and slashed at her with the

viciousness of a dagger. She barely kept her expression smooth. Alaric knew of her former marriage, was aware that her husband had perished in a car accident. But aside from her former in-laws, who had no desire to see the truth come to light, the details of her horrendous marriage and that horrific night had died with Miles.

Still, that word never failed to make her inwardly flinch. *Scandal.*

Her mother-in-law had screeched it at Clara in the bedroom adjoining Miles's master suite in his luxury penthouse, full of expensive paintings and sculptures that didn't go with anything but had signaled loudly to all visitors that someone with money and culture resided there. Temperance Clemont had looked the opposite of cultured as she'd threatened Clara with lawsuits, jail and other horrific consequences, including "a scandal she'd never live down," for not saving her son.

Temperance had at least been partially right. Clara had done what she'd done too many times with Miles—let her own fears stop her from doing the right thing. In this case, stop Miles from getting behind the wheel after he'd had so much to drink he'd barely been able to stand up.

But Temperance's accusations, that Clara had somehow orchestrated the event to get to Miles's money…that had been going too far. It had only been because she managed to snag a copy of the police report, the one proving that Miles had been drunk, before Temperance had had it buried that she had any leverage against her mother-in-law and her oil baron husband, Stanley. After she'd returned Temperance's threats with some of her own, they'd slipped away to one of their oceanside mansions and left her finally, blissfully alone.

Except for the sick feeling that developed in the pit of her stomach whenever she heard that word. That it was being flung at her by the father of her child made it ten times worse.

"Marriage is not the answer."

Alaric blinked. Had she surprised him? The possibility that he had expected her to thank him and quickly agree to turn her life, and that of the baby's, over to him chased away her nausea.

"It is the only answer, Clara."

Anger pulsed through her veins and gave her enough strength to sit up straight, bringing her within inches of Alaric. Miles had pressured her into getting engaged long before she was ready, and damn it, she'd let him. She'd been so lost after losing her mother, just a few years after losing her father, and had let her craving for a family override her gut feeling that her relationship with Miles had moved far too quickly, that while he was fun to be around he was not husband material. That one concession had led to another, then one more, until suddenly she'd had nothing left of herself but her name.

The penthouse, with its rooftop garden and indoor swimming pool, had quickly revealed itself for what it was beneath the glitter and expensive furnishings: a gilded cage. It had started out slowly, with Miles encouraging her to stay home and enjoy newlywed life, before progressing into ordering her to tell him her every movement when she left. His controlling demands had taken their toll to the point that she'd stopped going out unless he told her to accompany him somewhere. Easier to wither away in the penthouse than risk a furious tantrum from her husband.

The first time she'd left the house after his death, she'd paused so long in the lobby the doorman had approached to ask if she was all right. Stepping out into the blistering wind of a London winter had been so refreshing she hadn't been able to hold back her smile or the tears of relief that had followed.

Nothing, including a prince used to getting his way, would make her give up her independence again.

"Not for me."

"Because you've been married once before?"

"Yes. Once was enough."

His eyes swept over her face, assessing, probing, delving deeper than anyone, including Miles, ever had. She didn't flinch, didn't pull away as one hand drifted up to rest against her cheek. He'd touched her in far more intimate places a month ago.

"Why?"

"My husband was spoiled and self-centered," she replied matter-of-factly. "The man I dated was not the man I married. Marriage was not enjoyable. I don't see myself repeating the experience."

Alaric's face softened as she spoke, something almost akin to compassion lighting his emerald gaze. But the brief empathy disappeared at her refusal.

"Yes. You will."

She stood, her quick movement making his hand fall away and forcing him to move back. Was it wrong to take pleasure in knowing she'd literally thrown him off-balance? *Probably,* she thought as she walked to her door and held it open, *but I'm too tired to care.*

"No, I won't. I'm sick. You have a wedding reception to be at. I have no desire to keep you from being involved if you want to be, but I'm not marrying you." Pride at her ability to stand up for herself straightened her spine and strengthened her voice. "We'll discuss options in the morning."

Alaric drew himself up to his very imposing height. Broad shoulders that reminded her of the mountains beyond the palace that stretched up to the sky, tall, daunting and magnificent. Her body stirred as he stalked toward

her, each step slow and deliberate, muscles rippling beneath the fine cloth of his suit.

When he'd held her in his arms, cradled her body
against him as though she'd been crafted from spun glass
as they'd both drifted down from the incredible peak of
passion, she'd nearly wept. Wept from the sheer pleasure,
wept from how incredibly alive she'd felt...

And wept because, for one moment, she'd felt cherished. Cared for.

Dangerous emotions that could lead down a fatal path,
as she'd learned all too well. The difference was that, when
Miles had showered her with gifts and compliments, she'd
been starved for affection, left adrift by her parents' death
and feeling isolated among the bustling streets of London,
a far cry from the small town she'd been raised in. He'd
picked up a book she'd dropped outside the lecture hall at
the University of London, shooting her a thousand-watt
smile that had seemed like sunshine cutting through the
cloud of grief she'd been under since her mother's death
the year before. He'd insisted on walking her to class, then
taking her out to dinner, which had ended up being a private dinner cruise on the Thames. She knew now that her
responses, overflowing with gratitude and praise, had fed
into Miles's ego. They'd created a vicious cycle for themselves that had whirled them through their courtship so
quickly she hadn't paid attention to the steadily growing
warning signs until it was too late.

Now, no matter how incredible Alaric had made her
feel, no matter how much she enjoyed his company, she
knew that she didn't need it to survive. And she certainly
didn't want it when the so-called proposal was rooted in
necessity and, judging by the harsh set of Alaric's jaw,
anger.

Guilt punched through her own frustration. Alaric had
suggested more protection. But after she'd mentioned being

on the pill—*stupid*—they had both given in to the heat of the moment and eschewed any rational thought in favor of surrendering to lust.

She lifted her chin in the air as he stopped in front of her, staring down at her with hard eyes, quiet wrath radiating off his body.

"I am the heir apparent. 'No' is not an answer I'm used to hearing."

Was it wrong to feel disappointed in his reply? His world had been turned upside down in the last two months, from a long-lost sister and sudden royal marriage to his own engagement being broken and now a child on the way.

Still, the Alaric she knew wouldn't reply like a spoiled brat not getting his way, not when it was just the two of them. What if the man she thought she'd gotten to know, the man she'd felt closer to than anyone over the past few months, was just like Miles—an image she'd built up in her head?

"Then perhaps you need to hear it more often." She gestured to the open door. "Because that's all you'll get from me. I won't keep the baby from you. But I am not marrying you."

He stepped closer. She breathed in and was hit by a familiar scent: pine and spice, a sensual, masculine mix that had wound itself into her psyche since that night in the gym. Except now, after being surrounded by that fragrance as Alaric had placed an open-mouthed kiss to the pulse frantically beating in her throat, his tongue dancing over her skin with an expertise that had set fire to her as he'd moved inside her body, it was no longer just a casual aroma. It ignited her senses, stirred memories better left in the past and, worst of all, lowered her defenses.

What would it be like, she wondered for the span of a heartbeat, to say yes? To be married to a man she respected, who always acted in the best interests of his country and the throne? Who had shown her a side of passion she'd never imagined could exist?

Her hand drifted toward her stomach before she caught herself. What would it be like to have a father in her child's life? Something she herself had been so fortunate to have and had missed so terribly when cancer had cruelly snatched him away?

But what if she would be married to a man who, like her former husband, wanted what he wanted when he wanted it?

No, thanks.

He leaned down, his lips stopping a breath away from hers. For a moment she was seized with a mad desire to raise up on her toes and kiss him. Would it shock him? Would she experience satisfaction that she had thrown him off-balance again in less than a minute?

Or would he do what Alaric did best: take control?

Worry flickered through her. When it came to anything regarding his beloved Linnaea, Alaric had no problem sacrificing any personal gains if it meant a better outcome for the country. He'd dethroned his own father. What sort of definitive action would he take regarding her and their child?

"I have no desire to see this become a legal issue."

His voice trailed off, leaving a wealth of meaning lingering on the air as the hairs on her arms stood straight up.

"Don't threaten me, Alaric Van Ambrose."

"It's not a threat, Clara. It's a fact, the only route available if you decline my offer of marriage." Pity softened his gaze. She hated it. "It's not how I want things to proceed. But you of all people must understand why it's imperative that we marry and this child is not only protected but has a clear path to the throne."

Deep inside, the part of her that had fallen in love with Linnaea, that had adopted the country as her own and fought tooth and nail alongside Alaric the past seven years to free it from Daxon's selfish ruling, understood all too well.

But the thought of being pressured into another marriage made her feel as if she was being slowly but steadily pushed into a tiny room, one where the walls closed in until she could barely breathe.

Trapped until the day she died.

She started as Alaric's hand settled on her arm, firm and warm. Comforting. It shouldn't be. She should resist it all costs. She'd let Miles entice her into marriage against her better judgment. How she could be such a fool to let herself repeat the mistakes of the past?

"We'll meet at ten a.m. in my office." His voice was infinitely gentler, coaxing. It lured her in, made her want to believe that things could be as easy as saying yes. More hazardous to her heart than Miles ever had been. Even in her grief, some part of her had been aware that Miles's charm had only existed on the surface. She'd just told herself that it would get better with time, so desperate had she been to move past the grief of losing her mother and being alone in the world with no family of her own.

Stupid, stupid, stupid.

The qualities she liked about Alaric, his leadership, his integrity, his steadfast commitment to duty, were embedded in his character and as real as the child growing inside her. Even if the burgeoning intimacy between them was an illusion she'd created, she didn't doubt the abilities that had first stoked her admiration and, eventually, the crush that had developed. He was everything Miles hadn't been. Which made him infinitely more tempting, and twice as dangerous.

It wouldn't be hard at all to fall for Alaric Van Ambrose.

She started to rebut his offer of a morning meeting, but then conceded with a nod. Better to pick her battles, especially when she was facing down an all-out war.

"Ten a.m. Good night, Your Highness."

As soon as the door closed and she heard his footsteps recede down the hallway, her body drooped, her hand clutching the doorknob like it was a lifeline. She forced herself to breathe and summoned enough strength to wobble back to her bedroom. The thick comforter welcomed her with a pillowy embrace. Her eyes started to drift shut.

You have just a little over twelve hours to put a plan together, the rational side of her brain reminded her.

She would…after a little nap.

CHAPTER FIVE

THE DETERMINED KNOCK sounded at ten o'clock precisely. Despite his inner turmoil, a smile tugged at Alaric's lips. Clara was renowned for never arriving early or late, but precisely on time. It was why he had been so concerned by her tardiness yesterday.

The smile disappeared as he crossed the room with a determined stride. He respected that Clara was the one pregnant with their child. But it didn't stop the pride that filled his chest at the thought of finally having a child of his own to continue the legacy of the Linnaean throne. He'd barely been able to stomach the thought of touching Celestine, let alone creating children with her. Having a woman like Clara, one who was just as passionate about his country as he was, who exhibited qualities like determination, dedication and decorum, carry his child filled him with an emotion he had rarely experienced: happiness.

While he would have certainly changed the way their child's conception occurred, he couldn't regret the result. Not when he compared it to the alternative of being shackled to Celestine. Now the only thing standing in his way of achieving everything he'd worked so hard to build, including a proper royal marriage, was Clara's stubbornness.

He had never not achieved something he'd set his sights on before. He wasn't about to start losing now.

He opened the door. Clara looked up and blinked in surprise. He took advantage of her surprise to rake her with a swift gaze. She was still a touch too pale, a faint bruising beneath her eyes as if she hadn't gotten much sleep. But today, instead of glancing at her and then immediately focusing on his work, he noted the blue of her eyes, the contrast of her elfin face with the determined jut of her chin.

His mind drifted to his ex-fiancée. With coal-black hair, caramel-colored eyes and cheekbones that would have made Michelangelo weep, she'd landed on the covers of numerous magazines, lauded as one of the most beautiful women in the world despite her selfish nature and endless partying. He'd agreed with the critics, acknowledging her as physically stunning the same way he would admire a rare artifact. Only her beauty hadn't had a visceral effect on him.

The opposite of the unexpected awareness that had lodged its hooks into his skin the moment Clara had walked into that gym last Christmas. The awareness that had steadily grown, tunneling far deeper than he'd realized with the passing months, growing and morphing into a physical attraction that had exploded that night in his office. An attraction that even now burned as he looked at the mother of his child. The woman who, sooner rather than later, would be wearing his ring on her finger.

"Were you expecting someone else?" he asked drily.

"No. You usually say 'enter' instead of opening the door yourself."

"Things have changed."

A frown flickered across her face before she walked into the room and moved to her usual spot in the chair in front of his desk. She sat with the grace and aplomb of a queen.

Which was good, Alaric reflected as he followed her. Because he intended her to make her one.

"How are you feeling?"

"Better, thank you."

He sat in his chair, his eyes inadvertently drifting down to her belly.

"You're five weeks along?"

Something flashed in her eyes.

"Yes."

"And there is no other possibility?"

He kept his voice neutral, irritated at the relief that relaxed his muscles at the brief shake of her head.

"I'm assuming you could make a case against the birth control company."

A delicate pink stained her cheek.

"I... I was taking a sleep aid at the time. I didn't realize it could reduce the efficacy of the pill." She glanced down at her hands. "I'm sorry, Alaric. Truly."

When she looked back up, he nodded his acceptance of her explanation. Had it been any one of his former lovers, he would have suspected sabotage. But Clara hadn't tried to seduce him, hadn't tried to ingratiate herself in any way prior to their lovemaking. She was honest and forthright. More qualities that made her right for what he had in mind.

"So...eight months."

"Yes."

"A summer child."

"Yes."

"Will you marry me?"

One corner of her lips quirked. "No."

Admiration warred with irritation. Why did he have to break his celibacy streak with the one woman who would resist marrying a future king? His jaw tightened as his resolve strengthened. He hadn't pushed Celestine to the altar for a multitude of reasons, including his own guilt that he had essentially purchased a bride.

But this was different. The future of his child was at stake. He would go to hell and back to ensure that his son or daughter would be born with his name, his protection and the legacy of the Linnaean throne instead of the years of shame he'd suffered or the struggles Briony had grown up with.

His fingers curled into fists. Briony had claimed that her childhood was pleasant, at least until her mother had remarried, but money and security had been scarce. They'd fought for every little pleasure. Briony had struggled for months to pay for her mother's medical bills, working herself to the bone. Another result of Daxon's carelessness. He'd seduced Briony's mother, a college student studying abroad, without a care for the potential consequences.

The thought of Clara working long hours while living in some tiny ramshackle house while he resided in luxury in the royal palace made him sick to his stomach. He would not allow Clara or his child to go through a similar torture.

And it wasn't just his child's future at stake, either. It was Linnaea's future. He finally had the opportunity to chart a new course for the country, one that included a legitimate heir and a wife who would represent the country far better than her predecessor. More than once he'd wondered how Celestine would raise any children they had together. Part of him had hoped that she would continue her self-absorbed existence and leave their children to him. But that wouldn't have been ideal for their children, as he well knew, to have one parent who loved and guided them while the other barely acknowledged their presence. Once Briony had joined the royal household, he'd even toyed with the idea of not having children, of asking his sister and her husband to carry on the throne.

A frown creased his brow as he regarded Clara with a hooded gaze. She had always been an advocate for Linnaea. Perhaps she didn't understand the ramifications of what was at stake. It was no longer her decision to make, or his.

The urge to assume the mantle of Prince Alaric Van Ambrose loomed. But judging by the tense set of Clara's slender shoulders and her perch on the edge of the chair, going in guns blazing would only make her dig her heels in more. Better to start slow and make his case.

"Tell me about your first husband."

There. A blink, followed by the slightest tensing of her hands on the armrests. Whatever had happened between the Clemonts and Clara had left a mark. Judging by the tension now rolling off her slender frame, it had not been an entirely pleasant experience. He'd done quite a bit of reading on the late Miles Clemont, son of oil tycoon Stanley and former model Temperance Clemont, last night. Partly out of curiosity as to what kind of man would entice Clara Stephenson to wear his ring, but also research to arm himself for the unexpected battle she'd presented him with. She'd alluded to unhappiness in the marriage. Yet neither he nor his security firm that performed meticulous background checks had uncovered anything that would suggest what had occurred to give Clara such a negative view of matrimony.

By all accounts, the family had it all: wealth, prestige, good looks. Reviewing the numerous photos of Miles available online, mostly magazines and the occasional news feature on the work he had done with his father's company, it had been hard to picture him and Clara together. With a blindingly white smile against a deep tan and auburn hair combed back into a slick coif, Miles had oozed confidence and money.

What had Clara seen in him?

"His name was Miles Clemont. He was a consultant for Clemont Oil." She tilted her head to one side. "But you knew that already."

"We do extensive background checks on all of our hires."

"Then you know everything."

Her voice hitched up the tiniest fraction on the last word. No, he most definitely did not know anything.

"His death must have been hard on you."

"Yes."

Flat, emotionless. Anyone who took her at face value would have thought her cold and unfeeling. Most would have missed the rapid blink, the uptick of the pulse beating at the base of her throat. No, Clara was anything but impassive regarding her late husband.

"You were married for only a few months, correct?"

She looked away. "Yes. What does this have to do with our situation?"

"I'm trying to discern the reason for your refusal to see sense."

Her head whipped back around, her lips thinning as her eyes narrowed.

"See sense? Agree to marry my boss because of a one-night stand?"

His anger flared again. Anger at Clara for her ability to view their brief intimacy with detachment. Anger at her for resisting what should have been a cut-and-dried decision.

And anger at himself for letting one moment of weakness lead to this whole damn mess.

"A one-night stand that resulted in a child, Clara."

She ran a hand over her hair, dislodging the normally perfectly arranged coif so that a few strands of pale blond hair fell and framed her face.

"Women raise children on their own all the time."

"They do. But not children who will inherit the throne of Linnaea."

Her hand drifted down and settled over her stomach. Possessiveness filled his veins and nearly propelled him across the room to her side. He would protect Clara and their child. He might have made a mistake that night in his office. But he would be damned if he made any more that placed Clara in the position his father had placed women in.

"Is the thought of marrying your child's father truly so abhorrent?"

A tiny vee appeared between her brows. She wasn't as certain in her refusal as she wanted to appear.

"It's not abhorrent. It's… I never really thought about getting married again."

"Why?"

Her nose wrinkled a fraction, enough to let him know that her reasons weren't rooted in memories of marital bliss. He made a mental note to call the private security firm that conducted the checks for all of his employees, ignoring the prick to his conscience. He trusted Clara. He did. But after what he had been through as a child with his father, after years of dealing with Celestine's outrageous behavior, he would not go back through the hell of having another scandal touch his country.

Whether or not he liked it, his future wife's background needed a second look.

"I used to want a family, but then Miles died, I came to work here, and dating has never been a big priority. I guess I assumed my time had passed." She seemed to be choosing her words carefully. "Miles and I were very young when we got married. Too young. We could have made better decisions." Her gaze shifted to him, and steel flashed in her blue gaze. The show of strength sparked the sensual awareness that had never been far out of reach since that night in the gym.

"Many married couples don't enjoy matrimony."

The steel melted into something soft and sad. "Some do." She shook her head. "But you're right. Many couples don't."

"However," Alaric cut in, "I'm not suggesting a marriage based on the lies so many put forth in their over-the-top proposals. It's based on practicality."

"Practicality?"

"Yes. Facts. Marriage would provide our child with a legitimate claim to the throne. It would also extend the protection of this office to both you and our son or daughter."

She frowned. "Protection?"

"I am not without enemies. Marrying me would ensure you and our child are safe."

He stood and circled around his desk. His respect for Clara increased as she stayed where she was, not budging as he sat on the edge of the desk and left just a few inches between himself and her chair.

"What's your plan?"

"I just found out yesterday. I haven't really had time to make a plan."

He pounced. "So you were planning on remaining in the employ of the country of Linnaea? Or staying here and finding a new job?"

Her eyes widened slightly. "I…"

"And am I not to be allowed access to my own child?"

"No, that's not…" She shook her head. "I would never deny you, or my child, their father. I loved my father. I can't imagine not having had him in my life."

The crack widened.

"What about putting our son or daughter to bed? Being there when they skin their knee? Or bring home their first drawing from school?"

Her lips parted. "You… I never pictured you as…"

"A father?" His mouth curved up. "Until yesterday, you never had a reason to."

Pink tinged her cheeks. "True. You're just normally reserved. It's hard to imagine you kissing a child's knee to make it feel better."

"I accepted long ago that any marriage I entered into

would be for political reasons." His mother's tear-streaked face gazing out the window flashed in his mind. "Given what I've seen of love and passion, I had no interest in pursuing an alliance with so-called romantic roots. But I knew I would always be the kind of father mine wasn't."

Present, for one, he thought as he stood and walked to the window. How many times had he looked out a window waiting for his father to arrive, for dinner or a trip, only to be left watching as the sky turned from sunset gold to starry darkness? How often had his father chosen the company of a woman he'd just met over that of his own wife and, once she was gone, his own son?

It had been nearly twenty years since the last time he'd allowed himself to be disappointed. Twenty years and he still carried the token with him, wrapped in a red cloth in his billfold.

He'd been a child on the cusp of becoming a man, the ache of his mother's death still fresh. All he'd wanted was one ride on a Ferris wheel with his father. He'd watched the red cars of the Riesenrad from his hotel window, eyes fixed on the lights, ears ringing with the imagined music and laughter of families as they enjoyed the historic ride instead of the ticking of the clock as the minutes turned to hours.

He'd woken up to the sound of Daxon stumbling into the hotel room, a half-murmured apology making it out of his crusty lips before he'd dashed into the bathroom and slammed the door.

Few people could identify the day they had gone from child to adult. His would forever be burned into his memory.

Anger surged through him. Not being married to Clara, not being there for his child, would be walking in his father's footsteps.

"I will be a part of my child's life. That is nonnegotiable."

The words came out much harsher than he'd intended, but he didn't apologize. Clara was not a foolish woman. Even if she didn't know the full story of his painful childhood, she had to comprehend what kind of life could be waiting for a royal child born out of wedlock.

Silence reigned behind him. He waited. He excelled at waiting. He didn't want to hurt Clara, to force her. He wanted her to reach the same conclusion on her own.

But if push came to shove, he would fight.

The soft sigh behind him signaled victory. He stayed at the window.

Wait. Let her come to you.

"What if I agreed to stay in Linnaea? Signed some sort of custody agreement?"

"That does not resolve the issue of legitimacy as it pertains to our child's claim to the throne. Nor," he added as he turned back to face her, "does it solve the problem of the scandal that will rock this country, not to mention Europe, at the news that the future king's illicit liaison with his secretary produced an illegitimate child."

Sparks practically crackled in the air around her as she stood, her hands balled into fists.

"Executive assistant."

"What?"

"I'm *not* a secretary," she ground out. "I'm an executive assistant."

He stalked toward her, savoring the infusion of color in her cheeks, the crackling blue flames in her eyes as she held her ground.

"You type up documents. You answer calls. You manage my schedule." A slow, cocky smile spread across his face. "Sounds like a secretary to me."

She gave him an answering smile, sharp and full of

fight. "Is it common practice for you to make love to your *secretaries* on top of your desk?"

The barb found its mark as his anger swelled. He'd been so damned foolish. But, he resolved as he took another step that brought him within inches of her, he would make it right.

"You're the first. Although I wouldn't call that lovemaking."

One brow shot up. "Oh?"

He leaned in, inhaling the rosy, orange scent tinged with a hint of something woodsy that had become imprinted on his skin that fateful night. The smell of the fresh rose arrangement in the formal dining room had sparked memories of how smooth the skin of her thighs had felt as he'd lifted her onto the desk. A bite of an orange had him reliving the sensation of her lips parting for him, welcoming him into the sweet, hot heat of her mouth as she'd moaned every time he'd thrust into her body.

Their night together may have been impulsive and reckless. But as much as he should regret it, he couldn't. Not when it had felt so damn good.

"That was wild sex. Next time will be different."

She swallowed hard. Her tongue darted out, touching her lower lip in an unconscious gesture as her eyes locked on his.

"You can't seduce me into marrying you, Alaric."

"I'm not. But good sex would be a bonus to our arrangement."

A small laugh escaped as she looked down. He put one finger under her chin and gently but firmly tilted her face back up. At first, he'd wondered if there was something about him preventing Clara from saying yes. But it seemed like her resistance was rooted in something else, something from her past.

"What did Miles do to cause this aversion to marriage?"

The spell broke. The fire disappeared from Clara's eyes as she stepped back, replaced by the flinty hardness she usually exhibited when dealing with everything from an angry ambassador to a reporter caught infiltrating the palace.

"This has nothing to do with Miles, or my former marriage."

"Then what?"

No answer. She just stared at him with that unyielding gaze. It was ridiculous to feel hurt that she wouldn't confide in him, not when he himself loathed sharing any piece of himself beyond what the public saw.

But it did hurt. He had shared a part of himself that night in the gym, when he'd continued to batter the bag and let Clara see him without a shred of dignity as he'd let his emotions show in every punch, every blow.

Now, when the stakes were much higher than a simple holiday dinner gone wrong, when she was pregnant with *his* child, she was holding back from him and making what should have been a cut-and-dried situation tangled and messy.

"Keep your secrets, then, Clara. But if you truly think that you'll be raising our child on your own without my involvement, depriving him or her of his rightful inheritance, then you're not the woman I thought you were."

She flinched. A low blow, he knew, but an accurate one. How could she not see that her plan to be a single mother was a foolish one? Even dangerous when one factored in the threats that royals and dignitaries faced in the world today? She was not a stupid woman. What on earth was possessing her to reject his offer?

"You only want to marry me because you don't want people thinking you're like your father."

His body went cold. Judging by the draining of the color from her face, she knew she'd hit her mark with stinging accuracy.

"Alaric, I'm… I'm sorry…"

Her voice trailed off as he held up a hand.

"Don't apologize. You're right." He crossed to his desk, focusing on the neat stack of papers that required his attention before the end of the day. "Believe it or not, Clara, I truly want to be a part of our child's life. I want it to grow up without the daily pain I lived through. I want it to be safe and know that it's loved."

"And you need an heir," Clara added, a touch of bitterness in her tone. "It makes me feel like a broodmare."

"I do need an heir. But if we don't marry, I will marry someone else. The children I bear with whomever I marry will inherit the throne. Perhaps that won't matter to the child you carry. Or perhaps it will mean everything." He took the top packet of papers and pushed it across the desk. "I will do anything I can to make this arrangement acceptable for you. I've typed up a preliminary marriage contract. My lawyers made every clause in your favor to the best of their ability."

She stared at the contract as if it was a poisonous snake about to bite.

"A contract?"

"Prenuptial agreement. A common practice."

Slowly, she reached out and picked it up. Her eyes darted over the first page, widening with every sentence she read.

"You want us to get married within a week?"

"We're risking exposure of our tryst already with you being a month along. The sooner we get married, the better."

She flipped the page. "A fidelity clause?"

"One thing I have never tolerated is betrayal." Not after what he'd seen his mother go through. Marianne had been faithful to Daxon until her dying day, regardless of the numerous photos and tabloid articles. Each affair had chipped away at her already-fragile heart. She'd seen her commitment as a badge of pride, that she was doing the right thing by the man she'd married. Alaric had been torn between wanting to rage at her for letting Daxon get away with his perfidies and admiration for her grace and class, traits he had tried to emulate over the years.

Until he'd lifted his secretary onto his desk and ravished her like a wild animal.

"That clause goes both ways. You'll never have to be concerned about me straying. There's also a handsome allowance, the freedom to come and go from Linnaea as you wish."

One hand slowly went up to her forehead, the tiniest tremor visible in her fingers.

"I… I need time to think."

He looked down so she couldn't see the triumph in his eyes. They had gone from her stalwart refusal to considering his offer. He'd conducted enough business to know that if she had already started to reevaluate, it was only a matter of time before she gave in completely.

"I'll see you tomorrow morning, then. Ten a.m. again?"

He expected her to argue, to dig her heels in and ask for more time. But when he looked up, she merely nodded.

"Ten a.m."

And then she was gone, the door closing softly behind her. Instead of feeling exhilarated, he felt surprisingly bereft. Yes, he wanted to achieve his goals. But, he realized with a small amount of surprise, he wanted Clara to be happy, too.

He gave himself a mental shake. Given the past seven years and all he'd come to learn about Clara, from her spine of steel when dealing with feuding politicians to her deft handling of his father's antics, if she truly didn't want to get married to him she wouldn't have started to consider his proposal.

Better, he decided, not to look a gift horse in the mouth. By the end of the week, Clara Stephenson would be his wife, and another crisis would be averted.

CHAPTER SIX

CLARA GLANCED AT her wristwatch. Nine fifty-two. Twenty-four hours had passed far too quickly. Focusing on work for most of the day had kept the swirling mess of her personal life at bay. It had been a blessing until exhaustion hit her like a truck. She'd barely staggered up to her room, where she'd collapsed onto the couch and slept until a quarter past six in the morning.

Which had left her with less than four hours to make the biggest decision of her life.

Yesterday had thrown her for a loop. She had assumed Alaric's interest in marriage had been solely motivated by securing an heir to the throne. But he'd surprised her. Again. Alaric wanted to be a father. With that sentiment, he'd started a crack in the wall she'd built, a crack that had only widened over the course of their conversation.

She'd grown up wanting a family of her own. The more time she'd spent with Miles and his family, however, the more that desire had mutated into a commitment to not bring a child into the frigid atmosphere of the Clemont family. Temperance and Stanley would have inserted themselves into her child's life, ensuring he or she was raised as they saw fit. Miles had said he wanted children when they dated. But how could he possibly have had a child when he still acted like one himself?

The face he'd made when she'd try to take the keys from

him that night, when she'd begged him to let her drive, had reminded her of a toddler not getting his way.

"Don't tell me what to do!" he'd shouted before he'd backhanded her across the face.

Her hand drifted up to her cheek. Miles hadn't left a permanent mark, but his tantrums and self-indulgences had left plenty of wounds invisible to the naked eye.

In the years since Miles's death, she had kept people at arm's length, including potential friends and prospective romances. Marriage and children had been even further down the list of things she saw in her future. She wasn't a fool to believe that all men were so horrible. But she was a fool when it came to her own judgment. She'd made such a colossal error with Miles. What if she made another one with Alaric?

Another glance at her watch. Nine fifty-six.

Alaric was a good man in many ways. She knew that he was right, that marrying him would ensure the best possible future for their child.

But what about them? Could she really commit herself to another loveless marriage? He'd made it perfectly clear yesterday that it would be a business arrangement, another point in favor of the argument that she had read far more into their relationship of the past year. Yet the way he'd spoken about being a father…she wanted that for her child. She'd been so blessed to grow up with a father who had adored her. She'd lost a piece of herself when he'd died. Could she truly deny her son or daughter the chance to have a father like Alaric, one she sensed would fight for and love and care for them just as much as her own father had? All because she'd made mistakes in the past and was now letting her own fears and insecurities influence her decision?

And then there was the glaring fact that, if it did come out that Alaric had gotten his executive assistant pregnant, it could undo some of the considerable progress he'd achieved over the last few weeks. From stripping Daxon of his power to distancing himself from Celestine's antics just as Switzerland had agreed to throw both its support and its treasury behind the palace, Linnaea had made more advancements in just over a month than it had in the years she'd been working here.

Alaric always placed the country first. It was a role he'd been born to, and one he'd accepted long ago. She'd always worked with Linnaea's best interests at heart. She loved the country, the people.

But could she do the same as Alaric? Commit her entire life to the throne?

Her head dropped back against the wall with a dull thud. Instead of walking into this meeting with answers, all she had was more questions.

The numbers changed to ten o'clock. She stood, crossed the hall and knocked. Movements she did every day. But right now, she felt like she was moving through a dream, each gesture sluggish.

It didn't help that Alaric had changed the location of their meeting from his office to his private apartment. If he'd been trying to throw her off, he'd succeeded far too easily.

The door opened. Alaric towered over her, his face the same inscrutable mask he always wore, his emerald eyes dark and flinty.

Her heart thudded in her chest. Before that night in the gym, she'd acknowledged Alaric's handsomeness. He was, and always had been, devastatingly attractive. So were the abs on Michelangelo's statue of David. That didn't mean she was going to fall head over heels for a hunk of marble, living or not. Alaric had been handsome but cold, a leader who placed his people first but also ruthless when it came to decision-making. She had carried out his orders on more than one occasion while privately disagreeing with how he'd gone about it. He eschewed any type of emotion over logic, facts and data.

Seeing him as she'd seen him the night of the failed Christmas dinner—raw, rough, wild—had turned her appreciation into red-hot longing.

It hadn't just changed her physical attraction to him. He'd started to ask for her opinion more, confide to her the reasons behind his decisions. She'd glimpsed so much more of the man behind the prince. Here was a man who truly wanted the best for his people, who didn't want to make the mistakes of his predecessor who had made his decisions purely on emotion. She still didn't agree with his borderline obsession with keeping all feelings out of his choices. But she'd understood him better, respected his reasons and silently thanked the powers that be that her silly infatuation would never go beyond her own fantasies where she could risk getting her heart broken.

Then he'd looked at her, eyes alight with molten emerald fire, and she'd burned for him.

And now she was carrying his child. She was carrying his child and, she acknowledged as she walked into his apartment, she owed it to her child to give it everything she could. Including a father.

Her eyes wandered before she could stop herself. His suite was triple the size of hers, with floor-to-ceiling windows overlooking the mountains and a balcony facing the lake. Brown leather furniture trimmed in brass, thick burgundy carpets and drapes that made the room feel surprisingly cozy and a couple of carefully selected paintings of Linnaean landscapes.

She turned to find him watching her. She returned his frank gaze, concealing her surprise at the comfortable home he'd created for himself.

"Did you sleep well?" he asked as he gestured to a chair

in front of the fireplace, a thick blanket draped over one arm. She sat, resisting the beckoning warmth of the crackling flames and the buttery soft leather as she watched him sit across from her.

"As well as I could."

The tiniest quirk of his lips made something twist in her chest. Alaric's equivalent of throwing his head back and laughing. When she'd seen its appearance in various meetings over the years, it had always made her inwardly chuckle. Over the last year, she'd seen it more, chalked it up as a sign of their growing camaraderie that he was sharing something so simple and yet so important with her, a piece of himself no one else got to see.

"Before you tell me what decision stole your sleep, I'd like to share something with you." He reached out and grabbed something red off the end table next to his chair. He unwrapped the brightly colored fabric to reveal a small coin.

"Are you offering to buy my hand in marriage?"

"If I was into such outdated methods of persuading a woman to marry me, I would be offering far more than this." He stood, crossed the room and placed the coin in her hand. She peered closer. It was gold, the edges slightly worn, the image smoothed out by time and wear, as if the owner had taken it out of their pocket and touched it, tracing the delicate features of the Ferris wheel emblazoned on one side. On the other, elegant script read Riesenrad.

"The Ferris wheel in Vienna?"

She looked up to see Alaric's gaze fixated not on her but the coin, a naked pain in his eyes that shocked her.

"My father took me with him to Vienna after my mother died. I was fourteen." He turned away, shoving his hands into his pockets as he walked over to the windows and looked out over his domain. With his shoulders thrown back and his suit tailored to follow every hard line of his muscular body, he looked every inch the future king.

"It was the one time I remember him trying to be a father. He was in town for a conference and took me out to lunch, walks around Vienna between meetings. It was the most time we'd spent together. It made me think that perhaps my mother's death had changed things. On our last night, we were supposed to ride the Riesenrad."

A weight settled on Clara's shoulders, Alaric's pain seeping into her own body.

"I had a view of it from our hotel. I sat by the window for five hours, sure that he would walk in any moment and we would go." She sensed rather than saw the hurt pulsing through his body, tightening his muscles further as he tried to keep his emotions under control. "It was after midnight when he stumbled in drunk. He'd had a glass of wine at a reception, then another at dinner, and then he just didn't stop. He spent the evening with the wife of a dignitary."

What was there to say? Everything that came to mind seemed trite, meant to fill the silence versus offer genuine comfort. She had never experienced anything so horrific from her parents. Her marriage may have been a disaster, but her parents' union had been one for the storybooks, a relationship built on mutual respect and a deep-seated love.

And her father...her eyes grew hot. He'd been wonderful. Not perfect, but she had never doubted he'd loved her. He'd taken her to carnivals, on nature walks, had read to her at night and rocked her back to sleep when thunderstorms had spooked her.

What would it be like to have a father who not only didn't show any love or affection, but literally abandoned their grieving child in their hour of need?

The ache that had started yesterday when Alaric pointed out that not marrying meant her child would grow up without a regular presence from a father figure burst and filled her chest. She knew she would be a great mother. But if she had the chance to offer her child the kind of life she had had, one with a father who cared for them, would it be selfish to deny them that?

She rose and walked across the room. Alaric didn't move, didn't even show that he registered her approach, until she tentatively moved her hand from her stomach to his shoulder. His body flinched but he didn't move, didn't look at her. Slowly her hand relaxed, her fingers splaying across the soft material of his jacket.

How long they stayed like that, she couldn't say. Each moment stretched into the next, awkwardness gradually easing into a familiarity, a comforting space where they could both exist in their pain and confusion without having to fill the silence.

Her heart thudded. Alaric didn't want love. She wasn't sure she did, either. Her one attempt at love had meant relinquishing so much of herself. But this…perhaps this type of understanding would be enough.

Words rose to her lips. Alaric had confided so much in her. If she was truly contemplating saying yes, he deserved to know the truth of what had happened that night: the role she'd played in her husband's death. The threats Temperance Clemont had leveled at her before she'd left for the final time, to ensure Clara never found happiness with anyone again.

The words died on her tongue. The Clemonts hadn't been a part of her life for eight years. If they had truly wanted to sabotage her, they would have made a move before now. What was the point in bringing it up? Besides, she was already pregnant with the heir to Linnaea's throne. If she brought up the past now, it would introduce the possibility of scandal just as Alaric was finally distancing himself from his father's and fiancée's tumultuous pasts.

That's just an excuse, a nasty little voice whispered in her ear. *You're afraid.*

Her fingers tensed, pressed harder on his shoulder. Alaric was too lost in his own past to notice. Slowly, she eased her touch, relaxing her hand and breathing in deeply.

Yes, she was afraid. Afraid that if she told Alaric what had truly happened that night, he would look at her in disgust, the way he'd looked every time he'd seen a picture of his fiancée or had a confrontation with Daxon.

Every time he had to confront a *scandal*.

Finally, he turned. Her hand dropped and she stepped back, giving them both some much-needed distance.

"Do you keep the coin to remind yourself of his true character?"

Alaric's dark chuckle made coldness slither down her spine. She would never want to be on the receiving end of Prince Alaric Van Ambrose's wrath. The world was fortunate that he had chosen to use his razor-sharp intelligence and formidable will for good.

"I have plenty of reminders as to his nature. No, I kept it for my child." He plucked the coin from her hand and held it in his own, gazing at it for a long moment before he brought his arresting green gaze up and met her eyes. "As a reminder to myself to be a better father than mine ever was. As a reminder that something as simple as a ride on the Ferris wheel can mean more than all the sports cars and fancy suits and money in the world to a child."

His words ripped away the last vestiges of her initial refusal. She swallowed hard, turned away from him and walked back over to her chair. She didn't sit, ran her fingers over the soft leather. The touch grounded her, gave her something visual to focus on other than him.

"Then our child should count themself lucky to have you as a father."

Silence descended on the room. Her fingers drifted

down to the arm of the chair, tapped the brass buttons embedded in the material as she waited for him to reply.

Then, at last: "Is that an answer?"

She nodded, unable to speak past the lump in her throat. She had no idea if she was doing the right thing. So many questions and worries swirled in her mind. Would she and Alaric be able to make a marriage work? What if she wasn't a good queen? Even though she was not a Linnaean national, the country and its people had become very dear to her in the time she'd spent in the palace. The possibility that she would let them down just as they were finally clawing their way out of the darkness made her sick to her stomach.

And the baby...the most important aspect of this whole arrangement. Was this the right thing for her baby?

The man didn't even blink, just returned her nod with one of his own as if he had expected nothing less.

"Review this and sign it by this evening."

Her first proposal had gone very differently. Miles had proposed on bended knee at one of his parents' grand parties in front of several hundred guests, sliding the three-carat diamond ring on her finger as if it was the Hope Diamond and basking in the congratulations the guests bestowed on them throughout the evening. It hadn't felt like a proposal rooted in love. No, it had all been for show. Just like Miles, as she'd come to learn the hard way.

She'd always sworn that if she ever got married again, it would be very different. Who knew that it would be transactional, a signing of papers and a few exchanged words for the sake of legality and legacy instead of any romantic notions?

Perhaps this is better, her rational side consoled her. *There's no false hope. No ideas of love to let you down. You know exactly what you're getting.*

"You said yesterday you wanted to get married by the end of the week."

"Yes. I'll arrange for the ceremony to take place on Saturday." He pulled his phone out of his pocket and began to type something. "We'll prepare a small statement to be released after we've departed for a monthlong honeymoon. I don't want to detract from my sister's wedding."

A small smile tugged at her lips. It had been nice to see Alaric finally grow close to someone, especially someone like Briony, who had taken on her duties as princess with incredible aplomb despite having grown up across the ocean in a small town in Kansas.

"She'll appreciate the thought."

"It will also keep the spotlight on her and off the timeline of recent events."

Her smile disappeared. She should have thought of that, would have thought of it if her mind had been in the right place.

"A wise approach."

"The new public relations officer will handle the details of the press release."

"New officer?"

"I promoted your assistant, Meira, this morning."

The walls of her invisible prison shuddered, pressed in on her as her mouth dropped open.

"Meira?"

"Yes."

"But… I don't understand."

Alaric looked up from his phone and frowned. "What is there to understand? I will need to hire a new executive assistant. I offered Meira both your role and that of public relations officer. She chose the latter."

"Without talking to me first?"

The frown deepened. "I make decisions about palace staffing, Clara. I have for years."

The reprimand brought back the sharp sting in her cheeks from Miles's slap all those years ago.

"I should have been consulted."

"A minor change in staffing hardly seemed worth bothering you over."

Her mouth opened, closed, opened again.

"What if I had said no?"

He glanced up at her again with his eyes narrowed. "I told you yesterday, no wasn't an option. I made my decisions based on what the best choice was for everyone. Given your history, I knew you'd come to the same conclusion."

She pressed her lips together so he couldn't see her gnashing her teeth. She didn't know what ticked her off more, that he knew what decision she would make before she had or that he'd started making plans before she'd told him yes.

He must have sensed her consternation because he folded his arms across his chest.

"You told me yourself Meira wanted to eventually move into a public relations role. I listened and I offered her that opportunity." His phone pinged, drawing his attention off her. "Meira is working on the press release now. I'll send the details regarding the actual ceremony to you this evening along with the paperwork."

She tried to keep her tone calm as she voiced the fear slowly unfurling in her belly. "Am I to have all my responsibilities stripped from me then?"

Alaric blinked in surprise before a frown crinkled his brow. "No. I would hope you'd think better of me than that, Clara, after all our years together. You've seen how much of a role Briony has taken on as princess. Once we've navigated these first few weeks, we'll sit down to discuss what duties you'll have as queen." The frown deepened. "I have no interest in having a queen who is nothing more than an ornament. But we're to be married. You can't continue as my assistant."

She wanted to stay and argue. But what was the point? Meira had told her multiple times how much she wanted to work in the public relations office. She had become a dear friend, the first true friend Clara had had in years. She couldn't torpedo something Meira had been working toward just because she didn't like how it had come about. And Alaric's explanation for reassigning her duties made sense. She hadn't really thought about how her role in the palace would change, but it would need to change. She'd seen all the things Briony had taken on since she'd come to Linnaea. The to-do list for the future queen of the country would most likely be even longer and more intense.

Rational reasons for why he'd done what he'd done. None of it assuaged her growing annoyance with Alaric's princely manner. Had she thought his firm decision-making attractive before?

Because right now, it was just irritating.

She moved toward the door. She'd barely taken five steps before Alaric stepped in front of her.

"Clara."

Slowly, she looked up. Her gaze landed on his lips as her irritation melted away. Did he want to kiss her again? The thought left butterflies dancing in her stomach despite her frustration, anticipatory flutters mixed with a nervous quivering of what a kiss would mean. A gesture to seal the deal? A premonition of the intimacy to come? He'd certainly made his preferences for both fidelity and physical affection clear yesterday. But she thought she'd have time, time to get used to the idea of being married again, of being married to her *boss*, before they would touch again.

Because deep down, if she was being honest with herself, it hadn't just been her failed marriage to Miles or the circumstances around their child being conceived that had held her back from saying yes. No, it was how Alaric had made her feel when they'd made love, how sexy and beautiful and alive he'd made her feel as she'd come apart in his arms. The sensations had been so intense, so raw, had made her feel like her heart had been laid bare for him to see every bit of herself. Something she'd never experienced before, and certainly not one she had ever expected to experience with Alaric.

But to let someone who held so much power gain access to her body, let alone her heart, was terrifying. What if she couldn't keep him at arm's length? What if she made the same mistakes she had with Miles?

What if, what if, what if...?

"I'm very tired, Your Highness. Could we continue this discussion later?"

He knew she was lying. The man had a built-in lie detector, had used it to eject plenty of unscrupulous and deceitful business professionals, politicians and royals from various meetings over the years she'd worked for him. But right now, she didn't care. She just wanted to get away, to be alone with her tumultuous thoughts.

His hand came up, his fingers settling lightly on her jaw. She inhaled sharply.

"If you call me Alaric."

The smugness in his tone told her he knew exactly the kind of effect he was having on her, the heat that bloomed on her skin where his fingertips rested.

She narrowed her eyes. "Why?"

"I'm to be your husband. When we're in private, using my given name is appropriate."

"You're not my husband yet."

Something flashed in his eyes but disappeared before she could discern what it was.

"You said it once before."

Her entire body flushed. She had said it more than once.

Moaned it, borderline screamed it into his mouth as he'd sealed his lips over hers to smother her cry of ecstasy as he'd brought her to a level of exquisite pleasure she'd never experienced.

"I'd like to leave now, Alaric."

No sooner had his name left her lips then he stepped back. Cool air brushed her skin before embarrassed heat replaced the warmth from his touch. He was much more in command of himself than she was.

The what-ifs grew stronger as she brushed past him. She had made it to the door, her hand reaching for the knob, when his voice rang out once more.

"Is there anything else you want to share with me before we make this official?"

Don't panic. He can't possibly know you were there that night. That Miles is dead because of you.

She looked over her shoulder at him as casually as she could manage, striving to keep her panic buried. Part of her wanted nothing more than to confide in him, to finally unburden herself. Logically, she knew she hadn't intended for Miles to get hurt, let alone die.

But logic didn't banish her guilt. She had been the one to let him drive, who had let her embarrassment when he'd slapped her overcome common sense as he'd gotten behind the wheel and she'd climbed in the car with him. And ultimately it had been her actions that had led to the car accident that had claimed his life. She'd been weak when she needed to be strong. Because of that moment of weakness, a man was dead, a son buried in the ground. No matter how much she loathed Temperance and Stanley Clemont, their grief had been real.

The truth had stayed buried this long, survived Alaric's notoriously in-depth background checks and the lens of the paparazzi so frequently fixed on Linnaea's royal family. There was nothing to gain by sharing it now.

Nothing to gain and everything to lose.

"No." She forced a smile to her face. "Nothing."

CHAPTER SEVEN

THE DAY OF her wedding dawned bright and beautiful. Sapphire-blue sky, glittering white snow, and a lull in the brisk winter wind that had whipped down from the mountains and shrieked its way through the castle gardens the past few days.

Any other bride would have been ecstatic. Clara, however, could barely stand to look at her own reflection in the mirror. She stood at the window of her suite, her last night in the apartment she'd called home for the past seven years, her fingers resting on the cold glass of the window.

She'd tossed and turned all night. Was she doing the right thing? Should she tell Alaric about Miles? The accident? Could she make a loveless marriage work?

Yet if she did change her mind, told Alaric she couldn't go through with the wedding...where would that leave her? Her child? She'd be trading one set of problems for another.

"You look beautiful, Your Highness."

Clara forced a smile onto her face as she turned to Meira Laird, her former assistant and now officially the new public relations officer. The petite raven-haired young woman had come across as timid and shy when Clara had first met her a year ago when she interviewed her for the position of executive assistant to the executive assistant of the prince. Her quiet, compassionate nature concealed a talent for communication. It was why Clara had mentioned Meira's interest in public relations to Alaric.

She just hadn't anticipated Alaric moving forward without talking to her first.

In a matter of days, their relationship had drastically changed. As his executive assistant, she had felt respected. Alaric consulted her, asked for her opinions and, most importantly, listened to her.

Yet between his push to get married so quickly and now making changes in her staffing without talking to her, was the camaraderie and rapport they'd developed over the years going to be replaced by a dictator who made decisions for her? Her career had given her purpose after her unwanted time as a trophy wife. Who would she be without it?

An image of Miles's face appeared in her mind. Handsome, yes, made even more attractive by tucks and nips since he'd been in college. She'd been so lost after her mother's death, being truly alone in the world for the first time, that she hadn't noticed the signs until his ring was on her finger.

Not true. No, she had noticed in the months leading up to the wedding. Had felt uncomfortable with how he discouraged her from befriending anyone he didn't introduce her to. But she had wanted so desperately to be happy, to have the kind of marriage her parents had had, to not be alone, that she had looked the other way, gone along with his suggestions to avoid conflict.

Panic fluttered low in her belly. Was she doing the same thing now?

"You look a thousand miles away."

Clara shook her head and focused on Meira.

"I am," she confessed with a smile. "Sorry."

The few people Miles had allowed her to be friends with had snubbed their noses at her once she'd gotten rid of the

Clemont name. Trusting others, let alone herself, had been a challenge. Becoming close with Meira had been a saving grace she didn't even know she needed. She'd finally started to relax and enjoy life outside of work again. How quickly she'd come to trust and feel comfortable around Briony had been a result of her friendship with Meira, too.

What if her marriage to Alaric altered her relationship with Meira, too? What if she withdrew into herself and lost so much of the progress she'd made?

Meira approached her and slid an arm around her shoulders, giving her a comforting squeeze.

"This is different. He's different."

She'd confessed some of the details of her first marriage to Meira over the summer after one too many glasses of wine. Meira had returned the favor by sharing her own story of heartbreak, a young man she'd fallen in love with who had deserted her when her family had lost their fortune. The summer night revelations had bonded the two women.

"He's different in some ways," Clara agreed. "But if I wasn't carrying his child, we wouldn't be getting married."

Meira's eyes narrowed thoughtfully as she stepped back and smoothed the skirt of Clara's dress.

"I'm not so sure about that."

Clara turned away so Meira wouldn't see her rolling her eyes. Meira had been just as trepidatious as Clara about relationships until Briony and Cass had descended on the palace and surprised everyone by falling in love. Planning the royal wedding had brought on a severe case of romanticism.

"I am."

In the mirror she caught Meira's head shaking.

"I think you two have been mistaking respect and admiration for something more."

Clara laughed.

"What on earth are you talking about?"

"The way you two look at each other. How His Highness…" Meira's hands fluttered in the air for a moment as she tried to find the right words. "Softens around you. It's subtle, but it's there. He's more relaxed around you, and I don't think it's just because he respects your work."

She'd thought so, too. But based on how quickly he'd shifted back into being prince, how rapidly he'd decided her opinion didn't matter now that they were engaged, Alaric reserved his more personal interactions for friends or close acquaintances, not lovers or fiancées. It had been eight years since she'd been touched so intimately, and the only time in her life she'd enjoyed physical pleasure. Of course she would have a physical reaction to a man who could make her feel like that.

But romance? Emotional intimacy? No. Even she couldn't be so stupid as to make the same mistake twice and fall for a man who would never be capable of loving her. It was absurd to even contemplate the power-wielding, strict prince as having anything approaching romantic feelings for anyone. The few affairs he'd conducted when she'd first worked for him had seemed transactional, cold, businesslike. She'd booked enough dinner reservations and sent calendar invites to his paramours via email to know the man didn't approach relationships with romantic intent.

He may have been the best lover she'd ever been with—although she only had the one to compare with, and that wasn't saying much—but sex and love were two very different things.

She glanced at her reflection in the mirror and bit back a sigh. Not exactly the dress she'd envisioned a member of royalty wearing. She'd picked a cream- colored sheath dress with long sleeves. Simple, elegant, a far cry from the full-skirted gown Temperance Clemont had insisted she wear. Clara had wanted so badly to have a relationship with Miles's mother that she'd gone along with her future mother-in-law. The tulle of the underskirt had made her itch, and she hadn't been able to eat a bite of the lemon lobster fettucine because she'd been terrified of dropping food on the five-figure dress.

Still…she'd always thought that if she got married again, she would make sure it was in a dress she wanted.

Her eyes drifted to her window and the rooftops of the buildings of Eira, the city she'd come to call home. When she'd first started, Daxon's frequent appearances in the international tabloids had struck her as unprofessional and annoying. But as she'd dug deeper into her new career and been confronted with the full scope of the damage he'd caused, from the lack of affordable housing and quality jobs to damaged relationships with countries across the world that wanted nothing to do with a king who preferred to spend money versus rule, her work had become very personal to her. It had physically hurt to see deals fall through after one of Daxon's affairs was splashed across Instagram or to hear conversation about Celestine's latest tabloid feature dominate a conference instead of one of Alaric's carefully crafted economic proposals.

Shame crept up her neck and turned her cheeks red. She turned away from the mirror. What kind of queen was she going to be if she was feeling sorry for herself over a damned dress? Yes, things were looking up for Linnaea. A wedding dress for a future queen who never should have been queen in the first place was definitely not a priority.

With her focus back where it needed to be, Clara moved toward her bed to grab her coat.

"It's nearly time. We should head down."

Meira sighed. "I know he wants to keep this a secret and give Briony a little more time in the spotlight, but couldn't he have at least picked somewhere a tiny bit more romantic than his office?"

"It's not in his office anymore."

Meira's head whipped around as she narrowed her eyes. "Oh?"

"It's in the rose garden."

She tried, and failed, to keep her voice neutral. Alaric's text that morning sharing the new location had surprised her, too. She hadn't been able to deny the slight thrill that had pulsed through her at the thoughtful gesture, even if it had also confused her to no end. Was there a reason behind his sudden change of heart? Or was he simply trying to do something nice for his future wife?

A knock sounded on the door. Meira answered, murmured something to the person on the other side and turned back with a pale blue box in her hands, the lid topped off with a white bow.

"A footman just delivered this." Her voice held a touch of smugness as she gestured to the small white card on top. "Guess who it's from?"

"I can guess," Clara replied drily even as her heartbeat kicked up a notch. What could Alaric have sent her?

Meira set the box on a table. Clara lifted the lid and peeled back the tissue paper. Even she was unable to contain her gasp of surprise.

"Are those…"

Meira's voice trailed off as Clara let her fingers glide over the different materials inside. Her earlier excitement returned as a smile broke across her face.

"Wedding dresses."

Alaric glanced down at his watch. Two minutes to noon and no sign of his bride-to-be. Did the dress not fit? Had she misunderstood which garden? Or, worse, had she changed her mind and fled the palace?

Stop. He never questioned himself like this. He had not pulled the country back from the brink of financial disaster by engaging in self-doubt. There was a solution for every problem. No matter what happened today, he would fix it.

He focused on the looming escallonia hedges that surrounded the palace rose garden. In the dead of winter, the glossy leaves still held on to their green, a welcome splash of color beneath the snow. Come springtime, white and pale pink flowers would blossom, followed a couple months later by an explosion of color as the roses bloomed.

A more appropriate setting for a wedding, he grudgingly acknowledged. Briony had poked her head into his office last night. Despite his attempts at keeping his upcoming nuptials under wraps, his sister had found out and somehow knew about the baby, too. How, she'd refused to say, but his concern that she might be upset over her spotlight being stolen so quickly after her own wedding was invalid. Briony had been thrilled, pattering on about gaining a brother, a husband, a sister-in-law, and now a niece or nephew in such a short time.

Well, thrilled to a point. Once she'd learned of his plans for the ceremony to take place in his office, she'd nearly leaped across hid desk and strangled him.

"Seriously?" she'd cried. "Clara is carrying your child and you're going to marry her in your *office*?"

It had also been Briony's idea to surprise Clara with three wedding dresses from a designer in downtown Eira.

"She doesn't get to have a real wedding, Alaric. The least you can do is make it memorable for her."

Briony had a point. And it had given him the idea to summon the photographer from the palace's public relations office. Clara could have photos of the ceremony and, when news of their wedding came to light, he could produce the photos to combat negative press. The public loved royal weddings. With the right spin, an elopement in the rose garden would rise above malicious gossip.

He was about to glance down at his watch again when

he caught movement out of the corner of his eye. He looked up and froze.

Clara walked down the path toward him. The dress she'd picked, an ivory creation made of lace, clung to her svelte figure before gently flaring out around her knees and cascading into a train that made her seem like she was gliding down the path. A brilliant blue peacoat brought out the color of her eyes and made her pale gold hair glimmer against the backdrop of the snow.

She looked stunning. Like a future queen. When she drew alongside him, he reached out and tucked her gloved hand in the crook of his arm.

She smiled up at him, her eyes soft and glowing.

"Thank you," she whispered. "It's all so lovely."

Satisfaction warmed his chest even as shame threatened to snatch it away. Briony had been right. Two simple gestures had made all the difference in the demeanor of his bride.

As the judge began to speak, Clara's fingers tightened around his arm. He glanced at her. Her eyes were focused on the judge, her face smooth and her lips set in the barest hint of a smile. Despite her gratitude, there was nothing to suggest she thought of this marriage as anything more than what it was: an arrangement to provide protection for her and their child, as well as a secure path to the throne for his heir.

Why did that bother him?

Because, he realized as the judge continued to speak on the sanctity of marriage, that part of him that had been disappointed by Clara's resigned acceptance of her fate was also now longing for something…more. What exactly, he couldn't begin to fathom.

He blinked, realizing the judge was addressing him.

"…take this woman to be your lawfully wedded wife…"

He needed to take a step back from the emotional precipice he'd stumbled onto. Yes, the situation had turned out far better than he had anticipated. But it had still been the result of his loss of control. This was not a fairy-tale royal romance. It was a business arrangement meant to protect an innocent child and the future of the country.

As he slid the wedding band onto Clara's finger, he steeled himself against any further sentimental indulgences. Now was the time to reassume the mantle of leader and focus on what mattered most: guiding his country into a new chapter while preparing to become a father to the next heir to the throne.

He met Clara's gaze and gave her a small, aloof smile. "I do."

CHAPTER EIGHT

CLARA LOOKED DOWN for the seventh or eighth time since the ceremony at the simple silver band on her left finger. It was official. She was now Clara Van Ambrose, Royal Princess of Linnaea.

Wife.

Not a title she had expected to have anytime in the near future, if ever, and certainly not with Alaric.

Alaric. Her boss. Her *husband.*

After their wedding ceremony, they had posed for a few photos for one of the palace photographers. Another gesture that, despite her best efforts, had further erased some of her concerns and questions and replaced it with hope. Foolish, bright, lovely hope.

She'd barely caught her breath on the elevator ride up to his private quarters.

Their private quarters, she'd amended as she'd walked into them for the second time that week, a nervous fluttering in her chest. Alaric had hinted that their marriage would, in time, include physical intimacy. But surely he hadn't meant now?

No, she'd realized with a mixture of relief and disappointment as he'd given her a slight, distracted smile and then immediately hopped on his phone once the door had closed behind them. It was to prepare for their honeymoon to Lake Geneva. A honeymoon that, judging by his side of the conversation, was all about privacy and giving Alaric the ability to work.

Work that didn't include her anymore.

Less than an hour later, he'd escorted her down to one of the private cars he preferred over the luxurious limousine Daxon liked to ride in. The short ride to the airport had been spent with him switching back and forth between his phone and his laptop as she sat there. The couple of times she'd tried to jump in like she had as his executive assistant, to offer a reminder on upcoming legislation or a detail about a dignitary, he'd told her to stop working and relax.

"You're a princess, not my assistant."

He hadn't said the words cruelly, but they'd still cut deep. Was this what her new life was to be like? Just sitting around like some useless ornament for him to trot out whenever he needed?

Anger simmered below the surface on the one-hour-long private plane ride to Geneva. She never would have guessed by the way he'd welcomed Briony and her activism with Linnaea's education system that he would relegate his wife to the role of fancy bauble.

She couldn't help but wonder if it wasn't how he felt about the role of his wife, but how he felt about *her*. Despite the position she'd served in for the past seven years, she was essentially a commoner, the daughter of a mechanic and a teacher who had only landed in the upper echelons of society because she'd caught Miles's eye. Did Alaric think her capable of organizing his budget and typing his emails, but not of leading the country together?

By the time the plane landed at the airport, she wanted nothing more than to tell him she'd made a mistake, run to the nearest terminal and board the quickest flight home.

Except she had no home. She couldn't just go back to her apartment at the palace. The house she'd lived in with her parents outside of Southampton until her mother's death had been sold long ago to pay for the last of her university tuition. Both her parents had been single children, their parents dead before she'd even been born.

All she had left now was the man descending the stairs onto the tarmac—her husband—and the unplanned child growing inside her. Would it be her only one? Would she continue in her parents' stead?

It was enough, she decided morosely as he turned to hold out his hand to her, to make one thoroughly depressed.

Alaric glanced out the window as the helicopter he'd arranged to take him and his new wife to the lake house slowly descended onto the helipad.

His wife.

No need to get sentimental, he reminded himself. That didn't stop protectiveness from rearing its head as her fingers settled in his and she alighted from the helicopter. Her eyes widened as she took in the sight of the chalet.

"It's beautiful, Alaric."

His hand tightened around hers for a moment before he forced himself to ease his grip. It was the first time she'd spontaneously used his name. It shouldn't matter.

Didn't matter, he reminded himself as he guided her down the stone path from the helipad toward the house.

"The one purchase my mother oversaw. She spent a lot of time here."

The two-story mansion had been built in a private cove with a private beach on Lake Geneva. His mother had fallen in love with the shingled, pale blue exterior and white shutters adorning each window. The color was too bright for his taste, but he'd never been able to bring himself to change it.

As an added bonus, Daxon despised the place. It didn't matter that the house boasted six bedrooms, an indoor pool and five acres of lakefront real estate. Daxon had berated his wife for choosing a house that looked like it "belonged in a tiny town in Maine" and not in the holdings of a king of Europe. It had been one of the few times his mother had stood up to Daxon. Daxon had retaliated by purchasing a lavish home on Lake Como in Italy and dragging them there for a vacation at least once a year.

However, he reflected as the blades of the helicopter came to a stop and he looked out over the snow-covered grounds leading down to the water's edge, the marble floors and Greek columns of the Lake Como house had always felt more like a museum than a house. Despite his loyalty to Linnaea, even the palace had at times seemed like a prison, his future written before he'd even been born.

Here, in what Daxon had sneeringly referred to as "the cottage," had been the closest to home he had ever experienced.

It was, he realized with a small degree of surprise, the first time he had ever brought a woman here.

He glanced at Clara out of the corner of his eye. She'd been extremely quiet since they'd flown out of Eira. At first the silence had been welcome. Between delegating how best to use the funds provided by his brother-in-law's deposit into Linnaea's treasury and navigating the upcoming treaty with Switzerland, his list continued to grow.

Somewhere over France the silence had started to creep under his skin. Given Celestine's behavior and frequent portrayals in the media, he'd accepted over the years that when he finally did marry, his queen would do best by staying in the background of official duties. He knew plenty of royals and dignitaries whose significant others excelled at spending money, wearing the latest couture and providing heirs while keeping as far away from their spouses' official duties as possible.

But Clara had never been one to stay in the background. No, she'd surprised him from her first day when she'd flatly told him an email he'd dictated to her was too abrupt. He'd been so surprised by her critique that instead of firing her, he'd asked her what she would change. The resulting second draft had not only been much better, but had led to an improved relationship with the member of Parliament he'd been writing to.

So why, he asked himself, as the pilot circled around the helicopter and opened the door, had he shut her down on the way to the plane? She was a woman who done nothing but work tirelessly for his country, who had agreed to marry him to provide the best possible life for their child even when marriage to him had clearly not been her first choice.

Yet he was treating her exactly like he would have Celestine. The realization left a bitter taste in his mouth. But how could they possibly return to their camaraderie of the previous year? It had been pleasant, yes, but once the constraints keeping them in their proper roles had been removed, they'd lost control so quickly.

He'd lost control.

Just like his father.

His fingers moved across the keyboard, each tap a little more forceful than the last. Clara didn't even glance at him, her eyes trained on the winter landscape outside.

"My mother purchased this when I was ten."

"It's beautiful."

Beneath the monotone he detected a hint of genuine appreciation. A tightness eased inside his chest. He had been concerned about what she would think about the cottage, he realized.

"I didn't ask you about a honeymoon. I just picked the best location for privacy."

Clara shrugged, still not looking at him.

"I understand."

Disappointment unfurled inside him. He didn't like this

Clara—agreeable, bland, quiet. Yet he had been the one to shut her down in the car. He had taken her off all of her assignments, initiated the hiring process for a new executive assistant and planned their honeymoon without asking for her opinion.

An apology rose to his lips. The words lodged in his throat. He couldn't remember the last time he had apologized. It might very well have been years. He made decisions with enough forethought and planning that he was almost always right.

He knew he needed to say something. But how many times had he heard his mother apologize to his father? How many times had he heard Daxon take advantage of that apology, use it to twist Marianne to his will and absolve himself of his own actions? Apologies hadn't resolved conflict. They'd been weaponized, used to control.

The door to the helicopter swung open. The pilot snapped to attention. Before Alaric could make the leap of faith and apologize for his heavy-handed behavior, Clara stood and walked down the stairs to the helipad, her bright blue peacoat wrapped tightly around her.

He slammed the lid on his laptop more forcefully than he had intended. Their marriage might be one of necessity, but that didn't mean it had to be like the one he would have had with Celestine. The sooner he remembered that and stopped keeping Clara at arm's length despite pressuring her into marrying him, the sooner they could return to something close to the camaraderie they had achieved in the office. Yes, he needed to maintain awareness, not get drawn too deeply into the emotional aspects of marriage. But he and Clara had succeeded as a team for seven years, including the last year of heightened awareness and tension. They could have that again.

He could start tonight. He had planned on dining alone in the upstairs bedroom he'd had transformed into an office when he'd purchased the house from the royal treasury ten years ago. There was plenty of work to be done, but perhaps he could invite her to work with him, have her review some of the upcoming events that had been planned with the Swiss ambassador and his wife—

His phone rang, cutting off his thoughts. He pulled his cell phone out of his coat pocket and frowned.

"Yes?"

"When were you going to tell me you got married?"

Despite the deep-seated loathing he had for his sire, the weak rasp of Daxon's voice still unnerved him.

"There was no need to inform you at this time."

Daxon's cursing was cut off by a horrific-sounding cough.

"Damn it, Alaric, I'm still king of this country. You are my son and heir."

"Officially, yes. Neither of those roles entitles you to know anything about my personal life."

Something shattered in the background. The weaker Daxon got as the cancer advanced through his body, the more prone he'd become to hurling the nearest object at hand into a wall.

"It does when you follow breaking one of the biggest deals I made for our country by marrying your secretary! Osborne is furious with me!"

"The deal where you bound your son to a girl he'd never met to pay off your debts? Yes, I can see where you might want to ensure the exact details of that stayed quiet."

Up ahead on the snow-covered path, Clara paused, her head slightly cocked to one side. Was she listening to the faint twittering of white-winged larks in the trees nearby? Or could she hear his sordid conversation with his bastard of a father?

"I'm in Switzerland at the moment. We can discuss this later, although there's not much else to be discussed."

Silence descended, an unusual sound when Daxon was around. Then it was broken by a harsh, guttural laughter that made Alaric's skin crawl.

"Briony told me, you know. That you married your secretary."

His fingers tightened around his phone. Briony had become aware all too quickly of Daxon's cruel, selfish nature. Surely she hadn't told him everything. Alaric wouldn't put it past his father to sell the details of Clara's pregnancy to a tabloid to make a fast dollar, especially with his reduced financial circumstances.

"And?"

"I find it rich that my perfect son ended his engagement to one of the wealthiest, most beautiful women in the world to marry a pale, shrewish widow."

Protectiveness reared its head.

"You will not speak of my wife in such a manner. Ever."

"I'm sure you had your reasons. What they are, I'll never understand."

"Nor do you need to. Good night, Your Highness."

"One last thing. I can't help but wonder that my son married a woman from his own office so quickly after ending his engagement of nine years."

The smugness seeping from the phone was enough to make him want to throw the device into the lake.

"What are you implying?"

"Just that you can't have fallen in love in just a few weeks. That's not like you. How long have you and your secretary been screwing?" The damning question was followed by another wheezing laugh. "Guess you're more like me than you thought."

He hung up. Clara turned to look at him, her brow furrowed. He wanted to go to her, to take comfort in the touch of her hand on his shoulder or perhaps even lead her to the master suite, lose himself and his fears in the pleasure of her body.

A want that, if he gave in to, would only prove his father right.

"I have business to attend to." He walked past her. "I'll be in my office until late. The staff will attend to you."

It was better this way, he told himself as he strode through the snow. He had eight months until his son or daughter was born. Perhaps by then, he would have himself under control.

CHAPTER NINE

CLARA WOKE TO weak sunlight filtering in through the curtains. She blinked, confused by the white crown molding and robin's-egg-blue walls, before her mind registered her surroundings. It still took a moment to remember that she was in her husband's vacation home on Lake Geneva.

The husband she hadn't seen since the helicopter had taken off and left her alone with him and a small staff. He'd taken a phone call as they'd exited the aircraft. Daxon, judging by the dark glower on his face by the time he'd hung up. He'd seen her as far as the entryway before curtly telling her he had business to attend to and would see her at dinner.

That had been two days ago. Aside from the occasional glimpse in the hall, she hadn't seen him at all.

She closed her eyes and sank back into the welcoming embrace of the feather mattress. Alaric had made it clear that there would be no emotional entanglements where she was concerned. She just hadn't expected for him to withdraw from the relationship they'd had as boss and assistant. She'd agreed to marry the man who engaged in conversation with her, who shared his thoughts on improving Linnaea's job market and treated her like she had something intelligent to say.

Was it too much to ask that he extend her the same respect as his wife?

With a frustrated sigh she threw back the cozy blankets and moved to the window. Snowflakes danced against a light gray sky, adding another layer to the white powder already covering the grounds.

She'd spent the first day exploring the house. She'd fallen in love with its unexpectedly cozy charm, from the mahogany wood floors and matching planked ceilings to the massive bay windows in the living room set behind a burgundy couch heaped with pillows and rugs. The living room, kitchen and dining room all had their own fireplaces, as did each of the bedrooms and the library.

The second day she'd returned to the library, browsing through the books before settling on a murder mystery and curling up in an overstuffed chair by the fireplace. Before she'd taken complete leave of her senses and had sex with her boss on top of his desk, she'd spent many nights in her own apartment reading. But in the past month she'd thrown herself even deeper into her work, spreadsheets and schedules keeping her mind off what had transpired between them.

It had been hard to get into the story at first. But gradually she'd relaxed, enjoying the flow of the words and the escalating intensity as the heroine matched wits with a killer hiding in a cast of suspicious characters. Halfway through, as the heroine questioned several suspects, her eyelids had grown unexpectedly heavy. She'd woken nearly two hours later with a blanket draped over her and a fire roaring in the fireplace. Instead of making her feel cared for and cozy, it had enhanced her loneliness.

Which is why, she decided as she turned away from the window, today she would venture out. Getting outside, going into the nearby town she'd spied on their helicopter ride, would raise her spirits. Then tomorrow she would hunt Alaric down and they would have a conversation about her role as princess and queen-to-be. That he thought she would be satisfied with a life of leisure showed how little he really knew her.

Just a good reminder to not romanticize their relationship in any way.

With that empowering thought and a plan in place, she made quick work of getting dressed and went downstairs. A breakfast had been laid out in the kitchen, including an assortment of Swiss cheese tarts and quiches topped with everything from sautéed onion to chopped apples. Enough to feed an army. She wrinkled her nose at the waste. She'd never seen Alaric engage in excess demonstration like this. He wasn't stingy, but he eschewed any useless posturing or grand gestures if they didn't serve a purpose.

She grabbed a good old-fashioned bagel, spread some cream cheese on it and headed for the front door. A walk around the property would do her good. Then she'd visit the servants' quarters and, if the roads were navigable, would have the driver take her into the picturesque town of Rolle.

She was almost to the front door when a board creaked behind her. She turned as Alaric walked down the stairs.

Her heart leaped into her throat. In dark jeans, a navy sweater with the sleeves pushed up to his elbows and a trace of stubble along his jaw, he looked even more masculine than he usually did in his tailored suits. This Alaric looked rugged, dangerous and all too enticing.

Great job not romanticizing.

"Where are you going?"

"Outside."

He frowned.

"It's cold outside."

She widened her eyes. "What?" She turned and peered out the window. "It snows when it's cold?"

As she turned back, she smacked into a solid wall of muscle. She looked up into narrowed green eyes.

"You're pregnant."

"Yes, pregnant. Not an invalid. I've lived in Linnaea for the past seven years, and I lived in England before that. Plenty of cold winters that I ventured out in."

"Not when you were pregnant."

She wanted to back up, to put physical space between them. Being this close to him, feeling the heat radiate off his muscular frame and the brush of his hard thighs against her legs, made her body respond in ways she didn't want it to. But as soon as she did that, he would have the upper hand.

"Alaric, I've been cooped up in this house for two days. I'm going outside."

She brushed past him and moved to the hall closet. Inside were several new coats, all from brands she knew cost a small fortune. Just like the closet in her room, she thought with a slight sigh as she brushed them aside and pulled out her blue peacoat. She'd brought her own outfits. But Alaric had had someone go shopping for her and stuff the closet in her room with clothes by Versace, Prada and Chanel.

An uncomfortable thought invaded as her hands brushed against the lush velvet of an emerald-colored coat. Miles had done the same thing. At first, she'd accepted his gifts of luxury dresses and expensive jewelry with gratitude, assuming he was showering her with the things he was used to giving. It hadn't been until later when he'd gotten upset at her wearing her old clothes that she realized, too late, the gifts had been his way of molding her into the type of woman he wanted her to be.

Her stomach rolled and she nearly dropped the bagel she still clutched in one hand.

"Then I'm coming with you."

She tugged on her coat, wanting to put as much distance between her and Alaric as possible so she could think. But maybe this was their chance to clear the air. There were so many questions floating around inside her head, so many possibilities of what his sudden change could mean. Unfortunately, without talking to him, she wouldn't find any answers.

"That would be nice."

She looked up to see Alaric blink, the only indicator he was surprised but a gesture she knew very well after working so closely alongside him.

"All right. I'll get my—"

The shrill ring of his phone cut them off. He pulled it out of his pocket and grimaced.

"It's the Swiss ambassador's office."

Her heart sank. She'd spent a year working with Alaric to get the ambassador to agree to an in-person visit to Linnaea to see the country firsthand and all the progress Alaric had made. That the ambassador had finally agreed and come shortly after Alaric's half sister Briony had taken on Linnaea's broken education system had been a stroke of luck that had solidified a new relationship with Switzerland.

It should have been a huge achievement. Instead, it had been overshadowed by their night together and the subsequent weeks of trying to regain her professional foothold. And now…now she had completely been kicked out.

"You should take it. Maybe you could visit with him in person while we're here."

He nodded.

"We'll walk later."

She forced a smile on her face. "Sure."

But she knew later wouldn't come. At least not today. She waited until he was out of sight before she unlocked the front door and walked outside. The cold filled her lungs and gave her a sudden burst of energy, a surprising welcome from the oppressive warmth of the house.

As she walked down the steps and onto the snow-covered circular drive, she let her hand drift down to her belly. She'd only known for a week that she was pregnant. But whenever she thought about the child growing inside her, about holding him or her for the first time in her arms, she knew that no matter what happened with Alaric, she would love this child with every fiber of her being. Her parents had set the example for the kind of mother she wanted to be. If she could be even half the mom her own had been, she would be doing something right.

She'd agreed to marry Alaric because she thought he'd been serious about his intent to be a better father than his own. And, she acknowledged with a small degree of irritation, he would certainly be a better father than Daxon. He was nothing like his sire, even though she sometimes wondered if he ran such a rigid government because he was trying to stay as far away from the erratic rule his father had imposed for so many years.

The wedding ceremony, the dresses…those small touches had eased so much of her trepidation. She knew Alaric didn't love her. But seeing the evidence of his thoughtfulness, that he had meant what he had said about being involved and making their union a pleasant one for both them and their child, had made her cautiously hopeful.

But now…had she read too much into the wedding? Would he be involved in their marriage and their child the way he'd claimed he'd wanted to be? Or would he get so caught up in work he didn't have time for his child?

"No matter what, baby," she whispered to the tiny life inside her, "I'll be here for you."

CHAPTER TEN

ALARIC GLANCED OUT the window and saw with surprise that the sky had already grown dark. He glanced at his watch and swore. It was just after five o'clock. The conversation with the ambassador had taken nearly two hours, followed by a virtual meeting with one of his economic committees and then another meeting with his new brother-in-law, Cass.

Briony and Cass were honeymooning somewhere in the Maldives for three weeks, but Cass had proven to be invested in Linnaea's financial recovery, both literally and figuratively. His commitment was admirable given that Alaric's father had once kicked Cass and his family out of the country.

Toward the end of their meeting, Briony had appeared onscreen, radiant with a big smile on her face as she'd kissed Cass on the cheek and admonished him for working so late before their dinner reservation. Cass's indulgent grin as he'd told Alaric he'd follow up the next day before exiting out of the meeting had ratcheted up Alaric's guilt to new levels. The former playboy billionaire was making time for his wife and he couldn't even set aside five minutes to walk with his new bride.

After his conversation with Daxon, he'd kept his distance the first couple of days. Daxon's harsh laughter had echoed in his ears every time he'd even thought about

Clara. The tiny seed of doubt that had been planted after they'd made love on top of his desk had rooted itself deep in his heart, cunningly winding its way through his veins until it had leaped up and nearly strangled him following the phone call. To look at Clara and think that he had placed her in the same position his father had placed so many women, including Alaric's own mother, had made him so angry at himself he couldn't bear to be around her.

His anger had gradually subsided as he'd focused on work. When he'd gone down to the kitchen to grab a sandwich on the second day, he'd seen the door to the library open and found Clara sleeping in the chair by the fireplace.

Beautiful. That had been his first thought as his eyes had greedily moved over her sleeping form, from the gentle wisps of blond hair escaping from her bun to her dark lashes resting on her pale cheeks. She'd fallen asleep with a book in one hand and her cheek resting in the other. The urge to kneel before her, lean in and gently kiss her awake before scooping her in his arms and taking her back to the master suite had been overwhelming. He'd focused his attention instead on building a fire to ward off the chill seeping through the massive windows overlooking the lake and draping a blanket over her before returning to his office.

Eventually they would introduce physical intimacy into their relationship. He wanted more children. Hopefully she did, too. But when that happened, it needed to be the way his past relationships had been conducted, with a focus solely on physical pleasure. To act when he was feeling this muddled mix of emotions, of anger and guilt and a different type of attraction than what he'd felt for any other woman, was to court chaos.

However, not spending time with his wife was a cowardly move. He'd heard her move around in the adjoining suite that morning and had gone downstairs to join her for breakfast. He hadn't been expecting Clara to agree to his joining her for a walk. And he hadn't missed the disappointment that had flashed in her eyes before she'd withdrawn and told him to take the call.

He'd hesitated, almost invited her to join him...but he hadn't. Daxon's parting words from their last phone conversation had left their mark. It bothered him how much he missed spending time with Clara, her insight and attention to detail. The more he wanted to seek her out, the more he resisted. It had been easier when his engagement to Celestine had kept a barrier between them and he'd been able to just enjoy her company.

Yet by letting Daxon's insults guide his actions, he was giving his father power.

That disquieting thought followed him throughout the house as he searched for his wife. As each room proved to be empty, his frustration turned to concern. Where had she gone?

He pulled out his phone and tried calling her. Concern turned to panic when the call went straight to voice mail. A moment later, he dialed his head of security.

"Yes, Your Highness."

"Where is my wife?"

"She left two hours ago with the driver and Stefan. They went into Rolle."

Clara soaked up the ambience of the little bookstore as she pulled a particularly worn volume off a rickety shelf. The bookstore was in the basement of a restaurant, the worn brick walls and creaky wood floors a haven that had welcomed her with open arms. Even though her designated bodyguard, Stefan, loomed near the doorway, she'd politely but firmly him told not to follow her into the stacks of books.

It would take some getting used to, having a bodyguard shadow her every move when she went out. But for right now, with the low murmur of other customers' voices underlying the soft jazz drifting out from hidden speakers, she could pretend that she was just a normal shopper.

She'd cracked open the book and was scanning the pages when the back of her neck prickled. Pine overrode the scent of old books, wrapping around her with a sensual warmth that let her know exactly who was standing behind her.

"Good evening, Your Highness."

"What are you doing here?"

Alaric's growl made her shiver in a not unpleasant way. Although judging by the thinly veiled anger in his voice, he was not pleased at her trip into town.

"I'm trying to locate my wife, who apparently doesn't understand basic security protocol for members of the royal family."

"Perhaps I would be more familiar if my husband had enough time to say more than 'good morning' to me," she retorted before she could stop herself. If the man wanted to keep her at arm's length, fine, but to keep her prisoner, too? Absolutely not.

Alaric started to say something, but the arrival of a loud tourist group drowned out whatever he was about to say. He grabbed her by the elbow and steered her down the aisle away from the crowd. The narrow shelves zigzagged back and forth in a maze she could have spent hours exploring. Judging by how quickly Alaric was moving, though, she was done exploring for the day.

Claustrophobia pressed in on her. Was this to be her life? Cooped up in the palace or whatever residence they were hiding in, never allowed to go out and do anything resembling a normal life?

They reached the back of the store. Clusters of chairs had been gathered into reading nooks, including several with thick velvet curtains. Alaric guided her into one and undid the gold rope holding the curtains back.

"Do not let anyone within ten feet of us," Alaric barked over her shoulder. She barely caught a glimpse of Stefan turning to stand guard between them and the rest of the bookstore before the curtain fell.

Leaving them in a tight space lit only by the dim glow of a lamp. The intimacy of the space, coupled with the low lighting and the rich, seductive color of the curtains and matching chairs, reminded her of a bordello. It would be all too easy to allow the intimate atmosphere to prompt her into doing something foolish like kissing her husband.

She wrenched her arm free and sat in one of the over-stuffed chairs. The more distance between them, the better. Having an attack of hormones was not in her best interest right now.

"I took a guard with me."

"And failed to notify me that you were leaving the house."

Alaric prowled back and forth, his large frame filling up the small space. He reminded her of a caged panther with his dark hair, black V-neck sweater and matching pants. The sleeves had been pushed up to his elbows, revealing his powerful forearms.

"I didn't realize I had to ask permission every time I stepped out the front door."

"You're a princess now, Clara," he snapped. "A future queen, and carrying the heir to the throne. You can't just waltz off anytime you feel like it. Things are different."

"You're right." She stood and poked a finger in his chest. "Things are different. Let's talk about that, shall we? How long are you going to keep shutting me out and treating me like I'm some spoiled princess when I've done nothing but work my tail off to support you and your country?"

He stepped back. She remembered the first time she

had seen surprise flash in his green eyes. Her first day on the job when she'd offered a suggestion on an email he'd written, he'd looked thunderstruck, like no one had dared oppose anything he said.

"It was not my intention to shut you out."

"But you have." She wasn't going to let him make excuses. If he had a reason for taking away everything from her and locking her inside a gilded cage, she deserved an explanation. She had gone forward with the marriage in good faith, knowing it was the best decision for her child and for the country even if she'd had valid concerns. And this was how dared to treat her?

"What did I do?" She barely kept her voice steady through her anger and hurt. "I'm not Celestine, Alaric. Stop treating me like her."

His expression darkened, warning flickering across his face as his jaw tightened.

"Don't say that."

"Why not? You are. You've taken away my work, told me to relax, basically clipped my wings and stuffed me into a cage. I don't want to be worthless, Alaric. I want to be a partner. I want to keep doing my job."

"You are not worthless," he ground out.

"Yet you treat me like I'm not good for anything but sitting around and eating fancy treats all day." She cast a glance at the curtain and made a conscious effort to lower her voice. No mean feat when her heart was beating frantically, a headache starting to pound in her temples as she looked ahead to her future and saw nothing but confinement, restriction. "At least when I was your assistant we had tea together and even the occasional meal. Now that we're married, you disappear but seem to expect for me to be ready and waiting whenever you come calling. That's not how this is going to work."

She started to poke him again for emphasis, but he caught her wrist in his grasp.

"Don't tell me how things are going to go, Clara. I've always called the shots. Us getting married hasn't changed that."

"Then it seems I've made a mistake."

He froze. "What do you mean?"

"I'm not going to be a prisoner, Alaric. If our honeymoon means I'm going to be stranded in that house by myself for the next two weeks, I'm flying back to Linnaea tomorrow."

She started to pivot away. With a gentle tug he turned her back to him, slid an arm around her waist and pinioned her against his chest.

"Don't leave."

Words of protest rose to her lips. But beneath her anger, her brain picked up the slight hint of apology in his voice.

"Why not?"

He let out a deep sigh.

"I've never been a husband before. When I was engaged to Celestine, she made it perfectly clear in her communications to me what she expected of our relationship. She was to be taken care of financially and, as long as she conducted herself with discretion, would be allowed to do whatever she wanted. In her mind, I owed her since my father essentially bought her and her fortune. Guilt guided my actions."

Her past slammed into her present with sickening clarity. Miles had bought himself a trophy wife. Alaric had snagged himself a future queen. *No, Daxon was behind the contract,* she amended. Alaric was placing too much blame on himself for the arrangement with Celestine. But he had let it continue, even as he'd grown and matured. And now he'd entered into yet another contract with another fiancée he'd purchased, not for her wealth but for the child she carried. Worse still, he was treating her like she was his former fiancée and not the woman he'd been working alongside for the past seven years. That he had so quickly put her into the same box as Celestine, a woman who had seemed to glory in creating as much drama for Alaric as possible, made her chest tighten in pain and shame.

She'd made the same mistake. Again.

She tried to pull away. Alaric kept a firm grip on her waist.

"But you're right."

She leaned back and frowned.

"Are you ill?"

"Not to my knowledge. Why?"

"I think I can count on one hand the number of times you've told me I was right."

His chest rumbled against hers as he chuckled. "I'll mark it on my calendar. It will take me a while to learn how to navigate being both a leader and a husband. You've been a crucial part of this administration, Clara, and I don't intend for you to sit on a couch the rest of your life eating chocolates. I want you to be involved in Linnaea's future."

Ridiculous how such a non-sentimental statement could warm her.

"Well…thank you."

With her anger slowly subsiding, she became acutely aware of just how tightly they were melded together. The last time Alaric had held her this close, the muscles of his arm pressed against her back, she'd been arching against the thrusts of his body as he'd wrapped his fingers in her hair and kissed her senseless. The heat in her veins turned from a fiery burst of anger to a languid, seductive song that made her relax against him.

A growing hardness against her thigh signaled that she wasn't the only one being affected by their surroundings.

Slowly, she looked up. Alaric was staring down at her, his eyes glittering with intensity.

Just like the first, and only, time they'd kissed, she wasn't sure who moved first. Their lips met, one hand pressing against her back and the other sliding down to the curve of her hip, fingers urging her closer until she was straddling his thigh. She clung to his shoulders and sighed, opening her mouth to him. He growled and pressed deeper, his tongue sweeping across her lower lip before he claimed her in an intimate dance that made her heavy with desire.

When they'd kissed in his office, they'd moved at a frenetic pace that had left her breathless. They'd gone from a frantic kiss to him lifting her onto his desk, sliding her skirt up and trailing his fingers over the sensitive skin of her thighs. The moment he'd realized she hadn't been wearing panties beneath the tight evening gown, he'd shuddered and asked if she wanted this. She'd kissed him for an answer as her fingers had undone his zipper before wrapping around his impressive length. It had been incredible, but far too short.

Now, even though the world was just beyond the curtain and waited for them with all of its messiness, now they had a little time.

Her hands moved up to his hair, her fingers tangling in the thick, silky strands. She savored the texture, dropped one hand down to his neck and thrilled at the cords of muscle tight beneath his skin. As her fingertips grazed over his throat, he suddenly slid both hands under her thighs, lifted her up and spun around. Gently, he set her down on one of the chairs, his lips never leaving hers, as his hands drifted down to the hem of her shirt.

"Alaric…"

He froze. And then he was gone, releasing her so quickly she fell back into against the chair.

Alaric moved as far away as he could to the curtain,

his chest rising and falling as his harsh breathing filled the small space.

"Clara… I'm sorry."

"Why?" She stood, reached out to him, tried not to let her hurt show when he jerked away from her touch. Three days ago she hadn't been sure she was ready for the physical intimacies Alaric had hinted would come in time with their marriage. But now, after being reminded of just how truly good they were together, she wanted nothing more than to feel his body against hers again. To feel beautiful and sexy and alive. "We're married now, Alaric."

"I'm a prince. You're a princess. We're next in line to the throne." He gestured to the close confines of the reading nook. "This is beyond inappropriate. If we were to get caught, the media would rain hell on us. It's taken me years to build Linnaea's reputation back up, despite Daxon's and Celestine's efforts to ruin it. I don't want to risk that again."

Mortification stung her cheeks. She'd been concerned that Alaric had placed her in the same category as his ex-fiancée. But could she blame him when she'd ground her hips against his thigh with people just steps away, the same way Celestine had been plastered between those two men at the dance club in New York?

"I'm sorry, Alaric."

"It's my fault, Clara. I brought you back here."

Exhaustion settled into her bones and threatened to drag her down.

"We both made a mistake."

He stirred. "Clara, I don't think—"

"Could we discuss this later in a more private setting?" She nodded toward the curtain. "We've risked enough for tonight."

His mouth thinned into a grim line. He nodded and held back the curtain.

"Go. I'll wait a few minutes for you and Stefan to leave. I'll see you at the house."

She walked past him, keeping as much distance between them as possible. Thankfully there were no customers in sight, no one except Stefan, who stood ten feet away, his eyes scanning the shelves. When he saw her walking toward him, he all but snapped to attention.

"Ready to go, Your Highness?"

"Yes. I'm sorry if I got you in trouble, Stefan."

Stefan blinked in surprise, then bowed his head. "The prince was displeased, but he corrected me on protocol for future outings."

What future outings? she thought glumly as Stefan escorted her to the car waiting outside. It looked like, at least for the foreseeable future, she was truly going to be trapped at the lake house, just like Miles had confined her to the penthouse. After the incident in the reading nook, Alaric would probably disappear into his office for the rest of their honeymoon. And unlike her first marriage, where she'd stayed primarily out of fear and loneliness, now she had to stay for the sake of her unborn child.

At least she'd had eight years of freedom. She had just never pictured trading one cage for another.

CHAPTER ELEVEN

ALARIC HEARD HER before she walked into the kitchen. The soft padding of her footsteps on the wood floor, a gentle melody as she hummed a song. The domestic sounds calmed the heightened state of awareness he'd been in since last night.

Last night when he'd almost taken his wife for the second time in a very inappropriate place that could have caused a disaster.

What was wrong with him? He'd always conducted his previous affairs with the utmost care—faraway cities, upscale hotels that catered to elite clientele and operated with the highest discretion. His previous lovers had been enjoyable. But with Clara…once he'd tasted her, felt the delicious heat of her body and seen her come alive for him, she had become a drug he couldn't get enough of.

Worry slithered into his thoughts, the same worry that had been steadily growing ever since that night. If he was willing to risk everything he'd worked so hard for, everything the people of his country deserved, for a moment of passion, was he fit to lead? Or was he too much like Daxon at his core to be a good representative of the Linnaean people? He'd prided himself on his ability to remain in control. But perhaps it was because he hadn't been faced with the right kind of temptation until now.

A temptation he had married and was expecting a child

with. It wasn't Clara's fault that he behaved like that around her. But it was something he needed to regain control of. Fast. Avoiding Clara would only work for so long. They were married. The news would come out in time. Time to take control of the narrative.

Clara rounded the corner, her eyes focused on a book. Her blond hair had been gathered into a loose bun on top of her head, long strands already falling out to grace the back of her neck and frame her delicate face. Beneath an ivory cardigan she wore pale pink lounge pants and a matching top that clung to the curves of her breasts. Her nipples were pebbled beneath the thin material. His entire body tightened.

Stay focused.

Clara's head suddenly snapped up and her eyes widened as she took in Alaric standing by the kitchen sink.

"What are you doing here?"

"Good morning to you, too."

Her cheeks darkened to a rosy color. "Sorry. Um, good morning. Everything all right?"

"Yes. Why wouldn't it be?"

"It's just… I haven't seen you down here for breakfast since we arrived. I wasn't sure if someone saw…" Her blush deepened. "That is, if something made its way into the news…"

"No." He waved her worry aside. "Nothing like that. Can I get you something to eat?"

She blinked in surprise. "Um… I can get it myself."

"Clara, you're my wife. You're pregnant. And I've left you alone for three days on our honeymoon. I'm making you breakfast."

At last, she nodded.

"That would be nice. Tea and toast, please."

He arched a brow. "Aren't you supposed to be eating for two?"

She grimaced. "Hard to do when I wake up every morning feeling like I've just gotten off a boat in a thunderstorm. I'll eat more later."

He wanted to push, but judging by the queasy look on her face when she glanced at his half-eaten bagel covered in a liberal amount of cream cheese and piled with smoked salmon and cucumber, pushing would result in a very unpleasant morning.

He moved around the kitchen, the silence broken by the occasional clink of the teacup or the whisper as Clara turned a page in her book. It was, he realized with some surprise, a pleasant silence, one he didn't feel the need to fill with inane chatter. The last time he'd taken a lover to dinner—over two years ago—she hadn't stopped talking, from the time he'd picked her up at her hotel in Paris until he'd dropped her off after a theater performance. She'd coyly invited him up to her room, but he hadn't been able to muster even the faintest desire to join her in her bed.

He hadn't been with anyone since. Truthfully, even though he'd told himself it was his upcoming marriage to Celestine that had led to his streak of celibacy, he'd grown tired of the brief flings, the businesslike arrangement of his sexual encounters, the lack of a connection beyond mutual physical pleasure. Pleasure that had dulled over the years, each encounter bleeding into the next.

There had been, too, a dull throb that had grown into an ache with each rendezvous. He'd always held a part of himself back from his previous lovers, knowing nothing would come of their time together. Perhaps that was why he'd sought out the women he had: emotionally distant, independently wealthy, few mutual interests that would spark something beyond a pleasantly shared meal and good sex.

There hadn't been a single woman he'd been with over the years who would be like Clara was now: content to spend a few minutes in silence reading as he made her breakfast.

This was more what he had envisioned when he had proposed to Clara, this satisfying coexistence.

He set a plate with lightly buttered toast and a teacup in front of her.

"Thank you," she said with a smile as if he'd just given her a diamond bracelet.

That was one of the things he'd always liked about Clara, he reflected as he sat across from her. Despite her reputation for being his hard-nosed executive assistant, she could also be one of the most relaxed, easygoing people he'd ever met.

Which made his treatment of her the last few days even more unacceptable.

"What would you think about having dinner tonight?"

She looked up. "Dinner?"

"Yes."

A frown creased her brow. "Breakfast and dinner in one day. Why do I feel like you're about to tell me something bad?"

He chuckled. "Nothing so sinister. You were right. I've overreacted. While there will be more regulations on travel, I can't keep you locked in the house."

One dark blond brow arched up as her lips twisted into a sardonic smile that made his blood stir.

"Glad to know we're on the same page."

"It won't be the same as it was when you were my secretary."

"Executive assistant."

He bit back a grin.

"Yes, assistant. But, Clara, I do need to know when you're going to be gone. It's not some obsessive need to control you. The world is more dangerous for members of a royal family. Even though the majority of our country and

Switzerland support the treaty, there are those who are vehemently opposed. I have to keep you and our child safe."

She looked down at her toast for a moment before finally nodding. "I understand. I don't like it, but I understand."

"I know it's not what you probably envisioned when you married me."

"I never envisioned marrying you at all." A slight grin softened the sting of her words, although it disappeared quickly as her expression darkened. "It's just… I haven't told you much about my marriage to Miles."

Just hearing the man's name sent an unexpected bolt of jealousy through him.

"No, you haven't."

"I hinted that it was not a pleasant marriage." She pulled the tea bag out of her cup and watched it twirl back and forth, drops of amber liquid falling onto her plate. "He became very controlling. He didn't like me leaving his apartment in London without him or his mother accompanying me to wherever I was going. His mother picked out what I wore, took me to her hair stylist." She set the tea bag down and stared at the steam rising off the surface. "I wasn't my own person anymore."

Anger churned in his gut, along with the familiar uncomfortableness of guilt. Anger that Miles and his abominable-sounding mother had treated Clara so horribly, and guilt that, while not as extreme, he had been pushing Clara in a similar manner with his restrictions and lack of attention. He'd taken away her job, something she'd been very good at, because he had been uncertain of how he would feel working so closely with her now that their roles had changed. Not because it was the best thing for Clara or for Linnaea, but because of his own discomfort.

She looked up with a small smile. "When you told me I had to ask you about where I was going, I panicked. I was afraid I was falling back into a similar place I had been with Miles. But I understand the difference, the issue of security."

If he'd thought he couldn't feel any more guilty, her understanding only added to the weight pressing on his shoulders.

"I appreciate that, Clara. But I should have talked with you before issuing commands. We worked well together before this change in our relationship, and I should have trusted you by talking to you."

She paused for a moment before nodding once.

"Thank you, Alaric."

"There's nothing to thank me for. I didn't handle this well. Which is why I have two proposals."

A teasing light made her blue eyes sparkle. "The last proposal you made was certainly interesting."

"Nothing so drastic this time. The first is that I'd like for you to work with me today. I could use your insight on some of the communications going to the ambassador's staff and a meeting we're setting up next month with the president of the Swiss Confederation."

Her shoulders sagged in relief. "That sounds nice. I never thought I'd miss work so much." She tapped a finger on her book. "I've enjoyed reading, but this is much more time than I'm used to."

"Which brings me to my second point. Would you like to have dinner with me tonight? There's a restaurant just outside of Rolle."

"Are you comfortable with going out and being seen by the public?"

"It's something that needs to happen. I think it would be good for both of us to get out of the house, too, and see some of the local sights. Isn't that what a honeymoon is for?"

The local sight Alaric had picked for their dinner proved to be one of the most exclusive restaurants on the shores of Lake Geneva. Perched on a blufftop that overlooked the lake, the main dining room was dotted with intimate tables and flickering candles. A stone fireplace dominated one side of the room, while the other three featured floor-to-ceiling windows with incredible views of the country-side. Their waiter guided them around the perimeter to a private room tucked off to the side, complete with its own small fireplace and a table set for two. A vase with a red rose stood in stark relief against the white tablecloth, two small tealights flickering on either side of the vase.

Clara tried to ignore the whispers she heard behind them as the waiter pulled out her chair. When she glanced at the dining room, it was to see numerous heads whipping around in a fatal attempt not to be caught starting.

"I'm guessing we'll be featured on the morning news."

Alaric glanced at the curious diners and shrugged. "It was time. I had our public relations office send out a press release tonight anyway."

"You what?"

He looked up at her, his brows drawing together in a frown. "I'd asked you earlier about sharing our pictures from the wedding."

He had, she acknowledged. But she hadn't expected a full media campaign.

"I thought that would be something we'd do together."

"It's not like a standard civilian marriage, Clara. Anything that goes public like that has to go through our PR department."

She knew that. Of course she knew that. Since the department had been formed a couple months ago, she'd sent over numerous articles and sound bites for them to put together into a story or for sharing the palace's social media. But being restricted herself was going to take some getting used to.

Part of her wanted to fold in on herself, the way she used

to with Miles. It had been a habit she'd developed when they'd dated. Whenever he would shoot her down, she'd agree and withdraw. It avoided conflict and kept things at least manageable between the two of them. After her marriage, she'd swung the other direction, standing firm in almost every situation and not budging an inch. It had helped her on numerous occasions. But it had also kept people at arm's length. It hadn't been until she'd grown closer to Meira and started talking more with Briony that she'd realized just how much she'd used her supposed spine of steel to keep herself safe.

There had to be a compromise between the two parts of herself.

"Could I be involved in decisions like that?"

Alaric looked up from the menu in surprise. "What?"

"I understand the need to follow protocol," she said, her words tumbling over each other as nerves got the better of her. "I've lived it for seven years. I've enforced it more times than I can count. But I'd like to feel like a partner in this relationship as much as possible. Even just being told what's going to happen, instead of being told after the fact, would make me feel like I'm respected and not just an ornamental chess piece being moved around the board."

Alaric stared at her for a long moment, his eyes narrowed in thought. Part of her felt like she'd overstepped. But the other part, the part that had gone toe to toe with His Royal Highness, struggled to not say more and push her case.

Alaric surprised her by reaching across the table and grabbing her hand in a light grasp.

"A reasonable request. I will most likely need to be reminded from time to time."

She squeezed his fingers before letting go of his hand and picking up her own menu. "Thank you, Alaric."

The rest of the evening passed in a very pleasant fashion. Their waiter brought them dishes like Swiss onion soup, saffron risotto with creamy baked mushrooms and *Zurcher Pfarrhaustorte*, a tart stuffed with grated apples, toasted nuts and cinnamon and baked to perfection. For the first time since she'd known Alaric, their conversation didn't revolve around political deals or meetings or upcoming legislation. She told him about her parents, from reading in the corner of her father's mechanic shop while he worked on cars to summers spent at the beach with both of her parents. He surprised her by sharing memories of his mother and growing up in the palace, including one time when his mother had taught him how to slide down the banister in the main hall and he'd nearly taken out a visiting dignitary.

"She sounds like a wonderful mother," Clara said with a laugh.

"She was." Alaric's expression darkened slightly. "She was taken too soon."

Clara looked down at her half-eaten tart. She knew that the queen had passed away quickly and unexpectedly of a heart attack years ago. Judging by the look on Alaric's face, though, there was more to the story.

There always was.

She glanced toward the dining room again. Would Temperance and Stanley see the press release about her marriage? Would they connect the dots, that their former daughter-in-law had married the future king of Linnaea? They lived in Los Angeles now, a world away from Eastern Europe. But technology had connected the farthest corners of the earth. As much as she wanted to believe there was a chance they'd miss it, she imagined it was only a matter of time.

The real question was, what would they do when they found out? Would they leave her alone, as they had these past eight years? Or would they try to seek revenge, angry that their former daughter-in-law was trying to move on with her life?

She yanked herself out of the past. Alaric had just confided something intensely personal and here she was thinking about herself.

"Losing a mother is never easy." She glanced down at her stomach. "If...if it's a girl, we could name her Marianne. In honor of her."

The smile that broke across Alaric's face warmed her from head to toe. She'd never seen such joy on his face.

"I would like that, Clara. Very much. Unless you'd prefer to name her after your mother?"

"We could use her name as a middle name. It would work perfectly, actually. Rose."

"Princess Marianne Rose Van Ambrose. It is perfect." He cocked his head to one side. "You don't speak much about your parents."

Her chest tightened.

"It's hard to," she finally said. "They were..." She smiled even as she barely spoke past the lump in her throat. "They were wonderful."

Alaric reached across the table and threaded his fingers through hers in a gesture that, judging by his rapid blinking, surprised both of them. Slowly, she curled her own hand around his.

"They were older. My father contracted cancer. It ran in his family. He died when I was a teenager. And then my mom..." She focused her gaze on her plate. "It seems so stupid. Pneumonia. Something you hear about all the time but you think there's no way it could happen to your family. And then it does and you're alone and then you make foolish decisions."

Alaric's grip tightened on hers.

"Your marriage to Miles."

She nodded, surprised by how easily the words suddenly came. It had taken several glasses of wine to get to the point of confiding in Meira last summer. But somehow, sitting in the restaurant with Alaric holding her hand, she felt safe.

"I was lonely. Young. I didn't know hardly anyone in London. I mistook distraction from my grief for something more."

"Judging by the self-loathing in your voice, it's something you still haven't forgiven yourself for."

Her head snapped up. He stared at her, his gaze intense but kind.

"Not completely, no. It's hard to trust yourself or others after making such a big mistake."

Alaric's chuckle held a note of sadness. "I understand. I said something similar to Cass, actually, when he nearly torpedoed his relationship with my sister."

She laughed. "You gave Prince Cassius Adama relationship advice?"

"I did. And he took it."

"What did you say?"

The mirth disappeared from Alaric's face, replaced by a distant thoughtfulness. His thumb started to trace lazy circles on the back of her hand. Each subsequent stroke upped the heat slowly building inside her. Such a simple touch, but it made her feel cared for.

"That he was making decisions based on horrible examples he'd seen of relationships. That it was easier for him to stay withdrawn because getting involved was too scary."

Her mouth dropped open.

"That's…very insightful."

And almost frightening. He could have been describing her. Or, she realized with a start, himself. His parents' marriage, and his father's numerous affairs, were hardly sterling examples of love.

She gazed at him, her eyes running over the sharp

planes of his face, his full lips relaxed into a slight smile. He'd smiled more in the last hour than he had in the past year. He hadn't judged her for her hasty decisions.

She swallowed hard. Suddenly she wanted to tell him everything, to have him see her fully as no other person had.

He squeezed her hand again before he released it. The loss of his touch robbed her of her moment of confidence.

"Tell me more about your parents. It sounds like you at least had a positive example of a marriage."

She shoved her negative musings away and obliged his request, reminiscing about collecting shells and picnicking on the sand on a checkered blanket her mother had sewn. By the time Alaric escorted her out to the car, her good mood was restored.

Alaric sat across from her as he had on the ride in. She looked out the window as their driver navigated out of town. A few lights sparkled here and there in the windows of the elegant homes scattered along the water's edge. The pleasant hum of the car's engine, the dark interior and the heated leather seats made her drowsy.

I'll just close my eyes for a moment.

"Clara?"

A voice seemed to come from far away, a deep voice that wrapped her in a pleasant warmth.

"Mmm?"

"We're home."

"Mmm."

She didn't want to open her eyes, didn't want to get up. This was the most relaxed she'd felt in days.

A sensation that promptly disappeared when an arm slid under her legs and another slid around her back. Her eyes flew open as Alaric hauled her into his arms and got out of the car.

"Alaric, what are you doing?"

"Carrying you inside." He nodded to the driver, who was watching them with a smile on his face. "Good night, Frederick."

"Your Highness."

She buried her face in Alaric's coat.

"I'm mortified."

"Why?"

"You're carrying me like I'm a child."

"No, I'm carrying the woman who's carrying my child."

She thought he would set her down on the front porch. But he continued inside, up the stairs and down the hall as if she weighed nothing more than a piece of paper. Another unexpected moment that, like the sweet additions to their wedding, wound its way through her body and wrapped around her heart. Slowly, she allowed herself to relax in his arms, to savor the strength of his grasp.

It would be so easy to get used to being treated like this. So easy to let herself open up to a man who made her feel treasured with his surprisingly romantic gestures.

Finally, they reached her door.

"You can set me down now."

He opened the door and stepped inside. The room, which had felt as large as her apartment at the palace, seemed to shrink as he walked to the bed and gently laid her down.

"Good night, Clara."

He started to pull away, but she kept her arms looped around his neck. Whether it was the incredible food or the enjoyable conversation or her self-reflection at dinner, she couldn't say. But something emboldened her to lean up and press her lips against Alaric's.

"Thank you for a wonderful evening," she whispered as she started to pull away.

Alaric's hands slid into her hair and slowly tugged her back against him. He sat on the edge of the bed as he deepened their kiss, his lips firm against hers. Without the franticness of the first time they'd kissed, or the threat of discovery and the tension from their argument that had hovered over them the second time, there was nothing but a sense of delicious freedom and wantonness as she leaned into him.

She had intended to only kiss him. But when his fingers crept beneath the collar of her coat and pushed the fabric off her shoulders, she sucked in a shuddering breath. Was she ready for this? Could she sleep with her husband knowing that it wouldn't lead to anything more than the pleasant camaraderie they already shared?

His fingers slid under the strap of her dress, sending a shiver across her skin. He slowly continued to pull the dress down until she was bare from the waist up, sitting on her bed in a puddle of black satin. She opened her eyes as Alaric pulled back, his gaze shimmering with emerald fire as he grasped her hands in his and held her arms out away from her body. Her first instinct was to cover herself as her old insecurities rose up. He'd never seen her nude. What if he didn't like what he saw?

"You're beautiful, Clara." He released one of her hands to cup her breast, the soft touch sending heat spiraling through her veins. "So beautiful."

Her doubts fled. Only desire remained as she lay back on the bed.

"Make love to me, Alaric."

CHAPTER TWELVE

ALARIC STARED AT HER. For one frightening moment, there was nothing but silence.

And then his gaze moved down her body. His eyes glowed molten green as he caressed her naked body, each lingering look more intimate and scorching than the last. She reached down, sucked in a deep breath, and slowly pushed the rest of her dress off, including the silk panties that had clung to her hips like a second skin.

He didn't move, didn't flinch, just watched as she undressed for him. She felt wonderfully brazen, wanton and seductive, her hands gliding down her own body and back up as she slipped off her shoes and lay back once more against the pillows.

He took one step forward. She pushed herself up onto her elbows, her eyes drifting down to his hips. Any lingering doubts were banished by the hard evidence between his thighs. Despite her lying naked before him, a blush stole over her cheeks.

"I don't think our current situation is fair."

Was that her voice? Husky, low, seductive?

A wicked grin she would never have imagined Alaric was capable of if she hadn't seen it crept over his handsome face and made her belly tighten.

"What are you going to do about it?"

The challenge reverberated through her. She paused,

self-doubt creeping in. Their first time, their only time, had been when he'd been raw and hurting. What if their explosive chemistry had been the result of a moment in time? She'd only been with Miles. She wasn't experienced like she assumed Alaric's previous lovers had been.

Stop.

A tiny voice whispered the command in her ear. She listened, steadied her breathing and let herself relax, focused on the warmth of desire that had been building since he'd carried her inside the house. Her fears melted away as she slowly stood and crossed to him. When she pulled the hem of his shirt from his pants, her fingers grazing the chiseled muscles of his abdomen, he hissed.

"Taking your time?"

His growl rippled over her, emboldened her as she slowly undid his buttons.

"We didn't get much time in your office." She leaned down and placed a kiss to his bared chest. His body went rigid beneath her touch. "Now would seem an appropriate moment to go slow."

He stood still as she undid his tie, slid his shirt and suit jacket from his shoulders. He tensed but didn't stop her as she unbuckled his belt. She hooked her fingers in the waistband of his pants and boxers and slowly eased them down over his muscular thighs, the low rumbling sound in his throat sending an electrifying thrill through her.

When her fingers grazed his impressive length and she felt him swell even more against the slightest touch, an urge seized her. She sank to her knees.

"Clara, you don't have to…"

His words trailed off and ended in a guttural moan as she wrapped one hand around the base of his hardness and took him in her mouth. She loved the way his hips arched forward, his hands tangling in her hair as he groaned her name. When she looked up, it was to see him with his head thrown back, his jaw taut. He looked powerful, strong and on the verge of losing control.

Because of her. Because of how she touched him.

That carnal knowledge spurred her on as she cupped him, savored the ever-increasing hardness of his body.

"Clara."

He bit her name out. Strong hands reached down and hauled her to her feet, pressing her body against his, naked skin to naked skin. Her lips parted on a gasp just as he kissed her, his tongue sweeping into her mouth as he laid claim to her.

"Fair is fair, wife."

Before she could blink, he swept her into his arms and deposited her on the bed. He shed the rest of his clothes before joining her, caging her beneath his body. She started to part her legs. He kissed her again, swiftly, and then pulled back with a chuckle.

"Not yet."

He trailed his lips down her neck to her breasts, circling one globe and then the other with the tip of his tongue before capturing each peak in his mouth and sucking with long, drawn-out movements that made her writhe beneath him as her fingers tangled in his hair. He continued his sensual onslaught, moving down over her belly, her hips, until he paused just above her most sensitive skin.

Her thighs pressed together of their own accord. The few times she and Miles had had sex, it had been fleeting, a few thrusts for his own pleasure and then it was over. She'd never experienced a man touching her the way Alaric was touching her now.

He pressed a kiss to her core, an open-mouthed caress that made her body curve up into his touch before she could stop herself.

"Alaric."

He parted her legs, and she let him. How could she stop

him when he looked at her with gleaming eyes filled with male satisfaction and appreciation? Appreciation for *her* body. When he leaned down and his tongue danced over her skin, she cried out, asking him, begging him as the tension built inside her, wound her so tight as pleasure spiraled from his touch throughout her body.

Just as she felt herself on the edge of finally achieving release, he pulled back with a dark chuckle.

"Alaric!" she cried out, her hands reaching for him. "That's not—"

He moved up her body with lightning speed and pinned her to the mattress with his weight, one hand forming to the curve of her hip as the other smoothed the hair back from her forehead. He stared at her for a moment, as if seeing her for the first time, some unknown emotion glittering in the green depths.

"I want to be inside you this first time."

She blinked back the sudden hot tears at his words.

"I don't know if you remember, but we already did this once," she said with a cheeky smile to cover her emotional response.

"Our first time as husband and wife."

What did one say to such an unexpected and tender sentiment? He gave her little time to ponder the question as he pressed the tip of his hardness against her and robbed her of her voice. Slowly, he slid inside her, her body stretching to accommodate him, her hips cradling his thighs until he filled her.

He kissed her once more, soft and gentle, before he began to move with long, slow thrusts. She met every stroke, her hands caressing his back, her fingers gliding over his face as she kissed his jaw, his cheek, his nose, his lips.

The crescendo built inside her once more, taking her higher with every touch.

"Alaric…"

"Clara."

She burst into a thousand pieces, riding a wave of pleasure so intense she swore she saw stars. Her nails raked down his back, and he followed a moment later, burying his face against her shoulder as he shuddered in her arms.

He relaxed against her, the weight of his body keeping her pinned in place. She sighed as her fingers drifted languidly over his back, his shoulders, his neck, his skin covered in a fine sheen of sweat.

"I like slow."

His words teased a chuckle out of her.

"Me, too."

He lifted his head and shot her the most carefree, relaxed smile she'd ever seen.

One that faded a moment later as he glanced at the clock.

"It's getting late."

"So?"

He started to push up. "I should go." He waved his hand at the bed. "I don't…that is…"

She forced a smile to her face. "I understand. This was…nice."

He arched a brow. "Nice?"

"Okay, very nice."

He eased himself back down. "I don't know how to be a husband, Clara."

"I can't say I have that much experience being a wife." She gestured toward the door. "You were up-front with me, Alaric. I know what to expect and what not to. If staying here crosses a boundary for you, I don't want you to feel like you have to stay."

Even though I really want you to.

Miles had always kept a separate bed in his own master suite. She'd never woken up next to him. Not that she'd ever wanted to, not when she didn't know if she'd wake up in bed with the charmer or an abusive drunk.

But with Alaric…

She gave herself a slight shake. He wasn't comfortable. No point in entertaining what-ifs.

A frown darkened his face.

"It's not…" He glanced around the bed. "How about I lie here with you? Just for a bit?"

"Alaric, I'm a big girl. You don't—"

Before she could finish her sentence, he rolled to the side, slid an arm beneath her waist and pulled her against his chest. Even though they'd just made love, the intimacy of being pressed against him sent a languid wave of heat through her body.

She waited for a moment, then slowly let herself relax, her head dropping onto his shoulder as she shyly rested one hand on his chest.

"Just for a bit," she murmured as her eyes slowly closed.

It was still dark when Alaric awoke. Clara's breath feathered across his chest, her head resting just above his heart, one hand curled against his skin. He gave in to his first inclination, to gently trace his fingers up and down her back and kiss the top of her silken head. She murmured in her sleep and curled deeper into his embrace.

He had never fallen asleep with any of his past lovers, much less woken up in their bed. It was an intimacy he didn't entertain. With the clock ticking on his upcoming marriage to Celestine, there had been no point in risking a woman developing any affection for him. More complications and messy tabloid coverage had been the last thing he'd needed.

But, he realized as his fingers trailed down Clara's spine, over the curve of her hip, lingered on the slight swelling of her belly, he had missed out on something truly incredible in doing so.

He wasn't so blind to emotions that he had missed the disappointment in Clara's eyes when he'd started to leave, nor her attempts at insisting she was fine if he didn't stay. The part he hadn't shared, that had made him start to leave in the first place, was that he had wanted to stay. No woman had ever made him want to stay.

Until Clara.

He hadn't planned on falling asleep with her. But as he'd lain there in the dark, as she'd slowly relaxed against him and slipped into slumber in the circle of his arms, he hadn't wanted to disturb her. He'd told himself he would just rest his eyes.

And now here he was, in his wife's bed, not wanting to be anywhere else. Being at the lake house with her, without the busyness of the palace, the constant meetings and without his forced engagement hanging over his head, made him even more aware of the traits he liked about his wife. Her kindness, her support, her acceptance of him. Her argument, too, that she be allowed to resume her roles, had induced simultaneous feelings of guilt and an admiration made all the more potent by the tenderness creeping in with every moment spent in her presence. One of his chief regrets about Celestine had been how little she had cared about Linnaea. She had ignored or flat-out refused to attend any of the special events he'd invited her to, the last being the art museum opening in Eira in the fall.

Clara stirred in his arms, her fingernails grazing his chest and reigniting the spark of desire that had blazed into an inferno so intense he'd barely been able to breathe past his desire when she'd lain back on the bed and asked him to make love to her. He had an incredible wife who shared his passion for his country, who wanted to be involved, who was carrying his child.

Was it too much to hope that, at last, everything in his life was finally on the right track?

His hand drifted back up and grazed the underside of her breast. A soft moan escaped her lips. His fingers quested higher, drifted over a pebbled nipple with the lightest caress. Clara's eyes fluttered open as a slow smile spread across her face.

"Alaric?"

He gently rolled her onto her back, pinning her hips with his. She gasped and squirmed against his growing hardness. He reached up, grasped her wrists in one hand and held them above her head.

"Not fair," she laughed up at him.

"Perhaps this will be more to your liking."

He leaned down and captured one nipple in her mouth, grazing his teeth over the sensitive bud. She arched up into his touch and moaned his name. The sound of her voice stripped away any semblance of restraint. His other hand drifted down to the wetness between her thighs. He stroked her skin, slid one finger, then two, into her wet heat, nearly came undone when she clenched around him.

"Alaric, please!"

He nudged her thighs apart and slid inside, shuddering as she surrounded him, her bare breasts pressing against his chest while he continued to hold her hands captive above her head. Each stroke was just a bit harder, his rhythm quickening as his pleasure and desire soared to a fever pitch.

She cried out, coming undone once more. He followed a moment later. Molten heat flooded his veins. He released her wrists, meeting her halfway as their arms flew around each other, their lips pressed together until he couldn't tell where he ended and she began.

CHAPTER THIRTEEN

CLARA FOCUSED ON the screen of the laptop Alaric had procured for her, the words blurring. She'd reread the email she didn't know how many times. She cast a glance at the door he'd disappeared out of to take a call. Alaric's ringing phone had startled them both out of a deep sleep just after dawn. For a moment, she'd been too content wrapped up in the warmth of his arms and snuggled against his naked body to pay much attention. But when the unknown caller had called again, Alaric had answered with barely concealed irritation that had quickly turned to brusque concern. Daxon had taken a turn for the worse early that morning. The doctors said he was stable for now, but they'd reduced his time from a year down to just a few months at best.

As much pain as Daxon had caused, Clara hadn't missed the worry on Alaric's face as he'd spoken with the palace physician.

Finally, she slammed her computer shut. She needed to get up and move around, refocus before she did any more work. Selfish as it was, it wasn't just her concern for Alaric and Daxon.

No, after the physical and emotional closeness of yesterday, it was hard to keep the feelings that had been growing for the past year at bay. From making her breakfast and listening to her past to his happiness at her name suggestion for the baby and the incredible intimacy they'd shared last night, she was struggling to not let her emotions have free rein.

What, she asked herself for the hundredth time in the past twenty-four hours, was she feeling for her husband? Was it a naturally developing affection for her new partner? Or was it something more?

She heaved a frustrated sigh and headed for the door. She stepped out into the hall just as Alaric walked around the corner, one hand wrapped around his phone, the other curled into a fist.

"What happened?"

He shook his head.

"The old man's a damned fool. He's refusing most recommendations. Said he knows the end is near and he's going to live it on his terms, not some damned doctor's."

She reached out slowly and laid a tentative hand on his arm. When he didn't pull away, she moved closer and moved her hand to his back, rubbing gently at the tension knotting his muscles.

"I was about to go on a walk, get out and move a bit. Why don't you join me?"

He started to shake his head again.

"Alaric. I think it would be good for you. You're no good to anyone, especially yourself, if you're wound up."

Finally, he nodded. Five minutes later they were walking down the stone path that led to the house's private dock. She stayed silent, soaking in the sounds surrounding them: the distant chirping of a bird, the soft lapping of the water against the shore as a brisk wind danced across the water, the creak of the dock as they stepped onto the wood decking.

It wasn't until they'd reached the end of the pier, gazing out over the water, that he spoke.

"I hate him."

Her heart twisted in her chest. She'd never known any-thing but love for her father. She couldn't imagine hav-ing a father like Daxon, let alone fathom how Alaric had turned into the man he was today with such a selfish sire.

"I hate him," Alaric repeated, his eyes distant as he stared at the mountain peaks on the other side of the lake, "yet when I heard that he was so close to death, I felt sad."

She reached out, grabbed his gloved hand. His fingers lay limp for a moment before entwining with hers.

"Understandable."

His harsh bark of laughter echoed out over the water.

"How? How is it understandable that I feel anything akin to regret for that sad excuse of a human being?" His head whipped around, his face thunderous. "He killed my mother. Not outright murder, but he brought on her heart attack. Every time he ended up in the papers, one of his mistresses on his arm, she withered away a little bit more until there was nothing left. I have no doubt that his ac-tions caused her heart attack. The bastard didn't even visit her in the hospital, just showed up at her funeral to be in the pictures."

Clara's lips parted in shock. Daxon hadn't been as pro-lific in his romantic conquests in the years she'd been with the palace. She'd heard plenty of rumors, seen old copies of newspapers. He'd leered at her the few times she'd in-teracted with him personally. But she'd never personally been subjugated to the torment he'd put his son and wife through.

"He couldn't have known when he created that mar-riage contract that Celestine would turn into the woman she became. But sometimes, when I saw the pictures of what she was doing, it was like reliving the worst years of my father's debauchery."

"Why didn't you break it off sooner?"

"I couldn't. Linnaea needed the money our marriage

would bring in. It wasn't until Cass's offer of a dowry in exchange for marrying Briony that the possibility of breaking it off was on the table. Even then, I didn't want to break my word."

He said it matter-of-factly, the prince who had long ago accepted his fate to benefit his people. Her heart broke for the man who had sacrificed so much even as she felt herself falling over the edge, falling deeper for someone who had suffered time and time again to live up to his commitments.

"The more she appeared in the tabloids, the more I built my walls up. I felt nothing for her because by then I had closed myself off. But Daxon…" His voice trailed off. "There were moments growing up, times when I saw what my mother must have seen in him. It created a longing that, to this day, I still can't shake."

"He's your father." She squeezed his hand. "Even if it doesn't make sense logically, it's natural to want their love no matter how much they hurt us. There's a lot to mourn in a situation like this."

"Did you mourn Miles?"

The random question threw her. She started to pull her hand away, but he tightened his grip.

"Don't pull away from me, Clara." Sorrow made his voice heavy. "Not now."

She swallowed hard, trying to find the right words.

"In a way I did. I felt like I mourned more what I thought we had the first month we dated, the possibility of what could have been."

Alaric nodded.

"What might have been," he echoed. "Miles died outside of Chamonix in France?"

The lingering sense of nausea that was never far away spiraled upward and shot into her throat. She swallowed hard, noting his eyes flickering to her throat.

"Yes."

"A car accident."

He stumbled on his way to the car. Dropped the keys on the ground. She knew he was too drunk to drive, knew she should stop him. But she didn't. Because she was a coward.

"Yes."

He was fishing. She'd seen him use this tactic plenty of times in meetings, at political dinners, with his own father. He was good...very good at portraying himself as the one with all the answers.

She debated for a moment. If she gave him part of the truth, perhaps it would be enough to get him to back down.

"Miles was drunk." She looked down, allowing the guilt she lived with every day to finally show. "I...we were at a party at a friend's chalet. He grabbed the keys and slapped me when I suggested I drive." She rapidly blinked away the unexpected tears burning behind her eyes. "He was angry that I suggested he not drive in front of his friends."

"We do a background check on all of our employees. Miles's death showed as part of yours. I never saw anything about him being intoxicated."

"When you have parents as wealthy as Miles, you can make the police and the media say whatever you want."

Thank God she'd had the wherewithal to get a copy of the toxicology report before they'd manipulated the truth, tried to paint her as the perpetrator of the accident.

Although it wouldn't have been far off.

Sympathy shone in Alaric's eyes, as if he finally understood her.

If only you knew the whole truth. Would you still want to make love to me? Have a child with me when I cost someone his life because I was too weak to stop him?

"You feel guilty for not stopping him."

She wanted so badly to tell him. But what if he looked at her not with the tenderness of last night but with disgust? Daxon's affairs and Celestine's partying were nothing compared to a young man losing his life.

"Yes."

The choke in her voice was real. She didn't relive those minutes as often as she used to. But certain anniversaries, like his death and their wedding, brought them back with vivid force, along with a list of *should have done this* and *could have done that*. She could have not married Miles. She should have put her foot down about him driving that night. She shouldn't have grabbed the wheel…

"I'm sorry, Clara."

"Thank you."

He scrubbed a hand over his face. "I shouldn't have sprung that on you. I needed to focus on something else. Although it helps."

"It does?"

"Yes. Being able to talk. Being with someone who understands the complex pain of losing someone you don't really like but will still mourn in a way after they're gone."

A storm of emotions descended on her. A sense of freedom at having finally shared a small part of her story. Pride that she had at last had enough confidence to speak.

But beneath that little thread of light churned something far darker and dangerous: fear. She'd opened the lock on her past and let Alaric see inside. Eventually, she would have to tell him everything. It was the right thing to do and, after what he'd shared about the impact his father's scandalous behavior had had not just on the country but on Alaric and his mother, he deserved to know what had happened, to prepare in the event that the truth of Miles's accident ever came out.

She would have to…but not just yet. Alaric had revealed the effects Daxon's and Celestine's behavior had had on his views toward love and romance. He would never be able to let himself care for her the way she was coming to care about him.

But he did feel something, some sort of affection and respect that had strengthened over the course of their honeymoon. If she revealed the full truth too soon and, worse, that she had concealed so much from him, would he ever be able to forgive her? Would their fledgling relationship survive, or would it be crushed under the weight of her deceit before it had a chance to grow?

A breeze stirred the bare branches of the trees overhead. A shiver racked her body, although whether it was the cold or her internal struggle, she couldn't say. Alaric moved behind her and wrapped his arms around her, pulling her back against his chest. She banished her frightened thoughts and sank into his embrace, focusing on the weight of his arms, the dull thud of his heartbeat against her back, the lingering scent of pine she'd come to know so well.

They stood there until the tips of their noses had turned red with cold. They returned to the house as the sky dimmed. When he paused at the bottom of the stairs, she reached out her hand. He followed her up the stairs and into her room. He kissed her slowly, undressed her even slower. She returned each caress, pressing her lips to the sensitive skin of his wrist, savored the hiss of his breath at her touch.

When he laid her back on the bed and covered her naked body with his, she parted her thighs and arched into the thrust of his hips as he slid inside her. He held her in his arms as they matched each other's rhythm, deep languid movements that slowly carried them up to the peak of pleasure.

After, he tugged her into the curve of his body, his chest pressed against her back. She listened as his breathing deepened and he slipped into sleep.

But every time she closed her eyes, sleep eluded her,

chased away by the memories of that awful night when she'd yanked the wheel out of her husband's hands and sent the car careering off the road.

Would she ever escape her past?

CHAPTER FOURTEEN

BRIONY'S MOUTH DROPPED open as she walked into the lake house.

"This looks like something from the coast of Maine!"

Clara smiled. "I've never been to the States before."

"You'd love it," Briony assured her. "Little coastal towns with houses just like this. Big windows, wood interiors, porches galore." She enveloped her big brother in an enthusiastic hug. Clara watched as he returned her embrace, a smile teasing his lips.

As much as Clara had been enjoying her time with Alaric, it was good to see Briony and Cass. Briony had called asking if she and Cass could drop by on their way back to Linnaea from their own honeymoon. She'd missed her big brother, Alaric had said, the roll of his eyes belying the affection in his voice.

Clara had been apprehensive when Cass brought Alaric's long-lost half sister to the palace three months ago. Her concerns had lain primarily with Cass and what she saw as his manipulative attempts to get his family back into Linnaea. She'd been right, except that Cass had done something unexpected. He'd fallen in love with Briony.

Briony had been even more unexpected. A bartender who had paused her education degree to care for her stepfamily after her mother's unexpected death, she'd taken to royal life like she'd been born into it. She'd pursued the rebuilding of Linnaea's education system with a passion that had impressed even her stalwart brother. In just a few short months, she had proven to be what Alaric desperately needed: family.

Something he needed now more than ever Clara thought as Briony bounced over to her for a hug. Alaric had considered cutting their honeymoon short after Daxon's health scare. But the doctors had assured him that Daxon was stabilized. Having Briony's visit to look forward to and knowing she would be going back to Linnaea had helped him relax once more.

They started off most mornings with breakfast in the kitchen. Unlike the first morning when she'd come down to the professional spread laid out by the cook, Alaric cooked most mornings while she sat on a high-top chair at the counter and read. Mornings were spent tackling palace business. Even though Alaric had hired a new official executive assistant, she was performing many of the duties she had before.

Except this time, she thought with a smile, those duties were occasionally paused as she pulled the skirt of her dress up and straddled his lap, or Alaric lured her into the shower for a sensual rinse as he wrapped her legs around his waist and took her against the tiled wall. That afternoon on the dock seemed to have ripped away the last of their reticence, at least when it came to sex. They couldn't get enough of each other.

Aside from their romantic encounters, afternoons had become her favorite. They'd walked through the winding corridors of Geneva's old city center, explored the shops in Carouge shopping district and sampled fondue brought in by an exclusive restaurant in the coziness of the lake house's family room. They'd even spent one blissful afternoon planning out their new apartment at the palace, right down to the nursery decorated in a woodland theme that reminded her of the forest behind the castle.

And nights…nights they made love in her bed, falling asleep in a tangle of limbs.

It was the happiest she'd ever been in her life. So why, she asked herself as her sister-in-law wrapped her in a hug, couldn't she just be satisfied with what she had? Why was she wanting more when Alaric had made it clear that he had no interest in deepening their relationship emotionally? After his confession on the pier, there had been no more intimate talks, no more unburdening of feelings. There were times she caught him glancing at her with a slight smile, felt his touch linger as they made love.

And then there were the wedding photos. Meira and the PR office had done a spectacular job with the press release, releasing "exclusive" materials to some of the most reputable publications across the world.

The formal portraits after the ceremony had been lovely. But it had been a candid shot right before their vows, when Alaric had kissed her hand as she'd thanked him for arranging the more intimate details of their day, that had made her breath catch. The way he looked down at her, his gaze appreciative and warm as she'd smiled up at him, had confirmed the truth she'd been trying to avoid.

She'd fallen in love with her husband. She'd fallen in love, and she didn't know what to do about it.

As if she'd summoned him with her chaotic thoughts, Alaric came up behind her and slid an arm around her waist. She relaxed into his embrace.

"Dinner is ready," he announced, his voice a rumble against her back.

"Great." Briony bounced on her toes. "We barely ate on the flight over."

Cass shook his head as he smiled indulgently at his wife.

"I barely ate. Briony ate everything in sight."

Briony playfully swatted his arm. "Well, I am eating for two."

It took a moment for Briony's words to register. When they did, Clara's jaw dropped.

"You're pregnant?"

Briony nodded, her face radiant. "Sorry, we had this whole plan for telling you over dinner, but I just couldn't resist." She turned to Alaric. "You're going to be an uncle!"

Alaric swept her into a tight hug.

"Congratulations."

The rest of the evening passed a blur. Conversation shifted from what Briony and Cass had done on their honeymoon to the upcoming treaty with Switzerland. It wasn't until after dinner, when Alaric pulled Cass aside to talk business, that Briony and Clara got a moment alone.

"I'm really happy for you and Cass," Clara said as they sipped tea by the fire.

"Thank you." Briony patted her still-flat stomach. "It's a little hard to take it all in. Finding out I'm a princess, getting married, having a baby. I feel like I've lived three lifetimes these last few months." She leaned in, a conspiratorial gleam in her eye. "I couldn't help but wonder if you and I will be giving birth about the same time."

For a moment Clara just stared at her.

"What… I don't know what you're talking about."

"I saw you the day of our wedding." She motioned toward Clara's belly. "Your hand drifted down and laid across your stomach, just like I started doing as soon as I found out. And then I remembered the night of the dinner with the Swiss ambassador and his family." Her smile turned devilish. "When you and Alaric were comforting me, I didn't fully register the implication of your hair being all mussed when I came to his office. But then it all fell into place."

"You haven't told anyone, have you?"

"No, of course not! The only reason I even told Daxon that the two of you had gotten married was because he was spouting off about contacting Alaric's ex-fiancée's father and trying to get their marriage back on track." She scowled. "Alaric never should have been engaged to her in the first place."

Clara's initial panic abated, leaving her feeling a little dizzy.

"Alaric…you should know Alaric didn't cheat on Celestine. What happened between us happened after she'd broken off their engagement."

Briony laid her hand over Clara's. "My brother is one of the most honorable people I know. I never doubted his integrity for one second. But even if the sequence of events had been different, their engagement wasn't real. And judging by the photos I saw, she was certainly not faithful to him."

Clara's lips twisted into a grimace. She'd seen plenty of photos of Celestine Osborn, but that last one, especially knowing what she did know about Alaric's past, made her livid that a woman could act so selfishly and cruelly.

"She certainly seemed to like the attention," was the nicest thing she could come up with.

"The wrong attention. Now, your photos," Briony said, her voice lightening, "those were stunning."

Clara smiled as a pleased blush stole across her cheeks. "Thank you."

"I'm so glad Alaric listened to me."

"Listened to you?"

"Yeah, about moving the ceremony…" Briony's voice trailed off as her eyes widened for a moment. "I just mentioned the rose garden seemed really nice. I spent a lot of time there when I first got to the palace."

Clara's chest tightened with pain. She'd thought Alaric had come up with the idea to move the ceremony himself.

It had been the first gesture that had made her question if perhaps he saw their relationship as something more than just a business arrangement.

Except it hadn't been his idea at all.

Her chest tightened painfully.

"Did you suggest anything else?"

Briony glanced at her husband and her brother.

"I don't think—"

"Briony. Please."

Her sister-in-law's face fell. "The dress. And the photographer."

Numbness set in. Their wedding had been the moment she thought things had truly started to change. But now, to find out it had all been someone else's idea, made her feel like the biggest fool. Hadn't she just been asking why she couldn't be happy with what she and Alaric had?

"Clara, I'm sorry—"

"Briony, it's not your fault," Clara interrupted as she laid a hand over her sister-in-law's. "And it's not Alaric's, either. It was a lovely ceremony, regardless of who came up with what idea. I made an assumption and it surprised me to find out differently, that's all."

Briony watched her nervously. "Are you sure? You two seem so happy. I'd feel terrible if I ruined it with my big mouth."

Clara looked across the room as Alaric conversed with Cass. As if he'd sensed her watching him, he glanced over at her and smiled. Could she really hold a grudge for something that hadn't been done out of malice or hurt? Worse, how could she be upset with him when she hadn't been entirely truthful about her own past?

She had a husband who worshipped her in bed, made her breakfast every morning and had once more begun to treat her like a partner in work. She would be a mother before the year was out, and welcoming a niece or nephew, too.

She breathed in, her resolve strengthening. The wedding ceremony may not have been Alaric's idea. But she had so much more than she'd ever thought possible. She certainly had more with Alaric than she'd ever had with Miles.

Even if her husband didn't return her love, she had his affection and his respect. It would be enough.

It had to be.

"You didn't ruin anything, Briony." She smiled at Alaric before turning back to her sister-in-law. "I'm very happy."

Briony accepted her words with a relieved sigh and another apology before turning the topic back to baby names and nursery themes. She seemed to accept Clara's words.

If only Clara could accept them herself.

Alaric closed the door to Clara's room and turned, his body already anticipating finding his wife in bed waiting for him.

The bed was empty.

He glanced around the room, his pulse kicking up a notch. Clara had been fine until after dinner. After he'd finished talking with Cass and they'd rejoined their wives, she'd seemed a dimmer version of herself. Aloof, withdrawn, more like the Clara he had worked with for the first few years.

She'd engaged in conversation with Briony, chatted with Cass about the treaty, leaned into his touch as he'd sat next to her on the couch.

But something was different. As soon as Briony and Cass had bid them good-night, insisting on staying at a hotel in Geneva so as not to interrupt the honeymooners, she'd disappeared upstairs.

The muted sound of rushing water met his ears. He moved toward the bathroom door, pulling off his clothes as he went. It wasn't just desire guiding his steps. It was the unsettling notion that had flared up every now and then when he would catch Clara looking at him with sadness in her gaze, or staring at something in the distance, a haunted look in her eyes.

He needed to ask her. Part of him didn't want to press her or risk upsetting her. Yet he wanted to hear her answer, be reassured that she wasn't concealing something from him. The possibility that after all he'd shared with her, she hadn't trusted him with something created a gaping void in his chest that ached just at the thought of her not being honest with him.

Perhaps this was the result of giving in to his emotions more and allowing himself to experience his growing feeling of affection for his wife. It was hard not to wonder when this period of happiness would come crashing down and the next scandal or hardship would burst through the haven they'd created on the wintery shores of Lake Geneva.

He dismissed his worries as he opened the door. He moved to the shower, savoring the sight of his wife's nude body through the wavy glass. Her head was tilted back, wet hair plastered to her back as she stood beneath the waterfall stream, skin glistening. Suds clung to her full breasts as her hand drifted down, a bar of soap in her fingers.

Dear God, he was jealous of a bar of soap.

The door to the shower creaked as he stepped inside. Her eyes shot open, her lips parting in surprise before they tilted up into a small smile.

"Hi."

He stepped beneath the water and kissed her as if they'd been apart for hours instead of just minutes. She wrapped her arms around his neck, pressed her wet body against his in an intimate manner that made his hard length throb with need.

"Clara," he murmured against her lips. "Are you all right?"

She pulled back, her hands resting on his chest.

"I'm tired, but yes. It was nice seeing your sister and Prince Cass... Cass."

He chuckled at the slight wrinkling of her nose.

"It'll take some getting used to." His hand drifted up to smooth a wet tendril of hair back from her face. "You seemed down after dinner."

She blinked twice before her gaze darted off to the side, then back. A gesture so fast he would have missed it if he hadn't been watching her.

His chest tightened. There was something.

"Clara, what is it? Is the baby okay? Are you all—"

She went up on her toes and pressed her mouth to his. Her hands slid up his chest to his neck, then farther into his hair, fingers tangling in the wet strands. His arms cradled her close, his body demanding that he enjoy every bit of what she was offering even as his mind fought him, demanding answers.

"I'm fine," she whispered against his mouth between frantic kisses. "The baby is fine." She leaned back for one fleeting moment, the sadness in her eyes so acute it stabbed him to his core. "Have you ever been so happy you think there's no way it could possibly last?"

He stared at her. Had he voiced his own fears out loud? Or were they just so in tune, so much alike, that they were both terrified of accepting the happiness they'd found in this home by the water?

"Clara." His fingers firmed on her back, pulling her against his body until not even a sliver of daylight could come between them. "We've both been hurt. A lot. But that doesn't mean we're going to lose what we've created here. We're better people than the ones who hurt us, and we're not going to hurt each other the way they did."

This time her smile was more genuine, a small glimmer of her previous happiness creeping back in.

"You're right."

"I'm the prince. Of course I'm right."

He caught her laugh in another kiss, her mirth quickly turning to desire as he caressed her breasts, his hands sliding down her slick skin to part her thighs as he knelt before her and worshipped her core with his lips and tongue. She tasted so sweet, her soft cries growing louder, hips pumping against his mouth as he caressed her folds with long, slow licks.

When she came apart in his arms, he stood, hooking his arms behind her knees and lifting her up, pinning her against the tiled wall as he slid inside her. She gasped, clinging to him as he held himself deep within her.

"Alaric!"

She wrapped her legs around him and he let go of his control, their bodies joining as water streamed over them, the shower drowning out their cries of pleasure as they came apart in each other's arms.

CHAPTER FIFTEEN

ALARIC WOKE TO what had quickly become one of the most enjoyable parts of his day: the feeling of soft, warm skin pressed against his body. A quiet murmur brought a smile to his lips as Clara shifted, one arm draped across his chest, a leg firmly secured over his thigh. Silky strands of hair grazed his neck and sent a rush of heat to his groin.

He glanced down at his sleeping wife. They'd made love three times last night, including once in the middle of the night when they'd awoken pressed together in a frenzied passion of kissing that had ended with her astride his hips, hands pressed against his chest as she'd ridden him to the most pleasurable climax he'd ever experienced. As her own pleasure had taken hold and made her cry out, he'd reached up and placed one hand on her stomach. The intimacy of their lovemaking, the knowledge that she was carrying his child inside her, had intensified the pleasure coursing through his body. He'd come with a shout, pulling her down so that her naked body was pressed against his as he claimed her lips in a possessive kiss.

He had never experienced such sexual intimacy before. Any intimacy, really. After they'd spoken on the pier, it was as if a weight had been lifted from his heart he hadn't even known he'd been carrying all these years. Spending time with Clara, touching her, listening to her voice, all of it thrilled him. With no expiration date on their relationship, with her unconditional acceptance of all of his fears, she'd set him free.

Now if he could only do the same for her. The sadness in her eyes, the fear that something would come along to wreck the happiness they'd found, made him grateful her horrific excuse for a husband was in his grave. A sentiment most would probably find cruel, but he didn't care. The man had laid his hands on Clara, had used and abused her in her time of grief. That she had not only survived but become the woman she was today was a testament to her strength and resilience.

Now if she could only do what he himself was slowly learning how to do: let go of the past and embrace the gifts of the present.

She stirred once more before rolling over, taking a good portion of the thick blanket with her. Cool air prickled his skin. He leaned over, planted a soft kiss on her bare shoulder and rolled out of bed. Much as he wanted to wake her by sliding into her wet heat and seeing her eyes flutter open with desire as he moved inside her, she needed to rest.

He tugged on his robe and, with one last look at his future queen, closed the door behind him.

Perhaps, he thought as he walked into his suite, he could suggest she move into his bedroom. They'd slept together every night since they'd first made love as husband and wife. Another intimacy he had pictured himself engaging in, but one he had quickly become addicted to.

A fact that should bother him. He had been firm in his commitment to keep emotions out of their arrangement and reserve affection for their child. But the more happiness he found in the littlest of things, from her grateful smile when he made her a slice of toast to the satisfaction of once more working together, the more he found himself embracing the feelings developing. Affection, tenderness, warmth.

Briony and Cass had fallen in love, despite all odds. Yes, his mother had been destroyed by her love for his father. But Daxon was a different beast altogether. Clara was nothing like him. She was generous and honest and cared about the people of Linnaea.

And as she'd reminded him the few times he'd revisited and voiced his deepest fear, he wasn't Daxon. He wouldn't hurt Clara the way his father had hurt his mother.

In an odd way, Daxon's prognosis had also been a balm to years of hurt and resentment. Admitting to Clara that part of him still yearned for a relationship with a man who had been so cruel and selfish, and having her offer him nothing but support and acceptance in return, had made him feel…normal. There would always be regret that he and Daxon would most likely never repair their relationship.

At least Daxon had given him one thing: the motivation to never repeat his father's mistakes.

Linnaea's future was brighter than it had ever been. His sister was happily married and expecting her own child. He was married, and to someone he enjoyed being with instead of being trapped in a loveless business arrangement. He was going to be a father. Perhaps it was time to let go of the past and move forward.

His phone rang. He glanced down, then frowned. The screen identified the call as being from the Los Angeles area. Only a select few had his direct line.

"Yes?"

"Is this Prince Alaric Van Ambrose?"

The cultured yet snooty feminine voice immediately set him on edge. Disdain dripped through the phone.

"Who's calling?"

"My name is Temperance Clemont. My son was married to your wife."

She practically spat out the word *wife*. His entire body tensed. What little Clara had shared about her former husband and her in-laws had left him with the impression that Temperance and Stanley Clemont had spoiled the hell out of their one and only child, rendering him a useless human being who had tried to exert a childish control over the woman he should have revered. Every time he remembered Clara's face, the sadness and shame when she'd revealed Miles's behavior in the minutes leading up to his fatal accident, he wanted to strangle the man for daring to lay a hand on her.

"What can I do for you, Mrs. Clemont?"

"It's not what you can do for me, Your Highness, but what I can do for you."

He rolled his eyes. "I don't have time for melodrama, Mrs. Clemont. I understand your history with my wife is not a pleasant one, but I have no interest in dredging up the past."

"Even if a scandal could rock everything you've built for your country?"

Anger started to burn deep in his chest.

"I don't take kindly to threats."

"I'm not threatening," Temperance replied coolly. "I'm merely sharing valuable information."

"That your son died because he was drinking and made the poor decision to drive?"

Silence followed his bald statement. He didn't feel the least bit guilty. The woman had somehow manipulated Clara into thinking it was her fault that Miles had died when she had raised him to never take responsibility for his own actions.

"My son died because of Clara."

The ice in Temperance's voice could have frozen hell.

"Clara had nothing to do with it. If you're saying she's responsible because she didn't stop him from driving—"

"Clara's responsible because she was in the car with Miles when it crashed. The police found her fingerprints on the wheel."

Clara woke in a pleasant daze. She reached out, her hand brushing the empty space beside her. Disappointment filled her when she opened her eyes and realized she was alone. Who would have guessed how quickly she would get used to sleeping next to and waking up with her husband after sleeping alone for her whole life?

She stretched her arms above her head, wincing as her muscles burned. She hadn't meant to share her feelings with Alaric last night. But when he'd looked at her with such tenderness, when he'd been frightened for her and the baby, she hadn't been able to stop the words from flowing.

She slowly got out of bed and headed toward the sunken hot tub. As the tub filled with warm water and relaxed the parts of her body that ached from their night of amorous lovemaking, she finally acknowledged the truth she'd been trying to deny: she needed to tell Alaric everything. All she was doing was delaying the inevitable. He deserved the truth, had deserved it before they'd said their vows. She in turn needed to trust what he had said last night before he'd claimed her body with his own, that they wouldn't lose what they had created.

It wasn't until she was getting dressed that she saw the light blinking on her phone. A quick check showed that the text was from Alaric. Her grin dimmed a bit as she read the brief message.

Please come to my office when you're awake.

She checked her reflection in the mirror, smoothed her hair and headed down the hall. Not the sweetest of messages after the night they'd had. But he was still working very hard on the deal with Switzerland. Who knew what catastrophe he could have potentially woken up to.

She knocked on the door to his office.

"Come in."

Unease whispered across the back of her neck as she opened the door and saw him standing by the window with his back to her, his hands tucked into his pockets. Just two weeks ago Alaric had opened the door for her at the palace. "Things have changed," he'd said.

Had something else happened?

Stop being negative.

"Good morning," she said warmly.

He didn't reply for what felt like the longest time. Unease grew into alarm as she noted the tension in the column of his neck, the fierce set of his shoulders.

"Alaric, what's wrong?"

"When were you going to tell me you were in the car with Miles when it crashed?"

The world dropped out from under her. Bright points of light flickered across her vision as she sucked in a deep, shuddering breath. Somewhere in the recess of her mind she heard Miles's cruel laughter as she cried out a warning, as she reached for the wheel...

"What...what do you—"

"Don't deny it."

He continued to stare out the window. His voice, low and laced with icy fury, burrowed its way under her skin and lodged in her heart.

"I'm not denying it," she finally choked out. "Alaric, please, I have to tell you—"

"How many times did I ask if there was something you needed to tell me? When I bared my soul to you, did you take everything I had to give while not trusting me with your own past? Did you share the tiniest pieces so I wouldn't ask any more questions?"

Her throat tightened as she slowly sank into a chair.

"It had nothing to do with not trusting you."

"Didn't it?"

He finally turned. She wished he hadn't. His face, the face she'd caressed last night as he'd made love to her, was frozen into a mask of fury the likes of which she'd never seen. The jaw she'd kissed was now tight, his green eyes sharp and dark. Anger radiated off him and filled the room.

"No. I was… I've never told anyone what happened."

"Not even your husband?"

Her hand came up. He eyed it as if she'd covered her skin in her poison. Her arm dropped back to her side.

"Alaric, I didn't know how to talk about it. When we were married, it was made clear that this was going to be a formal arrangement. Sharing something like that…there's so much emotion and vulnerability."

"And when I told you about my past, about what my father did to my mother, you didn't think that was me displaying some emotion and vulnerability?"

Her eyes filled with tears. "It was, and it meant so much to me."

"So much that you continued to keep a secret from me? And not just one secret."

Confusion swept through her.

"What are you talking about?"

He stalked toward her, his eyes unblinking, his movements subtle but swift. Gone was the affectionate, loving husband she'd been accustomed to, replaced by a king-to-be who had retreated behind a wall of ice. His shoulders were rigid, the tendons in his neck taut as a vein pulsed beneath his skin.

"I'm talking about your fingerprints being found on the wheel of the car."

A dull roar built in her ears. How could he have possibly found that out? Alaric's lips moved, but she didn't hear a word that came out as blood roared in her ears. The world slowed down as her mind tried to reconcile between the past and the present. A memory flashed through her mind, a vivid image of her fingers curling around the wheel as she yanked, hearing Miles's shout as he cursed her, the car veering off to the side and the tree looming up out of the rain.

"What?" she finally gasped.

"Did you know there are suspicions that you caused the car accident to rid yourself of an inconvenient husband and inherit his money?"

Betrayal robbed her of her voice as she stared at him. He returned her stare with a frigid, unblinking stare of his own.

Finally, she swallowed past the tightness in her throat.

"Do you really believe that? That I'm capable of such a crime?"

"No." Her momentary relief disappeared as he continued, "But given that I only have one side of the story to go on, that my *wife* didn't confide in me, I can only go off what I was told."

The pieces fell into place with a resounding thud that wiped away the guilt she'd been feeling over not confiding in Alaric. There was only one person in the world who would have made such a horrific accusation.

"Did you call Temperance or did she call you?"

"It doesn't matter."

She looked up at him. Whether it was the shock or some leftover semblance of self-control, she managed to keep her voice level. "It does matter. It matters who called who, and it matters that instead of giving me a chance to tell my side of what happened, you automatically went off the word of a woman you've never met, a woman I told you made my life a living hell when I was with her son."

"You had your chance. Multiple ones, in fact." His eyes flickered. "I told you how important it's been to rise above the gossip Daxon and Celestine courted for years. I told you what the tabloids and press did to my mother. You know personally how much is riding on Linnaea being shown as a country rising from the ashes, not a nation run by spoiled despots. What do you think the media will do if they find out I not only married my secretary after I got her pregnant the night my fiancée broke off our engagement, but that I married a woman suspected of causing the accident that killed her wealthy husband?"

I won't cry. I will not cry.

Slowly, she stood.

"Is that what's most important here? Preserving Linnaea's image?"

"Don't twist my words," Alaric growled. "That's a part of it. You lied to me."

"I never lied."

"Concealed, distorted, however you did it, you didn't tell me the truth, Clara."

She closed her eyes to keep the tears at bay. She should have told him, should have trusted that he would listen to her as she had listened to him when he'd confided so much in her. But she'd done exactly what he'd told Cass not to: let her fears hold her back.

Now it was too late. She'd broken Alaric's trust. Temperance would never let her stop paying for what she imagined Clara had done to her precious son. The happiness Clara had so briefly found with her husband would now be forever out of reach. She could try to explain, but he'd just revealed he cared more about reputation and scandal than he did the truth.

She breathed in deeply and opened her eyes.

"Since Temperance filled you in on the details, it sounds like there's nothing more for me to say."

She turned and started for the door.

"Do not walk away from me, Clara. We aren't finished here."

"But we are." She stopped, her hand on the doorknob, and looked back at him. "You already have all the information you need. If it comes to light in the press, I'll work with the public relations department to mitigate the fallout as much as possible and will take full responsibility for whatever is needed to preserve Linnaea's image."

He ran a hand through his hair, the first sign that he wasn't in full control of his emotions.

"It's not just a public relations issue."

"No, but that seems to be a priority. Why else would you have taken Briony's suggestion to move the ceremony or take the wedding photos?"

She waited for him to correct her, to tell her it had been more than just for publicity.

But he remained silent, watching her with that hawk-like gaze.

Her hurt surged forth, took control of her tongue.

"Caring about how things look compared to how they are seems to run in the family."

She wanted to snatch the words back as soon as they left her mouth. His lips parted slightly as the full weight of what she'd said registered, essentially accusing him of his worst fear: that he was just like his father.

But before she could even begin to apologize, he pointed at the door.

"Go. The helicopter will be here in an hour to take you back to Linnaea." He bit out the words with a snapping fury that made her tremble. "We'll revisit this issue in time. But until I summon you, I don't want to hear from you, see you, nothing."

"Alaric, I—"

"You will refer to me as 'Your Highness.'" He walked around his desk and sat, focusing his gaze on his computer. "First names are for couples who share something beyond a formal arrangement."

"But I…"

Her voice trailed as the words welled in her throat.

I love you. I'm so sorry. I should have trusted you, trusted myself. I love you so much, Alaric.

"I'm sorry, Alaric," she finally whispered.

He didn't even look up.

"Goodbye, Your Highness."

CHAPTER SIXTEEN

THE MOUNTAINS OF Linnaea glittered in the distance. Clara kept her gaze focused on the snowcaps as the train rolled into the station. When the helicopter had arrived at the airport in Geneva, she'd taken one look at the private plane they'd flown in on and nearly burst into tears. Between the rapid unraveling of her relationship with Alaric and the pregnancy hormones, the thought of flying in the plane she'd flown with her husband on as they'd begun their honeymoon had been too much.

Stefan, poor man, had said he had to get permission from Alaric and the head of security. Clara had calmly told him she would scream that she was being kidnapped unless he took her to the station. Fortunately, he had obliged. She'd texted Meira a note to send him a bonus with his next check. He was good at his job, and he didn't deserve getting caught between two feuding monarchs.

A chill swept under the door of her private car as passengers walked past to disembark. Her skin pebbled beneath the thick wool of her sweater, but she barely noticed. She felt as cold inside as the ice glittering on the branches outside her window.

Had it been just twenty-four hours ago that she'd been cocooned in the warmth of her husband's arms after he'd made love to her? How had everything they'd been building over the past month fallen apart so quickly?

Simple. There wasn't anything between the two of you except a baby and good sex.

A lump rose in her throat. She knew better. Alaric may have felt nothing. But despite the cruel words she'd flung at him like daggers as she'd left, she loved him. She loved him so much it hurt.

Her phone buzzed in her pocket. She pulled it out to see an unfamiliar number on the screen. The text beneath alerted her to the fact that the call was from Los Angeles. Her chest constricted. Only two people would be contacting her from Los Angeles, and she had zero desire to speak with either of them. If Temperance Clemont was standing in front of her right now, it would be very hard not to slap what would no doubt be a very smug, self-satisfied expression off her face.

She sent the call to voice mail. A moment later, when it rang again, she turned her phone off.

Temperance may have succeeded in destroying what little relationship had been developing between Clara and her husband. But she would not let that vile woman have any more power over her life.

A private car whisked her from the train station to the palace. When she reached the floor that housed the royal family's apartments, she stopped. Where did she belong? The family suite she and Alaric had begun to decorate together from afar? Alaric's private apartment?

It could have been seconds or an hour before she slowly turned and took the elevator back down to her old apartment. The door swung open and, thankfully, her things were still in place. It would cause more gossip when she notified the palace staff that she would be remaining in her old suite until further notice. But given the media storm that was about to descend on the palace, she found she didn't really care anymore what others thought. Alaric had sworn he wouldn't divorce her. The next few months would be ugly, but eventually another royal would do something foolish or get married or have a baby. The spotlight would move off her and Linnaea. Alaric would continue to make progress in rebuilding Linnaea. And she would do whatever was needed to ensure she never hurt him or the people of her adopted country again.

Telling herself that didn't ease her heartache. Slowly, she eased herself into her favorite chair, the chair she'd been sitting in when Alaric had approached her with the pregnancy test in hand. That night, she'd thought there was no possible way she could ever co-parent with Alaric, let alone marry him.

Now she was over a thousand miles away from her husband missing him and the promise of a beautiful life together. She'd hurt him, not once but twice. He thought she'd lied to him. Even though she hadn't outright lied, she'd certainly concealed the truth. She'd known how much he abhorred scandal. He'd given her numerous opportunities to share what had happened, had shared his worst pains and biggest vulnerabilities with her.

And in a moment of pain, she'd hurled the cruelest thing she could have possibly said. If there had been any possible hope for reconciliation in the future, she'd ruined it with her nasty parting words.

...it was easier for him to stay withdrawn because getting involved was too scary...

She had wanted the benefits of a marriage without making the same investment Alaric had, withholding the worst parts of her own past out of fear while taking everything he had offered. She'd let her own guilt over not stopping Miles from driving, from spurring her to take action too late to save his life, prevent her from telling the man she loved the truth.

Alaric had been right. She hadn't trusted him to be

fair, to listen to her. She'd let fear rule her. Rule her and ruin her.

She brushed a stray tear from her cheek. Even though it hurt, the truth was finally out. She wouldn't have to move forward with the specter of his abuse and the circumstances of how he'd died looming in the background, overshadowing her new life.

That was a task she would start tomorrow. Tonight, she would mourn.

Silence greeted Alaric as he walked into the royal apartment. A quick glance confirmed what his new executive assistant, Geoffrey, had told him: Clara hadn't moved in. At first, when Geoffrey had called to report that Clara had ordered dinner be served to her in her old suite, he'd almost called her.

But what would have been the point? He'd told her that until he summoned her, he wanted nothing to do with her. She was following his orders.

It had been two days since Clara fled Lake Geneva. Two of the longest days of his life. The lake house had changed from a haven to a haunting reminder of the happy memories he'd created with his wife over the past few weeks. Memories that, even after he'd decided to return to Linnaea, had followed him on the plane ride home.

In the hours after he'd banished Clara, he'd been righteous in his anger, whipping through one task after another with ruthless efficiency. He had told her not once but twice how much his father's scandalizing had hurt him, had shared the most vulnerable parts of his past as he'd opened up to someone for the first time. And how had she repaid him? By keeping a scandalous secret from him. She had to have known something like that wouldn't stay hidden forever, especially now that she'd been thrust into the international spotlight.

He'd stayed up until nearly two in the morning when his eyelids had drooped and he hadn't been able to keep his head up. Somehow he'd slept until the sun crested over the horizon. The next thirty-six hours had passed in a blur of virtual meetings, phone calls and emails. He ate at his desk, typed brisk orders to Geoffrey and ordered the skeleton staff to leave him alone.

It worked until he'd woken up this morning, gotten out of bed and found one of Clara's silk robes tangled in the sheets.

How weak did it make him that he missed her? That he craved seeing her smile, holding her in his arms, talking with her about revisions the Swiss ambassador had made to the proposed treaty? His mother had longed for the Daxon she'd known briefly during their courtship, the man she thought she had fallen in love with. How many times had she said, "I just remember how things were. I know they can be better again."

Slowly, he walked down the hall to the suite of bedrooms. Three in total: a master suite with a bay of windows that overlooked the lake behind the palace and the mountains in the distance. A slightly smaller bedroom with equally stunning views.

But it was the third bedroom that made his chest tighten with pain. This bedroom had a connecting door to the master suite. This was the room for which Clara had picked out the soft green paint to serve as a backdrop for the white tree decals that re-created the forest behind the palace.

His fists clenched as he looked around the room. Clara had shared pictures she'd accumulated, from the white crib to the matching rocker in the corner next to a bookshelf stuffed with used children's books. He'd never thought about a nursery before. Nurseries were where babies slept, had their nappies changed and were nursed by their mothers.

But as Clara had talked about everything she'd envisioned taking placing in that room, the stories that would be read, the laughter that would echo off the walls, he'd found himself getting excited about a baby's room. Not just the room, but the sparkle in Clara's eyes as she'd talked, the affectionate way her hand had settled on her stomach as she'd talked about their child.

Had he been so blind as to her true nature? Or had Clara just made a terrible mistake, one that he'd overreacted to?

He surveyed the room one last time before turning and closing the door with more force than he'd intended. When Temperance had told him about Clara being in the car, his first reaction had been hurt. He had asked Clara multiple times if there was anything in her past that he should be aware of. He hadn't said anything about not marrying her, not providing for their child. He just wanted to know. He thought, too, that she had trusted him when she had shared Miles's drunken state before he'd gotten behind the wheel. It had been why he'd felt safe opening up to her after finding out about Daxon's prognosis.

Finding out that she had kept the full circumstances from him, not given him the chance to hear her side when he had bared the darkest parts of his soul to her, had been a stab in the back.

A shrill ring cut through the stillness. He pulled his phone out of his pocket and glanced at the screen. Ronan had taken it personally that he had missed the true circumstances of Clara's husband's death and had promised Alaric an update before midnight.

Alaric closed his eyes for a moment. Did he want to know what had truly happened?

He answered.

"Yes?"

"I've got it, sir."

"Good. When can I see it?"

"One of my men is being admitted to the palace as we

speak. He has a hard copy of the file. I didn't want to send it via email."

His hand tightened on the phone.

"Is it that bad?"

Ronan paused.

"Yes, Your Highness. It's bad."

Fifteen minutes later, Alaric was sitting in his office with a black file in hand, Ronan Security's initials tamped in red in the corner. He kept his gaze averted from the desk. He should have had it replaced before he left Lake Geneva.

He stared down at the folder. What would he find inside? As angry as he'd been the day he and Clara had fought, he hadn't for one second believed her capable of the accusation Temperance had leveled at her.

Didn't show it very well, did you?

The voice of his conscience whispered in his ear as he remembered Clara's beautiful blue eyes dull and wide with shock. He'd known as he'd berated her that he was being too harsh, that it wasn't so much the potential scandal that had dug its ugly talons into his heart but pain. He had started to open his heart to his wife. Finding out her deepest secret not from her but from her ex-mother-in-law had felt like a betrayal.

Slowly, he opened the folder. His heart stopped. The first image inside was of the car, a mangled black mess wrapped around a tree. In the background was Clara, strapped to a gurney as she was being loaded into an ambulance. Her face was covered in blood and scratches, her eyes barely open, tears streaking down her cheeks.

He ran a finger over her face as nausea built in his gut. His wife had gone through hell, first with a spoiled, abusive husband and then this. And how had he responded? By focusing on himself, on his pain and his past.

He spent an hour reviewing the contents of the folder.

The initial report stated that Miles had had a blood alcohol content three times the legal limit. An interview conducted with Clara in the hospital revealed that Miles had been driving recklessly, weaving back and forth across the road. Clara had begged him to stop. He'd steered toward another car. She'd grabbed the wheel, yanked it to prevent the other car from being hit. Unfortunately, she'd yanked too hard. Miles had lost control of the car and wrapped it around a tree. Other drivers on the road had corroborated Clara's account, stating that the car had been moving erratically for several kilometers.

Ronan had included a letter at the back. Within twenty-four hours, the Clemonts had bought the original report and paid off multiple officers and witnesses. One officer had kept a copy of the original and quit the department over the higher-ups allowing the Clemonts to change the narrative. When Ronan had started to dig deeper, he'd come across the officer's employment records and found that he'd quit shortly after the accident. Ronan had found him relatively easily living in Spain. The officer had been more than happy to provide the original report to Ronan and let the truth come out. He'd described Temperance and Stanley Clemont as "ruthless" and "heartless" when it came to their daughter-in-law.

They cared more about their son's reputation than they ever cared about her. She nearly died trying to save lives. But they tried to paint her as a murderess.

His body grew heavy with each passage he read until he could barely move. How could he have ever doubted her? How could he have been so cruel to her?

By the time he was done, he wanted nothing more than to run up to Clara's apartment, break down the door and beg her forgiveness.

He forced himself to stand and move to the window. Her parting insult had been accurate. Instead of acting rationally, he'd given in to his own pain and his own fear that once again scandal would plague his rule. He hadn't stopped to think about how differently Clara's circumstances had been: a woman caught up in a desperate situation created by her abusive spouse instead of his father's and ex-fiancée's self-indulgences.

Bile rose in his throat. Did he deserve her? One of his greatest fears had been that he was secretly like his father, that he would eventually cause Clara the kind of pain Daxon had caused Marianne. Hadn't he done just that with his actions over the last few days?

You are not your father.

How many times had she said that to him? He'd started to believe it before Temperance's phone call. Was he going to let people like Temperance, Celestine and Daxon ruin a future with the woman he loved?

Because he did love her, he realized with sudden clarity. He'd been falling in love with her for months. The intimacy they'd developed during their honeymoon had pushed him closer to acknowledging the depth of his feelings. Feelings he'd run from like a coward at the first sign of trouble.

As angry as he'd been at Celestine the night their engagement had ended, he really should be thanking her. If it hadn't been for the tumultuous conclusion to their arrangement, he never would have kissed Clara, never would have allowed himself to explore the emotions he felt for her.

Never would have finally opened his heart to love.

He flipped through the folder back to the first picture. Clara had been through so much: losing both her parents at a young age, going through an abusive marriage, restarting her life after a traumatic tragedy. And now he'd put her through another trauma. Did he deserve her?

No. No, he didn't. But he would spend the rest of his life trying to earn back her trust and, God willing, her love.

CHAPTER SEVENTEEN

CLARA WALKED THROUGH the rose garden, her boots crunching softly in the snow. Every time she'd woken up, which had seemed to be every hour, she'd grabbed her phone and checked the media sites to see if anything had been posted.

Nothing.

Around dawn she'd given up on sleep and gotten dressed in fleece-lined pants, a cozy sweater and her blue peacoat. Thin gray clouds covered the sky, creating a muted glow as the sun rose behind them. The palace had been quiet as she'd taken the elevator down to the ground floor and slipped out into the rose garden.

She ran a gloved hand over the leaves of the hedge. Just last month, she'd said her vows in this garden. If she'd known what was going to happen, would she have gone through with it?

Yes.

It was an easy answer. Those blissful weeks with Alaric, falling deeper in love and being loved in return for the first time in her life, were too precious to give up.

Alaric had come home last night. She'd been in her small window seat that overlooked the long drive that came up to the palace. When he'd alighted from the car, she'd pressed her face against the cold glass, drinking in the sight of him. She wanted to run to him, to throw her arms around his neck and be swept up into his embrace as she apologized for not trusting him. Perhaps, if he would have looked up, she would have done just that.

But he hadn't. He'd leaned in, said something to a dark-haired man she assumed was his new assistant—Geoffrey something—and strode into the palace. As if nothing in his life had changed.

She'd stayed in the window seat for another hour, staring out at the darkening sky, until hunger had sent her to the kitchen to scrounge for crackers and broth. Whether it was the events of the past few days, the pregnancy or both, she'd barely been able to keep any food down. It didn't help that at least once a day, Temperance tried to call her. The first couple of times, she hadn't left a voice mail. When she finally had, the accented voice had been smug.

"I warned you that you would one day pay for what happened to Miles."

The second and third voice mails had been a touch more emotional, as if Clara was offending Temperance by not responding and letting her vent her rage. She contemplated changing her number. But someone with Temperance's wealth, who probably had more money than the entire country of Linnaea, would just get her new number.

Better to let her tire herself out. She hadn't released anything to the media yet. Maybe she never would. To share that Clara was in the car that night would mean risking the discovery of Miles's state when he had been behind the wheel.

Her heart clenched. If only Alaric had talked to her instead of jumping to the worst conclusion. She could understand his hurt, see how he could have perceived her silence as a form of lying. But she couldn't understand why he'd immediately jumped to the worst possible conclusion. Even if he didn't love her, did he truly think so little of her after all this time?

Stop thinking about it. The more she ruminated, the

more upset she would get. She didn't need that for her-self or her child.

She sat down on one of the stone benches and looked around the garden. Right now, the pain was intense, es-pecially when her eyes flickered to the spot where she'd exchanged vows with Alaric and he'd surprised her with that gentle kiss on the lips. But the pain would fade with time. She would instead focus on the good that had come out of their union. A slight smile tugged at her lips. Spring mornings spent on a blanket with their child, reading books and eating strawberries as the gentle scent of roses wafted around them. Or perhaps lying in the grass during sum-mer and watching the star-filled sky.

She may not have the life she'd thought she would. But it could still be a good one.

"It's a beautiful place, even in winter."

His voice froze her in place. Had she imagined it? That deep, rich timbre of his voice as it washed over her and sent her pulse pounding?

Slowly, she turned her head. He stood just a few feet away, his hands clasped behind his back, his dark hair dusted with snow. Her throat tightened. God, she'd missed him.

"It is."

Her fingers curled around the seat of the bench. The coldness from the stone seeped through her gloves. No matter what, she would not make a fool of herself. They had to see each other eventually. Best to get it over with and move on.

"You look very pale."

She frowned.

"It is winter."

Alaric shook his head. "That's not… I meant you don't look well."

"The words every woman wants to hear when she's tired and nauseous."

Her nose wrinkled and she looked away. Great. Less than thirty seconds in each other's company and they were already snipping at each other. Was this how the rest of their marriage was destined to be?

She heard Alaric approach, shifted to the left as he eased himself onto the bench beside her to keep some space between them.

"You haven't been sleeping."

She shook her head.

She started as his hand slid over hers and gently eased her grip off the bench. She bit down on her lower lip as he threaded his fingers through hers. The simple act made her ache. Was he trying to punish her? Or was he trying to keep her calm before he dropped another bombshell on her, like asking for a divorce?

Her stomach rolled. Amazing how just three weeks ago she'd been fighting him against getting married. Now the thought of not having him in her life in any capacity left her shaken.

"I hurt you."

Her head snapped up.

"What?"

Alaric's eyes latched onto hers, his gaze moving over her face as if he hadn't seen her in decades instead of days. Slowly, his other hand came up. When she didn't move, his fingers settled on her cheek, cradling her with a gentleness that made her eyes grow hot.

"I hurt you, Clara. I let my own pride and pain and past overrule everything else." His voice grew thick as he leaned in, resting his forehead against hers. His breath came out fast and warmed her cheek. "Can I ever begin to tell you how sorry I am?"

She sat there, frozen in place, not wanting to pull away from his touch but unsure of how to answer.

"Clara, please say something."

The sorrow in his voice yanked her out of her shock. She leaned back, missed the warmth of his skin against hers as the winter air swirled around them. She had never in a thousand years imagined that he would apologize. Hope flickered in her chest.

But hope and apologies weren't enough. If this was the beginning of a new chapter, there had to be trust and communication.

She stood, gave his hand a squeeze and walked over to the fountain. She wrapped her arms around her waist as the words spilled forth.

"Miles was drunk a lot. I knew he'd struggled when we dated, but Temperance and Stanley managed it. I wanted to have a family again so badly that I looked past so many warning signs. Even when they became big flashing neon lights telling me to get out, I hung on. I'd put so much time in, I told myself, and perhaps things would get better when we got married."

She closed her eyes, remembering the shattering of glass the night of their honeymoon when he'd hurled a champagne flute at the wall in their hotel suite because she'd asked him to stay with her instead of going back to the reception to drink more.

"I was so stupid."

She sensed rather than heard Alaric stand.

"Plenty of people have made similar mistakes, Clara."

"They have. But this was my life. I knew better." She sucked in a shuddering breath. "Have you ever noticed how, once you've made excuses for one thing, it's easier to make excuses for the bigger things that follow? It starts with one too many drinks at dinner and ends with letting your husband drive away from a party drunk."

"With you in the car."

Anger pulsed in every word. But not, she realized with relief, at her. No, Alaric was angry at Miles for putting her in that position.

"I knew he'd had too much to safely drive. I'd asked him if he was safe to drive. He pulled me aside and slapped me across the face for embarrassing him in front of his friends."

Alaric's hands cupped her shoulders. She wanted to lean back into his embrace, to draw strength from his presence. But not yet. She needed to get this out, needed him to know the full story.

"I was so shocked and humiliated that I just got in the car." Her voice caught. "I got in the car, Alaric. I put all those people on the road at risk because I was embarrassed for myself. If I had put my foot down, Miles would still be alive. I didn't realize how truly drunk he was until he started weaving back and forth across the road."

She could still see the lines on the road, blurred by the falling rain and Miles's ever-increasing speed, disappear as he drifted across the road. She'd called out his name, seen him start then laugh off her discomfort as he'd pressed down on the gas pedal. He'd told her she was boring as he'd started deliberately going back and forth, nearly clipping the bumper of the car in front of them before speeding around them and almost crashing head-on into an oncoming truck.

"He kept going faster and faster. Another car was coming and he…he said if I would just trust him, he would get close without hitting them. That it was all a game."

She'd woken up to the sound of his shrill laughter echoing in her ears for weeks after the crash.

"I wasn't trying to hurt him. I grabbed the wheel…" Her hand drifted out, mimicking her actions from that awful night so long ago. "I didn't mean to yank as hard as I did. I was just so scared…"

Alaric's arms came around her, tight and strong. She should have resisted, but she couldn't anymore. She sagged back into his embrace, letting her head drop back against his chest.

"The last thing I remember is him shouting at me right before this awful screech, metal being ripped apart as the windshield shattered in front of my eyes. When I woke up, I was in the back of an ambulance being taken to the hospital."

Silence fell as Alaric held her. Snow drifted down, tiny flakes that dusted the sleeves of his jacket. The blanket of white snuffed out all sound and cocooned them within their own quiet corner of the world.

"What did Miles's parents do?"

She swallowed back the hurt that lodged in her throat as she remembered the first time Temperance and Stanley had walked into her room.

"I thought they were coming to support me. I was so grateful to see them. But then Temperance told me it was my fault that Miles had died, that I should have done more to stop him. When I told her that I had tried, she said I hadn't tried hard enough." She turned her head, snuggled into the curve of his neck. "When the police told her I had yanked the wheel away from Miles, she accused me of murdering him for his money."

Alaric spun her around with such speed she barely caught her breath before he drew her back into his embrace, one hand coming up to cradle the back of her head as he pressed his lips against her forehead.

"I'm sorry, Clara."

His words washed over her, loosened the knot inside her chest.

"Thank you. I never meant to cause the accident. But

I always wondered what if..." She sucked in a shuddering breath. "What if I had stood up to him? Wondered if Miles would still be alive. I didn't murder him, but I still killed him."

It was the first time she'd said the words out loud. They hung in the air, her full confession lingering between them.

She nearly came undone when he pressed the softest of kisses to her forehead.

"You made the only decision you could in one of the worst situations anyone could ever find themselves in. The only person responsible for Miles's death that night is Miles."

She sagged against him. He was offering her absolution, and, oh, how she wanted to accept it. But she had to make sure, one last time, that he fully understood what she'd done.

"I... I should have stopped him before he got in the car—"

"You were in a very abusive relationship, Clara. I saw my own mother withdraw into herself and make questionable decisions. Abuse strips us of who we are and leaves us with almost nothing to stand on." He kept one arm securely around her waist as he leaned back, capturing her gaze with his as he gently laid a hand on her cheek. "But you survived. You survived and look how strong you've become. I have no doubt the woman I married wouldn't hesitate now to step in if she saw someone in a position like that again."

A slow, tentative smile spread across her face even as tears finally escaped to trace their way down her cheeks.

"What changed your mind?"

"I already knew I'd made a colossal error before I got back to Linnaea. And then I reviewed the original file of the accident."

Her mouth dropped open. "But... I thought Temperance and Stanley had them all destroyed. I managed to get a copy of the toxicology report that showed Miles was drunk, but everything else… I thought it had been destroyed."

"One of the officers kept it." He placed another kiss on her forehead. "Clara… I can't imagine what you went through. I knew you were strong, but seeing what you experienced that night, and then having to deal with that witch in the aftermath…" He leaned back, a sad smile on his handsome face. "You don't know how strong you truly are, do you?"

"Just as you don't realize what an incredible leader you are."

Wind whipped around the corner of one of the hedges before he could answer. Clara shivered.

"Let's go inside. We can talk more where it's warmer."

She let him grab her hand and lead her back inside the palace. It was still early, but already she could hear the distant clang of pots in the royal family kitchen where a small staff was putting together breakfast for Alaric, Daxon and some of the higher-ranked officials who lived in the palace. A vacuum whirred down the hall as Alaric led her to elevator. A palace guard rounded the corner and stopped, standing back at attention until Alaric waved for him to be on his way. She didn't miss the slight hint of a smile on the guard's lips as his eyes drifted down to hers and Alaric's joined hands.

Linnaea had started out as a place to escape to, to put distance between her and London. But somewhere along the line it had become home.

Please let it continue to be home, she prayed as the elevator ascended. *Please let it not be too late for us to become a family.*

It took her a moment to realize that the elevator had taken them a couple floors above her apartment. As the doors whooshed open, she realized they were standing outside the door of the king's family apartment.

"Alaric…"

He turned and, before she could say another word, dropped to one knee.

"Clara, we have a lot to talk about. I have a lot to apologize for."

"So do I," she said shakily. "I should have told you—"

"Yes, you should have," he cut in gently, "but I should have trusted you." He reached out and grabbed her other hand in his. "But I'm going to do things differently moving forward. If you'll let me."

"Let you?"

"As your husband. Clara, would you do me the honor of letting me be your husband and show you every day how much I want you in my life?"

She couldn't hold back the tears this time. But at least they were happy tears, she thought as she nodded. He stood, cradled her face once more in his hands and kissed her. It was a kiss that nearly knocked her off her feet as his lips moved over hers, firm and possessive and yet so gentle and loving.

He pulled back. Before she could say another word, he opened the doors to the apartment, swept her into his arms and carried her across the threshold. The furniture was draped in plastic covers, the floor speckled with plaster dust, the walls half coated in paint.

She'd never seen anything so wonderful in her whole life.

"We'll be moved in by the end of next week," he said as he carried her up the curving stairs and down the hall. "I never want to spend another night without you in our bed."

She sighed contentedly and relaxed in his arms. "Our bed" had a lovely ring to it.

"Alaric, about what I said before I left—"

"You were right, Clara."

"But I wasn't! You are nothing like your father, Alaric."

He stopped in front of one of the doors and gently set her on her feet.

"I'm not. But in that moment, I was." He grabbed her hands and held them tightly in his grasp. "My history with my father, seeing what the negative press did to my mother, made me react in the worst way possible. I was hurt that you hadn't confided in me, angry after I'd shared what I had with you." He held up a finger as her lips parted to speak. "But that wasn't fair. Just because I chose to share something with you did not make you beholden to share with me."

"It wasn't that I didn't trust you. I just… I had never told anyone else what happened. I was so ashamed. I hadn't forgiven myself, so how could I possibly ask you to forgive me or understand what happened?"

"There's nothing to forgive, Clara. At least nothing I need to forgive you for. All I can ask is that you forgive me." He brought one of her hands up to his lips and pressed a kiss to her fingers. "I can't promise I won't say anything hurtful the rest of our lives, or that I won't make mistakes. But I can promise I will try every day to be the kind of husband you deserve and the father our child needs."

"And I will try to be the kind of wife who will support you and your country."

His proud smile filled her with warmth.

"You are already the queen Linnaea needs."

Before she could reply, he reached over and twisted the knob. The door swung open and her breath caught. The walls were painted a soft green. A white rocking chair sat in one corner, and a bookcase next to it was filled with books. Clara walked over to it, her chest nearly bursting with happiness as she saw the signs of love in the worn spines, the slightly faded covers.

"You remembered."

"Every word. In a few months, I'll sit in here and read to our son or daughter." He gestured to the rest of the empty room. "The rest of what we picked out is on its way. It should be here in—"

She cut him off by flinging her arms around his neck and planting a passionate kiss on his lips. He groaned and pulled her flush against his body, his hardness pressing against her core. She writhed against him, savoring the tightening of his arms around her waist.

"I think it's time, my love, for us to finally be together in our marital bed."

"My love?" she repeated softly.

He smiled, a genuine smile full of happiness and warmth.

"I forgot that part, didn't I?" He leaned down and pressed a sweet kiss to the corner of her mouth. "I love you, Clara."

"You do?"

"Very, very much. I think I have for a while. It just took time for me to see it."

Clara laughed. "Wait until I tell Meira."

Alaric frowned. "Meira?"

"She told me on our wedding day that she thought there was more between us than just a working relationship. She was right. I love you, Alaric. I've loved you for so long, and I'll never stop."

He led her into what would be their first bedroom together. Everything was just as they had planned two weeks ago, down to the oversize bed draped in cozy blankets. He undressed her with infinite care, trailing kisses from her neck over her breasts, lingering on her nipples before continuing down over the soft swell of her belly. When he pressed a hot, open-mouthed kiss to her core, she nearly came undone, her fingers tangling in his hair as she moaned his name. He lifted her up as if she were made of glass, laid her on the bed and made quick work of his own clothes before he covered her naked body with his. As he slid inside her, their bodies joining in a slow, sensual dance, she reached up and pressed her hand to his cheek.

"I love you, Alaric."

"And I love you, Clara." He leaned down and sealed their pledge with a kiss.

EPILOGUE

Six months later

CLARA RELAXED ON the chaise longue, shielding her eyes against the late-morning sun as she watched her husband lay out a checkered blanket.

"You really went all out for this picnic," she teased as he reached into the wicker basket.

"If we're going to have a picnic, we're going to do it right." He leaned over and cut off any further teasing with a firm kiss. "Who knows when we'll get a chance to have alone time again?"

He gestured at her belly, round and full. In less than four weeks, their daughter would be making her appearance into the world. It had been Alaric's idea for them to have one last getaway before they officially became parents.

She leaned back against the pillows he'd arranged for her and gazed out over the sparkling waters of Lake Geneva. They'd been to the lake house every other month since they'd reconciled that wintery morning. Some trips had only been for a couple days, while others, like their glorious trip in spring, had been over a week.

It had also been a haven for two major events: Daxon's passing and the revelation of Clara's role in the car accident.

Daxon's passing had, unfortunately, been expected.

He'd deteriorated quickly following Alaric and Clara's reconciliation and wound up in hospice care. As he was confined to his suite in the palace, Alaric and Briony had attempted to resolve their issues with their father. Alaric had come out tense and resigned. Briony had shook her head sadly when Clara had asked if she'd found the closure she'd been seeking.

"No. Sometimes people don't change. It's hard to accept that." She'd hugged Clara. "But we tried."

Daxon had passed two days later. Despite all the damage he'd wrought on Linnaea, Alaric and Briony had agreed to hold the customary funeral services honoring the passing of the King.

Alaric's coronation ceremony had been scheduled to take place two weeks after that. When he'd suggested they go public with the details of Clara's accident ahead of the ceremony, she'd panicked. Temperance's calls had decreased, but she had still left the occasional threatening voice mail, usually after an article had been published about her and Alaric or some picture had circulated on social media of them visiting one of Briony's schools or touring one of the many new manufacturing plants Alaric was overseeing.

There had been so much good happening for the country that the thought of her own past wreaking havoc on everything Alaric and his people had worked for her had nearly sent her into a tailspin.

"But what about the treaty? What about the fallout for Linnaea with all the media attention?"

"It's up to you, Clara. But this way, we can get everything out in the open. You have nothing to hide. Your people love you." He'd kissed her forehead. "I love you. We'll stand by you."

They'd given an exclusive interview to a star writer the week before the coronation. She hadn't shared everything.

Miles had still been her husband, and she had no desire to air all of his transgressions. But she had given an abbreviated version of what had happened that night, including that in her attempts to stop Miles from driving, they'd lost control of the car.

The interview had gone viral. While there had been some negative attention, the majority of the commentary had been incredibly supportive. When Briony had told an inquisitive reporter how brave her sister-in-law was to share her own experience and how she was doing even more by overseeing the development of a medical support system for alcoholics and their loved ones, the media had gone crazy. Donations to the newly established Linnaean Alcohol Recovery Group had surpassed seven figures in less than a week.

The calls from Temperance had stopped.

A sudden kick made Clara smile. Her hand drifted down to the swell of her belly as her daughter moved inside her. Part of her would always feel sorry for Temperance. The closer she came to giving birth, the more she couldn't imagine the hell Temperance and Stanley had gone through in losing their only child.

But, she reminded herself, she and Alaric would raise a daughter who was not only loved but knew how to treat others.

Alaric laid out plates of cheeses, strawberries and *basler brunsli*, the best chocolate cookies she'd ever eaten. He handed her a glass of sparkling grape juice.

"What are you thinking?"

She smiled. "That I'm really happy."

He clinked his glass to hers.

"You deserve every bit of happiness, my love."

* * * * *

COMING SOON!

We really hope you enjoyed reading this book. If you're looking for more romance, be sure to head to the shops when new books are available on

Thursday 24th November

MILLS & BOON®

Coming next month

WEDDING NIGHT WITH THE
WRONG BILLIONAIRE
Dani Collins

"It's just us here." The words slipped out of her, impetuous. Desperate.

A distant part of her urged her to show some sense. She knew Micah would never forgive her for so much as getting in Remy's car, but they had had something in Paris. It had been interrupted and the not knowing what could have been had left her with an ache of yearning that had stalled her in some way. If she couldn't have Remy then it didn't matter who she married. They were all the same because they weren't him.

"No one would know."

"This would only be today. An hour. We couldn't tell anyone. Ever. If Hunter found out—"

"If Micah found out," she echoed with a catch in her voice. "I don't care about any of that, Remy. I really don't."

"After this, it goes back to the way it was, like we didn't even know one another. Is that really what you want?" His face twisted with conflict.

"No," she confessed with a chasm opening in her chest. "But I'll take it."

He closed his eyes, swearing as he fell back against the door with a defeated thump.

"Come here, then."

Continue reading
WEDDING NIGHT WITH THE WRONG BILLIONAIRE
Dani Collins

Available next month
www.millsandboon.co.uk

MILLS & BOON

THE HEART OF ROMANCE

A ROMANCE FOR EVERY READER

MODERN

Prepare to be swept off your feet by sophisticated, sexy and seductive heroes, in some of the world's most glamourous and romantic locations, where power and passion collide.

HISTORICAL

Escape with historical heroes from time gone by. Whether your passion for wicked Regency Rakes, muscled Vikings or rugged Highlanders, aw the romance of the past.

MEDICAL

Set your pulse racing with dedicated, delectable doctors in the high-pre sure world of medicine, where emotions run high and passion, comfort love are the best medicine.

True Love

Celebrate true love with tender stories of heartfelt romance, from the rush of falling in love to the joy a new baby can bring, and a focus on emotional heart of a relationship.

Desire

Indulge in secrets and scandal, intense drama and plenty of sizzling ho action with powerful and passionate heroes who have it all: wealth, sta good looks...everything but the right woman.

HEROES

Experience all the excitement of a gripping thriller, with an intense ro mance at its heart. Resourceful, true-to-life women and strong, fearless face danger and desire - a killer combination!

To see which titles are coming soon, please visit

millsandboon.co.uk/nextmonth

LET'S TALK
Romance

For exclusive extracts, competitions
and special offers, find us online:

facebook.com/millsandboon

@MillsandBoon

@MillsandBoonUK

Get in touch on 01413 063232

For all the latest titles coming soon, visit
millsandboon.co.uk/nextmonth